"*The Changing Season* is a story that will bring you back to that awkward period of time between childhood and adult life. I highly recommend this book."
– Richard Paul Evans, #1 *New York Times* bestselling author, *The Christmas Box* and *The Mistletoe Promise*

"Manchester's *The Changing Season* will be to young adults what *Old Yeller* is to my grandson."
– Ed Asner, Actor, *Up, The Mary Tyler Moore Show, Lou Grant, Elf*

"*The Changing Season* is a thought-provoking coming-of-age tale that explores the complicated themes of love, faith, family and, above all, loyalty. Mr. Manchester's portrayal of a boy at the cusp of manhood is evocative and sympathetic."
– Susan Wilson, *New York Times* bestselling author, *One Good Dog*

"Heartfelt, emotional, and beautifully written, *The Changing Season* is captivating. Steven Manchester is one gifted storyteller!"
– Carla Neggers, *New York Times* and *USA Today* bestselling author, *Harbor Island* and *Echo Lake*

"In *The Changing Season*, Steven Manchester brings us a warm-hearted story of love and loyalty—both canine and human—and shows us what it really means to be a best friend."
– Teresa Rhyne, #1 *New York Times* bestselling author, *The Dog Lives (and So Will I)* and *The Dogs Were Rescued (and So Was I)*

"A heartfelt coming-of-age story—detailing the love between human and canine—that will resonate with readers. Highly recommended!"
– Jennifer Probst, *New York Times* and *USA Today* bestselling author, *The Marriage Bargain* and *A Life Worth Living*

"Manchester beautifully describes the undeniable love and bond between Billy and his canine best friend Jimmy. *The Changing Season* reinforces how making one wrong decision can be life changing and the consequences can have a ripple effect that profoundly impacts the lives of others."
— Laura Schroff, #1 *New York Times* bestselling author, *An Invisible Thread*

"Beautifully written, poignant, and bittersweet, *The Changing Season* is a wonderful coming of age story."
— Christine Feehan, #1 *New York Times* bestselling author, the *Dark* series

"With the skill of a master storyteller, Steven Manchester leads you on a journey where your heart will forever be touched. I know mine was."
— Steena Holmes, *New York Times* and international bestselling author, *Emma's Secret: A Novel*

"In this tender coming-of-age novel, newly minted high school graduate Billy Baker experiences love in all its manifestations— friendship, romance, complicated family bonds and an unexpected passion for hard work—and discovers within himself the strength to survive the excruciating pain the loss of love can bring. The Changing Season traces Billy's journey toward adulthood with sensitivity and generosity. It offers no easy answers, yet as Billy bids farewell to adolescence and steps into his future, the path before him is illuminated by courage and hope."
— Judith Arnold, *USA Today* bestselling author, *Father Found*

"Any novel in which a young man loves his dog as much as any of his other friends will always appeal to me, and I am sure it will also appeal to other dog lovers. I like that Manchester allowed the dog to be a dog, even an overweight dog. A fine read!"
— Dr. Jeffrey Masson, *New York Times* bestselling author, *Dogs Never Lie About Love*

"*The Changing Season* is one of those rare coming-of-age tales that in suspending time becomes timeless itself. Steven Manchesterʻs stellar post-modern take on the world of *A Separate Peace* and *The Catcher in the Rye* serves up a cautionary tale about the fleeting nature of youth, intoned with a light of hope piercing the darkness. As simple in structure as it is ambitious in message, *The Changing Season* is a profound study of the human heart, revealing that growing older does not necessarily mean growing up."
– Jon Land, *USA Today* bestselling author of *Black Scorpion*

"In *The Changing Season*, 18-year-old Billy Baker arrives at a crossroad: step into adulthood with all its pleasures and perils *or* remain in the innocent bliss of childhood. This memorable coming-of-age story offers something for every reader's taste. You'll laugh—and cry—but you'll feel amply rewarded to have taken the trip. I know I did."
– Ruth Harris, #1 Amazon and million-copy *New York Times* bestselling author, *Park Avenue* series

"Steven Manchester's coming-of-age novel elegantly captures the wistful yearning of childhood's inevitable end as well as the unavoidable goodbyes that come all too soon when we share our lives with dogs. *The Changing Season's* message is both hopeful and heartrending—those things that make up our most poignant memories are usually the things we must ultimately leave behind."
– Melissa Jo Peltier, five-time *New York Times* bestselling author (with former "Dog Whisperer" Cesar Millan)

"*The Changing Season* is a modern-day coming-of-age story filled with vivid characters and the page-turning pace of some earlier American works. I thoroughly enjoyed the read and highly recommend it."
– Bob Mayer, *New York Times* bestselling author, *Area 51*

The Changing Season

Steven Manchester

THE
ST●RY
PLANT

This is a work of fiction. Names, characters, places, and incidents either are the product of the author's imagination or are used fictitiously. Any resemblance to actual events, locales, organizations, or persons living or dead, is entirely coincidental and beyond the intent of either the author or the publisher.

The Story Plant
Studio Digital CT, LLC
P.O. Box 4331
Stamford, CT 06907

Copyright © 2015 by Steven Manchester
Jacket design by Barbara Aronica Buck

Story Plant Hardcover ISBN-13 978-1-61188-226-1
Story Plant Paperback ISBN-13 978-1-61188-241-4
Fiction Studio Books E-book ISBN-13 978-1-936558-69-8

Visit our website at www.TheStoryPlant.com

All rights reserved, which includes the right to reproduce this book or portions thereof in any form whatsoever, except as provided by US Copyright Law. For information, address The Story Plant.

First Story Plant Hardcover Printing: February 2016
First Story Plant Paperback Printing: February 2017
Printed in The United States of America
0 9 8 7 6 5 4 3 2 1

For Lou Aronica, my mentor and friend

Chapter 1

There was no other way to describe it; they were driving home in the middle of a torrential downpour.

"I can't believe we're actually graduating from high school in a couple days," Billy said, trying to alleviate the anxiety he felt behind the wheel.

"Well, I can believe I'm graduating," Charlie said, "but I'm a little surprised you made it." Besides being his childhood best friend, Billy knew Charlie Philips to be a quick-witted, happy-go-lucky clown who'd had a girlfriend by the seventh grade and three more by the time he and Billy had reached high school. Charlie was also the first to sample beer and the musky taste of cigarette smoke. He was a pioneer of sorts, a frontiersman amongst his peers.

Billy looked at him and grinned. *You're such an idiot,* he thought, before leaning in toward the windshield to identify the disappearing road. He really liked the rain this time of year because it helped ease his allergy symptoms. *But this is ridiculous,* he thought. *I'd rather sneeze my brains out than hydroplane home in this monsoon.*

The driver's side windshield wiper worked well enough, but the passenger side's wiper jumped an inch or so each time before surrendering and falling back to its starting point. There was so much rain it wouldn't have mattered anyway. The single wiper blade was as effective as someone pushing a hand across their body in a swimming pool to get a better look at the bottom.

"So you're thinking about switching your major for next year, huh?" Charlie said.

Billy nodded. *I have no idea*, he thought. "I've actually been kicking around the idea of becoming a video game designer," he said, trying not to shrug. "I can start in Liberal Arts and easily switch over later on, if I want."

Charlie laughed. "Just because you've spent your life playing video games, that doesn't mean you're smart enough to design them, you know."

"Gee, thanks," Billy said, still staring out the windshield. "Not all of us have had our future planned since the third grade."

"That's right," Charlie said, smugly. "Starting the Criminal Justice program in the fall is my first step toward finally joining the FBI."

Without ever seeing it, Billy hit a massive puddle—gallons of water collected in a crater shaped by the winter plows—that immediately halted their speed and yanked them half out of their lane. Billy's heart plummeted in his chest. For one brief moment, Mother Nature had taken control out of his hands and he knew it.

"Showers for the remainder of the night," the deep radio voice announced.

Billy shook his head and turned to Charlie. "Showers?" he said. "If it gets any worse, we'll be doing the backstroke home." Billy turned the radio off to concentrate on the vanishing road, while the heavy rains pounded off the side of the car.

"Relax, buddy," Charlie said, obviously amused by Billy's elevated stress level. "You need to stop worrying so much."

Billy looked sideways again and snickered. "Yeah right," he said. Until having to pick a college major, he couldn't remember the last time he'd worried about anything. Passing another blurry green exit sign, Billy did all he could to keep the nose of the beat-up Honda straight and proceed carefully down the slippery highway. He turned the windshield wipers to high and listened as the lone wiper kept perfect beat with his heart. The white reflective lines painted on the road sparkled like beacons in the night. Hypnotized, he hugged each one and couldn't wait to see the next green sign. "Three more to go and we're home free," he told Charlie.

Slouched down in the passenger seat, Charlie shrugged. "Hey, did I tell you that I got Mark good the other day?"

Billy shook his head.

Charlie sat up straight in his seat and laughed, excited to share his latest prank. "I told that girl he likes that I caught him using bathroom air freshener as cologne and she..."

Suddenly, the Honda's back end skidded, kicking the car onto the slightest angle. The skid lasted no more than a second or two, but it was enough time for Billy to watch his entire life pass before the rain-smudged windshield. It was a brief film. "This is bad," he said aloud and swallowed hard.

Charlie went silent—as if he'd just realized they might be in danger—and never bothered to finish his story.

In the silence, the rain only picked up, while the angry winds continued to play ping-pong with their lives. His white knuckles wrapped around the steering wheel, Billy slid to the edge of the driver's seat and slowly continued on. "Relax," he teased Charlie. "You worry too much."

The *EXIT 8—WESTPORT* sign glistened in the storm, indicating there were only two more exits to go. Billy felt more relieved with each mile passed and gradually slid back into the bucket seat.

"Hey, take me home, okay?" Charlie told Billy.

Billy was surprised. "You're not sleeping over?"

Charlie shook his head. "I can't tonight. I told my mother I'd sleep home." As Billy started to question it, Charlie added, "Hey, I'm going to need help valeting cars."

"What night?" Billy asked. "...because I can't lose my job at the Pearl."

"Yeah, what a tragedy that would be...getting canned from that Chinese slave labor."

Billy laughed. "It's a job," he said, "and I need every penny I can make for college."

"That's right...to become a video game designer," Charlie teased.

"Whatever," Billy said, annoyed.

Charlie smirked. "So your dad's not footing the bill, huh?"

"Yeah right," Billy said, returning the smirk, "right after I get the Porsche and my sister finishes grad school."

"I need you to cover for Ryan on Thursday night," Charlie said, referring back to the valet job. "He has some wedding or something." Charlie nodded. "We'll probably each make a hundred cash. Just be there at six o'clock."

Billy returned his friend's nod. "For a hundred cash, I'll be there," he said.

Five tense minutes later, they pulled into Charlie's driveway. "I'll see you in the morning," Billy said.

"Last day of school," Charlie said, smiling. "I wouldn't miss it," he joked before jumping out of the car and sprinting toward his front door.

Before his best friend had even reached the door, Billy lost sight of his silhouette in the rain. "Me either," Billy said and laughed, backing out of the driveway and beginning the final leg of the journey home.

At the blurry red light, he looked sideways and caught a glimpse of himself in the driver's side window. *And I am smart enough to design video games*, he told himself...*if that's what I actually wanted.*

Dripping wet but relieved to be in one piece, Billy returned home to find Jimmy, his other best friend, waiting for him.

Jimmy was so excited to see Billy that—as if his canine frame were made of rubber bones—his body bent in half from his tail wagging so hard. The dog barked and spun in circles a few times, unafraid to hang his heart out on his furry sleeve and show his love for Billy.

Billy quickly went to his knees. "Shhhh. We don't want to wake up Mom and Dad," he whispered to the dog, raking his fingers through Jimmy's heavy coat. "I'm okay, buddy," Billy added. "You missed me, didn't you?"

Jimmy barked again, answering the question. He smelled musty, like he'd just come in from the rain himself.

"Shhhh," Billy repeated and laughed.

Like most Americans, Jimmy—named after Billy's late uncle—was a mixed breed, a mutt—Labrador retriever blended with one or two unknown breeds. His shiny, raven-black coat was broken up by two white socks on his front legs and paws—and a discolored patch of fur on his hind quarter; it was an old battle scar, proof of his love and devotion to his family. A perfect white stripe ran down the length of his snout, and there was lots of snow on his muzzle and around his eyes, thick swaths of silvery fur that betrayed his advanced years and experience. His milk-chocolate eyes were soft and kind and his left ear stood up straight while the right one normally flopped onto his forehead. He had a thick barrel chest which didn't lose any girth all the way to his back hips. And his black bushy tail, dipped in white, was always on the move—as if controlled by some over-caffeinated puppeteer.

As Jimmy convulsed for attention, Billy rubbed his chest up and down—fast and hard—exactly the way the dog liked it. "Let's get a drink before we turn in," Billy told him and started for the kitchen, with Jimmy hobbling closely behind.

The two of them stepped into the dark kitchen. In the refrigerator's soft light, Billy placed the gallon of milk to his lips, tilted it toward the ceiling and took a few long gulps. In the shadows on the floor, Jimmy lapped at his water bowl, spraying back wash all over the worn linoleum. After placing the milk back into the fridge, Billy wiped his sleeve across his mouth and looked down at the sitting dog. "Do you have to go out, boy?" he asked, while the refrigerator door slowly closed and the kitchen went dark again.

As he limped past Billy, Jimmy's nails scratched across the floor. "Jimmy, your toenails need to be cut," Billy told the dog.

"You sound like a ferret on tile." Billy took a few steps toward the back door and laughed, realizing his own nails needed to be trimmed.

Jimmy waited at the back door to be let out. Years ago, the mutt had been trained to go out to the wood line to do his business. There was no need for an electric fence, just a little discipline and a whole lot of love. Jimmy always went out alone, did his thing and came back in without having to be yelled at or even summoned.

Billy opened the door. "Make it quick," he said. "It's bad out there." The rain was still coming down hard.

Two minutes later, the mildewed-smelling dog hurried back in, shaking the rain from his coat and tracking mud through the kitchen like a small monster truck.

"Oh Jimmy..." Billy complained, grabbing the paper towels and haphazardly wiping up the linoleum behind them.

After Billy relieved himself—and Jimmy waited by the bathroom door, being just as patient—the two of them stepped into Billy's bedroom. The room smelled like a mix of high school locker room and the moment a forgotten lunch box—that's been sitting in the sun for a full August afternoon—is opened. Billy huffed at the stench and looked down at Jimmy. Like a canary heading into a coal mine, the mutt didn't seem to notice; with his head down, he marched straight in.

A half dozen hip-hop posters covered the cracks in the plaster walls. The only window in the room was covered by an old throw blanket, which was intended to block out every ray of the sun, whether it was morning or noon. It was a tight space containing a single bed, a small desk supporting a television and video game console, a bureau and a closet that might have comfortably stored two-dozen outfits. Instead, it was used for storage. The spring-loaded door was rarely opened, though, as everything would have spilled out. It was also the door that Billy feared throughout his childhood: the monster's front door.

A bag of cheese puffs had spilled out from the bureau onto the floor and a box of pizza crusts sat on the desk chair. "Home, sweet home," Billy told Jimmy and snickered. With all that covered it, Billy couldn't remember the last time he'd seen his bedroom carpet. A year before, his mother had abandoned any hope for the room and refused to enter it again. "You want to live like a pig, then go ahead," she'd told him. "Whatever's not in the laundry room doesn't get washed." Besides Charlie and Mark, Jimmy was the only soul brave enough to enter the landfill.

Before swiping a mountain of dirty clothes onto the floor and jumping into bed, Billy shut off the light. The night light, however, stayed on for Jimmy—the timid soul.

Even though there wasn't nearly enough room for the two of them, Jimmy jumped up onto the bed beside Billy and immediately flipped onto his back. Billy laughed. Even now—at twelve years old—Jimmy wouldn't go to sleep until he got his belly rubbed. "Aren't you tired?" he asked the squinty-eyed dog.

Jimmy never answered. He just lay on his back, his chest heaving and tongue hanging to the side.

After pampering the spoiled elder for a few minutes, Billy asked, "What do you think about me going to school for video game design, Jimmy? I could pull that off, right?"

The mutt's eyes had already turned to narrow slits.

"...or maybe I should look into the culinary arts program?" Billy suggested, letting the random idea flop around in his head for a moment or two. "I could open up my own restaurant someday. It's not like we don't love to eat." Billy tried pushing the big oaf over. It was no use. He laughed, remembering when his mom—all those years ago—had tried to stop the dog from sleeping in his bed. "He's only going to get bigger," she'd warned, "and you'll never be able to move him."

"I don't care, Ma. Just let him stay," Billy had said. "I don't care if there's no room. I want him with me."

She'd smiled. "Okay, but one of these days you're going to regret it."

As the rain and wind battered the window, Billy looked sideways at old Jimmy and tried one last time to shove him over. But the dog was already snoring and wouldn't budge an inch.

Billy chuckled again. *You were wrong, Ma,* he thought. *I still have no regrets.*

Jimmy yawned once and threw his leg—connected to its giant paw—onto Billy's chest.

Billy stared at the ceiling and smiled. When he was a young boy, Jimmy was his whole world. Now, his four-legged best friend made him feel whole. *No regrets at all,* he thought and closed his eyes, waiting for the angry storm—pounding away at his window—to sing him to sleep. But before the darkness had completely enveloped the world, Billy had his final thought of the day. *To hell with culinary arts. Owning a restaurant would be way too much work.*

Billy awoke late for his last day of school. He looked at his alarm clock and realized he'd forgotten to set it. "Oh man," he grumbled, though he felt anything but panic. He yawned once and sat up, swinging his feet onto the sea of dirty clothes. Jimmy was already waiting by the door to start the day. "Early bird," he teased the dog.

The pair moped down the hallway to the kitchen. The house was quiet; Billy's dad was traversing the first long miles of a cross-country haul, his mom was already at Nick's Pizza Shop preparing the dough for the day and Sophie—his genius sister—was nowhere to be found. *She's probably at the library, getting a head start on some stupid summer course,* he figured, and smiled at the thought of her.

Essentially sleepwalking, Billy took Jimmy outside to do his business. Hours before, the rain had stopped and the dark clouds dispersed. It was bright and sunny, a beautiful day. Billy sneezed. While he waited for Jimmy, he yawned a few times and sneezed again—which led to a dreadful sneezing fit. Within seconds, his eyes were red and swollen, and there was a tickle in his throat that couldn't possibly be scratched. Even with the heavy rains that had passed through, the tree pollen covered everything—windshields, patio furniture, Billy's esophagus—in a fine green film. It was an annual three weeks of physical torment which offered only two choices: suffer through it or take the antihistamine that pulled his head into a dense fog and made his body feel as weak as a scarecrow's. Billy was still doing his best to suffer through it.

They hurried back inside. While Jimmy watched with beggar's eyes, Billy slathered a slice of toast in thick peanut butter. He ripped off a chunk and placed two aspirin tablets—prescribed on a temporary basis by the vet—in the middle to help Jimmy manage his arthritis and the other pains of old age. The dog inhaled it. "Jimmy, you're a peanut butter junkie," Billy said. "You really need help."

After feeding Jimmy the rest of the peanut butter toast, Billy filled the dog's giant bowl—the first of two helpings he received each day—before dumping half of a box of cold cereal into his own faded bowl. He'd only taken two bites before Jimmy's loud chomping halted him. The dog was inhaling the crunchy kibble like he hadn't eaten in a week. "Go easy, boy," Billy told him, shaking his head. "Nobody's going to steal it from you. I promise."

Jimmy's head popped up briefly to glance sideways. It was enough time for a mouthful of his breakfast to fire out of the side of his jowls, salad-shooter style. But the dog never missed a beat. He was a canine vacuum cleaner. Whether it was escapee kibble or those brown, snail-like stains—similar to what a baby's teething cookie leaves behind—Jimmy made good on mopping up his own messes.

"You're going to get sick eating that fast," Billy teased him. "And you're going to get even fatter."

By this time, the dog was nearly done vacuuming the kitchen floor.

Billy laughed. Jimmy's ideal weight was fifty pounds, but somewhere along the way he'd acquired a bad habit of snacking between meals, so he now tipped the scale at just over seventy pounds and bordered on obese.

Jimmy finally looked up, as if he realized he'd just been slighted.

"Sorry, big boy," Billy said, chuckling, "I didn't mean to insult you."

Without dignifying the comment with a response, Jimmy jumped right into his morning hygiene session. The big mutt was obsessive compulsive, always licking his paw and running it across his face and behind his ears. And he washed up three or four times a day, whether he needed it or not.

"Clean freak," Billy told him and, leaving the dog to his bath, returned to his cereal. The milk had already turned to a rich, chocolaty brown. *Perfect*, he thought.

It didn't take long to get ready for school. Being the opposite of Jimmy—somewhat hygienically challenged—Billy quickly brushed his teeth and washed his face. He then ran a brush through his hair three times or until he hit a knot he was in no mood to tackle. Just as he prepared to leave the bathroom, he paused in the mirror for a moment and gazed at his reflection through red puffy eyes.

At seventeen years old, he was already 6'2" on a wiry frame he was still filling out; he sensed it would be a few years before he wore it comfortably. He had brown hair, light mocha eyes and short-cropped hair that was tapered in the back, with sideburns sculpted in the shape of long, sharp fangs. He also had straight white teeth, thanks to two years of wearing braces and his father's overtime hours to pay for them. He reached up and rubbed his failed goatee, a sad patch of facial hair kept to conceal the final remnants of chin acne—just another cruel cost of passing through adolescence. "You need to get a real job," he told his reflection.

While Jimmy watched his every move—and was already fidgeting at the realization he was being left alone—Billy threw on a white V-neck t-shirt, a pair of worn jeans and a new pair of Nikes, purchased with his birthday money. He looked at his alarm clock again and whistled. "Wow, I'm really late," he said, and couldn't have cared any less if he were still sleeping.

He turned on the video game console, grabbed one of the controllers and sat on the edge of his bed. "One quick game won't hurt," he told Jimmy.

As if a switch had been thrown, the dog collapsed to his front paws.

Twenty minutes later, Billy paused the game and emerged from his fog.

Billy headed for the front door with Jimmy on his heels. They faced each other. "Sorry, Jimmy, but you don't need to walk me to school today," Billy said, referring to the daily routine they'd kept all through his school years. "I'm taking my car."

Jimmy whimpered and raised his paw six inches off the floor.

Billy threw his backpack over his right shoulder and took a knee. "I'll be back before you know it," he said, kissing the crown of Jimmy's silver head. "Just be good while I'm gone, okay?"

Jimmy whined.

"You'll be fine," Billy promised—as he'd promised each and every day for years—and closed the door behind him. After checking that it was locked, Billy sneezed hard. "Damn allergies," he complained.

Jimmy whimpered from behind the closed door.

The days of high school fun were quickly coming to a close. Billy Baker, Mark Diethelm and Charlie Philips stepped into their third period biology class. While Billy and Mark headed for the rear of the room, Charlie sat down in the front seat. It was an assigned seat—a punishment for constantly horsing around. He looked over his shoulder and grinned. "I'll never forget all the love we've experienced in this room, boys," he told Billy and Mark.

The class—Charlie's devoted minions—erupted in laughter. They all knew their teacher, Mr. Olivier, had missed his

calling. The old grump should have been an undertaker special-
izing in high school students.

Mr. Olivier caught the comment and informed the heckler,
"One more immature outburst like that and you're out of here,
Mr. Philips."

"I'm out of here anyway, Mr. Olivier," Charlie said, the
man's warning bringing out the smart-mouthed child in him.
"We all are." He grinned wider.

The laughter only grew louder.

Mr. Olivier shook his head in disgust and pointed toward
the door. "You first then."

Charlie stood, faced his classmates and took his final high
school bow. While the class erupted in applause, he slowly
strolled out of the room.

Billy looked at Mark. "And he wants to be an FBI agent."

Mark shook his head and laughed. "He's got a better shot at
making the FBI's most wanted list," he joked.

After class, Billy and Mark found Charlie waiting with his
girlfriend Bianca in the hallway—wearing his signature smirk.

"There's the perfect couple now," Billy called out, making
Bianca blush. Both of them had blonde hair and light eyes and
were as physically fit as champion swimmers. If either of them
had been called pretty, it wouldn't have been a lie.

"They look more like brother and sister to me," Mark mumbled under his breath.

Billy laughed before sneezing twice. He looked back at his
friend and laughed again. Tall and lanky, Mark had worn a five
o'clock shadow since the eighth grade; he'd been a big kid who'd
stopped growing long before his peers. His bushy eyebrows—
like protective awnings—shaded his already dark eyes, giving
him a mature look. His Adam's apple was the size of a baseball,
helping him retain his radio voice, which was deep and soothing—and would someday be loved by the women, but not yet.
"And you have the perfect face for radio," Billy teased him.

Mark never missed a beat. "When I grow up, Billy Baker, I
want to be just like you," he said. "This way, my mom..."

"You boys ready for lunch?" Charlie interrupted, as they approached.

"I know I am," Bianca said.

Charlie shook his head. "Sorry, babe, but we've been planning a *boys only* lunch for our last day of school," he said, "so we're heading over to Lina's Restaurant for a meal we can digest."

While Bianca folded her arms and began to pout, Billy nodded. "I'm ready," he said.

Mark shook his head. "Sorry, but my grandparents flew in this morning for graduation. I need to get home. The family's getting together this afternoon to spend time with them."

"Lucky you," Charlie teased.

"Lucky me is right," Mark shot back. "I actually like my family."

The jab was enough to shut Charlie's mouth. Everyone knew that Charlie didn't have a great home life. While his dad was out cheating, his mom was either in therapy or dabbling in script drugs and alcohol. All the while, Charlie and his sister were left to fend for themselves.

"Sorry dude," Mark said and meant it. "I didn't mean..."

Charlie waved it off. "It's fine," he said. "Now I'll only have to share my dessert with Billy."

There was polite laughter.

Mark nodded. "Have a good time without me," he said and disappeared into a thick crowd of students.

"Oh, we will," Charlie called out after him. "We will." He turned toward Bianca, who had already gone from pouting to angry. Billy stifled his grin as Charlie reached out to grab Bianca's hand. She pulled away from him and stomped down the hall after Mark.

"If it's going to be a problem, Charlie," Billy teased, "we can go out for lunch when you have permission. Why don't we just head over to the cafeteria and..."

"Whatever," Charlie said, punching his arm. "There's no way we're eating another meat surprise on our last day."

Lina's was only a small restaurant that served appetizers unloaded from a refrigerator truck. For some reason, Billy felt excited when they arrived at the place for lunch; it felt like he and Charlie had suddenly become adults. As they waited for a table in the fancy tiled foyer, Charlie whispered, "Man, is she cute!" referring to one of the waitresses' striking looks. He then looked toward Billy and grinned. "You should ask her for her cell number."

Billy half shrugged. "Yeah right, she's like ten years older than us."

"But of course you won't," Charlie added.

"Why would I, anyway? So you can sabotage me for some stupid laugh?"

"I wouldn't do that," Charlie said, but he could hardly contain his smile.

"Sure you wouldn't."

Just then, the hostess—an older woman wearing too much make-up—approached them with two menus in hand. "Are you guys together?" she asked.

Grinning, Charlie looked at Billy and nodded. "You could say that," he replied, "but somebody's afraid of the word *commitment.*"

Billy shook his head. "Here we go," he moaned, trying to suppress an ongoing sneezing fit. "Charlie, don't..."

But Charlie maintained his smile and gestured toward Billy. "He's so sensitive. He only has one feeling and I keep crushing it."

The heavy-set woman laughed, while Billy shook his head. "Don't listen to him," he told her, his face burning red.

"Okay then," she said, trying to stifle a laugh while leading them to a table near the window.

They took their seats across from each other. Charlie stared at Billy, while Billy struggled to avoid his friend's comical gaze—until they both started laughing. "And you wonder why I can't find a girlfriend," Billy said.

Charlie's face turned serious. "Don't give me that crap, Billy," he said. "You know I've never messed with you around girls our age. The reason you can't find a girlfriend is because you haven't found your testicles yet." He smiled. "And as soon as you do, you'll be unstoppable."

Billy stared at his best friend thinking, *For those who don't know Charlie...really know him...they'd absolutely hate him.* But beneath the sarcastic clown's rough exterior was a fiercely loyal and caring friend.

As they scanned the tall menus, Charlie said, "So your parents are throwing you a bash for graduation, huh?"

Billy nodded. "Yup, whether I want it or not."

Charlie shook his head. "Are you crazy? Graduation parties mean cards stuffed with cash."

"I guess," Billy said, trying to decide between the cheeseburger or the turkey and stuffing wrap.

"You guess?" Charlie replied. "You'll probably make more money at that party than you will all summer sweating your ass off at Oriental Pearl."

Billy shook his head. "I need to find something better than the Pearl," Billy said, "or I'll end up in tractor-trailer school in the fall." As soon as the words left his lips, he felt sorry for them.

"What's wrong with that?" Charlie asked. "Your dad's done all right for himself."

"I didn't mean it that way," Billy said, regretfully.

Charlie grinned. "So how much do you think Aunt Phoebe's going to give you?"

"Give me?" Billy asked.

"For a graduation gift?" Charlie added.

Billy laughed. "Who knows. Maybe..."

The pretty waitress approached with a smile. "You guys ready to order?" she asked.

Charlie snapped his menu closed. "Let me get the house cheeseburger with sweet potato fries and a Coke." He smirked. "By the way, how fresh are those fries?" he asked.

She glared down at him. "As fresh as frozen sweet potato fries can be," she said, her smile erased.

"That sounds perfect," he said. "I'll take them."

With a slight shake of her head, she scribbled Charlie's order into her notepad. "And you?" she asked, looking toward Billy.

"Give me the same thing, please," he said, stifling an oncoming sneezing fit, "but I want my burger cooked medium."

Finishing the order in her book, she hurried away.

"Go ahead, keep playing with people, Charlie," Billy said, sneezing once, "and you're going to eat a lot of food covered in spit."

Charlie laughed. "That's an old wives' tale," he said. "I don't think people actually do that."

"Sure they don't," Billy said, embarking on another sneezing fit.

"I was just messing with her."

"I know, but I'm pretty sure she didn't appreciate being messed with." He grinned. "I don't think most people appreciate it."

Charlie nodded in surrender. After a few moments, he broke the silence. "We've come a long way since freshman year, Billy Boy," he announced, grinning, "when you got stuffed into that gym locker."

"They were football players and there were three of them," Billy shot back. "And I think one of them was into his sixth year of high school."

While they both laughed, the waitress delivered their drinks.

Charlie's eyes went wide. "Remember Mr. Bulging Eyes?" he asked, taking a sip of his cola.

Billy took a deep breath. "I wish I didn't," he said, while his mind raced back to one of the scariest experiences of his short life.

It was supposed to be a joy ride, an innocent childhood prank, but it turned into a nightmare. They were fourteen years old when they took Charlie's father's car. Charlie drove, while Billy and Mark were willing passengers. They headed down the road and took a right toward a private lane that ran the length of the pond. Charlie punched the gas, squealing the tires and throwing up rocks, as he barreled down the narrow lane.

As they turned the car around, they saw that a mob of unhappy neighbors had gathered at the top of the road waiting to greet them.

"Oh crap!" Charlie said, as he drove back slowly to face their jury.

With his heart in his throat, Billy looked at Mark whose face was already bleached white. *This is bad*, he thought.

When they reached the yelling mob and stopped the car, Charlie cracked the window a few inches. A man with bulging eyes approached and, although his anger was understandable, the rage in his voice seemed incredibly inappropriate. While the boys became terrified, Charlie tried to remain calm.

The man wedged his fingers into the window and told them, "Get out of the car now! We're going to call the police."

"Go ahead and call the cops then," Charlie told the lunatic, "but we're not getting out of the car."

"Get out!" the man screamed, while his massive fingers pulled on the window, trying to break it. As Billy recalled, it was like being in a horror movie. And then Charlie stomped on the gas.

Mr. Bulging Eyes never let go and was dragged over several bushes before he was thrown away from the car. Charlie panicked. He took a quick right and started for the man's backyard. Billy and Mark looked back. By now, Mr. Bulging Eyes was up and running—with the rest of the neighborhood taking chase. "Oh shit!" they screamed.

Charlie kept his foot to the floor when they hit the soft lawn. The car began to sink. Grass and mud kicked up from the rear wheels, as the car began carving a tank trench into the furious man's yard. Just when it looked like they were goners, the car swayed right, then left, then right again until it bucked itself free. Charlie aimed for the road.

The mob was now screaming for blood. The boys looked back. Mark yelled, "Rock!" He and Billy took cover. A second later, a small boulder crashed through the rear window and landed on the back seat. They looked up. The giant was smiling. *He could have competed at shot put in the Olympics,* Billy thought.

They got to the end of the road, bailed out of the damaged car and sprinted for home.

For once, their parents' faces—and the police—seemed like child's play. They needed protection.

Billy returned to the present and grinned. "I think Mark crapped his Underoos that day," he said, wiping his itchy, swollen eyes.

"I think you're right," Charlie agreed.

Billy studied his friend's face. "He didn't mean anything about that comment, you know...the one he made about your family," Billy said.

"No shit, Sherlock," Charlie said. "Mark's the nicest guy I know."

"Gee, thanks."

"But he is, dude." Charlie's right eyebrow stood at attention. "Tell me he's not?"

Billy nodded. "You're right. That boy's way ahead of his time."

Mark never really fit into any one group or category— whether they were jocks, brains, motor heads or theatre rats. Instead, he drifted around, belonging to them all. And no matter where he landed, he proved to be a fiercely loyal friend. He was the earthy-crunchy type—very intelligent but not pretentious. And although he served as the butt of many jokes, it didn't seem to bother him. He was just comfortable in his own skin.

The waitress delivered their lunches, minus her original smile. As she walked away, Charlie inspected his burger and flipped a few of the orange-colored fries around.

Billy laughed. "And you want to be a professional investigator?" Billy asked, snickering.

"What?" Charlie said. "You're the one who said she might spit in my food."

Billy nodded. "Sure, but if I were you I would have checked my drink first," he said, shrugging. "It seems like the more obvious place to hock a nasty wad of spit."

Charlie considered it and slowly pushed his drink away from him. "So you're valeting with me tomorrow night, right?"

Billy nodded. "I told you already; I got your back."

As the waitress passed their table, Charlie flagged her down. "Excuse me, Miss, but can I please get another drink? I just found something floating in mine."

She scooped up his glass, looked into it and shook her head again. "Fine," she said.

The boys ate in silence, exchanging a few grunts and groans as they devoured their last high school lunch together. The waitress delivered the fresh soda. Charlie studied it for a few extended moments before taking a long drink.

Billy laughed. "Feel better, detective?" he asked, filling his mouth with fries.

"I do," Charlie said, taking another sip.

Before long, Charlie grabbed his midsection and grinned. "This was good," he said. "I'm glad we came here."

"Me too," Billy said.

As the waitress rushed by, she slapped the check onto the table.

Charlie grinned. "I don't think she likes me," he said.

"And who could blame her?" Billy said.

Charlie nodded in agreement, but quickly changed the subject. "I don't think I'm going to miss the lunches at school, that's for sure."

"Neither am I," Billy said and laughed.

Charlie stood, looked at the bill and threw some money onto the table. "I need to go find Bianca," he said, rolling his eyes. "I have a feeling she's going to make me pay for this lunch again." He took one last drink and started for the front door.

Billy nodded, watching his friend scurry out of the restaurant. Billy picked up the bill and added his money to Charlie's, throwing in a few extra bucks for the poor waitress' troubles. *It isn't much,* he thought, *but it's more than she would have gotten, if Charlie hadn't run his mouth.*

Charlie had been parking cars as a valet attendant for months and bragged about the job like he'd hit the lottery. "Tons of under-the-table cash to drive every car we could never afford," he told Billy and Mark. "It's a dream come true."

Right away, Charlie showed Billy the ropes. He jumped into the next car that pulled into the lot—a Cadillac—and wheeled it around the corner. As Billy watched—and the car owner disappeared into the nightclub—Charlie tapped the building before backing the Cadillac straight into a chain link fence. He jumped out, smiling. "Make sure you keep 'em parked tight," he said.

Billy shook his head, thinking, *We're going to get paid to abuse cars?*

Billy quickly learned that Charlie hadn't been lying. *This job is a blast.* A car pulled up. Billy opened both doors, offered the driver a numbered ticket and then parked the car in the massive lot. There were varied distances from the seats to the steering wheels, and most cars smelled like a mix of doggy bag food, cologne and perfume.

Once a patron left the club, they handed Billy their valet ticket. He ran into the lot, quickly searched out their car and drove it back to them—insuring to keep both doors open. For this alone, the average tip was two to three dollars. The small lot fit better than fifty cars snugly.

An hour went by when Charlie appeared with a man on his arm. He escorted the staggering man over to Billy and announced, "Mr. Rollins, here, is a customer who's not too happy about you denting his car. And he wants a few words with you." Without another word, Charlie turned on his heels and marched off into the shadows.

Instinctively, Billy apologized. "I'm so sorry, sir. Which car is yours?"

The man became enraged, flailing his arms and muttering words that were more than likely vulgarities—though Billy couldn't tell for sure. "Can you please show me the damage to your car?" he asked the inebriated man, feeling horrible about the situation.

The drunk spun on his heels and wobbled off into the lot, wandering through the rows of cars—occasionally going to his knees to search for something beneath them.

Confused, Billy followed, attempting to gain more answers with each row of cars they passed.

This went on for a few minutes until business started picking up. "Are you all done messing around, Billy?" Charlie yelled. "We have cars to park."

By then, Billy understood that he'd been playing the victim of another stupid prank.

Charlie later filled him in that he'd discovered the intoxicated man passed out in the gutter. He grabbed the stranger by the arm and helped him up. The man began slurring his words beyond recognition, while Charlie quickly deciphered that the drunk had lost his bottle of gin and wanted help finding it. "I have just the person you need to talk to," he told the wasted man and took him straight to Billy.

Billy laughed along with his friend. "You're going to get yours, Charlie. Trust me, it's coming."

It was one o'clock in the morning when Billy returned home. Jimmy was waiting for him at the front door. Although Jimmy was too exhausted to spin in circles and perform like some circus dog, Billy realized, *He still waited up.*

Billy closed the front door, went to one knee and scratched the black mutt's neck. "Good boy, Jimmy," he told him. "Did you have a nice night?"

The mutt sighed heavily.

Billy laughed. "That says it all, buddy. Let's go to bed." As they headed for Billy's dumpster of a room, he asked Jimmy,

"What do you think about me going to school for law enforcement? If Charlie can get accepted into the program, then I should..."

Jimmy yawned, more interested in sleep.

"You're right," Billy said. "It is a stupid idea."

Chapter 2

Billy couldn't take the sneezing and watery eyes anymore and finally surrendered. With the help of one tiny white pill, his aggravating symptoms were instantly alleviated, leaving his entire world covered in a thick coat of syrup.

The few days that led up to graduation flew by, filled with enough distractions so that little thought was focused on life or the future. Like mosquitos to a bug light, Billy, Charlie, Mark and Jimmy ended up in Billy's bedroom, engaged in multiple video game tournaments that started late in the afternoon and went deep into the night, without them exchanging one serious word. It was a bizarre tradition they'd perfected throughout high school, sharpening their tongues through witty banter.

"Can you buy men's clothes where you got that shirt?" Charlie asked Mark, as he stalked him on the screen.

"What's that?" Mark asked, in deep concentration.

Charlie quickly looked sideways. "What's the matter with you? Are you on a three-second delay or something?"

Billy laughed but never looked up from the game.

"Why are you even here, Charlie?" Mark asked, his eyes also locked onto the television. "The restraining order doesn't mean anything to you, does it?"

Although they heckled one another, each heated competition required their full and complete concentration.

"Restraining order?" Charlie repeated and snickered. "I do more around this house than Billy does. They'd never get rid of me."

Mark quickly looked at Billy, who nodded it was true. They all laughed.

"Whatever, Quasimodo," Billy said and leapt off the bed as he launched his attack on screen. "Got you, lollipop!" he screamed at Charlie. "You're dead."

Charlie threw his controller onto the floor and grinned. He clearly had an advantage in the verbal combat now and everyone knew it. "You know, Billy," he said, "if you're not gay, then you've got a lot of people fooled."

Mark had just taken a drink of soda and gagged, nearly spraying the liquid out of his nose.

"Yeah okay," Billy countered, still concentrating on the screen. "If there's such a thing as reincarnation, I want to come back as you, Charlie. You're my hero."

"Well, I'm not a very strong person, but I do possess an inner strength," Charlie quipped.

Mark nodded. "And he really likes pinwheels in autumn and the idea that no two snowflakes are the same," he added.

Billy laughed—just in time for Mark to deliver the fatal blow.

Mark threw his arms into the air in victory. "Champion again!" he sang, as a chorus of one.

"Yeah, for the next half hour anyway," Charlie said, resetting the game.

Billy turned to the newest champion. "Look at you, Marky Mark. You're so animated you should come with your own theme song."

"When you become a video game programmer, Billy, you should design one that half-wits like Mark can't win," Charlie said.

Billy glared at him.

"Video game programmer?" Mark chimed in. "I thought Billy Baker was going to be a candlestick maker?"

Both Charlie and Mark laughed.

"Don't worry about me, fellas. I'll be just fine," Billy said, nodding. "Trust me, I'm not worried in the least," he lied.

While the vicious mockery continued, they played game after game—until they were oblivious to reality.

On the morning before Billy's graduation, Billy and Jimmy awoke late. Amidst walls papered in famous rappers, Billy turned to his side. "Are you going to sleep the whole day away?" he teased the dog.

Jimmy yawned and awkwardly jumped down from the bed. Billy swore he saw the old mutt grimace before letting out a heavy sigh. Jimmy stood motionless for a few moments until he was sure he had his legs under him. He took a step, wobbled once, paused and then picked up the pace. Momentum carried him out of the bedroom to where he needed to go.

Billy literally rolled out of bed and sat yawning for a few minutes.

Jimmy barked, calling from the kitchen. From his urgent tone, he needed to go out to relieve himself and couldn't wait.

"Okay, okay," Billy said and popped up in his boxer briefs. He ran down the hall on feet that were not yet awake or filled with blood. The last few steps into the kitchen resembled a stomp dance gone wrong. When Billy opened the door, Jimmy bolted out and moved as fast as his elderly legs would take him.

"You're such a pain in the butt," Billy said, yawning.

Jimmy headed for the back of the yard and squatted.

"Right," Billy mumbled and turned to avoid the show. "You need some privacy."

After a healthy breakfast of two Pop Tarts, an antihistamine and a warm glass of root beer for Billy, and two peanut butter-covered aspirin, an overflowing bowl of kibble and some fresh water for Jimmy, the dog licked his paw and ran it across his face and behind his ears.

After Jimmy's bath, the two of them headed outside, Billy now properly attired in old sweat pants and a torn t-shirt.

Billy picked up the green Frisbee that sat on the deck and flung it into the yard.

Jimmy looked up at him like he was insane.

Billy laughed. "Sorry buddy," he said, "if you could toss it I'd shag, but..."

Jimmy slowly walked over to the Frisbee and grabbed it with his teeth. He carried it back to Billy and dropped it at his feet.

"That works for me, Jimmy."

The silver-faced dog lay down and yawned. He was too tired for anything but relaxing. Billy didn't mind. They sat together for a long while, both content to be in each other's sluggish company.

"Well, we did it, buddy," Billy said, breaking the silence. "We made it through high school." He threw his arm around Jimmy's back. "And this is going to be the summer of our lives."

Jimmy's eyes rotated up in a pathetic display of interest; no other part of him moved.

"We'll go for ice cream and long rides in the car and swimming at the beach," Billy said excitedly, "and we'll even go camping...your favorite."

Jimmy yawned again.

Billy laughed and lay on the deck beside him. "It's going to be a summer to remember," he promised. "You just wait and see."

They lay side-by-side for some time, eyes closed and content to share in the silence. Suddenly, in the stillness, the weight of an unknown future descended upon Billy. "It's what's going to happen after summer that I'm starting to worry about," he confessed aloud.

Jimmy immediately opened his eyes and looked at Billy, ready to listen.

"I mean, think about it...I'm supposed to know, *right now*, what I want to do for the rest of my life? Who I'm supposed to become?" He took a deep breath. "Until recently, the only decision I needed to make was what to order for lunch." He looked sideways at Jimmy. "I probably shouldn't worry, but I have no idea what I want out of life and it seems stupid to go to college and study something I may never care about...or use."

Jimmy whimpered.

"Relax. I'm not thinking about *not going* to college. It's just that I'd feel a hell of a lot better about it if I knew what I was going for, you know?"

The mutt squirmed closer, resting his chin on Billy's arm.

"Charlie's going to school for criminal justice. Mark's going for engineering." He sighed. "It seems like every one of my friends is excited about chasing after their dreams, but I..." He stopped and took in a few deep breaths. "I don't have a clue about what I should be chasing, Jimmy." He rolled his head back and forth on the deck. "And if growing up means feeling lost, then they can keep it."

This time, Jimmy sighed.

While a soft breeze sang in the blossoming trees, Billy closed his eyes and tried to quiet his mind; he tried to return to the blissful ignorance he'd spent his entire life enjoying. It was no use. He needed an answer to his dilemma. He needed to discover his passion.

Some time passed, enough time for Jimmy to settle into a peaceful nap. "What about social work?" Billy suggested, startling the dog from his slumber. "Mom's cousin, Paula, was a social worker and she's helped more people than you could count." He thought about it. "I like helping people."

Jimmy sighed again.

"All right, I get it," Billy said. "I'll keep working on it."

Beneath his maroon gown and cap, Billy wore khakis—pulled up to his waist for the special occasion—a button-down shirt, high tops and dark sunglasses, just like Charlie and Mark.

The unauthorized eyewear was their small display of rebellion against "the man."

The sky was blue and, although it was a beautiful day to the eye, the sun beat down mercilessly generating an unseasonably warm temperature. Billy's shirt collar was already saturated in sweat, stinging his neck. The fold-out chairs—a thousand in all—were packed tightly together on the lawn, allowing little room for anyone to breathe. Billy looked back at his parents and Sophie, who were already squirming in the heat. *I may not have finished at the top of my class like Sophie*, he thought, *but at least I finished*. He then turned to Mark. "There are a lot of pretty girls here today," he whispered.

Mark grinned. "Yup, and we've been with most of them every single day for the last four years."

Billy took another look around. *He's right*, he thought, *but somehow they look different today*. He couldn't believe how fast the years had whipped by. Not so long ago, he was being babysat by a goofy purple dinosaur named Barney and swearing that the white Power Ranger was the greatest hero of all time. And now, he was taking his final steps out of childhood.

After hearing an extended congratulations from the school principal, district superintendent and class valedictorian, groans amongst the crowd were beginning to grow in number and volume.

The keynote speaker finally approached the podium and, after thanking all the long-winded dignitaries and suffering faculty, he addressed the graduating class. "Yours is an entitled generation," he read from his notes and looked up. "And I'm here on behalf of my generation to apologize to you and to explain that the real world is nothing like the childhoods you're graduating from today."

Billy looked at Charlie and Mark and snickered. "This ought to be something," he mumbled.

"Yours is an entitled generation," the speaker repeated, "and it's not your fault. It's mine." He paused. "You see, my mom and dad made me do chores to earn an allowance. No clean dishes, no spending money. When I wasn't hustling to make a few dollars, I played Little League. But I never made the All Star team." He cleared his throat and shrugged. "When my kids started playing baseball, I threw a few games and let them win—something my dad never did. And today, everyone gets a trophy whether they deserve it or not.

"I swore my kids were going to have a better life—an easier time of it—and I'm pretty sure my friends, your parents, thought the same way. So we grew up, worked our way through college, got jobs and worked even harder to climb the ladder to a better job—until we could afford a down payment on a house that would take us thirty years to pay off. We got married and had kids—you guys. And we kept our promise. We gave you everything—sometimes before you even asked."

Billy turned right to see Mark looking at him. They rolled their eyes at the same time.

"When I was a kid, Christmas was a really, really big deal," the speaker continued. "Each year, we got a bike or some big ticket item. For my kids, it's actually tough for me to figure out what to buy them for Christmas because they already have everything. They..."

I hope Mom put the air conditioner on for Jimmy, Billy thought. *It's hot as hell today.*

"You have to learn to lose before you can win," the man rambled on. "You have to build a work ethic. Go out into the world and experience just how terrible manual and menial jobs can be...along with the pitiful pay. Only then can you completely commit to education and truly value it."

Billy actually chuckled aloud. *I work at the Oriental Pearl,* he thought. *You can't get much more manual and menial than that. And the pay...*

"I learned to solve problems and face bullies all on my own. But not you," the speaker said, "you..."

Is this guy for real? Billy thought. *He'll be lucky if he doesn't get booed off the stage.* He scanned the crowd. The entire audience—all thousand sweaty people—sat completely silent. Most of them looked dazed and confused. *Hypnotized by bullshit*, Billy thought.

Even in the awkward silence, the speaker was determined to finish his bleak message. "So let me tell you about the real world—what you absolutely need to know as you prepare to peek your head outside of this red-bricked sanctuary you've spent the last four years in.

"Not everyone makes the team. And trophies..." He shook his head. "Nope, you don't get them for just showing up. It's a very competitive world and there's no such thing as luck. In the real world, we never get what we wish for. We get what we work for. And that's *if* we stay at it long enough.

"No one, other than your parents, will fight your battles for you. And you'll soon discover that..."

Whoever hired this joker is probably going to hear it, Billy thought. *And I doubt they'll ever be allowed to book another speaker.*

"My job as a parent," he continued on, "my one and only real job is to prepare my children to thrive—even to survive—and because of my childhood dejections, I chose to coddle them instead. All the years they should have been building muscle and endurance to face the challenges of the world, I was..." The man's words drifted off. "Blah, blah, blah..."

Billy couldn't help it. Between the heat and his lack of interest, he kept zoning out. He looked around and saw that most eyes were glazed over in a zombie-like state; everyone was just trying to get through it, obviously hoping it would end soon. *I wonder how many parties me and the boys will hit over the next couple weeks?* Billy wondered.

The man turned up the volume, drawing everyone's attention back to him. "So I'll tell you exactly what I've told my kids. On behalf of my generation, I apologize for having failed you..."

The audience shifted uneasily in their chairs, some going as far as letting out grunts of disapproval. Billy was hopeful, thinking, *It looks like this self-righteous wind bag is about to wrap up.*

"Just don't be delusional and leave this auditorium thinking that your existence, up until this point, has been anything but a fantasy. The world out there is not nearly as kind or fair as what you've experienced thus far. *You*—not Mom or Dad—but *you* will have to work hard for everything you get from here on. *You* will have to take accountability for your own life. *You* will be the one who must..."

Billy sighed heavily and looked sideways at Charlie, who had his eyes closed.

The speaker looked up from the lectern and softened his tone for the big finish. "Some of my words may have come across as harsh, I know. But understand that my intentions are good and I don't want a lie to be the last thing you hear in this school." As if in prayer, he folded his hands together. "So please do me and my foolish generation a huge favor and let us off the hook. Please go out there and live the most accomplished and amazing lives any generation ever boasted. Don't be afraid to fail, especially in pursuit of something you feel passionate about, because that's where success can be found." He folded his papers and stepped down from his mahogany soap box.

There was some genuine applause—coming from some of the parents—but the audience's reaction was mixed at best. It was like they'd gotten slapped with one hand and hugged with the other. The speech was tough love in its strangest form and the aftertaste was a bitter one.

Although Billy clapped softly, he didn't like or appreciate the speech. He turned to Charlie. "This guy has no idea what the hell he's talking about," he whispered. "He's so full of it."

Billy looked back at his parents. Neither of them was clapping. Sophie, on the other hand, was grinning. *It figures she'd appreciate that speech,* he thought, chuckling to himself.

At the end of the graduation ceremony, Billy's high school class threw their caps into the baby-blue sky and watched as they floated down like certificates of freedom. Their scrolled diplomas were their tickets out of childhood—free passes into the real world. Billy looked around and scanned many of their faces—smiles he'd known since first grade. *Most are going on to college,* he thought, *and a few others into the military.* The reality of it made him feel sad. *At least we still have one last summer*, he reminded himself.

In the third row, Mom, Dad and Sophie were still hanging in there—even smiling. Billy marched straight to them.

He wasn't ten feet from them when his dad, Norman Rockwell Baker, barked out, "There he is, our high school graduate!" Billy's dad was tall and burly, with wavy chestnut hair and a square chin. Although he was handsome, his passion for food had bloated his midsection or "dinner muscle" as he liked to call it.

Billy stepped into his mother's embrace first. "We're so proud of you, Billy," she said and swayed with him amongst the sea of people like they were all alone. Margaret "Maggie" Baker had short-cropped auburn hair with a nice wave. Soft green eyes, with crow's feet at the corners, betrayed her proud Irish ethnicity. She was well-endowed with a full midsection and a big backside that she claimed was "a gift from the pizza shop." She wore very little makeup and although jolly was not a word often used to describe women, there was no better word to portray her. "So proud," she repeated, kissing Billy's cheek.

He let go of one hug and locked onto another, stepping into his father's open arms. The large truck driver slapped Billy a few times on the back like he was trying to dislodge a chicken bone from his throat. "Your mom's right," his dad whispered, the man's voice laden with emotion he fought hard to keep at bay. "We're real proud, son. Congratulations!"

Stepping back, Billy looked into his dad's misty eyes. They nodded at each other. It was a subtle exchange, but they both understood it meant infinitely more.

Billy turned and looked down at Sophie, his older sister. "You made it, Billy," she teased. "In spite of yourself, you did it." Billy laughed and they hugged. Sophie was shorter than him and cute, but her appearance was deceiving; she was as smart and intense as anyone Billy had ever known. And she was totally driven to make something of her life and become someone. "I'm proud of you, Billy," she whispered.

He felt his chest grow warm. Coming from Sophie, those five words meant the world. She'd been his rock since he could remember. "Thanks, Sophe," he said.

"And this is just the start for you," Sophie added. "You're going to do something amazing with your life, I just know it... once you stop being so lazy and grow up a little."

"Thanks," he repeated, feeling the sting of her backhanded compliment, "I think."

Billy's mom solicited the help of an elderly woman and the Baker family posed for several smiling photos. The family then stood in a circle for a while, wishing Billy "all the luck in the world" and discussing the incredible things that Sophie had predicted for him.

I hope she's right, Billy thought. As he listened and smiled, he felt a strange release from childhood. If he didn't know any better, he would have sworn he was now being spoken to with more respect—respect he had not yet earned. It felt awkward and a little scary.

His mom smiled. "That keynote's speech was unexpected," she whispered.

"And right on the mark for most of it," his dad added at his usual volume.

Billy snickered and looked at Sophie. Although she seemed a bit distracted and not her usual attentive self, she still nodded—surprising Billy more. "I think the man made some good points, too," she said.

After a few more photos, Billy said, "I should go congratulate my classmates. I may never see some of them again."

"Of course," his dad said, "go do your thing."

"Will you be home later?" his mom asked.

"Yup," Billy said and disappeared into the thick crowd to rejoin his friends, while his family headed home.

As Billy bounced off of people and excused himself a half dozen times, a pair of conflicting thoughts wrestled in his mind. *High school's finally over*, he thought, filled with excitement and joy. And then it hit him, freezing him in place for a moment. *Oh my God, high school's over*, he thought, feeling like a blanket of sorrow had just been draped over him.

He'd already shaken four hands and hugged three tearful girls when he was approached by Neil Jeronimo, a gifted stage actor and classmate since the first grade. "Where are you off to next year, Billy?" Neil asked.

"UMASS," Billy quickly answered. "I'm going to get some core classes under my belt and then I'm leaning toward pre-med," he fibbed.

Neil whistled. "Good for you. That's a lot of school." He shook his head. "You're a better man than I, Gunga Din." He paused in thought. "Wait a minute. I thought you hated the sight of blood. Remember that time in the fifth grade when you cut your arm in gym class and passed out." He laughed at the memory. "Some of the girls thought you'd actually died and..."

"Yeah, I got over my fear of blood a long time ago," Billy interrupted with a smile. "So where are you headed, Neil?" he asked, redirecting the conversation.

"Rhode Island College," he said. "I'll be majoring in Musical Theatre." His eyes looked like they were on fire when he announced it.

"Then it's off to Broadway, right?" Billy said.

Neil half shrugged. "That's the plan, anyway."

"You're going to make it big, Neil," Billy said and meant it. "I just hope you don't forget us little people when you do."

Neil chuckled, gratefully.

"Any chance I can score some free tickets to your first show?"

"You really think you'll need free tickets on a doctor's salary?" Neil teased.

Billy could feel his face blush. He quickly extended his hand. "I wish you all the best, my friend. I really do."

Neil shook his hand. "And I wish you the same, Billy."

As Billy walked away, although he'd never dream of musical theatre for himself, he felt envious of Neil. *At least he's excited about where he's heading*, he thought.

Billy drove home in his beat-up Honda—with its loud exhaust pipe and bumper sticker that read, *Free Tibet*—to find

Charlie and an excited Jimmy already waiting for him at the house. There was a bouquet of flowers sitting in a vase on the living room coffee table.

"Who are these for?" Billy asked, surprised to see them.

"Me," his mom answered, grinning. "Charlie gave them to me as a thank you."

"A thank you?" Billy said, looking at Charlie.

"I would have never made it through high school if it wasn't for your mom," he answered honestly.

She smiled at Charlie, before the boys started down the hallway to Billy's room.

"You brown noser," Billy said under his breath. "You're making me look bad."

"She gave birth to you, Billy, so of course she's always been there for you," Charlie said, "but she's been right there for me, too, and she never had to be." He nodded, gratefully.

It was a nice gesture and Charlie was being sincere, so Billy let it go at that. Without any further discussion, the three—Billy, Charlie and Jimmy—proceeded straight to the dump site to play video games. After four years, the decision had become involuntary. When they weren't muddling through homework, the boys played gaming tournaments that sometimes lasted late into the night. On many moons, while the wind tapped on the bedroom window, they stripped to their underwear and tried to beat the game before the sun peeked over the black horizon.

Billy was already into his attack when he yelled, "Mom, can you warm up some pizza bites for us? We're starving."

"They're easy enough to make," she called back from the living room. "I think you can handle it, Billy."

"Yeah, but they don't come out as good when I make them," he yelled back before looking at Charlie and smiling. "Besides, we just graduated and this can be part of our gift."

While they could hear her footsteps heading for the kitchen, Charlie grinned. "Yeah, that speaker dude was definitely full of crap."

Billy thought about it and smirked. "Whatever." He looked down at Jimmy. "Mom's good to us, isn't she, buddy?"

Jimmy nudged Billy with his nose.

"And can you bring Jimmy a snack too?" Billy screamed to his mother.

Charlie chuckled and shook his head. "Hey, I saw you talking to that crash dummy, Mr. McKee, at graduation," he said, referring to their old English teacher.

Billy half shrugged. "Yeah, so what?"

"Well, you're the only one in the whole school who would."

Billy offered a full shrug. "He's okay," he said, never letting on that Mr. McKee was the only teacher who'd ever showed any real interest in Billy's future or offered a single word of encouragement. Billy could still hear him: "Billy, although you do a pretty good job trying to conceal it, you're a really smart kid who has more potential than most kids I've ever known...and I've been teaching for years. It may sound clichéd, but you can honestly do anything you want, if you go and get it." The man smiled. "Now go and get it, Billy." These few simple words made Billy feel good—even special—and that one feeling was all it would take to remember Mr. McKee for the rest of his life.

"Remember when we had him for Driver's Ed?" Charlie asked, laughing.

Billy nodded, still concentrating on the video game.

"I screamed so loud one time that I thought he was going to piss his pants," Charlie said, laughing. "When we pulled over, I told him I saw a squirrel crossing the street and I thought we were going to hit it."

Billy laughed. "You really do need to be locked up," he said, before launching his final attack and winning the first game.

Just then, there was a knock on the door. "Room service, Prince William," Billy's mom said, followed by the sound of her footsteps fading away.

Billy looked at Charlie. "Can you grab our snacks?"

"Are your legs broken or something?" Charlie asked.

Billy nodded. "The doorway's as far as my mom will go. You know that."

Charlie opened the door. There were two plates of food and a stack of clean folded clothes sitting on the hallway floor. "You've got it rough," he teased Billy.

Billy laughed and looked at Jimmy. "We definitely do," he joked.

Charlie left after dinner, while Billy and Jimmy returned to the video game. There was a knock on his bedroom door. Billy looked up from the television screen to see his dad letting himself in. Billy paused the game again and watched as his father surveyed the disastrous room.

The old man shook his head. "How the hell can you sleep in here?" he asked, rhetorically.

Billy looked at him but didn't respond.

"Listen, I know we've had this conversation before but I wanted to remind you that your mother and I may not be able to help you as much as we'd hoped for college."

Billy nodded. "No problem, Dad."

"If I didn't have to pay half my damn check to the government," he interrupted.

"I get it, Dad," Billy said, cutting off the usual ramble.

"Any luck with scholarships?" the man asked, surprising Billy.

The old man's actually put some thought into this, he thought, and shrugged. "A few small ones that'll help me pay for books." He thought about it. "I'm still waiting to hear back from the VFW."

"The VFW? Oh, on that write-up you did about Grandpa?"

Billy nodded; even more impressed his dad remembered.

The big man offered a slight nod. "We would have had your grandfather around much longer if the government hadn't poisoned him with all those chemicals they used over there in the jungle."

Billy nodded again. It was an old story. "I know, Dad. It's terrible that..."

"What about a summer job?" he asked, interrupting again.

"I have the Pearl for now, but it's only part-time," Billy said. "I keep looking for something full-time but the jobs that were available last summer have already been taken by people who should be retired."

The old man shook his head. "Times are tough for everyone, Billy. It's sad. Mom and I will divide whatever we can between you and Sophie, but don't expect too much."

Billy nodded. "I won't, Dad," he said, thinking, *I never have.*

"Okay then." The big man looked at the video game before turning to leave. "I'll let you get back to your important business then," he commented, throwing his usual jab at Billy's questionable use of time. He closed the door behind him.

Before returning to his game, Billy turned to Jimmy. "He means well, I guess." He thought about it and shook his head. "But there's no doubt about it now. No matter how you slice it, I'm paying for college."

Jimmy placed his chin flush to the bed and threw his paw across his eyes.

"Exactly," Billy said and returned to the virtual world, where there was no need to worry about college—whether it be funding or which major to take.

The school year ended with a bang and the multiple house parties were sure to be a last "hoorah" for Billy and his fellow graduates. It was a time to make lifelong memories with old friends. The days of irresponsibility were quickly coming to an end. Billy, Charlie and Mark were graduating from boyhood and stepping into manhood—*or so we're told.*

The first graduation party, hosted that night, was filled with underage drinking and lots of girls. Bianca, Charlie's girlfriend, was also in attendance to ensure that Charlie didn't graduate too deeply into manhood.

Inside the massive house, the boys played beer pong on a custom mahogany dining room table, with Billy losing badly and having to refill his red plastic Solo cup several times. Before long, Bianca excused herself. "You boys are such fools," she huffed and left them to their foolishness.

When the boys had drunk their fill—and then some—they headed outdoors to play corn hole with beanbags or sit by the roaring fire pit to exchange stories of their glory days in high school.

"We're the only class to go undefeated in a food fight," Billy boasted.

"Which is the kind of stuff legends are made from," Mark kidded.

Everyone laughed.

"And what would you rather be remembered for, Mark?" Billy asked. "...the most consecutive wins on the chess club?"

Everyone laughed harder.

'Yup," Mark said seriously, "I would."

It was nearing the end of the party when Billy noticed that Charlie was unusually quiet. "What's wrong with you?" he asked.

Charlie pointed toward Bianca. She was talking with some kid named Dalton Noble, who lived a few towns over and had also just graduated from high school. "It looks like they're getting real chummy over there," he slurred, clearly upset. "I think she might be cheating on me, Billy."

Billy snickered. "Are you crazy? You guys have been together since freshman year when you almost caught her hair on fire in Ms. Dubrowski's chemistry class."

Charlie thought about it and smirked. "Yeah, maybe you're right," he said, before swallowing down the rest of his beer and marching over toward Dalton and Bianca. Billy watched as Charlie grabbed Bianca's hand and they headed out of the yard, his arm slung across her shoulder and her arm wrapped around his waist. Just before leaving, Billy and Charlie exchanged glances. Charlie smiled.

Bianca cheating? Billy thought, and snickered again. *You two will probably be married by Christmas.*

Billy was drifting through some happy fog when Mark approached. "Listen, brother, I'm going to be taking off too. Are you going to be all right?"

Billy took another sip of beer and nodded. "I'll be fine. I'll give you a call tomorrow. Maybe we can grab lunch at Nick's or something?"

"Sounds like a plan," Mark said and chuckled. "If you're up for it, that is." Billy was trying to process the joke when Mark pointed at his red plastic cup. "You might want to slow down a little, bro."

"I'm fine," Billy repeated.

"If you say so," Mark added and headed out.

It wasn't long before Billy stumbled and realized he'd had one too many to drink. *Oh shit, I'm so buzzed*, he thought, realizing that he was faced with a real dilemma. He took a seat and thought it over. *My house is only two blocks away*, he quickly justified. *I'll be fine if I just take it slow.*

Billy slid behind the Honda's steering wheel and took a couple of deep breaths. "We just have two blocks," he told the car and turned the ignition. The motor roared to life. After rolling down the window and turning up the radio, he pulled away from the curb. Right away, he discovered that the road was one big blur. While his heart began to pound in his ears, he slid to the edge of the driver's seat, turned off the radio and opened his eyes as wide as he could. *It's like I'm in the middle of a damned video game*, he thought and his heart pounded harder. Everything looked animated and hazy. There were cars parked on both sides of the road and he concentrated on keeping the Honda's nose pointed straight down the middle. With each car he passed—without hitting it—he sucked in another deep breath, until he was nearly hyperventilating. *You stupid bastard*, he scolded himself and drove like he was in a heavily populated school zone. It took forever to reach the one block mark. *Maybe I should just pull over and leave the car...walk the rest of the way home*, he thought, but he never took his toe off the gas—or his eyes out of the rearview mirror. *No cops*, he kept repeating in his head. *Please God...no cops.*

At home, Jimmy was waiting for Billy at the front door. After relieving themselves, Billy staggered straight to bed, with Jimmy hobbling closely behind.

Billy collapsed on the bed. *Thank you, God, for...for letting me get home...without...without getting pulled over.* The silent prayer drained whatever strength he had left.

He lay on his side staring at what looked like two Jimmys, while both Jimmys stared back at him. "Did you...did you have a good night?" Billy managed to ask the blurry dogs.

Both black mutts leaned in close until they became one and continued to stare at him.

"I know," Billy stuttered, "I know I...I know I shouldn't have driven home...after drinking so much."

Licking his paw and taking a quick bath, the patient dog seemed to listen to every word of Billy's heartfelt confession.

"It won't happen again, okay?" Billy slurred, closing his heavy eyelids.

Jimmy heaved a big sigh.

Billy opened one eye, while he placed one of his feet on the floor to try to stop the bed from spinning so fast. "Don't look at me like that, Jim...Jimmy," he muttered. "I said I was wrong, didn't I?" He gagged once, but choked back the urge to vomit. "I...I just wish this bed...this damn bed would stop spinning."

Jimmy touched his cold nose to Billy's and lapped his cheek a few times before nuzzling up close to him.

Billy closed both eyes again and took a few deep breaths. No matter what happened, Jimmy loved him—completely and without conditions. "That's my boy," Billy said. "That's...that's my good boy."

The room spun three or four more times before Jimmy's nightlight shrank to a tiny pinpoint and the world went black.

Billy awoke in the previous night's clothes. He slowly opened his eyes and felt like he was riding some evil roller coaster. His head felt heavy and unmanageable on his neck. He tried to sit up but nausea shoved him back onto the bed. Struck with fatigue and muscle weakness, his body was recovering from the thousands of healthy brain cells he'd assassinated the night before. He turned to his right to find Jimmy—just one Jimmy—staring back at him, the dog's face seemingly filled with disappointment.

Billy opened his mouth to speak when he sneezed instead. He immediately grabbed for his throbbing head. *I should take an antihistamine*, he thought, but decided it might actually be his final push into a coma.

An hour later, just past lunch time, Billy managed to make it to the kitchen table for breakfast. Jimmy broke off the escort to chow down a bowl of kibble.

"How was the party last night?" his mom asked, grinning.

His dad chuckled.

Real funny, Billy thought and placed his pounding head into his hands. He moaned once but the slightest sound was now amplified. *I'm never drinking again*, he promised himself and, though he didn't cross his fingers behind his back, he still knew the words were empty. *And I'm never driving drunk again.* This vow, however, he intended to keep for life. He took a few deep breaths, trying to stave off the urge to vomit. *I need lots of water and Gatorade to rehydrate...and Ibuprofen*, he thought. He sneezed twice and could feel his eyes growing puffy. *Oh great*, he thought, tempted to scratch his eyes out of his head.

His dad laughed at him. "Stay away from the egg salad today," he teased, making Billy gag and his mother laugh.

"That'll teach you, Billy," his mother said, appearing pleased over his misery.

Normal conversation sounded like a screaming match to Billy.

The old man nodded. "It's the only way to learn," he said. "Now he knows there's a tough price to be paid when you hit the bottle hard."

You should know, Billy whispered in his head but even that voice was too loud. While his parents continued to smile at him, he pulled himself up from the table and dragged his heavy feet down the hall to his bedroom. Jimmy matched his every painful step.

When Billy reached his door, his father yelled out, "And don't you ever drink and drive again! You hear me?"

The hypocrisy sprinkled a bitter metallic taste onto Billy's tongue. "I hear ya," Billy mumbled, thinking, *That's like Aunt Phoebe blowing smoke in my face and telling me to stay away from cigarettes.*

He closed his bedroom door behind him, climbed over a small mountain of dirty clothes and collapsed onto his bed— with Jimmy jumping in right beside him. "I'm all done drinking," he told Jimmy again.

The wise old dog had already closed his eyes, uninterested in Billy's false promises.

"I'm so done," Billy repeated before sliding back into his self-induced coma.

Chapter 3

On Saturday afternoon, Billy's parents hosted a barbecue to celebrate his graduation. Fold-out chairs were placed throughout the backyard and so many wonderful smells filled the spring air. The traditional Baker clam boil was simmering in a huge copper, oval-shaped pot—with wire screens resting on top to steam white fish in wax paper and boiled eggs wrapped in aluminum foil. This mouth-watering bounty competed with the distinct smells of juicy hamburgers, marinated meat and grilled chicken on a stick. Billy's mom and Sophie scurried around, taking care of each detail.

Potato salad and macaroni salad, slathered in mayonnaise and basking in the warm sun, sat in the middle of the plastic-covered table. Billy watched as his Aunt Phoebe made it her mission to shoo black flies away from the corn on the cob, bowls of potato chips and a platter of sliced watermelon. And then he spotted his little cousin, Jack. "Hey, Juice Box, you made it!"

Jack sprinted up to Billy, giving him a hug and a sealed card. "It's from Aunt Phoebe," the boy announced and petted Jimmy's head before running off to the inflatable bounce house Billy's parents had rented.

Billy looked up to find his eccentric, chain-smoking aunt smiling at him—and shooing away more flies. While she waited and watched, he opened the card and pretended to read the message. *Fifteen bucks*, he thought. *That ought to buy me two lunches on campus...maybe.* He grinned. *I'll have to show Charlie.*

He nodded gratefully and approached Aunt Phoebe to give her a hug. "Thank you so much for the generous gift," he told her, wondering whether he would ever get the ashtray stench out of his clothes.

"You're welcome, sweetheart," she said, planting her shriveled lips onto his cheek like a cold snail. "Spend it wisely, okay?"

Billy quickly excused himself and hurried over to a picnic bench, where his dad and Uncle Pete were telling the same stories they always told. The Boston Red Sox played on a transistor radio; Joe Castiglione's distinctive voice confirming that summer was just underway. While people talked and laughed above the table, Jimmy worked beneath it like a pilot fish on the under belly of a shark—trawling for scraps—scanning and devouring most leftovers before they ever hit the ground.

Billy headed into the house to relieve himself when he spotted Jack swatting something invisible in front of the living room window. "What are you doing, Juice Box?" he asked him.

"Catching bees," Jack said, swatting away.

Billy looked closer. The little boy was trying to capture dust particles floating around in the window's sunlight. "Keep at it," he told him. "You're doing a good job."

As she hurried past the two, Sophie laughed.

Throughout the afternoon, Billy and his underage friends sneaked swigs of beer, while his grandparents, aunts, uncles and cousins filled the yard with many different conversations going on at once. Kids played and Jimmy took chase, at least to the best of his limited ability. Some of the men played horseshoes, while some of their women looked on from the shade of the giant oak tree. But no matter what they were doing, everyone was smiling—as they shared in each other's company.

Suddenly, a water balloon fight broke out. In the past, Jimmy would have jumped right in. But not today. Today, he sat on the sidelines and watched through sad puppy eyes, his gray muzzle resting across his worn paws.

Many of Billy's friends came and went throughout the day. Each one of them greeted Jimmy, spoiling the old dog with lots of love.

"Any plans for the summer?" Bianca asked the group of recent graduates huddled together.

Charlie grabbed her around the waist. "I'll be spending most of my time with the woman of my dreams," he said, pulling her close to him.

"And who's that?" Billy asked.

Everyone laughed, while Charlie pretended to be angry.

Mark smiled. "I'll be taking a couple of intro courses at the local college to help me get a head start on next year," he announced.

"Of course you are," Charlie teased, "what else would you be doing?"

"Summer school?" Billy said, jumping in. "You can keep that, Mark. I don't want to learn anything this summer."

Bianca turned to Billy. "So what do you have planned then?"

"I plan on chillin'," Billy said and then smiled excitedly. "I have to get a real job, but whenever I'm not working I plan to be at the beach with Jimmy." He looked at the dog. "I also promised that I'd take him camping before I head off to college." He patted the mutt's head. "Jimmy loves our camping trips."

Jimmy sat back on his haunches, slobbering all over himself. He had just consumed a hamburger patty that one of the graduates sneaked to him. He looked up at Billy.

"Right, buddy?" Billy asked him.

Jimmy licked his chops and whimpered for another handout.

Mark bent down and rubbed the mutt's belly. "Looks like camping's not the only thing old Jimmy loves."

Everyone laughed.

"You need to stop eating," Billy scolded the dog, "or you're going to get sick."

As the afternoon grew late, Billy noticed Charlie and Bianca exchanging some heated words in the shadows of the yard. "You're wrong, Charlie!" Bianca squealed. "Yeah, I've talked to that kid a few times, so what? There's nothing going on between us."

"I know what I've seen," Charlie hissed. "Don't tell me what I've seen with my own eyes."

As their argument rose in volume, people began to take notice. *Oh boy, this isn't good*, Billy thought.

Sophie approached him. "Billy, you need to tell them to either knock it off or leave."

Nodding, Billy made his way toward them to break it up.

"Then you need to get yourself some glasses," Bianca countered. "If I wanted to be with someone else, I'd be with someone else. I wouldn't have to sneak around behind your back."

"Oh, you wouldn't, huh?" Charlie yelled; he was nearly frothing at the mouth.

Billy wasn't ten feet from them when Bianca screamed, "That's right, I wouldn't!" She stormed off, crying.

Charlie never took a step to chase after her.

As Billy approached, his best friend was shaking his head wildly, his face beet red and his eyes filled with rage.

"Whoa, Charlie, take a breath," Billy said.

Charlie looked up at him, the murderous rage still glistening in his baby blues.

Billy was hardly deterred. "What the hell was that all about?" he asked.

Charlie took that breath, and then another. "Nothing," he finally snapped back. "You know what, Billy, maybe it is a good thing we're all moving on from high school. A new start might be best for everyone..."

"Don't talk stupid, Charlie. You're pissed. I get it. But now you're talking out of your ass."

"Talking out of my ass?" Charlie said, his volume rising with each word.

"That's right," Billy said, "and you need to keep it down. You're going to end up giving my Aunt Phoebe a stroke."

Charlie opened his mouth to respond. Instead, Billy's last comment shut him up. "Shit, I'm sorry," he mumbled.

Billy tried to keep a straight face, but couldn't. "I'm playing with you. Aunt Phoebe has so many chemicals in her that she's going to outlive us both." He put his hand on Charlie's shoulder. "But kidding aside, I think you're dead wrong about Bianca."

"I don't think so, Billy. I get the worst feeling in my gut..."

"In your gut?" Billy interrupted, adding a snicker. "Without evidence, it's nothing but paranoia, brother."

Charlie shook his head. "I know what I know."

Billy opened his mouth to counter again but decided against it. *You guys have all summer to figure it out*, he thought and let it go at that.

It was approaching dusk when Charlie approached Billy, now wearing his mischievous grin. Billy looked past him to discover that a few more graduates had arrived. This time, one of them brought along a girl Billy had never seen before—a girl who stole his breath away.

She had curly blonde hair and caramel eyes. As if being pulled by a magnet, Billy strode—zombie-like—toward her. A closer look revealed a perfect row of teeth pointing to two adorable dimples and pursed lips. From the conversation, he'd gathered that her name was Vicki. For a few magical moments, he watched her from a distance. She was giggling at something someone had said when she began flipping her hair around, flirtatiously. Billy could feel his bottom jaw droop, as he slid deeper into the glorious trance.

As he continued to watch Vicki from a distance, his heart thumped hard in his chest. *Oh, my God*, he repeated in his head. He'd never experienced anything like it. He'd had crushes on girls before, but none of them ever made him feel like the world had suddenly run out of air.

As hope filled his heart, his mind sabotaged the moment. In the past, Billy had played the masochist, facing the demoralizing rejection of any pimply-faced high school freshman. *But that was a long time ago*, he told himself. *Things are different now. I'm different.*

He suddenly realized Charlie was still standing beside him— and smiling. Charlie studied the girl. "Take it easy, buddy," he told

Billy. "She's not that nice." Charlie assessed her some more and shrugged. "I've seen better legs hanging out of a nest."

"You must be blind," Billy said and then told himself, *Go talk to her. She's here...at your party. Go ahead. It's not like she won't talk to you. It's your party. Go...* But he couldn't do it. He just couldn't find the nerve to approach her and introduce himself.

Charlie chuckled—in some *I knew you wouldn't approach her* tone—and sauntered away.

Billy was still locked in a hypnotic state when he saw Vicki greet one of the guys at the party with a hug. *Oh no*, he thought and his stomach flopped, nearly kicking up the greasy drippings of his lunch. For that one horrid moment, every drop of blood drained from his heart, while gravity carried it to his feet. He couldn't recall ever feeling more disappointed. *Life can be so unfair*, he thought—the way it built up a man's hopes only to pull the carpet out from under his quivering legs. *Well, that's that*, he told himself, trying to shake the cobwebs from his head and emerge from his short-lived fantasy.

An hour later, Vicki left the party without as much as a word or glance Billy's way; without knowing he even existed. *Just my luck*, he thought and did his best not to sulk. *Man, is she beautiful.*

It was already dark when Billy's dad prepared the fire pit in the backyard. Many of the day's competing conversations came to a halt and, for a time, there was silence—followed by crickets and the wind flirting with the trees. Everyone grabbed a chair and set them in a circle around the pit. While the fire jumped to life—orange and red flames dancing wildly in the darkness—everyone settled comfortably into their respective places around the large circle. Billy took in a deep breath and thought, *I wish Vicki were sitting beside me right now.* It seemed odd to want to share something so badly with someone he'd never even spoken to. But it wasn't his mind that desired it; it was his heart. Again, he tried to shake it off and stay in the present. He looked around the circle and smiled gratefully. It had been a glorious day.

While he stroked Jimmy under the chin, the night's first fireflies revealed themselves. Whispered conversations led to chuckles from adults, a clear sign of good memories being recalled. Billy sat back with Charlie and Mark on either side of him and began to recall all the amazing times they'd spent together in this yard; the three of them playing manhunt in the dark—walkie-talkies and flashlights in hand—while the fading light made them feel like they could run twice as fast as they could; the old oak tree, which served as their tree fort; the hushed conversations and the lights that dotted the abandoned street. Billy inhaled deeply and smiled wider. Even if he'd never admit it to his nagging parents, he knew, *I had a very cool childhood.* He grabbed a stick, impaled a fat marshmallow and began roasting his first S'more.

While Billy assembled the sweet treat and took a bite, Jimmy nudged his leg with his nose.

"You can't have any, Jimmy," Billy whispered past a mouth full of graham crackers.

In the flickering light, the dog put on his best beggar's eyes.

"We both know what chocolate does to you," Billy said. He could still feel the panic that ran through the house when they'd discovered Jimmy had stolen a solid chocolate Easter Bunny and choked it down. Chunks of gold foil wrapper were the only evidence of his crime, until he became deathly ill. After two full days of whining and whimpering, Jimmy paid for his crime in full before returning to the land of the living.

As the flames danced in Jimmy's pleading eyes, Billy got up from his chair to get the dog another cold hamburger patty. "You're such a pain," Billy joked.

"And make it quick," Charlie called after Billy, rubbing the mutt's neck. "Our boy's so hungry, his belly's rumbling."

Mark laughed. "It sounds more like he's getting ready to explode."

There were several cherry-red embers still glowing in the pit when the backyard was finally abandoned to the moon. Although he was asked to stay over, Mark was one of the last guests to leave. Billy, Charlie and Jimmy headed for his bedroom—Charlie dragging a bulky air mattress behind him.

While Charlie kicked aside clothes on the floor to make room for his inflatable bed, Billy thought about all the time they'd spent together, years which had made them more like brothers than friends. *Charlie's pretty much grown up at our house,* he thought, and smiled as Charlie grabbed a clean t-shirt from his bureau.

Charlie shut off the light, just as Billy and Jimmy jumped into bed. As they all lay quietly for a few minutes, allowing the day's events to be etched into their memories, Jimmy's night light illuminated three prone silhouettes on the walls.

"What a day," Billy mumbled, breaking the silence.

"What a day," Charlie repeated, each word dropping off in volume from exhaustion.

As Billy contemplated the day's events, Charlie laughed. "What?" Billy asked.

"You should've talked to that girl," he said, yawning.

"What girl?"

"What girl?" Charlie echoed, suddenly awake again. "The one you were drooling over... that girl."

"I know," Billy said.

"You think too much. That's your problem."

I know, Billy thought. "What about you and Bianca?" he asked. "What the hell's going on with you two?"

Charlie's silhouette rolled over in the dim light and faced the wall. "I don't know what to think," he mumbled, "and I'd rather not talk about it."

"Okay," Billy said and gasped when Jimmy threw a big paw across his chest. "Damn, Jimmy," Billy said, grabbing for his chest.

Charlie laughed. "That a boy, Jimmy," he said, knowing exactly what happened without seeing it, "you slap him good for me."

There were a few more laughs, followed by three motionless shadows and then some heavy snoring.

Sunday morning limped in and Billy awoke at his usual time—late. Charlie had already left and from the sound of silence in the house, his parents were also gone. "They must be out at a yard sale or something," Billy told Jimmy, still lying prone on his back. "And Sophie's out dress shopping for Miranda's wedding," he remembered aloud.

The dog couldn't have cared less; he made a beeline to the kitchen door to relieve his body of all the garbage he'd choked down the day before.

"That was some party yesterday, huh buddy?" Billy said, opening the door. "I just wish I'd had the guts to talk to that girl, Vicki. She's absolutely gorgeous."

Jimmy bolted out.

Billy took one step out the kitchen door to discover the backyard was completely cleaned. *Probably Charlie*, he thought, *the do-gooder*.

After feeding Jimmy, Billy popped a tiny white antihistamine and headed for his video game while Jimmy started in on the day's first bath.

By early afternoon, the skies turned dark and threatened rain. Billy and Jimmy sat together on the living room couch, watching the Boston Red Sox get beat up pretty badly. It didn't matter. The Red Sox games were summer's background music, which had also served as the soundtrack for Billy's childhood. Outside, a light mist had turned to a soft rain that drummed gently on the roof, adding a heavy weight to each of Billy's eyelids. He looked at Jimmy, curled up on the other end of the couch. The dog yawned. Billy did the same before stretching out as far as Jimmy's barrel chest would allow. Billy's arms and legs felt like rubber bands. As the rain tapped on the window, he pulled a light throw blanket under his own chin. He inhaled deeply and smiled. "The count is full. And now, the pay-off pitch..." The Red Sox commentators' voices began to drift until their drone turned to distant voices. It wasn't long before the gray afternoon slipped into darkness and slumber.

An hour later, Jimmy's trembling body stirred him from his peaceful siesta.

"What is it?" Billy asked, still groggy.

The window above their heads flashed with lightning, followed by a loud clap of thunder. Jimmy closed his eyes tight and trembled. Billy grinned and pulled the frightened dog to him. "What a big baby you are," he said, while the thunder hammered at their ears. "Come here. It's only the angels bowling up in heaven." He chuckled.

While Jimmy nearly shivered his thick coat off his skeleton, Billy drifted back to sleep—their legs entwined.

In what felt like seconds, Billy awoke and wiped the drool from his face. He looked down the length of his body to find Jimmy sleeping peacefully. For a few moments, he lay beneath the warm cotton blanket, while his memory returned in fuzzy bits and pieces. Stretching out his sinewy muscles, it took a minute for reality to register and for his eyes to adjust to the dark afternoon. *It's amazing what a few extra hours of sleep can do for a guy's perspective*, he thought and looked at the TV. It was the bottom of the ninth inning and the score was still bloated against the hometown team. *Good*, he thought. *We didn't miss anything.* He threw the twisted blanket off his feet and looked out the window. Although the rain had stopped, the dark clouds still hovered. *We should probably still get up*, he thought.

Jimmy stirred and then yawned once. Billy watched as he stretched out his front legs, then torso, then hind legs—one at a time—before releasing a quiver that traveled the length of his body. It was like a ripple or wave, from his snout to his tail.

"Lazy dog," Billy told him and laughed. "It's time to get up. We have a video game to finish."

Sophie returned home, followed by Charlie. Billy's parents also returned from their treasure hunting with a bucket of fried chicken. Wearing a sour puss, Charlie took his seat at the kitchen table just as Billy broke the silence. "Sophie, I need to pick your brain about my class schedule in the fall," he told his sister.

"I'm happy to help," she said. "You're taking on a full course load, right?"

He nodded. "Yeah, but I want to stay away from the harder classes."

"Billy, as a Liberal Arts major, you're only going to take core classes your freshman year," she said, shaking her head. "And you might want to forget about taking the easy road from now on. College is a lot of hard work, so you might as well accept that right now."

Billy's mom and dad both nodded, but remained quiet—obviously pleased with how their daughter was handling the topic.

Damn, Sophie, Billy thought, but couldn't help but to grin. Even from atop her pedestal, she'd always been his compass.

"You want to go to college, right?" she asked.

He half shrugged. "I *need* to go to college," he mumbled, thinking, *Because I have no idea what else I'd do.*

"Yes, you do," she said, sternly. "And you *need* to take it seriously, Billy."

"Sure, Sophe," he mumbled and looked at Charlie, whose mind was clearly a thousand miles away from their conversation.

Before Billy could question him, Sophie redirected her attention to Charlie. "And what's eating at you?" she asked. "You haven't made fun of anyone or cracked one stupid joke since we sat down to eat."

Charlie looked at her, his once mischievous eyes looking wounded. "There's nothing wrong with me," he lied. "I just don't feel like talking, that's all."

"What? Charlie Philips doesn't feel like..."

"He doesn't feel like talking, Sophe," Billy interrupted, rushing to his friend's defense. "If he doesn't want to talk, then he doesn't have to talk. Let it go."

Every head at the table snapped up; something was definitely wrong with Charlie and now they all knew it.

There was quiet for a few awkward moments. As Billy's dad grabbed for another chicken leg, he said, "I kind of like it when we don't talk."

Everyone laughed—even Charlie. Jimmy, on the other hand, stood at the back door, whimpering.

Billy's mom tore another piece from her drumstick, wiped her mouth and got up to let him out. Not a second later, she screamed past a mouth full of chicken, "Oh God!"

Everyone sprang from the table and rushed toward the backyard to see what was wrong. It took a moment for the scene to register for Billy.

A raccoon had entered the yard and was picking through their trash cans when Jimmy caught him. To Billy's horror, Jimmy had cornered the masked thief.

"No, Jimmy!" Billy screamed. "Come inside, boy," he ordered.

But Jimmy wasn't hearing it. His hackles raised, the dog was bristling to take action. Jimmy had marked his territory long ago and was still willing to defend it—along with those he loved. Brow creased and eyes locked on his enemy, Jimmy's head was completely still. All of his senses were at full alert.

The courageous mutt bared his teeth. The raccoon did the same. Jimmy drew back for a moment, clearly contemplating his next move. For a second, he stood mannequin still, his head cocked slightly.

"Don't do it, Jimmy," Billy pled, terrified for his best friend.

Nose twitching and ears tucked back, Jimmy's tail went pin straight. A moment later, his body quivered and his tail twitched. It was slight, but Billy caught it. "No!" he yelled, knowing this was it. *It's go time.*

Ignoring all his pain, Jimmy lunged for the animal on the legs of a young, healthy dog. For a brief moment, he resembled the pup he'd been all those years ago. He tried to pin the raccoon, jaws snapping like an oversized, black piranha. This was followed by a blur of fur and teeth, the ferocious exchange pumping panic through Billy's body. It was awful—and awesome—at the same time.

"No, Jimmy!" Billy yelled again and realized his mom had echoed the same.

Evidently, the mutt had one last fight in him and he was hell bent on making it a good one. When it came to fight or flight, Jimmy was too old and tired to run away.

As fast as it had begun, it was over and the raccoon was scampering toward the shadowy wood line.

Jimmy started back toward the house, his tail held high but limping like the geriatric mess he was. When he reached the door, Billy went to both knees and hugged his panting friend. "You're my hero, Jimmy," he whispered, "and you just bought yourself a visit to the vet's office."

After receiving his rabies booster and a slew of other shots, Jimmy couldn't even lick his wounds in his own dog bed, which was located on the living room floor. Mrs. Pringle, the family cat, would not allow it.

It was both pathetic and comical. Jimmy was clearly capable of fighting a wild animal in the backyard to protect his family, but had it been Mrs. Pringle who'd done the threatening—and challenged the barking dog—Jimmy would have turned and run for the house with his tail tucked between his legs. This was a fact Mrs. Pringle had figured out years before. And from the day Billy's mom had bought Jimmy the red plaid dog bed, Mrs. Pringle had never allowed the good-hearted mutt to come within a foot of it.

Billy watched as this same scenario unfolded again. "You big marshmallow, you need to teach her who's boss," he teased, leaving it to Jimmy to deal with the feline bully on his own.

Jimmy wasn't three feet from the stuffed oval bed when Mrs. Pringle launched her attack, ears pinned back and teeth bared, hissing and swiping at him with paws that had been clawless since she was a kitten. Jimmy back pedaled. He tried to approach a few more times, but Mrs. Pringle defended the bed with the same ferocity each time. Jimmy finally gave up and lay at the base of the recliner, which seemed to suit Mrs. Pringle just fine.

Jimmy acted tough when he needed to, but his gentle spirit was no match for Mrs. Pringle's wrath.

Billy shook his head. The fact that Jimmy had just beat back a vicious raccoon seemed to lose some of its glory and Billy wouldn't have it. "Come on, you big bruiser," he told the dog. "Let's go get some ice cream. You've earned it."

Jimmy was up on his paws, strutting past Mrs. Pringle with his tail held high again—like he'd just won a second time.

As a reward for his selfless heroism, Billy took his best friend to Somerset Creamery, the best ice cream parlor in the county.

Billy ordered himself vanilla soft serve blended with a generous amount of peanut butter cups and some chocolate sauce to bind it all together, and a cone of vanilla soft serve for his drooling companion. As usual, though it looked like Jimmy really tried, he took two quick licks before he inhaled the entire cone into his mouth and gulped the whole thing down. He gagged twice, swallowed once more and then licked his chops—resting his pleading eyes directly on Billy's ice cream.

"That's it, Jimmy," Billy told him, shifting his sweet dessert from one hand to the other, away from the dog's reach. "You've had yours. You're all done."

The dog whined—either from wanting more and knowing he couldn't have it or from a massive brain freeze.

Going for ice cream is definitely a love/hate experience for Jimmy, Billy thought and chuckled, as he ate with his back to the mutt. After a few deep breaths, along with every ounce of his commitment and determination, Billy finished his giant frozen treat—throwing the cup and its red plastic spoon into the overflowing trash receptacle. "Your celebration's over, hero," he told the dog. "Let's go home. You need to get some rest so you can heal."

As they headed back to the rusted Honda, Billy stopped and looked down at Jimmy. "Do you think I'm cut out for the military?" he asked the mutt, while considering the idea seriously, himself. As they got into the car, Billy was already shaking his head. "I don't know," he mumbled. "They brag about getting more done before nine o'clock than most people do all day." He grinned at Jimmy. "We're lucky if we're even awake by nine, never mind out of bed." He started the ignition and the beater roared to life. He shook his head again. "I can't imagine a greater purpose than to protect my country. I just don't want to risk my life protecting some other country that's been at war since before the Bible was written." Billy threw the shifter into drive. "It looks like college is still the right path for me."

An hour later, Billy's bedroom door flew open and his dad barged in. "I have good news and bad news," he told Billy, grinning. "Which do you want first?"

Jimmy's ears stood up stiffly, ready to listen.

"The good news," Billy said, pausing his video game, "and you can keep the bad news to yourself."

The old man laughed. "I have a friend who has a friend who can get you an interview at Four Paws for a full-time summer position."

"The animal shelter?" Billy asked excitedly.

His dad nodded. "The same dog pound we got Sprinkles from," he teased, looking down at Jimmy.

The dog slowly sat up, seemingly taking offense.

Billy stroked Jimmy's neck. "And the bad news?" he asked reluctantly.

The big man grinned. "The bad news is that you might be shoveling shit for the next few months."

Billy smiled. "I've heard worse news," he said. "When's the interview?"

His dad shrugged. "Just head down there over the next few days. They know you're coming."

"Will do," Billy said, nodding. "Thanks, Dad. I really appreciate it."

His dad winked. "Don't mention it." As he reached the bedroom door, he pointed toward the video game. "Though it would be too bad if it cut into your play time," he said sarcastically.

Billy nodded. "It would be," he replied, returning to his game.

As the door closed, Billy looked at Jimmy and grinned. "What do you think about that, boy? Me working at the same dog pound we got you from?"

Jimmy lay back down, without approval or complaint.

"Well, I think it would be pretty cool," Billy said, before returning to the land of zombie-killing and hidden treasures.

Chapter 4

The Oriental Pearl had all the class of a gaudy casino. The exterior neon sign pulsated with a giant pearl that hovered between two fire-breathing dragons that had faced off years before to claim the prize. Inside the heavy glass doors, a thick plush carpet with swirls of red and orange covered every inch of the floor, while red and gold foil—accented in jade green—papered the walls. Big belly Buddhas and tall bamboo plants complemented the décor throughout. Light fixtures were made of hand-painted rice paper or some material fabricated to resemble it. And the bamboo partitions, separating several dining stations, were covered in the same material. Paper place mats printed with the Chinese horoscope allowed folks to discover whether they were born during the year of the dog, rat, pig or snake while they waited for their bowls of steaming lo mein and crispy egg rolls. And it was always loud in the place. Adult laughter was aided by empty Mai Tai glasses and scorpion bowls for two, while most children were essentially left unattended to play and scream. *Gaudy can't even begin to describe the place*, Billy thought. Yet, it was a favorite restaurant in town and a frequent stop for Billy's family. In all his years of enjoying the flaming pupu platters and shrimp fried rice, he'd never imagined working there.

Past the front counter—its glass case featuring souvenirs such as Geisha girl dolls, scroll calendars, Chinese fans and boxes of fortune cookies available in both chocolate and cardboard flavors—a ramp led to the kitchen. Red swinging doors opened into the bustling kitchen, where a maroon tile floor was always covered in a film of grease. Billy quickly found the obstacle to be a challenging one when putting away clean dishes and glasses.

And Billy washed those dishes for thirty dollars each Friday and Saturday night; sixty whole bucks for slaving away an entire weekend. Each night started at five o'clock and ended at two o'clock in the morning. He picked up every shift he could.

The job was Billy's first eye opener into the real world. No matter how hard he worked—and it had to be hard to keep up—he never made progress. He busted hump to spray down the dishes, load them onto the rack and slide them through the washer. From there, he made stacks according to geographic location within the vast kitchen before scurrying around to put them away. Silverware sorting was the most time-consuming, while glassware went quickest. Then, just when he thought he'd made a breakthrough, he looked up to realize, *I have to start all over again.*

Billy wiped the sweat from his forehead when he looked up to see that the dirty silverware tub was overflowing. As he sorted them face down onto the faded plastic rack, Lynn—an older, attractive waitress—approached the stainless steel shelf in front of him and sighed heavily. Billy glanced up quickly and smiled. Lynn scraped food from dirty plates into a giant, bag-lined trash barrel before stacking the plates within Billy's reach. "You haven't had a break yet, have you?" she said.

Without looking up at her, Billy shook his head and kept plugging away at the work in front of him. "Not yet," he said.

"And you haven't eaten?" she asked.

"Not yet," he repeated. "I'll grab something when it slows down."

"When's that," she asked, "at midnight?"

Billy pulled a hot rack of clean porcelain bowls from the industrial machine and laughed. "Probably," he said and slid the silverware rack into the steaming dish washer.

Lynn grabbed her empty tray and, before turning to serve another table, she said, "You should be out having fun with your friends, not sweating your butt off in this dump."

Billy chuckled again. "Most of my friends don't have to worry about paying for college," he said and looked up for a brief moment. "Unfortunately, I need this dump to get myself there." Billy laughed to himself. *Maybe that keynote speaker did have a few good points*, he thought.

"Good for you. You must want to go to college really bad," she said, before returning to her own exhausting duties.

As Lynn walked away, Billy laughed again. *Yeah, really bad*, he thought, mocking himself.

Oddly enough, Billy enjoyed the work, though he finally understood the complaints of those older than him. For the first time, he realized that when he used his muscles strenuously over an extended period of time, they actually started to burn. And he also enjoyed the camaraderie shared amongst the hard-working staff—which included snickers, sighs and rolling eyes exchanged when the boss wasn't around.

Billy put away the clean bowls and silverware and grabbed a beef teriyaki to munch on. When he returned to his station, two minutes later, a mountain of work awaited him. *Here we go again.*

It was half past midnight when Billy put away the last rack of clean glasses and headed for the front of the restaurant. While he waited for George Chu to pay him cash, he listened to the band, SNAFU, close out the night. The front counter was the perfect place to watch the frequent bar fights or the drunken women who sometimes exposed themselves.

"You'd better keep your blouse on tonight, Tina, or you're out of here for good," Steve, the bouncer, warned one of the girls.

Tina staggered a few steps, nearly falling down the three steps from the bar to the foyer. "You're no fun," she slurred, stumbling out of the place.

Yeah, Steve, Billy thought, disappointedly, *you're no fun at all!*

It was two o'clock in the morning when Billy and some of the other staff stepped out of the building to socialize in the parking lot for another hour or so.

Though crazy to some, the whole thing made good sense to Billy. While all of his friends were out partying on the weekends, he was working—or at least that's what others called it. To him, it was merely an early peek into adulthood.

The next morning, Billy awoke to find his brand new hundred-dollar Nike sneakers infested with ants; an army of small black creepy crawlers were attracted to the film of grease provided by the Chinese restaurant. *All because of some meaningless job*, he thought and told Jimmy, "It's going to take me a weekend and a half to pay for a new pair."

Jimmy's silhouette whimpered from the bedroom door, as if he were saying, *I really gotta go!*

"I'm coming, I'm coming," Billy said, picking up the rubber-soled ant hills on his way out of the room. *What a waste!* he thought. *I really need to land that job at the dog pound.*

After breakfast and Jimmy's morning bath, Billy decided to take the mutt for a walk. At an excruciatingly slow gait, they made it to the corner and stopped. "You want to keep going?" Billy asked him.

Jimmy collapsed into a half-prone, half-seated position, his tongue dancing to the rhythm of his heavy breathing.

"Yeah, me neither. I'm still beat from last night." He scratched Jimmy's head. "So what do you want to do then?" he asked.

Jimmy licked his chops once and then yawned—long and hard.

Billy chuckled. "A dog after my own heart," he said and turned back toward the house. "Let's just be quiet when we get back to the house. I don't want to catch any crap about us sneaking back to bed."

At the mention of *bed*, Jimmy picked up the pace.

Taking a break from his menial slave job, Billy prepared to meet Charlie and Mark at the last of the many graduation parties.

On his way out of the house, his dad caught him in the front yard. "Where are you off to in such a hurry?" he asked.

"Another graduation party," Billy said.

As if already disappointed, the old man took a deep breath. "Just make sure you don't drink too much," he said, exhaling deeply. "And you'd better not drive home drunk again!"

Although he nodded, Billy nearly choked on the hypocrisy of it all. For years, his father's drinking and gambling had taken a front seat to his own family, serious problems that took years for him to overcome.

As Billy jumped into his car, he instantly recalled a time when his self-righteous father struggled with his own addictions.

It was an ordinary Saturday when Billy's dad took him and Jimmy for a ride in the pickup truck, its two-tone look caused by the rust patches that were eating away at its once-green fenders. A bad exhaust leak made the beater roar, though the noise was nothing compared to the nausea they suffered from the fumes that seeped in. The rear of the truck was packed with junk, trash bags filled with empty returnable beer cans. His dad was a "collector" of sorts.

Billy loved spending time with his dad. Even if it meant he'd miss out on the thrills of a neighborhood man-hunt game or a spirited snowball fight, he loved spending time with him.

Wearing a day's worth of sweat and mud, Billy's neck was circled in a ring of dirt.

A tattoo with two love birds carrying a banner that read *MOM* bulged from his dad's forearm. For a man who grew up in the city, he loved country music and played his CDs over and over until Billy and Jimmy knew every twang. The truck was filled with smoke, both cigarette and exhaust. Billy or Jimmy didn't dare complain. His dad could be tough and, having his wits about him, Billy minded him. The big man said it was "respect." Billy later discovered it was actually "fear," an emotion which could appear very similar and have the same effect on a young boy. In any event, if his dad gave him the look to quiet down, Billy piped down.

As Billy recalled, Jimmy smelled as musty as ever, licking the truck's passenger window until it became one massive smudge. The old man liked having that mutt around. As a result, some of Jimmy's early days were spent in the passenger seat of that rusty bucket.

On this particular afternoon, in the sweltering heat, they pulled into the dirt parking lot of "the club." The old man shut off the truck, pulled the keys from the ignition and warned Billy and Jimmy, "I have choir practice with the boys, so be good and don't move. I'll be out in a few minutes." While Billy and Jimmy watched from the truck, the big man opened the building's red door and stepped in. The door closed behind him.

Billy and Jimmy sat there quietly, taking in what little surroundings were available—the cars in the lot. Those few minutes dragged into an hour and every new license plate that showed up was a real treat. Billy spent the time imagining who owned the unfamiliar car, while making up stories about their lives that he shared with his panting dog.

After at least two hours had elapsed, his dad stumbled out of "the club" with two bags of potato chips and threw them to Billy and Jimmy. "I just need to finish up," he slurred. "I'll be right back." With an eerie grin, he turned and staggered back toward "the club" where he disappeared behind its red door to conclude choir practice.

That damned door. Every magical time it opened, the hoots and hollers of people having fun spilled out. Jimmy and Billy hung out the truck window to listen. There was music and laughter and the crack of pool balls, and then the red door would close and the world would turn silent again. Billy hated when the door closed. He would have done anything to get behind that crimson door. He would have given anything to get in on the yelling and the laughter. For a few long hours, that one simple desire became bigger than anything he'd ever dreamed for.

Cramped in the truck, the games Billy played with Jimmy were ingenious, lasting until Jimmy's tongue went dry and whimpered his sorrow. Billy tried to nap, pleading with the poor animal to do the same. When that didn't work, he sang to his furry best friend. But most of the time, Billy just tried to ignore the rumbling in both their bellies. *An hour ago, the bag of chips seemed enough. But it would have been better had we been given nothing,* Billy thought defiantly.

As two hours rolled into three, at the risk of getting into some real trouble Jimmy and Billy grew braver. They stepped out of the truck and stretched their legs. For a few minutes, they played outside the heap of rust, careful to stay close. Billy grew so bold that he stole a peek through the windows of "the club." Still, he couldn't find the courage to get his head inside that taunting door.

Eventually, Jimmy began running around the parking lot and got real daring until the old man appeared from behind the red door and caught them. Furious, Billy's dad looked him in the eye. "I never ask you for anything," he screamed, "and when I do, you can't even sit still for a few minutes." Billy cried and when the sniffles subsided, the old man finished his smoke and wheezed, "Now stay in the truck. There are a lot of nuts out in the world and your mother would have my neck if I let anything happen to you." And after offering those pearls of wisdom, he returned for one last round of singing behind the blood-red door.

The sharp bite of his father's disappointment was nothing compared to the sense of betrayal Billy felt. It was an entire afternoon spent in a conflict of love versus hate. In the end, Billy decided to respect his dad for not coddling him. *He's teaching me to be a man,* Billy figured.

It took an eternity, but the payoff finally happened when his dad staggered out of the club with Slim Jims and pickled eggs that he delivered with pride. A strange man walked out with him, smoking a cigarette. The stranger watched as Billy's dad crawled into the truck. Shaking his head, he returned back behind the red door where all the fun awaited.

With one eye open, the old man drove Billy and Jimmy home. "Tell your mom we went fishing, all right?"

Petrified, Billy nodded. And he never spoke a word of it to his mother. It didn't matter. From the moment they pulled into the driveway, she knew. Saturday night was fight night at the Baker house. With the booze as her tag team partner, Billy's mom eventually won the brutal bout and sent the lying drunkard to sleep on his mother's couch for a few days.

Emerging from the old nightmare and baffled that the old man refused to remember, Billy started the car and looked back at his dad. *It must be pretty convenient to forget your own sins when you're judging someone else's*, he thought, shaking his head as he drove off.

At the party, while Billy held a red Solo cup—pretending to do some heavy drinking—he was strangely relieved that all the reveling was coming to an end.

It was dusk and, from the moment they'd arrived, Charlie was furious over something. "I'm so done with this bullshit," he whispered through gritted teeth. "Done!"

Billy caught the angry gibberish. "Everything all right?" he asked him. "If you need to talk..."

"No, I don't need to talk," Charlie barked, an unusual wrath glossing over his eyes.

"Okay, dude. You don't have to bite my head off. I'm just trying to..."

Charlie shook his head. "Just let it go, Billy. You have no idea what the hell's going on," he said.

"Then tell me," Billy said.

Without another word, Charlie guzzled his draft beer like he'd just returned home from a full combat tour in the desert.

He was staring at something—or somebody. Billy scanned the party but couldn't figure out what—or who—it was. He finally decided it didn't take a crystal ball to figure out why his best friend was so upset. *Charlie and Bianca have been fighting non-stop since graduation and she never showed up at this final shindig.* Billy decided to take his friend's advice and leave it alone.

While Charlie stared off into the shadows of the yard, Billy engaged in several different conversations. "So I hear you're going into teaching?" he said to Sandy, another one of his class-mates since elementary school.

She nodded. "I don't think I have a choice. My mother's an elementary school teacher, my grandmother was a high school teacher, her mother was..."

"Oh, I'm sorry," Billy said, "I thought..."

She slapped his arm. "I'm just teasing you. I've wanted to be a teacher since before I could walk."

Billy laughed. "Good for you."

"And I heard you're going to UMASS?" she said.

"I am," he said.

"What are you taking?"

"I have no idea," he said; he was so sick and tired of making up stories. "I'm enrolled in the Liberal Arts program for now. I'm just praying something comes to me sooner rather than later." Telling the truth felt good.

She placed her hand on his forearm. "I'm sure it will, Billy," she said, searching his eyes for a moment. "Have you ever thought about becoming a teacher? I think you'd make a great one."

"You do?" he asked, excited over the genuine suggestion.

She smiled. "I do." With a wink, she left him to talk to another friend.

A teacher? Billy wondered. Within seconds, his smile van-ished. *And spend the rest of my life in school?* He shook his head. *No, I don't think so.*

Forty minutes and three beers later, Charlie approached Billy and Mark. "I'm out of here," he announced, starting for the street.

Mark hurried after him. "What's the rush, Charlie? Maybe you should wait until..."

Charlie looked back, fury burning in his glare. "Mind your business, bro," he barked. "I'm fine."

"Are you okay to drive?" Billy asked his best friend, trying to keep up.

"What are you, my mother now?" Charlie hissed.

Something in Billy snapped. "Screw you, Charlie!" he yelled, halting his pursuit. "Go sulk somewhere else. I'm really getting sick of the drama anyway."

As Charlie jogged away, he never looked back. He was seething and in a very big hurry to go somewhere; it made Billy even angrier.

Mark tapped Billy's arm. "Things between him and Bianca must be worse than we thought."

"To hell with him," Billy said, madder than he'd been in a long time.

"I know," Mark said, "but I've never seen him this pissed off."

"He'll get over it," Billy said, taking a sip from his red cup. "To hell with him."

"I don't know," Mark muttered, shaking his head. "Something's up and it ain't good."

They returned to the party, with Billy cursing Charlie's name with each step.

The last light of the day had slid over the horizon and disappeared. Charlie was so enraged, he felt high, drunk on rage. He'd spotted Dalton hanging out in the shadows of the party and waited for him to leave. "It ends tonight," he hissed. "I'm done being played the fool." Sucking in short shallow breaths, Charlie's white knuckles threatened to crack the steering wheel in half. He was only a few minutes behind Dalton and—speeding like a maniac—he finally spotted the kid's silver Hyundai parked at a red light a few blocks from the party. Charlie's mind rushed with thoughts, confusing and nonsensical. He stepped on the gas and his car lurched forward. Pulling alongside Dalton, he screeched to a stop. After putting down the passenger window, he gestured that Dalton do the same. He did—reluctantly. Dalton's frightened face only confirmed Charlie's suspicions and made his rage grow tenfold. "Pull into that parking lot up ahead," Charlie told him through gritted teeth. He'd tried to sound calm, but it didn't come out that way.

"Why? What's up?" Dalton asked, his face flushed and his eyes enlarged from fear.

"I want to talk about you and Bianca seeing each other. I figure we can settle some things and..."

"I'm not seeing Bianca," Dalton yelled, his voice cracking.

If Charlie didn't know better, the kid even sounded convincing. "Bullshit!" Charlie yelled back. "Just pull into that lot so we can talk about it."

"There's nothing to talk about," Dalton said, his voice now high pitched, "and I'm not..."

"Pull the car over," Charlie screamed, "so I can beat you like a..."

The light was still red when Dalton punched the gas and squealed off.

"I was right!" Charlie screeched, stomping on the accelerator. "He's dead!"

Charlie was three car lengths from Dalton's rear bumper when Dalton took the Route 88 exit, a long stretch of two-lane highway that headed straight to the beach. "I got you now, you stupid bastard," Charlie yelled and got on the throttle hard.

It took five miles of high speed chase before Charlie was able to pull alongside his enemy again. Dalton's face was panicked. The Hyundai pulled away. Charlie glanced down at the speedometer. They were now exceeding one hundred miles per hour. "You're so dead, you son of a bitch," Charlie repeated, sliding to the edge of the driver's seat.

A mile later, he was at Dalton's rear bumper again when they hit a bend in the road. Charlie yanked the steering wheel into the turn, while Dalton's Hyundai stayed on its line and continued straight. Within seconds, Dalton was in the breakdown lane. From the moment his car hit the sandy shoulder of the road, it lurched right. In desperation, Dalton must have over-corrected when the car violently jerked left and then right again before skidding off the road and down a steep embankment. Charlie got on the brakes just in time to hear the loud crash. "Oh shit!" He screeched to a stop, pulled a quick U-turn and headed back to survey the accident scene.

In the quiet night, Charlie could hear the motor hissing, as if it were steaming mad. Other than that, there was an eerie silence; no moans or groans like he'd expected to hear. He got out of his car and started down the pitched embankment. Fifteen feet from the wreck, he could see that the destroyed Hyundai had struck a tree—which had refused to budge. Charlie stepped lightly to his left and the palm of his hand instinctively went to his mouth—to hold back a scream, the urge to puke, or both.

Dalton's upper body was half out of the windshield, lying on the car's crumpled hood—in a puddle of blood and brains. Even if the moonlight hadn't clearly pointed it out, Charlie would have been able to tell that a chunk of Dalton's skull was missing. *Missing*, he repeated in his head. He gagged at the sight of it but held the vomit back. Panic seeped into his racing heart before surging through his quivering body. "Oh God," Charlie gasped, "what did I do?" He braved another look at Dalton's fresh corpse and clasped his other hand over his mouth. *He's dead*, he confirmed. *I...I killed Dalton.*

Charlie wasn't sure how long it took but, when his wits finally returned to him, he scurried up the embankment. He fell once and then again before jumping back into his car. Hyper-ventilating, he looked up and down the desolate highway. He tried to calm his breathing, so he could think more clearly. *No one saw anything*, he decided. *There are no witnesses.* With the exception of a dark set of skid marks, nothing seemed out of the ordinary. He looked back toward the embankment and felt a belly of beer churn violently, threatening to erupt. He closed his eyes and took a deep breath. "This can't be happening!" he screamed. "No, God...please!" After pounding away at the steering wheel, he started the car, threw it into drive and headed toward home—crying hard the entire way. "I killed him!" he screamed. "I killed him!"

Just before reaching the car wash two towns over, he tried to console himself, thinking, *It was an accident, that's all*. But even he knew better than that. *I'm so screwed*, he thought and puked up everything that raged in his guts. *My life's over too*.

$\mathcal{B}$

The following afternoon, Billy—already willing to forget his anger toward Charlie—called his best friend's cell phone. It went right to voicemail. *That's odd*, he thought and then called the house. Charlie's mom picked up. "He's not here," she said. There was a pause. "I thought he was with you because he never came home last night."

Remembering Charlie's foul mood, Billy felt an eerie chill run across his skin, leaving goose bumps behind. "He probably just stayed at Mark's last night," Billy suggested before thinking, *He most likely sneaked into Bianca's house last night and slept over. Hopefully, they finally made up and put an end to this stupid bullshit*.

The woman sighed heavily. "I'm sure you'll see him before I do," she said indifferently.

"Maybe, but when you do see him, could you..." Billy began to ask when he realized she'd already hung up. "Thank you, Mrs. Philips," he said into the dead phone. "You really are a wonderful woman."

Billy headed off to Nick's Pizza for lunch. Nick's was located in a strip plaza, taking up two store fronts. From the time he walked in, the smells nearly bowled him over—pizzas, meat-filled calzones, and every sub you could imagine, from meatball to steak and cheese. The long, high-top counter was painted green, pitched in toward the floor. The counter was orange, the same obnoxious shade as Cinderella's pumpkin coach; it was ugly but inviting. On the counter, the cash register sang like a lark, while the tip jar contained only change and a single dollar bill that had been there for years as some pathetic, ineffective lure. A steel rack of potato chips sat beside a full tray of sweet baklava, which his mom brought home some nights. The floor tiles looked imported and expensive, a stark contrast to the homely wood paneling and Formica tangerine-colored counter.

Two sheets of plywood were hung over the two hot pizza ovens. Beneath them, Billy watched as his mom worked the flat paddle, sliding a pizza in and yanking two of them out. In a flash, she sliced and boxed the two pies and was taking an order with a phone wedged between her shoulder and the crook of her sweaty neck. Her hair was disheveled and, while spreading pizza cheese on a new pie, she looked up and saw him. Her eyes immediately lit up and she smiled.

After kissing his mom and placing his usual order—a large tuna sub, toasted, with extra provolone, lettuce and tomatoes—Billy headed to see Mark, who was already there.

The small dining room's walls were covered in Greek paintings of the Parthenon in Athens, as well as a few of the islands—Mykonos and Santorini—framed in gaudy gold frames. A few plastic floor plants, strung with small white lights that only twinkled when the set was just about to burn out, stood in the front corners. A dozen tables, surrounded by old wooden chairs, made the room look crowded. Mark was sitting in one of the back booths. Billy slid in across from him. "I tried calling Charlie but..."

"Did you hear about Dalton Noble?" Mark interrupted, an unusual urgency in his voice.

"Who?"

"That kid that lives in Berkley," Mark said. "He graduated this year too."

"Dalton...Dalton..." Billy searched his memory but couldn't place the name or face. He shook his head.

"The kid we saw at the party the other night, talking to Bianca."

"Oh yeah, right. What about him?"

"He drove his car into a tree off of Route 88 last night and killed himself."

"What?" A sick feeling tickled Billy's throat. "Are you serious? He's dead?"

Mark nodded. "Word has it that he left Jaime's party drunk and drove home."

"He was at Jaime's party last night? I never saw him there."

Mark nodded. "I saw him briefly, but I don't think he stayed long."

"And now he's dead," Billy thought aloud, immediately considering how life could change course at a moment's notice; one choice—good or bad—could alter a path that seemed so sure just moments before.

Without warning, a teenager sitting in the next booth jumped into the conversation. "My brother knows one of his cousins and she said he might have been texting when he drove off the road."

Billy tried to shake off the creepy sensation that ran through him. "Damn," he said. "That's messed up."

The teenager's acne-faced friend added, "They say Dalton was a great kid. He was supposed to go to UMASS in the fall on some academic scholarship."

"UMASS? That's where I'm going," Billy said, feeling the weight of the tragic news. "That sucks!"

Billy's mom entered the dining room to deliver Mark's small onion and mushroom pizza. Catching the tail end of their conversation, she shook her head. "What a tragedy." She looked at Billy and Mark. "You kids have your whole lives ahead of you."

"We know," they said in unison.

She peered harder at them both. "I'd better never hear about either of you drinking and driving again!" The last word carried a sharpness—comparable to a violent threat—which was not her usual style.

"We won't," the boys sang in chorus again.

She looked at Billy, her eyes searching for a promise.

"Never again," Billy vowed, his words strong and true.

She nodded and the usual sparkle reappeared in her eyes. "Come get your tuna sub," she told Billy. "It's probably done by now."

Billy pointed toward Mark's pizza. "Why does he get special treatment?"

"Come and get it," she repeated, turning on her heels. "Or I'll eat it."

Mark laughed.

Billy sighed heavily and pulled himself out of the booth like he was preparing to head off to a double shift at some rock quarry.

When he returned with his lunch, Mark asked, "Do you want to catch that new stalker movie tomorrow afternoon?"

Billy shook his head. "I wish," he said, his mouth already full, "but I can't. My dad set up an interview at the animal shelter...for a full-time summer position."

Mark smiled. "Cleaning shit for the summer. Good for you, Billy."

Billy took another big bite of his sandwich. "Whatever," he muttered. "I need the money."

As if he'd just remembered the start of their conversation, Mark asked, "So you talked to Charlie?"

Billy shook his head. "I tried calling him, but..." He stopped, feeling a wave of anger swell inside of him again. "Screw Charlie," he said, before diving back into his lunch.

Billy pulled out of Nick's Pizza's parking lot and, instead of steering left toward home, he turned the wheel right toward the beach. Some morbid sense of curiosity was prodding him to visit the scene of the tragic accident. For whatever reason, he felt compelled to see it.

As a lifelong resident of Westport, Billy had learned to avoid Route 88 in the summer. While the smarter townspeople traveled the back roads to get to the banks of the Westport River, or the dunes of Horseneck Beach, those who didn't know any better took their chances and traveled Route 88 at their own risk. *Whether it's because of a drunk driver or some knucklehead in a hurry to go nowhere,* he thought, *somebody always dies.*

Billy traveled the first few miles and could already feel the warm air beckoning the sun-worshipers to the ocean. Each year, thousands answered the call and made the dangerous trek.

As he drove, Billy considered the insane trip. Starting at the north end, there were five intersections to get through. Each set of lights was an obstacle, but if you could avoid being broadsided by another anxious beach comber then you still had to maneuver through the hills of winding asphalt. The speed limit began at fifty-five miles per hour and tapered down to forty. Normally, these signs were ignored and many drivers exceeded it by twenty to forty miles per hour more. For those who were in a real hurry, they were allowed to pass at almost any point in the road. It was absolute lunacy and that craziness had cost the lives of many people.

Besides guard rails and the woodlands which lined both sides of the highway, the only scenery to behold was the white crosses that marked their victims' final moments on earth.

Just as he could taste the salty air on his tongue, Billy hit a bend in the road and spotted two police cruisers securing the accident scene. He slowed the Honda to a crawl and craned his neck to take in all he could. There wasn't much to see; beyond the flashing blue lights, a set of dark skid marks led off the road, down an embankment and into the woods. But it was enough to turn his stomach. *A kid, my age, died right here just a few hours ago,* he thought. *That's nuts.* In his mind, he tried picturing what might have happened. Instantly, he imagined Dalton lying trapped in his crushed car, bleeding to death—alone and afraid. His eyes swelled with tears and he looked skyward. *Bless him, Father,* he silently prayed, *and please ease his family's pain.*

A couple hundred yards down the road, Billy spotted a large, bald man squatting in the opposite breakdown lane; he was clearly surveying another set of tire marks. *Is he a cop?* Billy wondered. He supposed it would have been odd otherwise, but the man wasn't wearing a police uniform.

Upon reaching the next intersection, Billy circled back like one of the seagulls that called out in the distance. He drove past the accident scene one last time—slowly. Although the bald man was gone, the queasy feeling in his stomach returned as he passed the two police cruisers. *Dalton had his whole life ahead of him*, he thought. *What a terrible way to die.*

He was nearly home when it dawned on him. *I have my whole life ahead of me*, he thought. *Thank God.*

Billy got home and noticed that Sophie's bedroom door was closed. *She must be home*, he thought. *Her car's in the driveway.* With Jimmy on his shins, he headed for the door. Billy lifted his fist to knock on the door when he heard Sophie talking to someone and laughing. "I wonder who she has over?" he said to Jimmy and knocked. There was no answer. Instead, her laughter grew louder. Billy knocked again and yelled, "Sophie?" Again, there was no answer. Curious, he slowly opened the door to discover Sophie lying on her bed, staring up at the ceiling and laughing. While Jimmy bound into the room, Billy quickly scanned it. *There's no one else in the room*, he thought and watched Sophie push Jimmy off her bed. He then glanced at her desk, where her cell phone was sitting—unused. "What are you doing, Sophe..." he began to ask.

"Nothing. Why?"

"I just heard you laughing."

"So what? I thought about something funny," she said, shooing Jimmy away from her—which Billy had never once seen her do.

"But you were talking to someone," he said, confused.

"No, I wasn't."

"Sophe, I've been standing at your door, listening to you talk to someone. And then you..."

"Then you must be hearing things." Her face instantly changed from happy to mean, a rarity for her. "What's your problem, Billy? I can't laugh anymore?"

"I never said that. But you..." He stopped, catching a faint whiff of some oddly familiar scent. *It smells like pot*, he thought, but he immediately rejected the idea. *No way. Not Sophie.* "What the hell's that smell?" he asked.

"I've been burning incense," she fired back. Now enraged, she sat up. "You know what," she barked, "just close my door behind you and take Jimmy with you!"

Billy grabbed the whimpering dog and escorted him out of the room. At the door, Billy stopped and watched as his sister looked back at the ceiling and began giggling again.

Billy closed her door and stood with his back against it. He looked down at Jimmy, who was still upset. The look in the mutt's dejected eyes said it all. "Don't take it personal, buddy," Billy said. "It's definitely not you." He shook his head. "She's the one who's screwed up over something."

Jimmy looked at Sophie's door one last time, before ambling off to Billy's bedroom—where the world made much better sense.

Chapter 5

On the morning of Dalton's funeral, the long slow procession crawled past Billy's house. He stood in his front yard, with Jimmy by his side. He'd contemplated attending the ceremony, but he really hadn't known Dalton. "It would have been weird if I went to the funeral home," he whispered down to the mutt. A black station wagon, overstuffed with flower arrangements, was followed by the polished hearse, carrying the remains of a life that had barely gotten started. Billy shook his head and vowed, "I'll never drink and drive again." As the brake lights illuminated the rear of the hearse, Billy recalled his grandpa's peculiar advice: 'Never laugh at a passing hearse because someday it'll be you.' He looked down at Jimmy again. "It could have been me in that casket, buddy." He shook his head again. "Never again! I don't want to be like Dad. Remember those days, Jimmy?"

The dog whined.

The shiny black family car crept by next. Billy got choked up for the faceless shadows that sat behind the dark, tinted glass. *I can't even imagine that kind of pain*, he thought sadly. And the parade of cars that followed—each with its headlights and flashers on—lasted for nearly ten minutes.

Jimmy sat up on his haunches with his head bowed—as if he were aware and showing his respect for the tragic human loss.

From beat-up clunkers—clearly owned by Dalton's young friends—to nicer rides driven by those who'd made their money, the ten minutes it took for them to pass was more than enough time for Billy to take stock of his recent mistakes. He also thought about all his friends who texted while driving—shocked that some of them were still walking amongst the living—and added that to the promises he'd made to himself. "No more texting and driving," he told Jimmy.

The dog's eyes stayed fixed on the cars driving by.

Watching all the young kids in the long parade, Billy imagined it was like a second graduation or some morose high school reunion that was taking place much too early. "Never again," he reminded himself and headed back into the house to get ready for his first real job interview.

Four Paws Animal Shelter—the local pound—was located on a dead end, and it was at the very end where the tar had been ripped up by seasons of bullish snowplows. The town didn't even patch the road, never mind tar it. Billy steered the tired Honda into the shelter's bluestone parking lot and smiled. *This place changed my life*, he thought, picturing Jimmy as a small pup. Shutting off the ignition, he took it all in.

The building was made of cinder blocks, painted drab green, and the roof's dark shingles needed replacing. A chain-link fence sprung out from both sides of the building, clearly meant to enclose the entire backyard—whether to keep the animals in, the humans out, or both. The cinder block fortress could have easily been located on a military installation; it was cold and impersonal. Two small windows were located on either side of the drab bunker, with a gray double door in the center. The doors were filthy; scuff marks on the bottom and dirty handprints up top. *Oh man*, Billy thought. His first impression of the place was abysmal.

One step into the place and the smells—urine, pine cleaner, feces, and more pine cleaner—overpowered all the other senses.

Billy stopped short and gave himself a minute to adjust to the rancid odors. An old, dull linoleum-tiled floor, which had probably been yellow at one time, was undoubtedly original to the building. It didn't appear it had ever been waxed, which made good sense. *But I wonder if it's ever been mopped?* Billy thought.

A reception area with an unmanned desk welcomed visitors. It wasn't a big area; there was an industrial clock, a calendar with kittens, which hadn't been flipped and was two months behind, and framed prints of dogs running in an open field. Everything looked old and unkempt, except for the fish tank which burst with vibrant colors in the corner of the dull world. The sparkling turquoise blue was home to a dozen small fish of different shapes and colors. Billy spent a minute bent at the waist, watching them swim and play.

A small office was located to the right. The walls were paneled brown, the floor tiles, a blah gray. Even the sun that filtered through the windows seemed gloomy. The door was cracked open a bit to the room on the left; Billy could tell it was being used to store file cabinets and supplies.

Once Billy became acclimated to the smells, his sense of hearing was pushed to the forefront. A muffled orchestra of barks, whines and cries seeped out from beneath a green door he couldn't wait to peek behind. He knocked a few times on the mysterious avocado-colored door and waited. The barks and cries continued. *There's no way anyone could ever hear me knocking,* he thought.

Suddenly, the door opened and a short, stout woman stood before him. Billy felt nervous. "My...my dad said he arranged an interview for your open summer position?" he blurted. From the look on the lady's face, he wondered whether his father had confused this place with another.

The embroidered name on the woman's shirt read *Arlene*. With two dogs under foot, she carefully looked Billy over, spending most of the time in his eyes.

Arlene Uslander had dirty-blonde hair pulled back into a ponytail. With kind, brown eyes, she dressed like she worked at the zoo. She wore a tan khaki outfit with a button down shirt, green braided belt, cargo pocket shorts and thick socks inside a pair of worn work boots.

Oh boy, Billy thought, fighting off a wave of skepticism.

"Do you love animals?" she asked bluntly.

"I do," he said, already bent at the waist, petting her dogs.

"That's McGruff, my boyfriend, and the mangy looking one is King," she said, introducing Billy to her four-legged companions.

Boyfriend, Billy repeated in his head and smiled. "Nice to meet you guys," he said, scratching both of their necks.

"Do you have any?" Arlene asked.

"Do I have any..."

"Dogs, cats...animals at home," she clarified.

"Two," he said, smiling. "A dog and a cat. The cat's name is Mrs. Pringle. She's my mother's," he admitted, shaking his head at the foolish name. "My dog's name is Jimmy," he added, a sense of pride returning to his smile.

She studied his face and her eyes softened. "Looks like Jimmy means a lot to you," she said.

Billy shook his head. "Actually, he means *everything* to me," he said, nodding. "We adopted Jimmy from this place twelve years ago and he's been my best friend ever since."

"You're hired," she said matter-of-factly and extended her hand.

"I am?" Billy asked, unsure whether she was pulling his leg. "There's no interview?"

Arlene smiled again and gripped his hand for a remarkably firm shake. "You just passed it."

"Really?" he said, still trying to process the fact that he'd landed the summer job.

"Really," she said. "You ready to get started?"

He nodded. "Yes, ma'am."

She laughed. "I'm no ma'am, as you'll soon find out. Call me Arlene."

He nodded. "I'm Billy."

She nodded. "Okay then, Billy, why don't we get started with a tour of the place, so you can meet our diverse clientele." She smirked. "And then we'll start you on hosing down the kennels."

"Sounds good to me," he said.

"Until you see how messy those kennels can get," she teased.

"Not a problem there," Billy said confidently. "I've been cleaning up after Jimmy for years."

Arlene had her hand on the green door's knob when she stopped and turned back to face Billy. "You can bring him to work with you if you want," she said.

"Bring who?" he asked.

"Jimmy."

Billy felt a bolt of joy rip through him. *This is too good to be true*, he thought. "Really?"

"Really," she said, chuckling at his reaction. "We actually like having dogs around here."

He nodded, feeling foolish and happy at the same time.

As Arlene opened the door, she said, "Welcome to the pound." She stopped and turned. "Actually, the word *pound* makes me laugh. This is a shelter."

Billy nodded.

"Outside our doors is where life will pound the hell out of you."

Billy chuckled and, as they stepped inside, he realized his first impression of Arlene was completely off. After spending fewer than five minutes with her, he could tell she was a wonderful human being: caring and kind. And from the way she treated the two dogs that clung to her shins, the soft-hearted caretaker obviously loved animals. *They're not just her passion*, Billy immediately decided, *they're her purpose.*

The animal shelter's back room was also constructed of cinder block, painted hospital white, with brown-painted steel-framed doors and windows, all of it screaming government funding.

Once they reached the kennel area, the worn linoleum transitioned to a polished concrete floor. Beneath twenty-foot ceilings, the interior kennels stood eight feet high, secured by chain link doors. From the first look, Billy's memory was jarred and he immediately returned to the day—all those years ago— when he'd picked Jimmy as a family member.

Walking into the cell block, competing scents of urine and disinfectant hung in the air. A wide variety of four-legged inmates, filling the cells on both sides of the drab green corridor, awaited their fate. Some were crying, while others had surrendered in a heap on the floor. The younger ones appeared oblivious to their grim surroundings.

In the furthest corner kennel, a black mutt with white socks was sitting, licking his paw and washing his ears and face.

"At least this one's clean," Billy's dad joked.

The dog stood, walked to the kennel door and placed his right paw up on the silver mesh, right where Billy's hand rested on the other side of the cold steel.

Billy's entire body tingled.

"And clever too," the old man muttered under his breath.

Although the black dog didn't have the striking features of some of the other dogs and was a little bigger than the other puppies that frolicked in the cell beside him, he clearly used what he had—his brain.

Billy remembered his father taking a long look at the dog. "Looks like he's mostly Labrador retriever with something much smaller mixed in...maybe ground hog?"

Billy's mom slapped her husband's arm and laughed.

The old man shrugged. "His mother could have been half wolverine, half squirrel. Whatever he is, the one thing I know for sure is that he's no pure blood." His dad looked the dog over again. "Yup, he's definitely a mutt."

"He's so cute," Sophie said.

The shelter's caretaker nodded. "This one's a sweet-tempered dog with a good disposition," he said before opening the cage door.

Billy and the dog lunged for each other, Billy wrapping the panting dog into his arms. "He's perfect," Billy said and stared into the dog's chocolate eyes. "Jimmy's perfect."

"Jimmy?" his dad repeated. "Are you serious? What about Bear or Rufus...or even Brutus?"

Billy shook his head.

"What about Sprinkles?" the old man teased.

Billy shook his head.

"Jimmy?" his dad asked.

"Jimmy," Sophie confirmed.

Billy nodded.

Jimmy licked Billy's face, as if offering his sticky seal of approval.

The big man laughed. "Okay then, let's go home, James," he said to the mutt.

"No, Dad, it's Jimmy...after Uncle Jimmy," Billy insisted, referring to his dad's older brother who had only survived eleven hours after birth, and who Billy had always felt sorry for because he'd been cheated so badly. "Jimmy," Billy repeated firmly and that was it.

Returning to the present, Billy noted that stainless steel half walls separated each kennel and each pen was three feet wide but deep all the way to the rear door. Every kennel had a run that was half inside the building and half outside. A small door led to an outside run, hooked by a rope that could be pulled to lift the door and allow an animal out. Billy was surprised to find that it was a sanitized environment.

"These kennels house the bigger dog breeds," Arlene said, "and are cleaned with a garden hose." She grinned.

Billy nodded, noting that the smaller dogs were stacked in two rows of cages. One stainless steel food bowl and a similar water bowl were placed in the rear of each cage, along with a small blanket.

Arlene stepped into a separate room that housed cats in stainless steel cages, three rows—stacked one on top of the next—with newspaper-lined trays. She pulled out one of the trays. "This is where we keep the goodies," she teased Billy.

He laughed.

"Even though we provide each cage with a litter box, most still make a mess," she explained. "The cleaning can be a little more challenging on the third row, so make sure you don't tilt the tray too far forward. Then you'll be wearing it and mopping up the floor afterward."

Each cage was filled with multiple cats. Arlene explained, "Although the cat carriers are intended for individual animals, we do everything we can to keep families together." She shook her head. "Some shelters have stopped taking cats altogether. There are just too many requiring resources that aren't available."

Billy mirrored her shaking head, thinking, *Arlene's obviously not one of those people.*

As they continued the tour, one of the cages displayed a peculiar sign: *Cat Quarantined.*

"What does that mean?" Billy asked.

"Cat flu," Arlene explained. "Outbreaks are common at any shelter. But trust me, through years of trial and error, we've learned that it's not worth trying to isolate an animal and disinfect the area. It's a waste of time and effort."

"So how..."

"Animals with the flu are left to the treatment of their own immune systems," she finished.

Billy nodded, as he learned that other small animals—bunnies, iguanas, guinea pigs, gerbils, hamsters, chinchillas—were occasionally housed in small cages or carriers where there was no room elsewhere.

"We also have a few cages for domestic birds," Arlene said, "and they're usually occupied."

"This place is amazing," Billy commented.

Arlene smiled. "I think so too." She pointed back to the ramp that led to the reception area. "We use our supply room to allow potential adopters to get a good look at the animals."

"I can't wait to see that," Billy said, realizing this new job promised the highest of highs—from young families to the elderly adopting a new furry family member—to the lowest of lows: the threat of animals being euthanized.

Arlene nodded. "The adoptions are definitely the upside of this job and you'll see plenty of them." When she smiled, her eyes misted over. "I still get emotional at every adoption."

"Are there a lot of them?" Billy asked.

"We average a half dozen a week," she said, nodding. "We're also affiliated with several organizations that accept specific breeds, usually pure breeds like golden retrievers, poodles, boxers, collies, and chihuahuas." She stopped and looked into Billy's eyes to hammer her next lesson home. "The name of the game is for us to find each animal a home. And with our limited resources, every day they stay here they're eating us out of house and home."

Billy laughed. "My grandpa used to use that same line when he teased me and my sister," he said.

Arlene laughed. "A fellow scholar," she joked, before continuing with her lesson. "We usually find a permanent family for the pure breeds right away."

As they made their way out back, Billy saw that there was a good-sized yard—more dirt than grass—which Arlene said was used for socializing.

"The locked gates help protect against accidental escapees," she explained with a grin. "We don't want any of these four-legged bandits slipping out over the wall."

Billy laughed, but also nodded that he understood the reasoning. He then noticed that the outside kennels were covered, from the run door to the cement pad. *These should be easier to hose down*, he thought.

As if reading his mind, Arlene said, "You'll pick up on the rest as we go along. For now, you ready to grab the disinfectant and clean some kennels?"

Billy nodded. "I am."

She chuckled. "If you want to put in a few hours today, that's fine. But I'll start you on the schedule next week...give you a few days to relax before you become my official slave. How's that sound?"

"Sounds perfect. Thank you."

She chuckled at his enthusiasm. "You're going to do well here I think," she said, adding a wink.

"I'll do my best," he promised, happy to be hanging up his ant-infested dishwashing sneakers.

"What more can I ask for?" she said, before searching his eyes one last time. She smiled. "It's as easy as herding cats," she said, winking again.

When he returned home, Billy told Jimmy the good news. "We both got the job at the animal shelter, old man. We're going to be working together!"

Jimmy collapsed to the ground and rested his chin on his folded paws.

Billy shrugged. *Jimmy's got a point*, he thought. *It's like getting paroled from prison only to go back years later and work there.* He stroked Jimmy's muzzle. "It'll be fun, buddy. You'll see."

The weary dog never responded.

Without giving it any thought, Billy called Charlie to share the good news. His cell phone went straight to voicemail. "Charlie," Billy said, "give me a call when you get this. I have some really good news." He thought about it. "Listen, bro, let's put the bullshit behind us. Just hit me up when you get a chance."

Billy hung up and dialed Mark's cell.

"Hello?" Mark said.

"I got the job!" Billy blurted. "The place is awesome and Arlene, the boss over there, says I can take Jimmy with me to work."

"That's cool, but how does the old-timer feel about that?"

"We'll see," Billy said, laughing. "I just told him about it and he doesn't seem all that enthused over it." Billy petted Jimmy's back.

"So when can we catch that stalker flick?" Mark asked. "It's supposed to be a good one."

Billy thought about it and sighed.

"There's brief nudity," Mark added.

Billy laughed. "I have one last shift at the Pearl and then we should have plenty of time."

"Cool. Just give me a call and let me know when you can do it. You know how much I love brief nudity."

"You're not alone there, bro," Billy said, laughing again. "I'll let you know when I free up."

"Later, Billy boy."

"Later, Mark."

Billy got off the phone and checked his email. He stood in shock. "Holy shit, I won the VFW scholarship for five hundred dollars," he said aloud. "Sweet!"

Jimmy sat up, as if waiting to hear more.

Billy had entered an essay contest hosted by the local VFW. The theme was, "A veteran who has made a difference in your life," and it was the first time he'd ever written from his heart.

His grandfather, his father's dad, was a combat veteran who'd served in Vietnam and suffered every day for it until his final breath.

Billy looked down at Jimmy. "It seems Grandpa's still looking out for me," he said, feeling blessed, before returning to the computer screen. "You're invited to the VFW Hall, Post 8502, to receive your award," he read aloud, "and to present your essay, along with a few words of thanks." Instantly, his breathing became shallow and his heart began to pound hard in his chest. He looked down at Jimmy again. "Maybe this isn't such a good thing after all," he muttered. On one hand, he was thrilled about the five hundred dollars; on the other, he was freaked out beyond words. "Present my essay in front of an audience?" he pondered aloud and felt his throat constrict.

Jimmy nudged Billy with his muzzle a few times.

"Not now, Jimmy!" Billy snapped, overwhelmed with angst.

The mutt nudged him again, refusing to be ignored.

Feeling dizzy, Billy reached down and petted him; it was enough of a distraction to stop the growing panic. It was exactly what Billy needed to start breathing again. "I'm sorry, buddy," Billy said, rubbing the scruff of the mutt's neck.

Jimmy nudged him one last time, as if to say—*No worries. I'm right here with you.*

Billy felt so much better already and laughed at the dog's cleverness. "Thank you, Jimmy," he said, continuing the well-deserved massage. "You're a good boy."

On his last night at Oriental Pearl, Billy kept his head down and his eyes on his assembly line. Long ago, the shared snickers and sighs amongst the staff had evolved into inside jokes. Most were waitresses—females who worked their beautiful butts off. At seventeen, it was all Billy's eyes would let him see. Their ages ranged, but to the raging hormones of a young adolescent it didn't matter. Billy was an intimate member of the clique, taking part in the jokes about the cooks who didn't speak English.

"They're such pigs," Lynn said, complaining about them.

Billy smirked. *But she's right*, he thought. *They are a strange lot.* The Chinese cooks were heavy gamblers: vulgar men with nudie calendars of busty American women. Each one of them tried to get in cheap grabs of the waitresses, laughing amongst themselves in their foreign gibberish. Other times, they would explode in anger and threaten to lash out with their blood-stained cleavers. *Very strange people*, Billy thought, *but I love their calendars.*

"You want a drink?" Lynn asked Billy.

He nodded. "How 'bout a Shirley Temple?" It was lemon lime soda with a splash of sweet grenadine syrup.

Lynn laughed. "Yeah, I don't think so," she said.

Five minutes later, she returned with a full tray of dirty dishes, along with a whiskey and cola. "I got you a real drink," she said, smiling, and placed it up on the top shelf.

Billy grabbed it and put the cold glass to his lips. He coughed, choked and cringed as the slow burn traveled the length of his throat. While Lynn looked on, smirking, Billy took another swig and smiled. "It must be an acquired taste," he told her, gagging again.

"Must be," she said, laughing all the way out of the kitchen.

The night was so busy that it faded into a mountain of dirty dishes, glasses and silverware that could not be conquered—until last call.

While Billy waited to be paid, he scanned the crowd. *No fights tonight*, he thought, disappointedly. *And no drunken girls gone bad.* He grabbed a fortune cookie and cracked it open. As he munched on the bland cookie, he read, *Expect a season of change*. With a shrug, he put the fortune into his pocket and said goodbye to the Oriental Pearl: the greatest job anyone could have ever hated.

On the ride home, he called Charlie's cell phone. It went right to voicemail. *Even though it's late, Charlie always picks up*, Billy thought, waiting for the beep. "Charlie, it's Billy. Give me a call just as soon as you get this. Don't worry about the time. I'll be up for a while. I haven't heard from you in almost a week and I'm starting to wonder what's up." He paused, realizing he no longer harbored any anger toward his friend. Instead, he was growing concerned. "Just call me, okay?"

Billy hung up the phone and took it slow going home. A mile down the road, he could hear the faint sound of sirens in the distance coming up from behind him. He peered into the rearview mirror. A pulsating glow of red and blue was growing larger by the second. He quickly pulled the car onto the shoulder of the road. In a flash, two enormous fire trucks were followed by a wailing ambulance, the three vehicles chugging by like some runaway train. Goose bumps covered Billy's arms and the small hairs on the back of his neck stood at attention. *There's something big going down*, he thought, *and the cavalry is on its way.* He was impressed and filled with respect at the responding troops.

Billy pulled back onto the road and, for the rest of the ride home, considered what it might be like to join the ranks and become a fireman or paramedic. *It's so awesome what they do*, he thought, *all the people they help*. But he didn't feel the passion he'd hoped he'd feel. There was definitely a deep respect and admiration for the calling, but he somehow knew it wasn't his.

But what the hell is my calling? he wondered, as the internal struggle continued.

Sitting in the corner chair of his darkened bedroom, Charlie listened to Billy's message and could feel another round of tears start down his cheeks. *Starting to wonder what's up?* he repeated in his head. *I killed a kid, Billy...that's what's up*. As the tears turned to heavy sobs, his body convulsed at the same gruesome pictures that played over and over in his throbbing head: Dalton's body was lying on the car's smashed hood, submerged in a growing puddle of blood and gray matter. *Oh my God*, Charlie thought, *a chunk of his skull was missing*. He jumped out of the chair and began dry heaving. *Missing*, he repeated, torturing himself.

Just then, there was a knock on his bedroom door. "Charlie, what's going on in there?" his mother asked. The doorknob jiggled a few times but the door remained locked.

Charlie dragged his sleeve across his mouth and took a deep breath. "Nothing, Ma! I'm fine. Just leave me alone."

The doorknob jiggled again. "That girlfriend of yours better not be in there, Charlie. I swear I'll..."

"Bianca and I broke up, Ma!" Charlie interrupted. "I just need some time alone, okay?"

"Good," the woman muttered. There was a moment of silence, followed by the sound of fading footsteps walking away from his door.

Charlie collapsed to the floor and placed his head into his hands. *Dalton's entire skull was crushed*, he thought, and began dry heaving again.

It took a long time before the newest wave of anxiety had passed. In the darkness, he punched the first few numbers into his cell phone when he stopped. "I can't bring Billy into this," he whimpered to himself. "I...I can't do that to him." He cleared the numbers from his phone, slid down to the floor and rolled himself into the fetal position. *I'm all alone now*, he realized, weeping like a child who'd lost all hope. *And it's exactly where I deserve to be.*

Chapter 6

In the morning, as Jimmy prepared to jump off the bed and face a new day, he winced in pain. Billy studied the dog for a few moments. *Jimmy's still healing from his combat wounds,* he thought and told him, "We don't have to start at the shelter for a few days, so we should spend some time together...just you and me."

Jimmy was a creature of habit, thriving on routine. After receiving his new arthritis pill hidden within a glob of peanut butter, he devoured the day's first cup of food within seconds. Although it looked like he tried to be neat it was no use. As Jimmy lapped from his water bowl, Billy took a few steps back; without wearing a poncho, he would have gotten soaked. On the upside, the extra water helped Jimmy get started on his morning bath.

While Billy waited for his partner to finish bathing, he spotted a note on the table. It was addressed, *Billy.* He opened it and read: *Billy, let's look at your class schedule when I get home tonight. I also want to make sure you've applied to all the grants you're entitled to. Even if you've missed deadlines, we can still set you up for next semester. Love ya, Sophie.*

Billy folded up the note and smiled. *Love you, too,* he thought.

After taking a very short walk, Billy and Jimmy ended up in the backyard. "Want to play?" Billy asked the dog.

Jimmy got down on his elbows, butt up and tail whipping around—ready to pounce. He even offered a low growl, like he actually meant business.

Billy laughed. "Who are you kidding, old man?" he asked him. "It's been forever since you've tried to spring an ambush on me."

In response, Jimmy kept his backside high in the air and front legs on the ground, preparing to lunge.

"Don't go hurting yourself," Billy told the mutt, letting him off the hook. He threw Jimmy one of his squeaky plush toys.

Jimmy trapped the toy with his front paws and nosed it a few times with his snout. Finally biting into it, he jerked his head violently back and forth, trying to dismember the small stuffed animal. And although he growled, his tail never stopped wagging.

"Big bad dog," Billy teased, getting onto his knees. He massaged Jimmy's thick neck.

Jimmy flopped down, out of breath; his tongue hanging out of the side of his mouth.

While the dog panted loudly, Billy joined him on the ground and stroked his heaving chest. "Now this is more your speed," he said.

That afternoon, with Jimmy riding shotgun, Billy pumped eight dollar's worth of gas into the Honda. For the time being, it was all his budget would allow.

After fastening his seat belt, Billy and his sidekick hit the back roads of Westport for a nice long drive. They were just underway when Billy looked to his right and laughed. "You really love your car rides, don't you?" he told Jimmy.

The silver-faced mutt never answered. Instead, he kept his entire head hanging out of the passenger side window. His eyes were squinted and his ears were flopping in the wind, like two flags fluttering in a wind storm. Billy remembered trying it once as a kid, but he didn't last all that long outside the window. The rush of air stung his eyes until he could no longer keep them open.

"Be careful," he told Jimmy, but the dog was in his glory— enjoying the open road like the free spirit he'd always been.

They were five miles from the beach, the salted air already teasing their tongues, when the Honda sputtered a few times. Billy took his foot off the gas and then reapplied pressure. In response, the Honda shook and convulsed like it was suffering some terrible seizure. Instantly, the dashboard lit up like a Christmas tree with every dummy light, while the car slowed to a crawl. Billy steered the Honda to the side of the road before it gasped one last breath, sputtered and died.

Billy put the gear shifter into park and tried to start it again. "Damn it!" It was no use. He looked at Jimmy. "Looks like we need to call Triple A," he said and pulled out his cell phone to dial his father.

The phone rang twice before his dad's baritone voice answered. "Hello?"

"Dad, it's Billy. I took Jimmy for a ride and we broke down."

"Where are you?" the old man asked.

"Main Road," Billy said, looking out his window, "between the Apothecary and Lees."

"I'll be there in ten," his dad said and hung up the phone.

Billy tossed his cell phone onto the dashboard and grinned. His father wasn't perfect by any stretch—*but if I called him from the moon,* Billy thought, *he'd still come and get me.*

Jimmy pulled his head back into the car and looked at Billy, as if awaiting an explanation for the delay.

"Sorry, buddy. We tried," Billy told him. "We'll have to go to the beach another day."

Jimmy whimpered softly before sticking his head back out of the window and licking at the salty air. As he did, Billy noticed that the car's inspection sticker had expired a month before. *Oh no...*

Billy waited up late that night but Sophie never came home. He turned into bed, wondering where she was and cursing his junk car. "The last thing I can afford right now is a new water pump," he told Jimmy, "but it doesn't look like I have a choice. Either that or I buy new sneakers and start walking everywhere." He thought about it and shook his head. "The inspection sticker's going to have to wait though."

Jimmy sat right beside him in the bed. He turned once, twice, three times—scratching frantically before finally lying down. It was as if the dog was burrowing, creating a nocturnal nest. Jimmy then curled both his head and tail under his chest, while he cuddled up against Billy.

Billy stroked the mutt's coat, noticing that the older Jimmy got, the more he sought out body heat. *On the upside*, Billy thought, *at least he doesn't squirm or wiggle around half the night like he did when he was young.*

"Sorry again about the beach, Jimmy," he whispered. "I'll make it up to you."

Jimmy nuzzled closer to him.

Billy closed his eyes and prepared to drift off with his best friend. Suddenly, a simple thought crossed his mind: *The scholarship presentation is in two days!* His eyes flew open and a wave of panic rushed through his body.

Jimmy sprang up and looked at him, whimpering once.

"It's okay," Billy said, breathing deeply, "I'm just really freaked out about having to speak in front of an audience."

Jimmy licked his cheek, before lying back down and nuzzling close to Billy again.

"At least that's one thing you'll never have to worry about," Billy told the considerate dog, trying to calm his negative thinking.

Jimmy nuzzled even closer, until they could feel each other's heartbeats; he turned his head and kissed Billy's cheek again.

Billy closed his eyes and wrapped his arm around the big oaf. He took a few deep breaths. "Thanks, buddy," he whispered. "I appreciate the support."

There were maybe two-dozen people in attendance—an elderly audience that looked harmless and kind. But somehow, it didn't seem to matter. Billy's short, shallow breaths quickly turned to hyperventilating. His extremities tingled with an overload of oxygen, while his mind raced back and forth like a hyperactive child without direction—or medication. His face felt numb and, each time he swallowed, he realized his mouth was empty of saliva—which he knew was desperately needed to deliver his presentation. He was sweating profusely and kept mopping his forehead with the white wash cloth he'd concealed in his pocket. Pure fear and jolts of panic rocked him to the core. He tried to affirm to himself, *You're going to do fine. This is nothing...just a couple of rows of nice old guys waiting to be thanked.* But feelings of doom and gloom immediately contradicted those thoughts. *This isn't worth five thousand dollars, never mind five hundred,* he thought. He was fighting his own war—logical mind versus pounding heart, and his feelings felt so much stronger than the lies he kept telling himself.

When he finally stepped up to the podium—having to tell both of his legs to move—he took a deep breath and felt like he was going to vomit. There was no decision now. *Backing out is no longer an option,* he told himself. Then, somewhere in the terrifying haze, he pictured Jimmy licking his cheek, followed by a small voice in his head that whispered, *Screw it.*

He unfolded his speech and cleared his throat. "Give More Than You Take by William Baker," Billy read and couldn't believe it when he heard his own voice speaking. "Since I was a young boy, my grandfather taught me that freedom never comes free and that patriotism matters very much. Without it, the United States of America would not be the greatest country on earth."

One silver head after the next nodded in staunch agreement.

"Grandpa said that patriotism is the glue that has held us together since the original New England patriots stood up against the British and fought for our liberty. Patriotism is what kept us strong during the Great Depression, each World War, the Civil Rights Movement and other times when we were challenged to show our true character. And no matter how sad or tragic things get in the world, it is still the glue that binds Americans together today. Whether it's standing up to show your respect during the National Anthem or standing up like my grandpa did to protect the weak from the strong, I believe that patriotism is the spark that inspires Americans to stand up for their beliefs and their rights. I also think that patriotism and pride are what *keep* people standing, even when they get scared or tired of fighting."

The nods grew more pronounced.

"I'm so blessed for the lessons my grandfather taught me."

Several men applauded, throwing Billy off a bit.

He took a breath and continued. "My grandfather's death was one of the toughest experiences I've ever endured," he said. "Sitting in the funeral home, surrounded by my family and others who knew him, I did not hear one word spoken of the wealth he'd accumulated throughout his life. Instead, people spoke about his service and the great sacrifices he'd made for our country in Vietnam. They also talked about the role he played in their lives and about some of the generous things he did for them. As I sat there pondering his life, I thought about the things that should truly matter and I continually asked myself, 'How much is enough?'"

As Billy read his essay aloud, the entire experience felt surreal—like he was watching himself speak from the safety of some invisible window.

"The dollar sign and the value we've given it has hypnotized our society into thinking that quantity is much more precious than quality. We've looked past what used to be important to become a greedy and selfish nation. As I drive through certain neighborhoods, I see large mansions with a fleet of fifty-thousand-dollar cars parked in their driveways. Not even ten minutes later in another town, you can find a single, homeless mother standing outside of a liquor store, begging for enough money to feed her children. It amazes me how people within the higher class of our society are so blinded by the gleam of their shiny new cars that they can't see their fellow Americans suffering each and every day.

"You cannot buy true love with a dollar bill and there is no cost for real friendship, so why is it that we all strive to make as much money as we can when the things that truly matter in life hold no price tag? As early as I can remember, I've always been told, 'Give more than you take.' As I've grown and matured, this phrase continues to ring even truer for me with every step I take. I realize I haven't been around a long time, but I also know that this is one of the most important things that we, as human beings, can do—give more than we take. And according to my grandfather, 'It is in that act of giving that we can build an extraordinary life.'

"Years from now, when I've drawn my final breath, I want people to say the same things about me that they said about my grandfather, the patriotic veteran. I want to be remembered for the good I've done and for the positive roles I've played in others' lives. I don't want people to talk about my awards or my possessions because in the end, those things aren't important. I want to leave this earth with a set of bonds that I've forged with people who have meant the world to me—bonds I can carry with me wherever I may go. Ultimately, that's the most important possession in any human being's life."

Billy paused and took a deep breath.

"My grandfather lived his life within the *we* society, where most people thought of others before themselves, building America into the great country that it is today. His generation faced difficult times and overcame many challenges to prove its true character. I, on the other hand, have been born and raised within the *me* society, where most people consider themselves before others and value the accumulation of material objects over building human relationships. I'd very much like to help change that."

There was more applause, much more.

Billy paused to offer a smile of gratitude. "Since my earliest memories, I can remember my grandpa saying, 'To be truly happy, you have to serve a purpose higher than yourself.' I think my grandfather would be proud that I have confirmed my values and that I intend to spend my life making a positive difference in the lives of others, rather than just feeding some greed for material wealth."

Billy took a big breath and vowed, "If I receive this scholarship, which will undoubtedly help me to achieve my college education, I have every intention of serving a purpose greater than just myself."

When Billy finished reading the essay, he looked up; his collar was drenched in sweat. Everyone was smiling—and clapping. He couldn't believe it. *I did it*, he thought. *I didn't piss my pants or die or even pass out. I actually did it.* He bowed his head in appreciation, as the audience continued to applaud and the five hundred pounds he'd carried around all week lifted off his shoulders and floated away. He took a deep breath; it felt like the first one in days.

Billy stepped into a crowd of old veterans that offered one slap after the other on his back.

"Good for you, son, honoring your grandfather like that," one of them said. "I'm sure he'd be real proud of you, if he were still with us today."

Billy nodded politely. *But I wrote what I had to in order to get accepted into college*, he thought truthfully. He hadn't lied or exaggerated about his grandfather. In fact, to him, the man had always walked on water. *But as far as myself*, he thought, *I have no idea what the afternoon holds, never mind the future beyond it. And I have no idea what I want to do with my life.* As he received another pat on the back, he was hoping his purpose would find him. *Because I have absolutely no idea where to look*, he thought.

Billy called Charlie again—and then again. The calls not only went unanswered but were unreturned. Charlie was creating some significant distance between them. *But why?* Billy wondered. *I know he and Bianca are on the rocks, but that shouldn't have to come between us. And that stupid argument we had at the party was nothing. We've had much worse fights.* He just couldn't make any sense of it. Undaunted, he left Charlie one voice message after the other. Within a few short weeks of their graduation, his best friend had all but shrunk away; there were no more all-night gaming marathons, watching the sun rise with orange cheese-puff powder covering their t-shirts. Billy was beside himself, alternating between confusion, anger and sadness—each emotion getting its fair share of his attention. *But Charlie's my brother and I need to figure out what the hell's going on with him*, he thought. *Whatever it is, something's wrong.*

With Jimmy riding shotgun, Billy drove over to Charlie's house and knocked on the front door. Charlie's mom answered it. "Do you know where he is, Mrs. Philips?" Billy asked.

She shook her head. "You just missed him," she said, taking a long drag from her cigarette. "He's been talking about selling that car of his. I think he went out to clean it again."

Billy shook his head in disbelief. "Charlie loves that car. Are you sure?"

She nodded, blowing a plume of smoke through the screen.

"No way," Billy muttered aloud, fanning the blue smoke cloud away from his face. *Something's definitely wrong*, he now knew for sure.

"He left a few minutes ago," she concluded, taking another drag. "Who knows when he'll be back."

As the screen door closed an inch from Billy's nose, he felt a terrible darkness creep into his soul. *Well, I know I'll be back tonight, Mrs. Philips,* he thought, *and I'll wait as long as it takes until I talk to Charlie and find out what's really going on.*

Billy got back into the Honda. Jimmy looked at him, as if awaiting an update. "Charlie's not home right now, but he'll be back." He patted the mutt's head. "And we'll be waiting for him when he does, boy."

Billy picked up his cell phone and called Mark.

"Hello?" Mark answered.

"Hey, it's me," Billy said. "I'm just leaving Charlie's place. He's not home...again." He shook his head. "I need to drop Jimmy off at home and then I'm heading over to Nick's. Why don't you meet me there?"

"Did Charlie's mother shed any light on why he's been avoiding everyone?" Mark asked.

"No," Billy said, "but while I was second-hand smoking one of her cancer sticks, she did tell me that he's out cleaning his car because he's talking about selling it."

"No way!" Mark blurted.

"That's what I said."

"I'll meet you at Nick's in ten."

"See you there," Billy said, pressing down on the accelerator.

As Billy stepped through the door at Nick's Pizza, he noticed Tony working the pizza ovens. *Ma must be in the back,* Billy thought.

Nick didn't own Nick's Pizza, Tony did—which Billy always thought was odd. Tony spotted Billy and yelled, "You ready to say goodbye to the Chinese and come work for me?"

Billy smiled. "Can you imagine me and my mother working together? She'd..."

"...kill you," Tony said, completing the sentence and laughing.

Billy laughed along with him. "Actually, I'm all done working at the Pearl. I just got a job at the animal shelter."

"Good for you," the olive-skinned man said.

Tony was a good man, with raven-black hair greased back in sweat. For most people, he wore a constant scowl that Billy's mom swore was nothing more than a disguise. Billy knew better too. *He's a sweetheart.* Tony wore an old, stained polo shirt—revealing his hairy arms—beneath a once-white apron. He was short, with hair protruding from his ears and a good-sized nose that had clearly been broken at least once.

"You having the usual," Tony asked, "tuna sub with provolone, toasted?"

Billy nodded. "Yes, sir."

Tony threw up one of his meaty hands. "You got it, buddy."

Billy nodded his gratitude. *Tony's in a good mood today*, he thought, *so lunch is definitely on the house again.*

Billy discovered Mark in the usual corner booth, finishing up a small mushroom, onion and cheese pizza.

"So you got your car fixed?" Mark said, as Billy took a seat across from him.

"Yeah, it needed a new water pump," Billy said, shaking his disgusted head. "My old man just put it in."

"Well, that's good."

"Yeah, that's good all right," Billy repeated. "I had to borrow the money from him and you know how he is when it comes to handing out loans."

"As long as you got wheels," Mark said, smiling. "And I'm guessing you survived the presentation at the VFW?" he said, changing the subject.

"Barely," Billy said. "I can't remember ever feeling that nervous, bro."

"At least you got paid for it," Mark teased.

"That's true," Billy said, "but there must be easier ways to make money."

Mark nodded. "So what do you think is really going on with Charlie? I've called him a few times but haven't heard a word back from him."

Billy shook his head. "I know. Same here. I just can't figure it."

"And he's talking about selling his car?" Mark asked, still surprised by this.

Billy nodded again. "According to that sweet woman he calls his mother, yeah...he's been cleaning it up, getting it ready to sell."

Mark snickered. "Well, you have to consider the source there." He shrugged. "She's never had a clue about what's going on in Charlie's world and I don't think she's ever cared."

"True," Billy said, feeling a little bit better. "But why hasn't he returned our calls?"

"You know Charlie," Mark said. "He's probably knee-deep in some sickening drama with Bianca."

Billy chuckled, feeling better still—and realized his friend was doing all he could to make him feel better. *Mark cares about other people*, he thought, *while most of the kids our age only care about themselves.*

"And sometimes Charlie isn't the most considerate person," Mark added, laughing, "or the smartest."

Billy nodded. "I know. My dad says Charlie's like a monkey trying to make music with one cymbal." Billy's eyes drifted off and his face turned serious. "But he's always been there for us when we've needed him."

Mark nodded. "Ain't that the truth. I remember when Troy Cabral was bullying me. Charlie was afraid of Troy, too, but he stood right by my side."

To Billy's surprise, his eyes misted over. He immediately turned in his seat, hiding it from Mark. A moment later, he offered a fake laugh. "I remember Troy telling Charlie that he was going to pound the both of you and..."

"...and although it was just a mask," Mark jumped in, "Charlie smiled at Troy and told him, 'You'd better bring some people.'"

Billy nodded, remembering every vivid detail of that fateful day. "Troy stood there for the longest time, studying Charlie and trying to figure out whether he was bluffing."

Mark grinned. "Either way, it worked."

Just then, Tony appeared with a large tuna sub. He placed it down in front of Billy and winked. "All set," he said and walked away, wiping his hands on his stained apron.

"Wow," Mark said, "aren't you special?"

Billy grinned comically. "Something my mother needs to remember."

Mark laughed.

After taking his first few bites, Billy blurted, "I hope Charlie's all right."

"He is," Mark said. "He just needs to get crap slapped."

"Crap slapped?"

"It's when you slap someone so hard they crap their pants."

Billy laughed. "Yup, that's exactly what he needs."

Mark's smile turned serious. "I'm sure it's something to do with Bianca and he just needs some time alone. He'll come around."

"That's probably true," Billy said, tearing another chunk out of his sub, "but I plan on finding out for myself tonight."

"How's that?" Mark asked.

"I'm going to camp out in front of his house until I see him and can ask him what the hell's going on."

"An ambush," Mark said, "I like it. You need back-up?"

Billy shrugged. "It's your call, if you want to come along. It might be a long night, though."

Mark grinned. "I'll call you later and let you know."

Billy nodded and dove back into his sandwich.

As they ate, two teenagers—Chris and Joel—were sitting in the next booth, discussing Dalton's death. "My Uncle Brandt works at the police department," Chris said, "and he says the toxicology report showed a slight trace of alcohol; one beer, two at most. But Dalton definitely wasn't drunk. And there were no drugs in his system."

Billy looked up from his lunch and listened in.

"Maybe he was texting?" Joel suggested.

Chris shook his head. "From what I'm told, the kid's last text was sent just a few minutes after he'd left the party. Dalton had told a friend that he'd catch up with him in the morning and that he was tired and heading home."

"In the opposite direction?" Joel said.

Billy inhaled deeply. *In the opposite direction,* he repeated in his head. *That's odd.*

Charlie stepped into his house to find his mother sitting at the kitchen table, chain-smoking a pack of cigarettes. "So you finally broke up with that girl?" she asked, without a hint of empathy.

"Yeah, Ma, we're not together anymore. Are you happy now?"

She shrugged. "Well, I never really liked her, Charlie. You know that."

Charlie shook his head and headed for his bedroom.

"Listen, you need to call your friend back. He keeps calling and he even came by the house looking for you."

Charlie stopped and looked back at her. "Who?" he asked. "Billy?"

"That's the one," she said, trying to find a place in the overflowing ashtray to poke out her butt. "Call him back, Charlie. He's starting to become annoying."

"Yeah, I'll call him, Ma," Charlie lied. "The last thing I want is for you to be annoyed." He started for his bedroom again.

"Sulking in your bedroom's not going to make anything better," she called out, lighting a new cigarette.

Charlie shook his head, thinking, *At this point, there's nothing's that could make anything better.* He slammed his bedroom door behind him and collapsed onto his bed. *There's nowhere to run,* he told himself, *and nowhere to hide.* Fresh tears streamed down his cheeks. *And life will never be the same again.* He reached under his bed and retrieved an old shoebox. Lifting it onto the bed, he removed the lid and pulled out his dad's .38 revolver, the same handgun he'd stolen from the closet two nights before. He swung open the pistol's tumbler to reveal six silver-tipped bullets. *All it's going to take is one of these, Charlie, and the nightmare ends.* He spun the tumbler once and clicked it back into place. The tears were flowing faster now. *It was an accident,* he told himself for the millionth time, but those words were as false as the first time he'd thought them. *But I didn't want Dalton to die,* he screamed in his head. *I didn't want that!* With a trembling hand, he grabbed the snub-nosed pistol and placed the muzzle flush to his forehead. *Just one moment of courage,* he thought, *and...* He was applying pressure to the trigger when he dropped the gun and stood, panicked. *I almost did it this time,* he realized. Another millimeter more and his brains would have been splattered all over his bedroom walls for his mother to clean up. The truth of it had him hyperventilate so hard that he nearly passed out. Amongst a thousand jumbled thoughts, he told himself, *I need to go...anywhere but here.* Filled with panic, he ran out of his room, toward the front door.

"Where do you think you're going again?" his mother asked, shrouded in a cloud of smoke.

Without a word, Charlie threw open the front door and just kept running.

It was an hour past dusk. Billy parked the Honda just down the street from Charlie's house and turned off the ignition. "It looks like it's just you and me, big boy," he told Jimmy. "Mark called and he's not going to make it." Jimmy sat up straight and stared out the windshield, like he knew he was on an official stake out.

"So are you ready to start the new job at the shelter?" Billy asked the dog, breaking the silence.

Jimmy sighed heavily.

Billy laughed. "Yeah, I hear ya. I wish we didn't have to work either." He shrugged. "Who knows, it might end up being fun?"

Jimmy turned his head and sighed again.

"I guess it is tough to teach an old dog new tricks, huh?" Billy teased.

Jimmy faced him and lifted his paw.

Billy shook it. "That's hardly a new trick, Jimmy," he said, patting the mutt's shoulder. "You really need some new material."

Suddenly, Jimmy stood up straight; his ears also stood at attention. A low growl rumbled in his diaphragm, as he focused on something Billy could not yet see.

"What is it?" Billy asked.

The rumble continued.

A few moments passed before Billy could make out the silhouette of an older woman, walking her dog on a leash; it was a boxer dressed in a pink sweater.

Billy laughed and looked at Jimmy, who was now trying to inhale the female dog through the windshield. "Relax, buddy," he whispered. "She's cute, but you don't want to make a fool of yourself."

Jimmy didn't care; his body twitched and convulsed, as he whined to get out of the Honda and meet her.

The woman and her dog walked right past the driver's side, causing Jimmy to leap into Billy's lap and jam his snout out of the half-opened window. "Whoa," Billy gasped, pushing the dog off his crotch. "Take it easy."

By now, Jimmy had worked himself into a full-blown tizzy and was crying to be freed.

Billy laughed, patting the mutt's back. "There's nothing shy about you, Jimmy, I'll give you that," Billy said, feeling a bit jealous, "but what do you think you'd do if you caught her, old-timer?"

Jimmy's rear end shook back and forth, anxious to give it one last shot.

"I wish I were as brave as you," Billy said, picturing Vicki. *I wonder how she is?* he thought, before turning back to Jimmy. "I'm the one who needs a girlfriend," he said. "You just need more sleep." He laughed.

Once the boxer had vanished into the distance, Jimmy returned to the passenger seat and the task at hand. For the next few minutes, they sat quietly together, watching the house. But it didn't take long before they were both antsy and fidgeting.

Billy thought about being trapped with Jimmy inside his father's pick-up truck, all those years ago, and squirmed in his seat. "Let's go for a walk," he told the mutt. "There's no way we're going to sit here all night."

Billy headed down the sidewalk, while Jimmy hobbled to keep up. They paced three or four times across the street from Charlie's house when Billy swore he spotted Charlie from a distance. "It's him," he told Jimmy, whose tongue was already flopping around like a mud flap in a rainstorm.

"Charlie!" Billy called out. "Charlie..."

Jimmy's black nose began twitching, investigating Billy's claim.

Billy picked up the pace, leaving Jimmy behind a few feet to catch up.

"It's him!" Billy confirmed and took off at a full sprint. As he approached Charlie, he was both excited and furious to see his oldest friend. His blood raced through his veins. And then he felt something else: concern. *Damn*, Billy thought. *Charlie looks like he's aged twenty years.* "Where the hell have you been?" Billy asked, as Jimmy caught up to them, panting. "And why haven't you called me and Mark back?"

Charlie immediately started to cry, disarming Billy.

Jimmy approached and sniffed Charlie before licking his hand.

As none of them were prepared to stand still for this exchange, they began to walk together.

Charlie shook his head twice and opened his mouth to speak but nothing came out.

"What..." Billy started to ask.

"I split up with Bianca," Charlie blurted.

"Oh man," Billy said, placing his hand on his best friend's shoulder, "I'm sorry to hear that, bro." He nodded. "I knew things weren't good between you two but I didn't realize..."

"But that's not the worst of it, Billy," Charlie managed between sobs.

Billy stopped short and swallowed hard. "She's...she's pregnant?"

Charlie shook his head. "I wish it were that," he muttered.

Billy was at a complete loss now. "Then what is it, bro?"

It took a few minutes before Charlie could compose himself enough to speak. "I...I was chasing Dalton that night and I...I'm the reason he drove off the road," he explained through convulsions. "I'm the reason Dalton's dead, Billy," he added, weeping mournfully.

"No way," Billy said, in shock. As though his friend had just admitted to cheating on a final exam, Billy tried to shake it off. "That's not even funny, Charlie."

"I know it isn't," Charlie said, his voice now a desperate whimper. "It's...it's..." He broke down again in a terrible sob.

The sight of it stole Billy's breath away. All at once, he internalized Charlie's confession and understood, *There's no coming back from this*. He opened his mouth but the silence hung between them. It was as if the permanence and the darkness punched Billy square in the gut. He looked at his childhood friend, his brother, and helplessly watched as Charlie collapsed to the sidewalk, rolling himself into the fetal position, and began wailing over the days and nights of torment he'd suffered alone.

Jimmy immediately responded, licking the spots on Charlie's face that his hands weren't covering.

Billy dropped to his knees and placed his hand on Charlie's shoulder, but the gesture seemed futile. "It'll be okay," Billy said, trying to soothe his friend.

But they both knew better. There would be severe consequences to Charlie's actions, consequences that would impact his future in unthinkable and dreadful ways. Everything that had taken place up to that point—childhood lessons, school, everything—felt like it was all being flushed away, circling the bowl as they huddled together on the sidewalk.

Jimmy alternated his licks between Charlie and Billy.

"It was an accident," Charlie finally managed through the sobs. "...a stupid accident."

"How did it happen?" Billy asked.

Charlie shook his head, violently—like he was trying to rid his mind of the grotesque memory. "For weeks, I'd been thinking that Bianca was screwing around on me with Dalton. When I left Jaime's party that night, I went looking for him and..." He stopped.

"And?" Billy asked.

"...and I finally spotted him parked at a red light. When I told him I wanted to talk, he took off."

"And you chased him?" Billy asked.

Charlie nodded. "We were flying down 88 when..."

"Oh, Charlie," Billy said, feeling like he was going to vomit.

"It was an accident, Billy," he repeated, as if trying to convince himself, as well.

"If it was an accident, Charlie," Billy replied, "then why haven't you gone to anyone...to the police and reported it?"

Charlie looked up at him. His face said it all. It wasn't just an accident. "I can't live like this anymore, Billy," Charlie moaned, continuing to sob. "I've even considered..." He stopped.

Not three steps out of high school and Charlie's heading straight to hell to pay for a few moments of thoughtless rage, Billy thought. He could already feel the weight of the dark confession sitting on his shoulders—like a secret he wished he'd never been told. "We'll figure something out," Billy said, now sitting on the ground beside a convulsing ball of flesh that was voted class clown just a few weeks earlier.

"Do you think so?" Charlie asked, his voice sounding like a four-year-old's.

"I do," Billy lied. *Oh God,* Billy thought, as his mind spiraled with one outcome after the next, each one of them leading to a very bad place.

As though he didn't know what else to do, Jimmy kept licking them both.

Before Charlie returned to his seclusion, he told Billy, "Promise me you won't tell a soul about any of this."

"But Charlie, you need to..."

"Promise me, Billy!" he cried, "...please!"

"I promise," Billy said, "I promise...but this isn't going away, Charlie. You know that, right?"

Without another word, Charlie disappeared back into his own personal hell.

On the late drive home, Billy continued to weigh the options in his head. No matter how hard he searched, there didn't seem to be any positive outcome to the nightmare. "This is so crazy," he told Jimmy. "Charlie and I were just talking about our futures." He shook his head. "I mean, we were just playing with Mr. Olivier in biology class, for God's sake."

Jimmy came out of the passenger window and rested his gentle eyes on Billy, offering his full attention.

Billy's eyes bulged with tears. "And now he's killed someone."

Jimmy sighed heavily.

"There's no coming back from this, buddy," he said, before giving it some more thought. "I just can't see how."

Jimmy's gaze stayed locked on his friend.

Although Charlie had committed the tragic crime, Billy's thrashing heart was already telling him that this was going to be his moral dilemma as well. "This sucks so bad," he thought aloud. "So bad..."

A mile down the road, Billy wiped his eyes and looked down at his four-legged confessional and advisor. "What the hell should I do?" he asked.

Jimmy yawned once but maintained his gaze, remaining silent.

Chapter 7

Still shaken to the bone from the previous night's discovery—and a full night's loss of sleep—Billy sat in line at the service station, hoping to get an inspection sticker for his tired Honda. Instead, for the same thirty-five dollars, the mechanic stuck a black rejection sticker on the inside of the windshield. "We can't give you a sticker until you get everything fixed."

"Everything fixed?" Billy said, his mind racing to the cost of the water pump he'd recently replaced.

"You have a broken headlight, broken windshield wiper and bald tires on the front." He shook his head. "What did you think, the car was going to pass?"

"I was hoping it would," Billy said.

"You need to get it all fixed before the car passes inspection," the mechanic repeated.

"And how much will that cost?" Billy asked.

The grease monkey shrugged and looked the car over, doing the math in his head. "We can throw some retreads on the front. A new headlight and wiper motor repair...around a hundred and a half, I'd say."

"Oh man," Billy muttered. "I'll need a few weeks to get the money together."

The guy nodded. "We'll be here when you're ready."

Billy pulled away and looked at his co-pilot—Jimmy. "This is unreal," he complained. "We're starting a new job today and we're already behind the eight ball."

Jimmy kept his eyes on the road.

Jimmy walked into Four Paws animal shelter like he was heading off to his lifelong factory job. Billy watched to see if any old memories registered for the mutt, but Jimmy was completely unaffected—until they reached the avocado door and all the sounds behind it had his ears on end. He whimpered once and looked up at Billy, his eyes glassed over with fear.

"Relax," Billy told him, "you're going to make lots of friends here."

As Billy opened the door, Jimmy whimpered once more before reluctantly limping in.

Arlene approached—with her two dogs, McGruff and King—and went straight to her knees to greet Jimmy. While McGruff and King nearly sniffed the fur off the back end of him, Arlene spent a few solid minutes of uninterrupted attention on Jimmy. She stroked his hind legs. "Let's see if we can't work some of those knots out of you, old man," she said.

Jimmy was completely torn; he loved the massage but was freaked out by the two dogs sniffing his backside.

Billy smiled. "See, Jimmy," he said, "new friends."

Jimmy looked up at Billy with more than a little doubt in his eyes.

Billy petted both McGruff and King, while Jimmy watched with a possessive eye.

Arlene stood, handed Billy a t-shirt and looked down at his shorts. "You can wear khakis or jeans and this is your uniform." The green t-shirt had *Four Paws* printed on the front. She looked down at Jimmy. "And you, sir, can stay in the buff like the rest of them." She laughed heartily.

Jimmy looked up at Billy, the doubt turning to fright.

When Arlene turned, Billy offered the dog a slight shrug.

While Jimmy was getting acquainted with his two new aggressive friends, Billy worked side by side with Arlene, feeding animals and cleaning cages. "Four Paws is a non-profit organization," she said, kicking off Billy's informal orientation. "It relies on donations, fund raisers, adoptions, and dedicated benefactors to keep the shelter in operation. We don't receive any state or federal funding."

For whatever reason, Billy was surprised by this.

"We work hard to give the animals more time on this earth," she said, shaking her head. "Many municipal shelters are so crowded they can't keep lost or stray animals for more than a few days." She stopped and looked at Billy. "Can you imagine humans being chemically terminated before receiving trash bag funerals?"

Billy shook his head.

"We believe there's a home out there for every animal we take in, if we only take the time to find it." She winked. "And we do. In fact, we like to say we give animals *a new leash on life*."

Corny, Billy thought, but he was relieved that Four Paws didn't euthanize animals.

"People interested in adopting have to come visit the animal in person, no exceptions," Arlene said.

"Who wouldn't come visit an animal they're trying to adopt?" Billy asked.

She looked at him. "Trust me, by the end of this summer, nothing will surprise you."

Billy nodded. *We'll see*, he thought.

"In many shelters, money dictates every decision and, if an animal isn't adopted within two weeks, it will be destroyed."

Billy stopped and stared at his new mentor. *Whoa...* This fact bothered him more than anything else ever had. "Are you kidding me?"

"I wish I were," she said, shaking her head. "We take in a thousand or so orphaned pets each year, even birds, guinea pigs and snakes—which make me squirm in my own skin."

"Me too," Billy confessed.

"When they arrive, we give them a quick visual exam," Arlene said. "Each of the animals is confined until they've been checked out by the vet and received any medical treatment they might need. Once they're cleared, we release them into the general population and get them acclimated."

Straight into the general population, Billy repeated in his head, amused by the prison reference. He nodded that he understood, before looking down to make sure Jimmy was okay.

The elder dog was like a magnet, stuck to his shins; Jimmy's eyes were as wide as Billy had ever seen them.

As she worked, Arlene instructed, "The larger breeds get a full scoop of food twice a day. The little guys, a half scoop two times a day."

Billy looked down at Jimmy again. "Just like Jimmy, minus the scraps."

She laughed and continued her lesson. "It's important we create as comfortable an environment as possible for these lost souls. Social contact and positive stimulation have proven to be major benefits when maintaining an animal's well-being." She gestured toward the other room. "We have cages for those who must be segregated and monitored, for one reason or another. But just as soon as we can integrate them back into the community, we do." She looked toward McGruff and King. "These are pack animals and without the pack, whether it be other dogs or a new human family, they cannot be complete."

"I understand," Billy said, petting Jimmy's head. Billy then noted that the feral cats were also exiled to one of the back communal rooms, as far away from the shelter's main population as they could be. He questioned it.

"Those that cannot be domesticated will have to be sent to a protected feral colony," she explained, shaking her head.

As they completed the feeding, Billy also noticed that—although Arlene said she was worried about when the next shipment of supplies would arrive—she dumped a half scoop more into each dog's bowl. Billy questioned this with a raised eyebrow.

She shrugged like a kid who'd just been caught in the proverbial cookie jar. "I'm just trying to make up for all the meals they didn't get."

He laughed, thinking, *Arlene obviously likes to fatten up her furry guests.*

"As I've said, we try to find permanent homes for our animals," she said, changing the subject, "but for those animals that are very young or need extra medical care, we also work with a list of good folks who are willing to provide temporary foster homes."

"That's cool," Billy said and stole a glance at Jimmy, who was clearly overwhelmed.

Their next stop was "the day spa": a grooming area set up in a corner of the main room where the pups got primped and bathed. It contained a tub, hose and stainless steel bench with a leash hook-up. "It's just another above and beyond service we provide," Arlene explained, with a wink.

Billy smiled.

"But I wouldn't get my hopes too high if I were you," she added. "The volunteers get the fluffy, feel good jobs like dog walking and grooming." She smirked. "And you're an indentured servant who's being paid to do the dirty work...literally."

He laughed.

She turned to him to wrap up her tutorial. "For now, what you need to know is that we provide the very best care we can while also matching orphaned pets with new homes. We also provide services like implanting microchips, which are permanent." Clearly impressed by the technology, she nodded. "A scan of any lost animal can identify them. That, along with pet licensing, helps reunite owners with their lost pets." She looked down to see if Jimmy wore a tag. "Good boy," she said.

Billy wasn't sure whether she was referring to him or the dog.

"Once every two weeks, the vet comes in and we offer low cost vaccinations. We also provide affordable spay and neuter surgeries to the public to help control pet overpopulation." She nodded. "A lot of people don't know this, but the surgery helps animals live longer and healthier lives."

"Good to know," Billy said.

At the end of the day, Arlene asked Billy, "So what do you think?"

He smiled. "I think I'm really going to like it here, but..." He paused.

"But?" she repeated, surprised.

Billy looked down at Jimmy. "But I don't think he cares too much for the place."

Arlene collapsed to her knees in front of Jimmy and began massaging his arthritic haunches. "He'll get used to the place," she said, studying Jimmy's soft chocolate eyes. "...or maybe he won't."

Billy dropped Jimmy off at home, fed him and then ran over to Nick's to get a bite to eat. He grabbed his tuna sub and wasn't even through the dining room door before Mark was sharing the big news. "You missed it," he announced.

"Missed what?" Billy asked.

"Some police detective, Swanson, just left here. He was asking all kinds of questions about Dalton Noble."

Although Billy's heart plunged into his gut, he did what he could to maintain a calm, even face. "Questions?" he asked. "What kind of questions?"

"He wanted to know if Dalton was having any problems with anyone." Mark shrugged. "If we'd heard him argue with anyone recently, crap like that."

"Problems?" Billy echoed, still standing.

"I told him I didn't think so," Mark said, shaking his head. "I even asked him if he thought Dalton's death was something other than an accident."

Billy's blood froze, slowing in his veins. Once he caught his breath, he tried to remain indifferent.

"He told me he was just trying to cover every base, that's all."

"Every base," Billy reiterated, his mind rushing out of control.

"He said he believed it was an accident, but was just making sure."

"Wow," Billy said, nearly falling into his seat. "That's messed up."

"So did you end up talking to Charlie last night?" Mark asked, obliviously. "Did he give you a good excuse for dodging us?" he asked with a smirk.

For a moment, Billy was deafened by a shroud of fog that felt suffocating.

"Well, did you see him?" Mark prodded.

"He broke up with Bianca," Billy finally blurted, spending more time looking at his lunch than at his friend.

"I hate to say I told you so, but..."

"He's a friggin' mess, Mark. You should have seen him."

Mark's grin disappeared. "It sucks. I get it. But he doesn't have to go underground. Couples our age break up. It happens." He shook his head. "It's not going to help him heal, if he keeps avoiding everyone."

Billy nodded. "I agree. But I think we should give him a break for now. He's in a lot of pain."

"Did he give you any details?" Mark asked.

Billy shook his head. "Not really," he lied. "He just said that he needs to lay low for a while until he gets his head together."

Mark nodded. "Fair enough, I guess." Smiling, he threw the last pizza crust into the cardboard box. "How's the new job? Did you have to shovel shit?"

Billy nodded. "It's a job," he said, "and anything's better than the Pearl."

"If you say so," Mark said, finishing his soda. "Listen, the Fourth of July parade starts at ten o'clock in the morning on Saturday. What time do you want to meet?"

"Fourth of July parade?" Billy repeated, finally looking into Mark's eyes—and still trying to recover from his state of shock. "I'm not going to any lame parade."

"Lame?" Mark snapped back. "Do you realize how many girls are going to be at that parade?"

Billy considered it, struggling to take another bite of his tuna sub.

"What are you going to miss," Mark asked, "a few hours of sleep?"

Billy nodded. "That's right."

"Well, too bad," Mark told him. "You're going. I'll be at your house at nine to pick you up."

"Nine in the morning?" Billy asked, his voice raised an octave.

Mark laughed. "Nine o'clock in the morning, Sleeping Beauty," he confirmed.

With a single nod, Billy ate in silence for a few minutes, his mind fixated on Charlie's dark confession and now a snooping detective named Swanson. *I need to let Charlie know*, he thought, panicked, and pushed the rest of his lunch away from him—afraid that he might lose more than just his appetite.

It was July Fourth and America was celebrating the birth of its freedom. Billy and Mark stood on the corner of South Main and Middle streets. Both sides of the barren street were lined with flag-waving spectators. Shops were closed for the day and stone-faced policemen patrolled on horseback, keeping the swaying crowd off the paved street. Screaming children sat atop the shoulders of short-sleeved fathers, while women chatted in tight groups. Suddenly, a siren wailed in the distance. All eyes went big. The parade was underway.

Leaning in to steal the first glimpse, a squeal traveled down the line. "They're coming!" someone announced. And so they did.

The horn of a Model T Ford led the way. Evidently, Mayor Joe Sherry had appointed himself Grand Marshal and was propped up on the back seat, waving furiously. By the look on his wife's sour face, she hardly shared his enthusiasm. Other politicians marched behind their leader, shaking hands.

Jumbled groups of every culture followed suit, proudly displaying the colors of their native countries. Italian, French, Irish and Portuguese flags bobbed along. On America's Independence Day, it didn't make sense.

There was a loud bang.

Everyone jumped, but not nearly as high as the policeman's horse. Some delinquent had tossed a firecracker at the poor animal's hooves before melting back into the thick crowd. Once the cop's spotted partner calmed down, they took chase. To Billy's surprise, the crowd cheered them on.

Oblivious to the heart-thumping interruption, milk trucks and farm tractors, transformed into creatively decorated floats, crept along. Uncle Sam and Betsy Ross waved and threw candy to the crowd. As children scurried and wrestled each other for the sweet loot, Billy waved back at Miss Ross. "She's really cute," he told Mark.

A Boy Scout troop marched in sync, while rougher-looking boys dressed in Little League uniforms moped by. A line of antique cars was carried in their wake, their paint so buffed that the sun's reflection actually hurt the eyes. A small group of young girls halted the procession. While they performed a brief tap dance number, Billy hurried back from the hot dog cart. He was just in time to catch the high school marching band play "When the Saints Come Marching In" completely off key.

Just then, a bright red fire engine opened up on the crowd, playfully dousing everyone with a powerful stream of cold water. Women screamed in delight, while drenched children waited for the handfuls of candy to be thrown. The firemen nearly laughed themselves off the rear of the truck before pouring their generosity onto the crowd of victims. Buckets of twist-wrap candy rained onto the glistening black street. Billy laughed at the spectacle. *Maybe this isn't so lame after all*, he thought, deciding he'd never admit it to Mark.

When the fire engine's siren moaned down to silence, the haunting sound of bagpipes took its place. Grown men, dressed in skirts, played a melancholy tune. Mark chuckled openly at their chosen outfits, causing a stranger with a peculiar twitch to tap him on the shoulder. "That's the police band," the man pointed out in a rasp, before returning to the statue he'd been earlier. Billy laughed. Mark's face was as bright as the fire truck that soaked them.

A roaming band of clowns followed the police, pleading with tiny dogs to jump through hula-hoops. At the conclusion of the hilarious show, the big-shoed jokesters dumped buckets of confetti on everyone. With the water from the fire truck, the confetti stuck like feathers to tar. "People really love throwing things on the Fourth of July, huh?" Billy said aloud.

Mark laughed.

In search of the opposite sex, Billy was scanning the mass of people across the street when a convoy of military vehicles returned his attention to the parade. Giant green trucks rumbled along, their billows of heavy smoke painting the blue sky black. An ancient one, towing an enormous cannon behind it, forced the twitching statue to speak again. "That's a Howitzer," the stranger whispered hoarsely, "and when she sneezed, the Gerrys and Japs soiled their trousers." He finished with a twisted grin and returned to his stoic stare. Billy and Mark looked at each other. Without a word, they shuffled down the sidewalk a few feet. The commentating was becoming a bit too spooky.

Behind the odd-looking vehicles, a drum and bugle corps echoed an ancient cadence into battle. Groups of men marched in step to every beat. Some wore uniforms; others, rows of colorful medals pinned to their swollen chests. Banners read: VFW, AMVETS and the wars in which they served. The oldest of them, the few remaining warriors of WWII, took the lead in the back of three convertibles. Upon their passing, the crowd stood silent in a show of awe and respect. Then it happened. As if on cue, the street exploded with spine-tingling cheers. Korean War and Vietnam War veterans followed their predecessors. Behind them, soldiers dressed in desert camouflage—men and women who had served in Iraq and Afghanistan—brought up the rear. Two of these warriors pushed their buddies' wheelchairs, while another saluted the crowd with his remaining arm.

Billy glanced at Mark to catch his friend's eyes misting over. It was the perfect fodder for teasing, but Billy remained silent, reflecting upon his own grandfather's heroic service. Both friends understood: if it weren't for the sacrifices of the men who marched before them, July Fourth would have been no more than another hot day in hell. The crowd continued to roar.

Billy was submerged in a daydream of serving his country in Iraq or Afghanistan—perhaps fulfilling his life's purpose—when he looked up and saw her. The sight nearly pulled him to his knees. He knew right away this strange effect wasn't due to the raw excitement of the day, the sheer respect felt for the soldiers who marched, or even the seasonably warm temperature. It was definitely caused by the angel who stood across from him. *It's Vicki!* he realized. Her curly blonde hair was blowing recklessly in the breeze. When Billy finally caught his breath, he glanced up to find a police horse approaching. Without realizing it, he'd wandered out several feet onto the parade route.

"Get back on the sidewalk," the grimacing cop ordered.

Billy nodded, but a racing pulse had his thoughts all boggled and hazy. With another stern look from the cop, Billy finally did as ordered. He glanced right to find Mark smiling at him.

"She is some beautiful, huh?" Mark said, pointing at Miss Fall River, the pageant queen who'd just ridden by on the back seat of a '57 Chevy convertible.

"You're not kidding," Billy managed. His giant pupils were still hypnotized by the stunning creature before him—*Vicki*.

"And the car's not too shabby either," Mark said.

Billy's forehead wrinkled and, for the first time, his eyes returned to his friend. "What car?" he asked.

Of all places, the parade ended at the high school, where there were food booths being attacked by an onslaught of parade-goers. The lure was no match for even the strongest willed. "Let's go check it out," Billy said, trying to coax Mark.

"You mean to look for Vicki, right?" Mark asked.

"So you did see her?" Billy said, surprised.

"Of course I saw her," Mark said. "I figured she'd be here today." He shook his head and smiled. "Why else do you think we're here...because I enjoy standing for hours in the scorching sun?"

Billy grinned at his friend's cleverness and consideration. Mark was absolutely selfless before being selfless was a cool thing. With a nod of gratitude, he told Mark, "Let's go." They followed the stampede in.

It was a junk food junkie's paradise. The smells of popcorn, fried dough, French fries and everything you'd never find in Ma's kitchen filled the air. The boys bought an early lunch before starting on their quest to find Billy's blonde infatuation.

It didn't take long. Billy had just stuffed the last half of a corn dog into his mouth when he spotted Vicki. She was standing near the Fraternal Order of Police dunk tank with her friend. *Go talk to her, you chicken shit!* he told himself. *You're never going to get the chance again.* Wiping his mouth with the back of his hand, he nodded at Mark and then rushed over.

Ten feet from the girls, Billy could feel his face burn red. It took a moment before he drummed up the courage to look at Vicki and catch her gorgeous caramel eyes shining back at him.

After a quick hello, it took six throws of a baseball and almost all his pride before Billy submerged the heckling victim—a muscle-bound cop—into the water. *It was well worth it!* he thought, blushing as both Vicki and her friend clapped for him.

The angel smiled. "Nice to see you again," Vicki said, indicating that she'd noticed him at his graduation party.

Billy was taken aback.

Giggling, she pointed at her friend. "And this is my friend, Emma."

Emma smiled.

Small talk gradually led to an awkward stroll. Vicki smelled as sweet as candy apples. Billy couldn't get over it. She was so easy to talk to and even easier to listen to. *And she's even prettier than I remember*, he thought. The whole time, he couldn't take his eyes off her.

Billy fought past the fear of rejection and confessed, "I was hoping I'd see you again."

"You were?" she asked, grinning.

He nodded. "Yep."

"Me too," she said.

Billy was taken further aback. "Really?" he asked. "We never got a chance to talk at my party. I didn't even think you noticed me," he added, feeling stupid as soon as the words left his lips.

"Of course I noticed you," she said, wearing the cutest grin. "You don't think I came here today because I like parades, do you?"

Billy could feel his face blush again. *Oh my God*, he thought, *this cannot be happening to me. It's too good to be true.*

"So what should I know about Billy Baker?" Vicki asked, wearing a smile that tested the strength of his knees.

"Not much to tell," he said, clearing his throat. "As you know, I just graduated from high school and I'll be going to college in the fall."

"What's your major?" she asked.

"Liberal Arts," he admitted, slightly embarrassed. "I really have no idea what I want yet." It still amazed him how self-conscious he felt about his lack of direction in life.

"There's still plenty of time to decide," she said, smashing his discomfort.

"What about you?" he asked.

"I've been accepted into a nursing program in the fall." She shrugged playfully. "I've wanted to be a nurse since I can remember."

"So you've always wanted to help people, huh?" he asked, impressed.

"Nah, I just like the white uniforms," she joked.

Billy laughed. *And she has a sense of humor too*, he thought. *This is unreal.*

"I just started volunteering at a nursing home to prepare myself for some of the gross stuff." She shook her head slightly. "I hope I can get used to it."

"Well, if it makes you feel any better," he said, "I just took a job at the local animal shelter, cleaning out cages for the summer."

"That does make me feel better," she teased.

"Good," he said.

"An animal shelter, huh? I love animals."

"Me too," he said. "I've had my dog, Jimmy, since I was a kid. He's so awesome. You should see some of the crazy things he can do."

Vicki stopped for a moment, peering into Billy's eyes. "I'd love to," she whispered.

Billy felt his knees wobble once more. "You will," he promised.

There was a giant bouncer set up for little kids and, though Billy and Mark would have surely tackled it without the girls around, they pretended not to even notice it.

Whether it was the warm air, the way the sun was quietly setting over the bay, or the sweet sounds of children at play, people seemed to embrace the rare feeling that, if only for the day, everything in the world was good. For Billy, however, the desperate hopes for love had surfaced and he couldn't remember feeling more alive. He took a few deep breaths and finally took the plunge. "Are you seeing anyone right now, Vicki?"

She searched his eyes for a long moment. "I was hoping... *you*," she said. Her eyes sparkled when she smiled.

Billy was speechless. When he'd composed himself, figuring there was enough oxygen to carry his words, he asked, "What about that guy you hugged at my party? Is he..."

She laughed, halting him. "Oh my God...no! That's Wyatt. We've been friends since the first grade. He's like my brother."

"Friends?" Billy repeated and laughed, feeling relieved. "That's good," he mumbled.

Vicki laughed again before diving back into his eyes. "Emma and I are going to South Kennedy Park to watch the fireworks tonight. Do you guys want to join us?"

Excitement ripped through Billy's body. He looked sideways at Mark, whose face betrayed a hint of disapproval. Billy's eyes went wide and he quickly leaned in toward his friend, giving him the unmistakable look that he needed his friend; now more than ever, he needed a wingman.

Mark lost the sour puss and smirked in surrender.

"Great," Vicki said, returning to Billy's eyes.

"What time?" Billy asked, trying to sound cool and collected.

"Just before it gets dark," she said. "We'll wait for you near the water fountain on Broadway."

Mark and Emma both nodded, seemingly uninterested in the plan or each other.

Billy and Mark arrived at the fountain an hour before dusk. "You're so pathetic," Mark told him. "She said *just* before dark."

"It is before dark," Billy countered with a weak shrug. "Besides, you're the one who started this whole thing."

Mark's eyebrow rose.

"Which I really appreciate," Billy added, taking a deep breath. "I don't want to miss her, okay?"

"Relax," Mark told him. "I'm just playing with you."

As they waited, Billy and Mark kicked through the litter that covered the ground until arriving at a stage that hosted local talent—with Billy constantly looking back at the fountain on Broadway. They stayed for nearly ten minutes before Billy decided, *There is no local talent.* People sang off key, children danced while tripping over their own feet and through it all, the audience struggled to hold back the laughter. Even if he'd wanted to, Billy couldn't have laughed. He was too busy monitoring the water fountain.

And then he saw her. *It's Vicki!* His heart raced and threw off his breathing. He took three quick steps toward her before he stopped and decided to watch. While Emma was shaking her head and laughing at Vicki—much like Mark had done all day—Vicki was craning her neck left and right, like she was searching for him. The sight of it stole the rest of the air in Billy's lungs.

When Billy and Mark finally approached, Vicki's eyes lit up. It made Billy feel like the luckiest man amid a crowd that was growing thicker by the second. "You made it," he said.

"I was just going to say the same thing about you," Vicki said.

As Vicki and Emma led the boys toward the bay—with Billy sneaking a couple of looks at Vicki's backside—the four walked through South Kennedy Park where young lovers cuddled on blankets and parents yelled for their kids to sit still. There was a sea of people, most lying on their backs, watching as the fireflies blended in with the stars above. On the bay, anchored boats drifted in circles waiting for the show to begin, while the burnt smell of sparklers filled the air. Even the distant sounds from the carnival wafted over on warm breezes. Billy decided, *It's the type of night wasted on anyone but lovers.*

Vicki staked a piece of lawn, making sure she sat beside Billy.

A few kids lit off some bottle rockets, causing the girls to jump.

Laughing, Mark turned to Billy. "At least they're pointing them into the air instead of at each other like we did when we were kids."

Billy laughed.

"You fired bottle rockets at each other?" Vicki asked, grinning.

Billy nodded. "Just to maim and disfigure," he said, "never to kill."

She laughed again and, as each moment passed, the darkness crept in closer. Suddenly, Billy noticed that Vicki was doing the same. While a fire engine waited at the base of the giant hill, a man dressed in an overstuffed jumpsuit set up his fireworks. *It's going to be a while yet*, Billy realized and leaned his head on one elbow to begin a conversation of whispers. Vicki's eyes sparkled at every word.

Billy learned that Vicki was seventeen, five months younger than him, and had just graduated from Somerset High School. He discovered that her favorite food was pizza, her dream was to live on the beach with her twelve children and she absolutely hated people who lied. "And I love classic movies," she said.

"You do?" he asked, trying to sound happy about it. "...like *Casablanca* and *Gone with the Wind*?"

"No," she said, "like *Dumb and Dumber* and *Wedding Crashers*."

"No way," he said excitedly.

"Way," she said.

"That's awesome! I love those stupid movies, but my knucklehead friends never want to watch them with me."

She laughed. "Well, I guess they're not real knuckleheads like you and I are."

"You know what I mean," he said.

She placed her hand on his arm. "I love mindless comedy," she said, "and the more stupider, the better."

"The more stupider?" he asked, grinning.

"That's right," she said grinning. "And I'd watch them with you."

Billy swallowed the golf ball which had instantly formed in his throat. "That would be awesome," he mumbled.

An hour whipped by and, to Billy's surprise, he had learned only a fraction of what he wanted to know about Vicki. When she asked him about himself, he almost felt it a waste of time. She pleaded, playfully, so he rambled on and it felt wonderful. *No one's ever been interested in my past or my dreams for the future*, Billy thought. While they spoke, he realized he was actually seeing Vicki for the first time. *She's so beautiful*, he thought. Besides the dirty-blonde hair and caramel eyes, there was something more he just couldn't place. Unashamed, he searched her face longer than he'd ever looked for anything.

There was a loud boom, while the sky lit up with red and blue fireworks.

The first set of fireworks illuminated the dark skies. "Oooh," the crowd moaned.

Billy and Vicki lay on their backs and watched.

There was another boom. Vicki reached for Billy's hand, folded her fingers into his and left them there. His entire body tingled from a rush of pure joy.

The next set of fireworks was a mixture of red and green, like the giant petals of a flower blooming before their wide eyes. "Aaah," the crowd responded in glee.

Billy couldn't help it any longer. As they held hands, he turned to steal a peek at Vicki, but found he was too late. She was already staring at him; the fireworks reflected in her soft eyes made him swallow hard. He smiled. She giggled innocently, squeezing his hand tighter.

There were multiple booms.

Billy and Vicki watched the rest of the show in each other's eyes. It was absolutely breathtaking. Suddenly, the truth hit him and nearly melted his heart. Although Vicki was as pretty as the next girl, only when he studied her eyes did he discover the truth: *Vicki's real beauty is on the inside.* In just a few hours, she'd tattooed his heart, leaving an indelible mark.

"The fireworks are over, Billy," Vicki whispered, "and Mark and Emma have left." She giggled. "Actually, everyone's left."

"Who?" he asked with a smile, but he never left her gaze. To him, the show had just gotten started.

When they finally left the park—walking hand in hand—Billy asked Vicki, "Can I call you?"

"Yes, please," she said smiling and punched her number into his cell phone.

"When can I see you again?" he asked.

"As soon as possible," she said, stopping to meet his eyes. "Listen Billy, I really like you, I do, but if I'm not around all that much over the next few days, please don't think it has anything to do with you."

"Oh okay," he said, feeling his heart sink. *This really is too good to be true*, he thought.

"My family's going through a tough time right now, so..."

"What is it?" he asked, genuinely concerned—and equally excited that she was telling the truth.

She shook her head.

He grabbed her hand. "You can tell me," he said.

"But we've only just met and I don't want to ruin..."

"You won't ruin anything," he promised, giving her hand a squeeze. "Honestly, Vicki, you can tell me," he whispered.

She took a deep breath and her eyes filled. "My Aunt Lily recently attempted suicide and was just released from the hospital."

"Oh, my God," Billy said, at a loss for any other words. "I'm so sorry," he finally managed, now feeling stupid that he'd allowed his doubts to surface so quickly.

Vicki was quiet for a bit. Billy could tell she was trying to contain the strong emotions that were bubbling just beneath the surface. "Ever since my cousin Dalton died in a car accident, the family's tried to heal, but..." She stopped again, on the verge of crying.

Billy gasped. *Dalton*, he echoed in his head, his blood curdling. *Dalton was Vicki's cousin?* Shock threatened to wrestle him to the sidewalk. While Vicki struggled to maintain her composure, Billy whispered, "So Dalton was your cousin?" He was desperately hoping it wasn't true.

"Yeah, my first cousin," she confirmed, her eyes glistening with tears. "My aunt hasn't been able to accept that he died in a drunk driving accident." She paused. "According to the autopsy report, Dalton had very little alcohol in his system."

"I didn't know your cousin, but I heard he was a great guy," Billy said, trying to be as supportive as his pounding heart and dry mouth would allow.

"He was," Vicki said, turning quiet again. She was clearly torn up over her cousin's death, as well as her aunt's unrelenting grief. "Dalton's funeral was the saddest thing I've ever experienced," she whispered.

"I bet," Billy said, not knowing what else to say.

She shook her head, quickly wiping her eyes. "I saw you standing in your yard that day, watching us drive by," she said, smiling slightly. "You were with a black dog."

"That's Jimmy," he said, giving that sorrowful afternoon some thought. "Like I said, I really didn't know Dalton, or I would have..."

She grabbed his arm. "It's fine, Billy," she said, "I understand."

"I'm so sorry it was your cousin who died in that terrible accident," Billy whispered, meaning it on more than one level. "And I really hope your aunt is able to find some peace soon." He nodded. "Whatever you need, I'm here for you." He then pictured Charlie's guilty face confessing his terrible sin and felt like he was going to vomit.

"Thank you, Billy," Vicki said, "you have no idea how much that means to me."

Billy did what he could not to puke up all that churned in his gut.

It was late when Billy—exhausted and filled with so many mixed emotions—called Mark's cell phone. "Thanks for having my back today, bro," he said. "I owe you, big time."

"Have you guys already made plans to see each other again?" Mark asked rhetorically.

"We have," Billy said. He couldn't have concealed the excitement in his voice if he'd been held at gunpoint.

"You like her a lot, huh?"

"Now there's an understatement," Billy said, wanting desperately to confide in Mark about all he was feeling; about how he was falling for a girl he was already keeping the truth from. *But I can't*, he thought. *I can't even tell Mark. I gave Charlie my word.*

"Well, that's it then," Mark said solemnly. "Between the new job at the pound and the new girlfriend, there's not going to be any time to..."

"I thought about that," Billy said, interrupting him. "I'm sorry, bro."

Mark snickered. "Don't be. I'm just busting your chops." His voice turned serious. "I'm pretty sure it's supposed to go down like this." He paused. "Now I need to go find a girlfriend I guess."

"What about Emma, Vicki's friend?" Billy asked, still struggling not to spill all the poison that boiled inside of him.

Mark snickered again. "I meant a girl who knows how to smile." He paused for a moment. "Why? Did Emma say something about me?"

"No," Billy said, grinning. "I'll see you soon, Mark."

"Sure you will," Mark said, though they both knew Billy was stretching the truth on that one.

Billy hung up. *If only Dalton wasn't Vicki's cousin*, he thought, and suddenly felt like strangling Charlie.

Chapter 8

Billy awoke from very little sleep. Before his feet hit the floor, he texted Vicki. *I couldn't stop thinking about you all night*, he wrote. *I really had a great time at the fireworks and like I said at the end of the night, I'm here to listen whenever you need to talk.* He hit send, looked at Jimmy—who was already waiting by the door—and swung his feet off the bed. "You should have been there, buddy," he told the old mutt. "It was the most incredible night of my life."

Jimmy whimpered, his only concern to relieve his bladder.

Billy followed the limping dog down the hall and was suddenly pummeled with a vicious combination of guilt and fear. "But wouldn't you know it, her cousin was Dalton...that kid Charlie ran off into a ditch." He shook his head at the absurd enormity of it. "...the kid who died," he whispered.

Jimmy kept right on hobbling.

"And Dalton's poor mom just tried to take her own life," Billy added, shivering at the thought of it. He shook his head again, trying to push the thought to the back of his mind. He pictured Vicki's face and focused on it. "Do you believe in love at first sight, Jimmy?" Billy asked, opening the kitchen door. "Well, maybe it was love at second sight." Jimmy lunged into the yard. Billy followed him out, which was unusual. "Well, I do," he told the squatting dog. "I believe it as much as I believe anything else in this world."

Jimmy finished his business and scratched at the earth a few times.

"As much as I believe you're a peanut butter junkie," Billy added.

Seemingly unimpressed, Jimmy moped back toward the house.

"We've only just met, Jimmy, but..." He shook his head. "I wish I could explain to you how I feel about her."

The dog paused at Billy's feet for a moment, cocked his head sideways and shot a look that made Billy grin.

"It's crazy, buddy, I know," Billy said, "but I've never felt this way about anyone before. Vicki's so beautiful and sweet and I couldn't sleep at all last night because I couldn't get her out of my head...and you know how much I love my sleep."

Jimmy headed for the kitchen, more interested in his crunchy breakfast than listening to Billy's mushy confession.

"Fine, don't believe me if you don't want to," Billy said, as he followed the big mutt into the house. "But just wait until you meet her. You'll know exactly what I mean."

As Billy prepared Jimmy's peanut butter-laced medication, his cell phone buzzed. It was a text from Vicki. "I couldn't stop thinking about you either," he read aloud. "I'm going to visit my aunt today, but I can't wait to talk to you when I get back. I'm so happy I went to that parade." Billy paused. "So happy," he repeated. Overwhelmed with emotion, he looked down at Jimmy and smiled. "See, buddy, I told you she was special."

Jimmy stared blankly at him, licking any remnants of peanut butter from his drooling jowls.

Billy read Vicki's text message again and again. "She couldn't stop thinking about me either," he said, picturing her sweet face. As a smile began to work its way into the corners of his mouth, it instantly disappeared. He shook his angry head. *Friggin' Charlie,* he thought, *you're the reason Vicki has to go visit her suffering aunt.*

After breakfast, Billy picked up his cell phone and called Charlie. The call went straight to voicemail. "Charlie, it's Billy. Call me as soon as you get this," he said coldly. "We need to talk." He paused and lowered his tone. "There's something you need to know." As he hung up, he looked down at Jimmy. "Now let's see if he calls me back."

Billy had worked and saved and finally returned to the service station to get the Honda fixed. It cost one hundred and sixty-two dollars to receive the coveted bright orange inspection sticker, buying him and the clunker another legal year on the open road. While the grinning mechanic slapped the sticker on the inside of the windshield, Billy told Jimmy, "What a waste of money!"

On their ride to work, Billy called Charlie's cell phone again. During the first ring, he told Jimmy, "I need to convince Charlie to turn himself in to the authorities."

Surprisingly, Charlie answered on the second ring.

"You need to do the right thing," Billy immediately prodded his friend.

"Are you on a secured line?" Charlie asked.

"What is this, *Mission Impossible*?"

"Somebody could be listening."

"Who," Billy asked, "your mother?" He looked at Jimmy and shook his head in disgust.

"The cops," Charlie said.

"Sure...without a warrant. Now you're paranoid too?"

"You're the one who told me that some detective was asking Mark questions about Dalton. You don't know who might be listening in, Billy."

"You're right, Charlie. I don't know!" Billy said, upset enough to slide to the edge of the driver's seat. "What I do know is that hiding in your house is only going to make people suspicious and what happened that night is never going to go away until you tell the truth and face it."

Sensing the tension, Jimmy sprang up in the passenger seat and began to whine.

"Now who's talking crazy?" Charlie asked.

"Do you want to live your whole life looking over your shoulder," Billy asked, "wondering whether someone's tapped your phone? Well, do you?" Billy felt lightheaded. "Screw that!" he said, pulling over to the side of the road to continue the call.

"That's easy to say, Billy, when you're not the one who might have to serve time."

"Listen Charlie, what happened that night can never be undone. The only thing you can control now is how you face it. This isn't the Middle Ages. Eventually, that detective's going to figure it out and then you'll look even guiltier for not coming forward on your own with the truth." He paused. "Not to mention, Dalton's parents have a right to know what happened to their son." Billy felt terrible saying it. *But it has to be said,* he thought, thinking about Vicki and the pain her family had already endured. "I called you last night and left you a message...telling you there's something you need to know."

"Yeah?" Charlie said, reluctantly.

"Well, I think you should know that Dalton's mom tried to commit suicide."

By now, Jimmy was shuffling back and forth in his seat, as agitated as Billy.

Charlie gasped loud enough to be heard. "How...how do you know that?" he stuttered.

"It doesn't matter how I know, Charlie," Billy said. "But it's true. The woman is so distraught that she wants to end her own life."

Charlie was crying so hard he could hardly speak. "I...I have to go," he finally managed.

"Go where?" Billy asked. "Charlie, please don't hang up. We can..." Silence stopped Billy from going on. He looked at his cell phone. Charlie had ended the call.

"Damn you, Charlie!" Billy barked. He took a deep breath and thought about his dilemma. It didn't take long before the same solution—the only solution he could see at the moment—rose to the surface. *I can't rat him out,* he decided. *I just can't do it. He needs to come clean all by himself.* Billy pictured Vicki's face and swallowed hard. *I just hope it's not too late when he does.*

Before reporting to work, Billy texted Vicki, *I'm thinking about you.*

After doing a load of rancid laundry, he began hosing out the kennels, his thoughts alternating between her and Charlie. *I need to do whatever it takes to talk some sense into Charlie and convince him to do the right thing,* he thought, feeling awful that he needed to keep a dark secret from a girl he was falling for.

He and Jimmy had been working for nearly an hour before Arlene approached. "How are you doing?" she asked. Billy paused and she picked up on it. "What is it?" she asked, taking a seat and massaging Jimmy's coat while she waited to hear the reason for his sour mood.

"It's not the job," Billy said right away. "I like the job. I do."

"Well, that's good," she said, petting Jimmy, "but I can see that something's eating at you."

Billy shrugged. "There's just so much going on right now," he said, still working as he talked. "I can't even begin to explain it."

"I'm here, if you need to," she offered sincerely.

He nodded, remembering how he'd told Vicki the same thing. "I appreciate that," he said, smiling. "Believe it or not, I feel better just by being here. This place..."

"...is a safe haven," Arlene said, finishing his thought. "...for all of us." She studied Billy's face for a few moments. Just as it was starting to get awkward, she said, "When the world kicks you to the ground, all you can do is stand back up, grit your teeth and get back at it." She nodded. "We all get beat on, Billy, that's a given." She gazed into his eyes and lowered her tone. "It's the decisions you make when you're down that make all the difference."

Although her generous lesson did not completely apply to his problem at hand, Billy still internalized it and nodded gratefully. As he pulled the hose into another dog run, he said, "I'm...I'm just really happy to be working here."

She smiled. "Some people don't know this, but this shelter has served as a refuge during several emergency evacuations." She nodded proudly. "There've been a few times when we've provided pet boarding during a natural disaster."

"Really?" Billy asked.

She nodded. "After Hurricane Katrina wiped out the Gulf Coast, many of the displaced animals were sent north. We took in quite a few until we found them new homes."

"Wow, that's great," he said.

Just then, one of the dogs in the yard, an Akita named Dallas, approached and barked. Billy looked at the dog and then back at Arlene.

"Around here, bow wow and meow mean the same thing." Grinning, she looked at Dallas and then back at Billy. "He's saying *thank you*."

Billy laughed. "You're welcome," he told Dallas.

"You don't speak dog or cat?" she asked.

"Some dog," Billy admitted. "I never really learned cat, though."

"Well, we'll need to fix that, won't we?"

"I'm willing to learn," he said.

She nodded. "I couldn't ask for any more than that," she said, as she stood. "My offer stands, okay?"

He looked at her, confused.

"I'm a good listener," she said. "I'm heading out on a road call right now, but I'm only a phone call away if you need me, okay?"

Billy nodded gratefully. *I wish I could tell you, Arlene, and get some of this weight off my chest*, he thought, *but I already have a pretty good idea of what you'd tell me anyway.* He returned to hosing down the kennels and, as the mundane task numbed his mind, he pictured Vicki's angelic face, working his way down her body. *How could someone be so cute and so sexy at the same time?* he asked himself, allowing his thoughts to linger on her body. *So damned sexy!*

An hour passed before Billy finished the kennels. While he left Jimmy in the yard to play, he searched out Arlene for a new assignment. He found her in the cat room, talking to one of the newly caught alley cats.

"You little hussy, Jezzabelle," Arlene told the plump striped cat, as she placed her into one of the cat carriers. "We're going to get you spayed and see if we can't slow down the cat population in this town."

While Jezzabelle moaned, Arlene talked to the animal like she was speaking to some promiscuous teenager. "That's right, girl," she said, "your party days are over." She looked up to find Billy holding back a laugh. She grinned. "I bet you never realized all the stuff you could learn by working here?"

Billy nodded. "So you're going to give me *the talk*?" he joked.

"Do you need *the talk*?" she asked, her face serious.

He shook his head.

"Good," she said, "because I would have had to find your father and slap him."

"You can still do that," Billy half joked.

"Daddy issues?" she asked, half joking.

"Not really," Billy said, shrugging.

She creased her brow, waiting to hear more.

"No more than anyone else, I guess," he added. "My old man's no saint, but he can be a good guy when the spirit moves him."

She smiled. "That's good," she said, "because there's nothing worse than having to jump through hoops for a saint." She winked. "Trust me, my mother was a saint and it wasn't easy."

Billy nodded.

She sighed. "I can smell some nasty cat carriers that are calling your name," she said, grinning.

He smiled. "I'm on it," he said and, as he walked away, his mind was brought back to his father and the first time he'd been introduced to the birds and bees.

Billy—nine years old at the time—spotted Jimmy mounted on the back of a brindle-colored female stray, humping her. "Jimmy, get over here!" he screamed.

The young mutt glanced once at his master before turning his head, ignoring Billy for the first time in his life.

It bothered Billy something terrible. "What's he doing, Dad?" Billy asked.

His dad grinned. "Slick Jimmy must have run out of gas and she's just towing him in," the old man explained.

Billy leaned in and watched Jimmy's jerky motions for a moment. "Why does he keep pushing her like that, Dad, to make her go faster?"

"It looks that way," his dad said, his grin turning into a full smile.

Billy watched—until Jimmy jumped off the female's back—never realizing he was missing something. "Get over here, Jimmy!" he yelled again.

Panting and wild eyed, the dog finally did as he was told; he was too fired up, however, to pay attention to Billy's scolding—or the old man's laughter.

Billy emerged from the memory and laughed. *Jimmy's glory days are long gone*, he thought, *but I'm really hoping mine have just begun.* He returned to work, while his thoughts were completely on Vicki and her beautiful body.

As Billy was finishing up for the day, Arlene approached him. "Are you in a hurry to get home?" she asked.

He half shrugged. "Not really. Why, what's up?"

She smiled. "We have an adoption this afternoon. The family's on their way here right now."

"Who are they adopting?" Billy asked, excitedly.

"Roxy," Arlene said, referring to a gentle Rottweiler mix.

"Jimmy and I would love to stay. Is there anything I can do to help?" he asked.

She shook her head. "Just watch and let me know if it's as amazing as I think it is."

He smiled. "Okay, you're on."

While Mr. and Mrs. Dube made their donation to the shelter and filled out the proper paperwork, Abigail Rose—their seven-year-old daughter—never let Roxy go. "I'm going to love you for the rest of my life," the little girl told the big, tongue-wagging mutt.

And she will, Billy thought; he just knew it. Although Jimmy was antsy to leave for the day, Billy watched the entire process closely, surprised to feel his eyes well with tears.

At one point, Arlene looked at him and grinned.

Billy turned his head, pretending to be unaffected.

As the Dubes left, with their newest family member in tow, Arlene turned to Billy. "Well, what did you think?"

"You were wrong," he said.

Arlene was clearly taken aback. "I was?"

He nodded. "It was even more amazing than you described."

She laughed, giving it some thought. "It is, isn't it?"

He nodded. "Absolutely amazing," he repeated.

Billy and Jimmy were on their way home from an honest day's work. They weren't twenty feet from the animal shelter when Billy called Vicki's cell.

"Hello?" she answered.

"Hi, beautiful," he blurted and waited.

"I was hoping you'd call me."

"You were?" he asked, his body temperature rising a few degrees.

"I've been thinking about you all day," she said, nonchalantly. "How was work?"

Billy smiled and, in that one moment, it felt as if they'd been together forever. "Really good," he said. "I'm still learning the ropes but, from what I've already seen, I'm glad I took the job. Jimmy and I actually stayed past our shift to see our first adoption. It was so cool!"

"Oh, how cute," she said. "I wish I'd been there with you."

"Me too," he said, smiling. "So how was your day?" There was a pause. It was enough time for Billy to remember the nightmare, to recall that Vicki had planned to visit her aunt. His heart sank.

"I've had better days," she admitted, sighing heavily. "I ended up going to my aunt and uncle's for a visit. It was so sad."

Billy wanted to say something—anything to make her feel better—but he remained quiet, waiting for her to share more.

"My poor uncle's eyes were so sunken and hollow," she said. "He obviously hasn't slept in days. And I've never heard his voice sound so sorrowful." She stopped, clearly trying to collect her emotions.

"I'm so sorry," Billy whispered.

"The moment I walked into the kitchen, I noticed there were a dozen casserole dishes sitting on the table...just left there, not even put in the fridge. My poor Aunt Lily was sitting in the living room, staring off into space. I guess the doctor prescribed some sedatives to help her cope with the grief. I tried talking to her, but when I looked into her eyes I could tell she wasn't really with me."

"Oh man," Billy mumbled, the anxiety swelling within him.

"My uncle talked to me for a while, but all of a sudden it was as if he remembered his son was gone forever and his eyes went blank again."

"I'm sorry," Billy repeated, "I really am." He had no idea what else to say.

Vicki cleared her throat. "Actually, I'm the one who should be apologizing to you. I didn't mean to..."

"Stop," Billy interrupted. "I already told you...whenever you need to talk, I'm here to listen."

"Thank you," she whispered; to Billy, her voice sounded like the flutter of angel's wings. "So what kind of dog got adopted?" she asked.

Billy had to think about it, switching gears in his mind. "A mutt," he said, "a big, beautiful mutt named Roxy."

"That's great," she said. "I hope Roxy found a nice home."

"I think she did," Billy said, his mind racing; he was trying to figure out how to cheer her up. "Hey, what do you think about letting me take you out tomorrow night?"

"I'd love that," she said. "Where are you taking me?"

"Well, I could tell you but that would ruin the surprise, wouldn't it?"

She giggled, making him feel better already. "It would," she whispered.

"How 'bout I pick you up at six o'clock?"

"I'll be ready," she promised.

"Good," he said and hung up. *Now where's the perfect place to take her*, he thought, *to make her feel as special as she makes me feel?*

After he and Jimmy played tug-of-war with a bathroom towel, Billy got ready for the big night. He rubbed a glob of purple gel into his unruly hair and opted to comb the thick mop to the side. *It looks different*, he decided in the mirror. *I like it.* Not yet understanding the wisdom of "less is more," he filled the bathroom with body spray; the cloud enveloped him, before settling onto him like some overpowering adhesive. After filling his pockets with a set of car keys and an anemic billfold, he headed for the kitchen.

He was halfway down the stairs—out of his mother's view—when his mom yelled out, "My God, Billy, did you use the whole can?"

He stepped into the kitchen.

"You need to go outside and walk some of that off," she said, her face serious.

"It's that strong?" he asked.

She nodded, her nose cringing in a display of repulsion. "Trust me, it's going to have the opposite effect you want." She grinned. "Is it the girl you've been talking to late at night?"

He nodded.

"You've been logging some serious time on the phone with her, huh?"

"Whenever I can," Billy admitted. "Whenever I can't see her."

His mom's grin widened. "What's her name?"

"Vicki," Billy said and couldn't help but smile.

"You want to attract the girl, Billy, not repel her...right?"

Sighing heavily, Billy turned on his heels and headed back up to the shower. "Two showers in one day," he told Jimmy. "It's got to be a record."

"And if you wear a belt, you won't have to keep pulling up your pants," his mom called out. "I'm just sayin'."

Billy shook his head.

Back in the bathroom, Jimmy looked up from the linoleum floor, holding the towel in his mouth.

Billy rubbed his head. "Sorry, buddy, but I need to get moving. We'll play again tomorrow, okay?"

Jimmy sat on his haunches, refusing to drop the towel.

"Okay," Billy said, trying to yank the damp cloth from the mutt's powerful jaws, "but we only have a minute."

Jimmy stuck his backside up into the air, growled deeply and shook his head back and forth—pulling the towel out of Billy's hands and making him laugh.

As Billy and Jimmy returned to the kitchen, his mom said, "Come by the pizza shop for dinner and I'll set you and Vicki up."

"No thanks, Mom. I appreciate it but I have other plans."

"Oh yeah, and what's that?"

"Agave in Bristol," he said nonchalantly.

"Well, excuse me, Mr. Big Shot," she teased, squeezing the back of his neck. "How come you've never taken me to Agave?" she kidded.

He smiled. "I really like her," he said, understating his true feelings.

"I can tell," she said, grinning. "Are you taking her back here after dinner?" The grin overtook her face. "Maybe she can help you clean your room?"

"Are you kidding me?" He shook his head and smiled. "I'd never show her my room."

"Well, at least you have enough sense to know it's a pig sty," his mom said, grabbing her purse. "Have fun and don't be too late," she said at the door.

He nodded. "You either," he teased.

She laughed loudly. "I wish."

Billy was right on her heels, with Jimmy escorting him to the front door. Taking a knee, he kissed the limping mutt. "You can't come with me this time, buddy," he said, rubbing the dog's thick neck, "but I promise to tell you all about it when I get home, okay?"

As the door closed behind Billy, Jimmy's melancholy whine faded to a soft whimper.

Billy had borrowed Mark's convertible, got it washed and vacuumed—which was part of the deal—and filled the tank with enough gas to hand it back at the same pitiful level.

Ten minutes later, he was parked out in front of Vicki's house. He took a deep breath. There were four cars in the driveway. *Everyone's home*, he thought and suddenly felt a pang of fear rip through him. He took a couple more deep breaths and, as he fixed his shirt, he shook his head. *I should have worn something else...something new.* He took a few steps toward the door, while his heart pounded hard in his ears. *Relax*, he told himself. *It's only a date.* As he reached the front door, another voice added, *Yeah, with the girl of your dreams. Now don't screw this up!* As he knocked, his breathing grew shallow, making him feel light-headed. *And I should have brought her flowers. I'm so stupid!*

Just then, the door opened and a tall, distinguished looking man—Vicki's dad—was standing there. "Billy?" he asked.

Billy held his breath and nodded.

"Come in," he said, "Vicki's just finishing up. You know how girls are," he added, raising an eyebrow.

By now, the world was spinning. Like a sheep led to its slaughter, Billy followed Vicki's dad into the living room, taking a seat on the leather couch, as instructed.

"So where are you taking my little girl tonight, Billy?" he asked, seriously. "I suspect she'll be in good hands..."

"Ummm...we're going to..."

Smiling, the lanky man slapped Billy's knee. "Relax, I'm just playing with you."

Oh man, Billy thought, *this guy's a ball buster.*

The grinning man added, "Vicki was raised to make good decisions and her mother and I trust her completely. If she likes you, then there have to be good reasons...so I like you too." He winked. "...unless you prove her wrong."

Billy nodded and, at that moment, felt some of his anxiety evaporate. As he waited for Vicki, he decided he liked her father. *He's a funny dude*, he thought. *And I can picture me busting some kid's balls, if I had a daughter who'd just started dating.*

Vicki's brother, Barry—a big, muscular kid a year younger than Billy—entered the room and quickly sized up his sister's date. "What's up?" he mumbled, with a nod of his head.

"What's up?" Billy said, returning the nod.

Barry left the room just as Vicki entered.

Billy instinctively stood, wiping his sweaty palms on his pants. *My God, she's beautiful*, he thought and scanned her body, spending a few extra moments at the curvy parts. Suddenly, he remembered her dad was still sitting there, watching him. Billy quickly looked away from Vicki, pretending not to ogle her. After an awkward moment, they started for the front door.

"Take good care of her," Vicki's dad told Billy, his grin returning.

"I will, sir," Billy said, seriously.

As Billy held open the car's passenger door, Vicki smiled. "A gentleman," she commented, impressed.

They drove slowly down Route 103, with Billy's breathing returning to normal; as each telephone pole passed, he felt like they were flying high above the clouds.

Agave had a gorgeous view of the bay, peppered in moored sailboats. The sun was just going down in the west, directly in front of their table, and the powder-blue sky was alive with gliding seagulls. They were seated at the outside terrace under the giant pergola, draped in white fabrics, with potted flowering plants climbing up the cedar posts. The round glass-top table, with linen napkins, was surrounded by four comfortable wicker chairs. Even with the salty breeze blowing straight at them, the air felt warm. A tarred path separating the terrace from the bay allowed joggers, walkers and bicyclists to pass them by.

"Very nice," Vicki said, almost to herself.

Referring to the restaurant's full tequila menu, Billy joked, "Do you think the waitress will card us?"

Vicki nodded. "I do."

Billy pointed out several of the tiny birds—chickadees—that darted back and forth beneath the tables in search of crumbs. "Did you know that that's where chicken nuggets come from?" he said.

"Gross," she said, laughing.

"That one's name is sweet and sour and his brother, over there, is honey mustard."

She slapped his arm.

"How about I order us a four piece as an appetizer?"

"You're crazy," she said, squeezing his arm and leaving her hand there.

Billy couldn't remember feeling this happy—*ever*.

When the waitress returned to the table, he ordered, "Two colas with lemon." He looked at Vicki. "And let's get the Agave

Nachos," he added, knowing that the appetizer could have fed an entire family.

After putting a small dent in the giant cheesy appetizer, Vicki ordered a pear gorgonzola salad.

"That's it?" Billy asked.

She pointed to the glob of nachos that had quickly grown cold. "How much do you think I can eat?"

He laughed, looked at the young waitress and ordered, "Grilled chicken penne in pink tequila sauce."

As the waitress walked away, Vicki said, "So you got your tequila after all, huh?"

He laughed. "I did."

They dined and watched the sun set over the sailboat-filled water. As they played adults, talking and laughing and eating, they took their time with all of it.

At one point, Vicki leaned across the table and grabbed Billy's hand. "Thank you," she said, before looking out onto the bay. "This place is so beautiful. How did you find it?"

"It took a little research." He shrugged. "No big deal."

She squeezed his hand. "If you did research, then it is a big deal." She stared at him and her eyes shined.

It took a moment for him to catch his breath.

"Thank you," she repeated, taking several pictures with her cell phone.

Although Agave was a great location, Billy hardly noticed. His undivided attention and focus was on Vicki. The people seated around them could have committed the most heinous crimes and Billy would never have been able to identify any one of them in a police lineup. There was only Vicki. *She's so gorgeous*, he thought.

The waitress bounced over with a chocolate lava cake. Within seconds, the sauce-stained plates were cleared, every breadcrumb scraped away—allowing plenty of room for the shared dessert.

A half hour later, Billy grabbed the black faux leather billfold and proudly paid their bill, leaving an adult-sized tip. He ran the cloth napkin across his mouth one last time and smiled. "You ready to go?" he asked Vicki.

"Not home, I'm not," she said sincerely.

His entire chest heated up, making his face burn. "Good," he managed. "Me either."

As they stood to leave, Vicki asked the waitress, "Can you please take our picture?"

They posed in front of the water; Billy's arm around Vicki's shoulder, her arm around his waist.

Billy was so ecstatic he felt like he'd drunk a half bottle of tequila.

It was dusk when they drove to Colt State Park, past the massive bull statues that guarded the iron ornate gates. Billy parked the ragtop.

For the next half hour, they walked along the water, sharing their brief lives as they went.

"So you still have no idea what you want for the future?" Vicki asked.

Billy looked at her and smiled wide. "I wouldn't say that anymore." He nodded. "I know *exactly* what I want."

She squeezed his arm and laughed. "Great answer, but I was talking about school."

He thought about it for a moment. "No, not really," he admitted, feeling a bit embarrassed. "But I'm praying it'll come to me."

"I'm sure it will," Vicki said, placing a soft kiss on his cheek. "I bet as soon as you stop worrying about it, it will come to you and you'll know exactly what you want."

"Man, I hope so," he sighed. "What about you?" he asked. "Have you gotten used to taking care of the elderly at the nursing home?"

"Vomit and bed pans, what's not to love?" she joked, before throwing off a small shrug. "What I have learned," she added, getting serious, "is that I'll clean vomit and bed pans all day long, if that's how I can help people."

"Good for you," he said, falling even deeper for her.

For a while, Billy rambled on, talking like an auctioneer— still trying hard to sell what Vicki had already purchased.

At one point, she stopped and rested her gaze upon him. "Shhh," she whispered. "I'm here, with you, and there's no other place I'd rather be." She leaned in a few inches, enough to reveal her romantic intentions.

With his heart pounding hard in his ears, Billy's dry lips nearly missed hers. When they parted, he remained close, locked onto her sparkling eyes. *She gives me chills*, he thought, shivering. After another sweet kiss—this one, wet and satisfying—he reached out and grabbed her hand. *This is so incredible*, he thought.

Smiling, she tightened her grip.

After some contented silence, Vicki looked up at the majestic sky and innocently commented, "I think God has done a wonderful job." She looked at Billy. "Do you go to church?"

"I used to." As if stalling for time, he looked around. "I love the message. It's the messenger I have a problem with. I don't think today's church is what God truly intended." He grinned. "Not that I can speak for Him."

Vicki returned the smile. "You mean *Her*, right?"

Billy laughed.

"Actually, I don't think God is either," she said. "I believe that wherever there's love... that's God."

Billy nodded. *Then he's here with us right now*, he thought.

As they settled back into the car, Billy gazed at Vicki. *She smells so good*, he thought, as he put the convertible top down. They turned back onto the road, still laughing over the chickadee nuggets, when he put his hand on her leg. It felt smooth to the touch. *Oh God*, he thought, while something stirred inside of him. He quickly pulled his hand away. Instead, he grabbed for her hand and watched as her hair whipped in the summer wind. The radio was at the perfect volume so they could enjoy the sounds of the night, as well.

As they drove, Billy stole several sideways glances at her, realizing he had never felt so happy or filled with such joy. *I don't really know Vicki...Well, not yet anyway,* he thought, but his feelings for her were so strong already. *Is it because she's my first real girlfriend?* he wondered, *or...* He quickly decided not to overanalyze and ruin it. *Maybe love isn't meant to be justified or explained?* He looked sideways again and concealed the screams of euphoria that scratched to be freed from the back of his throat.

There was no moon and the few stars that twinkled above had suddenly disappeared. In the dark, the air temperature suddenly changed and felt much cooler. As they drove down a short stretch of highway, it began raining. For a few seconds, it was just a shower—and then the downpour came. Unable to do anything but drive and find a safe place to pull the car over, Billy glanced to his right. Vicki was already soaking wet. "I'm sorry," he started to say when she began to laugh hysterically. He laughed along with her, the cool rain already penetrating his clothes.

As they approached a highway overpass, Billy parked beneath the steel and concrete shelter and put on the emergency flashers. They were both drenched, and so was the interior of the car.

"This is so crazy!" Vicki said, her voice electrified from excitement.

After Billy put the top up, he and Vicki remained parked for a few minutes—laughing.

When the laughter shrank to a few giggles, he looked into her eyes and shrugged. "Sorry," he said again.

She pushed the dripping hair out of her eyes and shook her head. "Please. This is..." She stopped and dove deeper into his gaze. Then, in one sudden movement, she slid toward him, leaned in and kissed him on the lips—much more passionately than at the park.

He kissed her back, feeling even more drunk on the moment. *Oh, my God,* he thought. *I love the rain.* He pushed back hard on her mouth, his tongue dancing wildly with hers.

When they finally pulled back onto the highway, the storm had passed. Billy drove into the parking lot of a convenience store, parked and turned to Vicki. *She looks even more beautiful soaking wet,* he thought. "I'm sorry, but there's no way I can bring this car back to Mark like this," he said.

"Of course," she said, "we can clean it together."

After spending three dollars for a dollar roll of paper towels, Billy joined Vicki to sop up the interior of the car. At one point, he looked up and saw her staring at him; she was smiling. *I never realized that cleaning could be so much fun,* he thought and saw that she was still staring. "What is it?" he asked.

She shook her head. "Nothing," she said. "It's just...I can't remember the last time I felt this happy."

Billy stopped a childish squeal from leaping off his diaphragm. "Me too," he said, shrugging. "Although I think we could have driven through a hurricane and it would have been a blast sharing it with you."

Vicki smiled widely and, when they finished, surveyed their work. "I think it's the best we can do for now," she said.

Billy nodded in agreement. "Mark will never know," he joked.

Vicki laughed. "Sure, if he doesn't drive it for a couple of weeks."

Billy laughed along with her. "I'm not worried about it. When I tell him what kind of night this was, I'm sure he'll understand." He looked up at her, realizing just how revealing his comments were and how very little—his thoughts or feelings—he was holding back.

Her smile vanished and she dove back into his eyes, with an intensity that stole his breath away once more. "I'd understand if I were him," she whispered.

As they drove home—soaked to the bone—Vicki echoed Billy's thoughts. "Tonight was so much fun," she said.

"I know," he said, "which is good 'cause Mark's never going to let me take his car again."

They both scanned the car's interior; the seats and carpets were saturated with water.

"Oh man," Billy said and they both started laughing again.

Not wanting the night to end, he drove her home at a snail's pace. And he sensed Vicki felt the same. They were surely going to be together again and there would be other amazing nights. *But not this night*, he thought, holding her hand tightly. *We will never have this night again.*

After sharing a short, sweet kiss at the door—being respectful to anyone who might be watching—Billy whispered, "Thank you for tonight. It was..."

"...perfect," she whispered. "I know." She hugged him. "But I'm the one who should be thanking you."

"You're welcome," he said. "I'll call you tomorrow."

She shook her head.

"No?" he said, his heart rate immediately changing.

"Call me when you get home," she said, kissing him again. "There's no way I'll be able to get any sleep tonight anyway."

He nodded, before floating back to the borrowed ragtop. *There's no way I'm getting any sleep tonight either*, he realized.

The drive home was a confusing one. With the top down and the warm night reminding him of their date, he wanted to take it slow. But he was also looking forward to hearing Vicki's voice again. He got on the gas and took the short way home. *Jimmy's going to love this one*, he thought, wearing a smile that felt like it might actually explode off his face.

Billy returned home and headed straight to his room to crash. While Jimmy waited patiently for some long-overdue attention, Billy changed into dry pajama bottoms and called Vicki's cell phone. "Hey, do you miss me yet?" he asked, brushing his wet hair back.

"Just as soon as you dropped me off," she whispered.

"Me too," Billy said, feeling his chest grow warm. "I'll be thinking about you all night."

"I hope so," she said.

He smiled widely. "Well, goodnight then."

"Goodnight," she whispered.

Billy could still hear her breathing. "Are you going to hang up?" he asked.

"You first," she said.

He smiled. "No," he whispered, "you first."

Vicki giggled, making Billy do the same. It would have been embarrassing had it been anybody but Jimmy listening.

"Goodnight," she said again—in the sweetest voice Billy had ever heard.

"Goodnight," he repeated. "I'll send you a text just as soon as I get up in the morning."

"You'd better," she said.

"Okay then," he said, "goodnight." As if he were in pain, he closed his eyes and ended the call.

When he opened his eyes again, Jimmy's silver snout was an inch from his. Billy laughed. "Sorry, buddy," he said, scratching the dog's thick neck for a few minutes. Yawning, Billy took off his damp shirt and was about to toss it onto the floor when he caught a whiff of Vicki's perfume. Instead, he rolled the shirt into a ball, shoved it into his face and inhaled deeply. "Ahhh," he exhaled. *It's Vicki*, he thought, collapsing onto his bed where he inhaled Vicki's scent and made Jimmy whimper at the unusual behavior. Between breaths, he told the fidgeting dog, "I love her, buddy. I really do. I know we just started seeing each other, but I can't help how I feel." He thought about it and nodded. "I love her so much it hurts."

Sighing heavily, Jimmy stuck his own snout into the shirt for a smell.

"She's so amazing, Jimmy. I can't stop staring at her when I'm with her and sometimes I'm telling her my deepest thoughts without even realizing I'm doing it." He looked at the dog. "And you know I've never done that. I usually keep my thoughts to myself." He shook his head. "But not with Vicki. Nope, with her it's like I feel free to tell her whatever I'm thinking or feeling." Billy scratched Jimmy's head. "You just wait 'til you meet her."

Jimmy plunged his black nose deeper into the balled shirt to get another whiff.

"She's so beautiful," Billy added, "and I love her voice." He laughed. "Even the way she laughs at my stupid jokes...It makes me feel like the luckiest guy in the whole world. And her smell..." Billy dove back into the shirt with Jimmy, where they were both lulled to sleep by Vicki's distinct scent.

Chapter 9

In the morning, after texting Vicki back and forth for twenty
minutes—his nose still buried in the damp, perfumed shirt—
Billy caught the time. "Oh shit! We have to get ready for work,
Jimmy," he said, feeling rattled for the first time in his life about
running behind. "We can't be late." While Jimmy watched on,
curiously, Billy sprang out of bed.

Billy had already discovered that the new job at the animal
shelter had less than ideal hours. Scheduled to start early in the
mornings and work on the weekends, there was less time for
hanging out with friends—just as Mark had predicted. *But Charlie's all but disappeared,* Billy thought, *and Mark's taking summer
classes.* There was also no time for the things he once loved—
like video games and sleeping in. But since Vicki had entered his
life, those things were going to take a back seat anyway and he
knew it. He looked at his cell phone, awaiting a reply from her.
It's the time away from Vicki that's the worst, he thought.

It took all Billy had just to drag himself into the shower.
Minutes later, rich Columbian coffee grabbed whatever senses
were still dull and shook them to sobriety. As Billy cradled the
hot mug, he shook his head. *This is nuts,* he thought. *Who gets up
and goes to work this early?*

He looked down at Jimmy, who was fidgeting with a breakfast that had been served much too early. *He's also struggling with the new routine,* Billy thought.

The Honda's rotted exhaust had finally given way. The car was obnoxiously loud and getting louder by the day, sounding like a country tractor pull screaming into the night.

A mile down the road, Billy picked up his cell phone. Alternating his attention between the road in front of him and the phone, he punched in numbers and waited until four rings led to Vicki's outgoing message. He listened to her sweet voice and smiled. At the beep, he cleared his throat. "Hey, beautiful," he said, "I was wondering if it would be okay if Jimmy and I swung by your house after work. Just call me when you get a chance. I can't stop thinking about you and I need to hear your voice." He hung up, looked down at Jimmy and shrugged. "Well, I do."

The mutt yawned.

As they drove, Billy asked the dog, "What do you think of me becoming a writer?"

Jimmy never even looked up; he was sitting quietly in his seat, looking like he dreaded going back to the shelter.

Billy thought about it and snickered. "Nah, probably not," he said. "It seems like a whole lot of work for very little pay." He sighed. "But if not writing, then what?"

Jimmy kept his head buried in his dirty white paws.

They were just pulling into the shelter's stone parking lot when Billy called Charlie's phone three times before he answered. "Bro, you need to man up," he pleaded the moment Charlie answered.

There was silence.

"Are you there?" Billy asked.

"Yeah, I'm here," Charlie whispered.

"You need to tell the cops about what really happened that night, Charlie."

"I don't think so," Charlie said.

"But you..."

"Billy, you're not going to dime me out, are you?" Charlie asked, his voice thick with fear.

"Of course not. I'd never do that. You know that!"

"Good." Charlie took a deep breath. "I just need to do this my way, okay?"

"And what way is that?"

"I...I don't know yet."

There was a pause. "You're going to have much bigger problems if you don't..."

"What the hell do you know about problems?" Charlie snapped at Billy.

"Just do the right thing, Charlie," Billy said, thinking, *You have no idea the problems you've already caused me.*

Charlie replied with the usual dial tone.

"Selfish bastard," Billy hissed. "Why should other people have to pay for *your* sins?"

Billy's shift had just started when a woman, Mrs. Thompson, was dragged through the front door by a tank that resembled a Rottweiler. Billy immediately thought of Roxy. As Mrs. Thompson leaned back, hanging onto the thick leash with every ounce of her strength, she told Billy, "Help me, please."

Jimmy immediately stood behind Billy, trembling at the sight of the giant.

Arlene's robust laugh echoed off the walls. Billy turned to see her standing behind him. She proceeded right to the Rottweiler and grabbed his leash. "What can we do for you?" Arlene asked Mrs. Thompson, awaiting the obvious.

Once she'd calmed her breathing, Mrs. Thompson explained, "I brought Roger in because he's too big and awkward around our small children." She shook her head and her eyes glassed over from honest care and compassion. "He's a good boy, a big baby, and he doesn't mean it, but he's going to end up hurting someone bad...or killing one of us."

While Jimmy peeked out from the safety of Billy's legs, Arlene knelt before the massive Rotty and studied his face. As she played with him, she was able to safely touch the dog's ears, mouth, tail, legs and belly. The Rottweiler was young, maybe two years old, but he was enormous, weighing well over one hundred forty pounds.

A prime example of new dog owners not doing their homework, Billy thought, realizing he'd already learned quite a bit from Arlene.

Jimmy still shook violently behind him.

Arlene and Billy spent a few minutes with Roger, while Jimmy shrank into the corner of the room, as though he were trying to make himself invisible. It was long enough to know Roger had a great temperament. He was non-aggressive and in good health.

"We have space available," Arlene told Mrs. Thompson, who appeared instantly relieved. "The next step is for you to fill out a questionnaire that'll give us information about Roger. I'll also need your vet's phone number so I can retrieve the big boy's medical records."

Mrs. Thompson nodded gratefully.

"Rottweilers can be as hard to place as Akitas, Chows, Dobermans, Pit Bulls and Shar Peis." She winked. "Luckily, I know a guy who knows a guy."

Mrs. Thompson laughed; it was more an extended sigh of relief than anything else.

"There is a surrender fee we charge for turning in an animal," Arlene concluded. "This will help to defray the cost of Roger's stay while he's here with us."

"Name your price," Mrs. Thompson said, completing the questionnaire like she was claiming her lottery winnings.

Billy looked down at Jimmy, who was still quivering in fear, and realized, *He's already had enough of this place.*

Stepping lighter than when she'd arrived, Mrs. Thompson closed the shelter's front door behind her. Arlene turned to

Roger and said, "I know just the family for you, Zeus." She bent down and re-checked the giant dog's undercarriage. He still had his God-given jewels. "A breeder," she confirmed. "They're definitely going to love you."

"What do you mean?" Billy asked.

Arlene explained, "Zeus is one lucky boy..."

"Zeus?" Billy asked. "I thought his name was Roger."

She shook her head. "There's no way this titan's leaving here with the name Roger." Arlene had a knack of picking the perfect name for a dog; if they were older and attached to a ridiculous name then she wouldn't muddle with it. But if they were still young enough to take on a new identity, she made it part of her mission to select the right name.

Billy laughed and took a knee to calm Jimmy down. "You're okay, buddy," he whispered.

"I know a breeder who's looking for a new stud." Arlene examined the four-legged ogre and grinned. "And with a specimen like him...before it's over, he's going to father a hundred offspring." She brought Zeus into the back, making Jimmy's heart rate slow to normal.

That afternoon, as Billy began socializing two new dogs, Arlene peeked her head into the back. "Billy, what do you think about helping me with our newsletter?"

He looked up. "Of course," he said. "Is it online?"

She half shrugged. "Kind of."

"Kind of?"

"We have a website, but it's dated and needs some serious TLC."

"I can take a look at that too," he said. "Once we throw some lipstick on the pig, I'll post the newsletter there as well."

Arlene chuckled at the pig reference, before returning to the issue at hand. "Wow, if you can get all that done, I may ask for your help with one of our many fundraisers."

"What fundraisers?" Billy asked.

"With the help of lots of volunteers, we run an annual dinner and silent auction, an arts festival, a casino trip, a couple different wine tastings and my favorite, our Santa Paws event. We host a pancake breakfast and have Santa Claus there to take pictures with children and their pets."

"Very cool," Billy said. "I'll have to go when I'm back home on Christmas break."

She nodded. "Your ticket's on me."

"So what do you need help with?" he asked.

"We do pretty good running the events, but it's spreading the word that's always been our challenge."

"Do you promote the events online," he asked, "like on social media?"

She shook her head again, blushing.

"I'm on it," he said, making her face glow.

As Arlene walked away, Billy contemplated all the time and effort this would take. He smiled. *I can't think of a better way to spend my time*, he thought, *than to do whatever I can to help these animals. If it helps them find good homes, then I'm all in.*

At the end of the day, Billy watched Jimmy lying in the shadows of the yard, a safe distance from the animal community. He lapped at his hind legs, as if trying to lick the aches and pains of old age away. *Dogs are pack animals and there's a hierarchy, a social order*, Billy contemplated, scanning the yard, *but Jimmy's too old and tired to try to claim his spot*. Instead, the aged black mutt refused to play and take part in any of the foolishness. "Jimmy," Billy yelled, "come on, boy, it's time to go home."

Jimmy's reflexes weren't what they used to be. He stood slowly, stiffly, and made his way toward Billy. When he got close enough, Billy could see the joy in the dog's eyes—to be leaving. Unfortunately, his broken body could no longer tell the same story.

"We've worked hard enough for one day," he told the senior canine, and he didn't have to tell him twice.

Jimmy made a beeline toward the front door.

On their way out, Billy caught Arlene in the supply room. "Everything's done," he said, "we're taking off for the day."

She looked up from her clipboard and nodded. "Make sure you spoil that dog with some love tonight." She winked at Jimmy.

"Every night," Billy said, smiling. "Are you out of here soon?"

She looked down at the clipboard and sighed. Arlene got paid for eight hours a day, but usually worked closer to twelve. "It'll be a while yet." She grinned. "It's a good thing I record my favorite shows."

Billy laughed. "We'll see you in the morning," he said.

"I'll be here," she replied and, before returning to the task at hand, she reached into her back pocket, retrieved a white envelope and handed it to Billy.

"What's this?" he asked.

"Your paycheck." She grinned. "You didn't come in every day as a volunteer, did you?"

He smiled. "No," he said, and was surprised when a strange thought crossed his mind: *But I would have been just as happy volunteering.*

With Jimmy taking the lead, Billy left the shelter. They weren't even at the Honda when Billy tore the envelope open and looked at his first paycheck—being "on the books." His eyes went wide. It was much less than he'd expected. *What the hell?* he thought. *Some of it must be missing.* As he slid into the driver's seat and fired up the screeching monster, he turned to Jimmy. "I'm not sure there's much of a difference between being a volunteer or a paid employee."

The mutt collapsed into the passenger seat, where he rolled himself into a ball and closed his tired eyes.

"Long day, huh, boy?" Billy asked, pulling out of the lot.

Jimmy yawned, but kept his eyes closed.

Laughing, Billy looked at his cell phone. There was a text from Vicki. His heart rate sped up. *I'd love to see you guys after work,* she wrote. *Come over as soon as you get out.*

Cruising along on cloud nine, Billy swung by Vicki's house—with Jimmy playing the napping co-pilot—and shut the wailing clunker down.

Vicki hurried out into the driveway and went wide eyed when she spotted the old dog. "Bring him in," she said excitedly, already scratching Jimmy's neck.

"Are you sure?" Billy asked, while the mutt sprang to life.

"Of course I'm sure," Vicki said. "He's beautiful." She kissed Billy.

Getting his second wind, Jimmy craned his neck out of the passenger side window and sniffed Vicki's hand. He immediately gave his approval with a whipping tail.

"See, I told you she was awesome," Billy whispered to the dog.

Jimmy's tail was going so fast, it nearly knocked him off the seat onto the passenger side floor.

Billy laughed. "I get excited when I see her too," he whispered, stealing a glance at Vicki's round behind, "but you don't have to overplay it."

From the moment they sat together on the living room floor, Jimmy was very attentive to Vicki and she was eager to return every ounce of it back to him.

"I think he has a crush on you," Billy told her, looking at Jimmy who was lying on his back and waiting for his belly to be rubbed.

"Do you blame him?" she teased, petting the dog's undercarriage.

"Absolutely not!" Billy said seriously.

"I was joking," she said.

"I wasn't," Billy said, getting to his knees to hug her.

Within the heat of the embrace, Vicki whispered, "I love you, Billy." It was the first time either of them had said it.

It was so unexpected, so pure and magical, that he got choked up and couldn't speak for a long moment. *I love you too,*

Vicki! he screamed in his head. *I love you with everything inside of me.* But the words were wedged sideways in his throat. He coughed once, twice, but still nothing came out.

While Jimmy whined, Vicki pulled away just enough to look at Billy. There was panic in her eyes. Clearly, she was expecting to hear an immediate response—a confirmation that her feelings were matched and mutual. But when she gazed into his eyes—which were swollen with tears—her eyes lit up and she smiled.

"I love you too," he finally managed. "I really do."

She collapsed back into their hug. "I know," she whispered. "I can see it in your eyes."

He squeezed her tight. "I love you more than I could ever say."

"I know," she repeated. "Me too."

Jimmy whined louder.

Vicki kissed Billy and kept right on kissing him until Jimmy began to howl for having to share her attention. Vicki returned to rubbing Jimmy's belly and told Billy, "Sorry, but it looks like Jimmy's my new boyfriend."

Billy looked down at his best friend. By now, Jimmy's eyes were shut tight and his tongue was nearly dragging the floor. "You big bum," he told the spoiled mutt. "You're killing me."

While Vicki giggled, Jimmy couldn't have cared less; one of his hind legs quivered in ecstasy. "Does Jimmy do any tricks?" she asked.

"Sure. He'll do anything for a treat. He gives his paw, sits, lies down and he used to play dead." Billy shrugged. "But now it takes him so long to get back up that you'd need to bring him a T-bone steak to see that one."

She laughed.

"And he has a beautiful smile," Billy added.

"He can smile?" Vicki asked excitedly.

Billy looked at Jimmy. "Let Vicki see those pearly whites, buddy."

On cue, Jimmy's lip curled into a snarl and he bared his teeth.

"Oh my God," she squealed, "how did you..."

"When he was a puppy," Billy explained, "he used to show his teeth as a warning. It was so funny that our family started to make a big deal about him having such a pretty smile." He shrugged. "And as you can see, Jimmy's an attention junkie, so it caught on and became a habit after that."

"And kisses?" she asked. "Does he give kisses?"

"Oh yeah. You can get as many of those as you want just by asking." Billy chuckled. "We've always figured he might have a touch of French poodle in him because Jimmy's a big kisser."

"Just like you?" she teased.

Billy searched her eyes. "Well, I hope I'm a little better than he is."

She laughed. "I'll let you know," she said and leaned into Jimmy's face, prepared to meet the slobber.

Billy sat back and watched in awe. *Jimmy's falling in love with Vicki*, he thought, *unlike his terrible behavior toward my first crush.* Billy remembered how the young, jealous dog had jumped on Olivia Reney—which he'd never done to anyone—and covered her pretty dress in enough dirt and mud to guarantee she'd never return. After Olivia had stormed off, Jimmy got yelled at and then went off to pout in the corner. In the end, life returned back to normal, which was clearly what the clever mutt had wanted. *I was all his back then*, Billy thought. This time, Jimmy seemed to better accept the natural course of things. *Either that, or he's more interested in Vicki than he is in me.* Billy laughed, as the dog lapped away at Vicki's wet cheek. *And I really can't blame him.*

Jimmy quickly glanced at Billy before slathering Vicki's face with another coat of spit.

While Billy allowed them their time to bond, he took account of his relationship with Vicki. *I feel high whenever I'm around her*, he thought, *and everything else just fades away when we're together.* Billy watched her play with Jimmy and smiled. *She's become my best friend.* The smile quickly faded when, somewhere deep in the back of his mind, Billy realized, *But it's only temporary.*

Interrupting the love fest between her and Jimmy, Billy mentioned it. "I'm so bummed we're not going to the same school in the fall. I'll be away at UMASS in Boston and you'll be at Quinnipiac all the way in Connecticut."

"I know," she said, grabbing his hand, "but we have right here, right now...together." She kissed him. "Besides, we'll stay in touch through texts and Skype, right? And I plan on coming home every vacation...if you want to spend them with me?"

He nodded. "Of course I do," he said.

"Okay then," she said and kissed him, quickly changing the subject.

Billy kissed her back, while Jimmy wailed his disapproval and pawed at them both to be included. When Billy finally surrendered Vicki's attention to the whining mutt, he took a few minutes to look around the room. Amongst other family photos, he spotted a framed picture sitting on the fireplace mantel, a much younger Barry and Vicki smiling from the glossy photo. There was also another boy—their age—smiling in the picture. Billy thought about it and immediately felt every ounce of joy drain out of him. *It must be Dalton*, he thought, a wave of guilt crashing into him and wrenching his stomach sideways.

Vicki broke free from Jimmy's kisses for a second. "Do you want to watch a movie?" she asked.

Billy instinctively nodded. "Sure," he said, "but your parents?"

"They're out for the night. And my brother's never home, so we have the whole place to ourselves."

Something in Billy's loins stirred at the possibilities. Still, he was reluctant to accept the offer.

"What is it?" she asked.

"I'd love to stay," he said, "but Jimmy hasn't eaten."

"Does he like steak? We have leftovers in the fridge."

"Are you kidding? Jimmy could eat his weight in steak," Billy said.

"Well, we don't have that much, but there should be enough to hold him over."

Billy nodded.

"And how about I make you and me a quick meal?" she suggested.

"You don't have to do that," Billy said, thrilled he was going to eat too.

"I know I don't." She got up, leaned into his face—until he could inhale her—and kissed him hard. "I want to."

"Thank you," he said, his loins filling with a surge of hot, rushing blood.

She grinned like an angel. "I love breakfast food any time of the day. Are you up for some eggs and bacon?"

"It's my favorite meal," he said.

She kissed him again. "Give me ten minutes and we'll eat."

"Can I help?" he asked.

She shrugged. "You can keep me company in the kitchen if you want."

Billy got up and went into the kitchen with her, with Jimmy scratching across the tile behind them.

Jimmy devoured his steak within seconds.

Billy looked down at the mutt and shook his head, embarrassed. "He's already been fed once today," he said. "You'd think..."

"He's just a hungry boy," Vicki said, dishing out the last of the beef to the dog. "He worked hard today." She patted the mutt's head.

Billy laughed. "Yeah, he worked hard today, all right. Jimmy hates that place."

"He does?" she asked.

Billy nodded. "I'm pretty sure he does."

Vicki petted him again, while Jimmy took his final bite and began vacuuming the smudged floor. Laughing, Vicki finished cooking the eggs and bacon. She and Billy then sat at the kitchen table, eating in silence like some old couple.

Billy couldn't remember feeling more content. After a second glass of orange juice, he pushed his empty plate away and smiled. "Thank you, Vicki," he said. "That was great."

"You're welcome," she said. "You should try my pancakes for lunch sometime." She stood, grabbed the plates and headed for the kitchen sink.

Billy couldn't help it; he stared at her rear end and nodded. "I'd love to."

She looked over her shoulder and giggled, knowing exactly what he was thinking.

With the DVD player loaded and a bowl of popcorn filled to the brim, Vicki snuggled between Billy and Jimmy on the couch, picked up the remote control and clicked it once. The opening scene to *Dumb & Dumber* began to play.

Billy looked at her. "Are you serious?" he asked, delighted with her film selection.

"Dead serious," she said, kissing him. "It's one of my all-time favorites."

Side by side, they laughed at every stupid joke and physical prank. Billy laughed so fiercely his stomach hurt. *I've never laughed this hard*, he thought and looked to his right to find Vicki bent in half, holding her side. He laughed even harder, until he couldn't breathe. While Jimmy watched on, Billy and Vicki held each other and rolled around on the couch in sheer hysterics.

After settling down and finally controlling themselves, Vicki pulled a throw blanket over them both and snuggled in closer to Billy.

The heat of her body made Billy squirm with anticipation. He wasn't laughing as hard now. Instead, he was completely focused on the source of the heat.

Long before the movie credits began to run, they were making out, passionately. Billy's breaths were short and quick; he recognized Vicki's breathing matched his—with the occasional groan thrown in. With his tongue buried in her mouth, he reached up and placed his hand on her right breast. She moaned and squirmed at his touch, moving in toward him. While Jimmy began to whine, Billy massaged her heaving chest and tried not to pass out from the oxygen overload.

Vicki finally threw the blanket off them and jumped up. "Whoa," she gasped, trying to catch her breath. "We have to stop before..."

"I know. I know. I'm sorry," Billy said. "I couldn't help it. I just..."

She dove back into his lap. "Don't you dare be sorry," she said. "I wanted it as much as you did." She took a deep breath and exhaled slowly. "Still do," she added.

Struggling to be a gentleman, Billy stood and escorted Jimmy to the front door. It took forever to say goodnight to Vicki. "Thanks for dinner and the movie," he whispered between kisses. "I don't think I've ever laughed so much in my life."

"Me too," she said, kissing him back. "I'm glad you're not turned off by my stupid sense of humor." She shrugged playfully. "It's not my fault my dad raised me like a boy."

"A boy?" Billy said, kissing her neck. "You're the furthest thing from a boy I've ever known."

She moaned again, making him feel like he was ready to explode. "I've never wanted to be with someone as much as you, Billy," she whispered.

He took a few deep breaths to get his feet under him. "I should go before..." Grinning, he raised his eyebrows.

She laughed and nodded in surrender. Going to one knee, she gave Jimmy the final kiss of the night. After wearing some heavy dog slobber, she asked the mutt, "Can you please give me a smile before you go home, Jimmy?"

The dog curled his front lip and bared his teeth.

She laughed. "Good boy," she said, scratching his neck a few more times.

On the way out, Billy caught a quick glimpse of the photo that stared back at him—judgmentally—from the mantle. *No matter how good things get, Dalton's never going to go away*, he thought. *One way or another, he's always going to be around.* Billy's mood plummeted from ecstasy to depression in one single breath.

On their way home, Billy caught some flashing blue lights in his rearview mirror, quickly closing in behind him. "The police can't be pulling me over," he told Jimmy. But when the cruiser got inches from his rear bumper and blasted its siren, Billy's heart jumped into his throat. "No. No," he said aloud, "this isn't good."

Although Jimmy tried to jump up to investigate, it took him a moment or two to get to his haunches. A low growl began to rumble in his diaphragm.

"Shhhh, Jimmy," Billy said, quickly pulling over to the shoulder of the road. He shut off the ignition, silencing the earsplitting clunker. With trembling hands, he leaned over the passenger seat—pushing the big mutt out of the way—and grabbed the car's registration from the glove box. Just then, the cop pounded on the passenger side window, making both Billy and Jimmy jump.

The dog began barking his head off, his nose pressed to the passenger's side window and his teeth bared.

"No, Jimmy," Billy reprimanded in a strained whisper, leaning over again and trying to roll down the window. "You're going to get us into more trouble."

The cop's silhouette disappeared from the window, while Jimmy continued to snarl and yap.

A moment later, there was a knock on the driver's side window. "License and registration," the police officer demanded.

By now, Jimmy was losing his mind.

With the blinding spotlight flooding his rearview and side mirrors, Billy fumbled to slide his license out of his wallet. "Yes, sir," he mumbled. It was the first time he'd ever had to speak to a cop, making his breathing shallow and his heart thump hard in his chest. As his sweaty hand passed the license and registration over, he spotted the legal inspection sticker in the corner of the windshield. *At least I'm okay there*, he thought, not feeling as much relief as he'd hoped.

"Any chance you can get the dog under control?" the cop asked.

Billy half shrugged. "He's just scared, that's all."

The cop shook his head and peered at Jimmy, who was wailing away. "Do you know why I pulled you over?" he asked in a deep, authoritative voice.

Billy shook his head. "I know I wasn't speeding..."

The man nodded. "No, you weren't. But I'm sure that folks in the next town over can hear you driving around within the speed limit."

Billy swallowed hard, making Jimmy growl.

"Stay in the car, both of you," the cop said. "I'll be right back." He disappeared, lost in the blinding light.

Billy turned to Jimmy. "Are you crazy?" he asked the incensed mutt. "You're going to get us both locked up."

Jimmy's barks were reduced to whimpers.

"Shhhh," Billy told the dog through gritted teeth.

Jimmy finally calmed himself.

They sat in relative silence, Billy's window cracked enough to hear the police radio squelch a few times followed by garbled voices, their messages unclear. Minutes—or what seemed like days—later, the cop reappeared in the driver's side window, startling both Billy and Jimmy again.

While Jimmy started in on his tantrum again, the cop handed back the license and registration to Billy, along with a ticket.

"Oh no," Billy said aloud.

"Your driving record's clean so I've only issued you a warning this time," he yelled over the dog.

"Thank you, sir," Billy stammered.

"Get the exhaust pipe patched up," he yelled. "Nobody wants to hear all that noise."

"I will," Billy yelled back, while Jimmy nearly frothed at the mouth.

The cop peered at Jimmy again. "He's not very well behaved, is he?"

Instantly, Billy's nervousness was replaced by the instinctive need to defend his friend. "Actually, he's a very good boy. You're just scaring him."

The cop shook his head again. "The next time you get pulled over, it's a seventy-five dollar fine," he promised.

"That's a half week's pay," Billy blurted.

Jimmy barked his objection.

"Just get it fixed," the officer said. "I'll be watching out for you." Without another word, he disappeared back into the bright light.

"Great," Billy said under his breath, as the cop headed back to his cruiser, "just great." Then it hit him. "No more iced coffees or frozen lemonades," he told Jimmy, who was just starting to wind down. "I can't afford them and get the car fixed too." He shook his head. "Unreal."

Billy waited another minute before the cruiser's spotlight went black and the rotating blue lights faded. The cop pulled back onto the road, driving away. In the welcome darkness, Billy started the ignition and cringed when the motor roared to life, howling into the night like the ferocious beast it was. He looked at Jimmy. "Thanks for trying to help," he told the mutt, "but next time, let me take care of it...or we'll both end up in jail."

Sighing heavily, Jimmy lay back down in the passenger's seat.

Billy and Jimmy pulled into their driveway to find Sophie sitting alone in her car. Billy shut off the roaring Honda and knocked on her side window, making her jump; it was a reaction that seemed a bit extreme to Billy. "Sorry," he said through the glass, "I didn't mean to scare you." He then laughed, thinking she was kidding for leaping out of her skin. But he quickly realized she wasn't kidding. "Are you coming inside?" he yelled.

She shook her head, but didn't roll down the window. "I'm listening to music," she yelled back.

Billy paused in the silence. *What music?* he asked himself, shaking his head. "Whatever," he said, before heading for the house. "Come on, boy," he told Jimmy.

The dog followed but looked back at Sophie every step of the way.

Billy's dad was half asleep in his recliner, watching the tail end of a late movie. "Where have you been?" he asked, indifferently, and yawned.

"At Vicki's," Billy said.

"Jimmy too?"

Billy nodded. "I think he likes her more than I do."

The old man laughed.

Billy pulled his check from his wallet and handed it to his dad. "I'm not sure if I should ask Arlene about it, but..." He shook his head. "I think some of my pay's missing."

The old man studied the check and grinned. "It's not missing, Billy," he said, "it's been taken by the government." The grin turned to a cynical chuckle. "Welcome to the world of paying taxes, son. It sucks, doesn't it?" His face turned serious, almost angry. "Now you know what it feels like to help pay for people who'd rather stay in bed and sleep than go to work and carry the same weight we do." His grin returned. "It makes you think about the world a little differently when you have to help pay for its problems, doesn't it?"

Billy nodded. It was a hard slap of reality. *I never got taxed cutting grass, delivering newspapers or washing dishes*, he thought and headed to his bedroom—where he could rewind every second of his night with Vicki and then text her until he and Jimmy passed out.

Chapter 10

By midweek, Billy approached his mother. "Mom, can I borrow a few bucks until I get paid again?"

"For what?" she asked, not paying any real attention to the request.

"Flowers for Vicki," Billy blurted, excited and leery of her response at the same time. "I should have brought her some on our first date, but I didn't think of it at the time."

His mom looked up and grinned. "It's nice that you want to bring your girlfriend flowers, Billy, but I'm broke until Friday. Go ask your father."

His heart sank. "But Mom..."

"If it can't wait, then you need to ask your father for the money." Smiling again, she grabbed her purse to go to work.

Billy shook his head and headed for his room to weigh his options.

That afternoon, Billy caught his dad in the driveway, tinkering under the hood of his truck. Billy took a deep breath and approached the old man. "Dad, can I borrow a few bucks until pay day?"

His dad came out from under the hood and looked at him, wiping his greasy hands on an old, dirty rag. "What do you need it for?" he asked, setting his eyes upon Billy.

Billy's mind raced. "Ummm...for gas. I'm almost on empty."

The big man smirked; it was the same stupid grin his mother had just worn. "How much do you need?"

"Twenty bucks," Billy said reluctantly.

"Twenty bucks?" his dad repeated, reaching for his wallet. He pulled out a crisp green bill and extended it toward Billy. "That ought to get you somewhere."

"Thanks, Dad," he said, snatching the money out of the man's massive hand.

"You know this bank's closed until the loan's paid in full, right?"

"I know, Dad. I know. You'll get it back on Friday." Billy turned to leave when he caught his father's smirk again. *Shit,* he thought, *Mom must have told him about the flowers.* But the thought left him as quickly as it came. He was already spending the twenty dollars in his head. *Fifteen bucks for the flowers and I'll throw five into the gas tank so I'm not a liar.* He smiled widely, already picturing Vicki's excited face and the kiss that was sure to follow.

Billy stepped into Nick's Pizza and looked up at the giant plywood menus. "Vicki will definitely want a pizza," he thought aloud, "but what kind?" He half shrugged and looked down to see his mother hard at work.

"Let's get going on that Streamline Realty Group lunch order," she yelled, managing the small pizza shop like a seasoned football coach.

And the place runs like a machine, Billy thought. His mom was tough but kind and had high expectations of her staff, especially when it came to customer service. As there wasn't any real competition in town, the shop did a high volume of business. Prices were good and the quality of food even better. From the dough to the sauce, the ingredients were fresh. They even baked their own sub rolls for their famous meatball hoagies. Although his mom would never cheat Tony a penny—no discounts or free-bees—she made it up in the absurd quantities she served: over-stuffed sandwiches, loads of pizza toppings, and salads with extra dressing thrown in.

With a smile, Billy caught her attention and quickly placed his order. "Large tuna sub, with provolone, toasted."

"That's different," his mom teased.

He grinned. "And a small cheese pizza," he added.

Her right eyebrow jumped. "Hungry today?" she asked.

He shook his head. "The pizza's for Vicki. I'm bringing her lunch."

The heavy-set woman smiled. "So *to go* then?"

Billy nodded. "Yes, please."

"I thought you were broke?" she said.

Billy smirked. "Dad just let me borrow twenty."

"What about the flowers?"

Billy nodded. "I need to pick them up after I leave here."

"Lunch and flowers...that's a lot to ask of twenty dollars," she teased. "You must be swinging by the cemetery for the flowers."

Billy chuckled at her twisted sense of humor. "We'll see what this lunch costs me," he said, "and whatever's left will go toward the flowers...and some gas for the Honda."

"Gas too?" she said, whistling. "Someday, you need to show me how you do it."

Billy shook his head, trying not to blush.

She laughed and gestured toward the dining room. "Mark's over there. He was giving me a hard time about not seeing you for a while." Billy's mother played the role of mom for lots of the town's teenagers—Billy's friends, as well as others who fre-quented the shop.

Billy opened the sliding glass cooler and grabbed two bot-tles of iced tea from a rainbow of different soft drinks. "I'll go see him," he said, exhaling deeply.

From the moment he entered the small dining room, Mark yelled out, "Look who's here! My long, lost friend William Baker has come to have lunch with me."

Billy shook Mark's hand and took a seat across from him. "Well, not quite," he admitted.

Mark looked at the two bottles of water. "Vicki?" he asked.

Billy smirked. "I'm meeting her at the park."

"A picnic," Mark teased, "how sweet."

Billy blushed slightly. "Sorry, bro, I know I haven't been around."

Mark laughed. "Will you stop," he said. "I was just messing with you." He studied Billy's face. "She seems like a great girl. I'm happy for you guys."

"Vicki's not like any other girl," Billy said.

"How do you know?" Mark asked, grinning. "It's not like you've been with anyone else."

"You know what I mean."

"Actually, I don't."

"I can't stop thinking about her and when I do, even for a moment, I get excited all over again...because I realize we're actually together." He shook his head. "Between you and me, I still can't believe she's with me."

"You're not the only one who can't believe it," Mark said, laughing.

"Gee, thanks."

"Relax," Mark said. "Don't go getting all sensitive on me."

A grin replaced Billy's scowl. "What do you say we hook up on Saturday and..."

"Can't," Mark answered. "It's Nathan's send-off party. He's heading off to boot camp next week."

"Oh yeah, the party I wasn't invited to."

"Yup, that's the one." Mark worked a mischievous grin into his face just to torment his old friend.

"Whatever," Billy said, smiling. "Lunch on Friday then?"

Mark nodded. "I'm always here, bro." He matched his friend's smile. "By the way, I ended up going to see that stalker movie all by myself."

Billy cringed. "Sorry about that," he said. "How was it?"

"Besides the brief nudity, it sucked," Mark said.

They both laughed.

"Oh, and you just missed Charlie. He was in here a little while ago."

Billy was taken aback. "Charlie was here?" he asked, his mind sent into a spiral. "That...that's good."

Mark nodded. "Yup, it looks like his heart's finally on the mend and he's decided to come out of hiding."

Billy was at a loss for words. "That's good," he repeated. "I'll have to go see him soon."

"He was asking if I'd seen you...if we'd talked recently."

Billy's eyebrow rose.

"I know," Mark said. "I thought it was strange too." He shrugged. "I just figured he's been out of commission for a while, so I didn't bust his balls too hard."

"That's good," Billy said for a third time, trying to avoid the topic any further. "Well, I have to run, bro."

Mark smirked again. "That's right, you have a tea party to get to."

Shaking his head, Billy stood, shook Mark's hand again and headed for the counter to grab the small pizza box and a warm sub wrapped in orange paper, sticking out of a thin brown paper bag.

When he took out his wallet, his mom shook her head. "I got it, money bags," she whispered.

"Thanks, Mom. You're the best."

"I bet you say that to all the girls," she joked.

He shrugged. "Well, definitely one other girl," he said.

She laughed again. "Go have fun," she said, before returning to the frantic orchestra she conducted. "Where are we with that Streamline Realty Group order?" she barked.

As Billy stepped out of the place, he laughed. *Mom has such a loud, obnoxious voice,* he thought, knowing it was just another souvenir from her years of playing general on the lunch rush battlefield.

Vicki had told Billy to meet her at the park at noon. He had no idea what the day promised, but he didn't care. *She's going to be there and that's all I need to know.*

When he first spotted her, a wave of pure joy washed over him, making him feel giddy. He actually giggled. Vicki was seated on a blanket that she'd spread out on the ground. There was a wicker basket—obviously filled with goodies—as well as plastic plates and cups. "So we are having an official picnic," Billy said aloud, a statement he would have mocked not so long ago. He pictured Mark's face and chuckled. *But now*, he thought, *I can't think of a better way to spend an afternoon*. He hurried to her.

Juggling the pizza and tuna sub in one hand, he proudly handed Vicki a small bunch of flowers with the other.

She was taken aback. "That's so thoughtful of you, Billy," she finally said. "They're beautiful. Thank you."

He smiled, pleased with her reaction. "But not as beautiful as you," he said, kneeling on the blanket and giving her a long kiss.

"Thank you," she repeated, once they came up for air.

They quickly settled into their little corner of the world and began picking away at their lunch. "You never talk about your family, Billy," Vicki said. "Why?"

He shrugged. "Because I'd rather talk about you and me," he answered honestly.

"But your family *is* who you are or at least where you came from. And I want to know everything I can about that."

He shrugged again. "My sister, Sophie, and I have been close ever since I can remember. She's been acting strange as hell lately, but there's nothing she wouldn't do for me and that's definitely a two-way street."

Vicki squeezed his arm, clearly touched by the sentiment.

"My mom's the coolest person ever. What you see is what you get with her."

Vicki nodded. "My dad's been taking me and Barry to Nick's Pizza for years," she said. "I've always loved your mom."

Billy smiled. "Me too."

She squeezed his hand tighter.

Billy took a drink and stared off into space for a moment. "And then there's Jimmy," he said with a smile, "who's been more like a brother to me than a pet."

Vicki smiled. "He's easy to love, that's for sure. You must have some funny memories, growing up with him by your side."

"I do," Billy said, nodding. Suddenly, he was filled with excitement over the mental pictures he was anxious to share. "Each winter, Jimmy knocked down every snowman Sophie and I made, before we were ever finished. Now that I think about it, I'm not sure we ever finished building a complete one."

Vicki laughed.

"Once, we got as far as putting on the carrot nose before I heard Jimmy rounding the house and picking up speed. The big oaf sounded like a train, chugging along at full speed. Then, like a football linebacker, the crazy mutt barreled the snowman over into a cloud of white powder." Billy laughed. "I remember standing there, holding the snowman's two stone eyes and wondering why Jimmy loved to torture me."

Vicki laughed harder.

"I'd yell at him, but the funny dog just tilted his head toward the sky, snapping his jaws like some demented piranha, trying to eat as many snowflakes as he could."

"Those are great memories," Vicki said.

Billy nodded, still entranced in the past. "At Christmas time, Jimmy always drank from the tree stand and dried out one pine tree after the next, turning each one of them brown. Although he got yelled at by everyone in the house, it was like he couldn't help himself...like he had some awful thirst that needed to be quenched, regardless of the consequences." He chuckled at the fond memory. "At night, Jimmy and I would lay on the couch, hypnotized by the twinkling lights on the Christmas tree. The ornaments were like our family album, telling our history. From the painted pine cone I made in first grade to the ornaments my mother bought at every place we visited throughout New England..." He shook his head. "There was so much for me and Jimmy to look at." Billy looked up to find Vicki staring at him and smiling. "What?" he asked.

"You're just cute, that's all," she said. "I love when you tell a story and get all excited. You look like a little boy."

He shrugged. "When our family took down the tree each year," he added, "most of the ornaments were lying on the floor behind it and many of the branches were snapped in half." He laughed. "Christmas tree stands are definitely Jimmy's favorite watering hole."

Vicki laughed along with him until they sat in the quiet for a few moments. "What about your dad?" she asked, breaking the silence. "I don't think you've ever talked about him."

Billy's eyebrow rose. "There's not much to tell, I guess. He's always on the road, working, and..." He stopped.

"Do you have a problem with him?" she asked, studying his eyes. "Daddy, son kind of stuff?"

He laughed. "Not really." He thought about it. "My old man isn't perfect by any stretch, but he's always been there for me when I've needed him."

"Well, that's good."

"It is," Billy agreed. "There was this one time when Jimmy got hit by a car and I thought I was going to lose him..." As Billy shared the details with Vicki, his mind completely returned to that fateful day. He could still feel every emotion as strongly as he'd felt them back then.

Billy was around ten years old and had just returned home from a week at summer camp. Jimmy was so excited to see him that his body was nearly folding itself in half from his wagging tail. As cars whooshed by between them, Billy screamed for the dog to "stay!" But the excited mutt bolted out into the street, sprinting toward a long-awaited hug from his master. Billy remembered how he'd closed his eyes tight just as the car's front grille was inches from Jimmy's torso. All at once, there were screeching tires, a loud thump and a pitiful whimper—and then everything went quiet. Billy could still feel the panic that had welled up inside of him; how his feet felt like they were chained to the sidewalk. No matter how badly he'd wanted to, he couldn't move.

And he couldn't breathe, making him feel dizzy and nauseous. Finally, something released inside of him and he managed to run to Jimmy's side. The dog was wheezing terribly, struggling to take in oxygen.

A half hour later, the vet came out from behind a swinging door and reported, "There's some internal bleeding and it's bad. We could operate and try to save him, but it's going to cost twelve hundred dollars."

"What?" Billy's dad screeched, already shaking his head. "How much to put the dog down?" he asked.

Everything in Billy's body seized up at the mention of killing Jimmy. "No!" Billy screamed.

"But he's suffering, son," the old man said, going to one knee to look Billy in his tear-filled eyes.

Panicked, Billy looked to the vet. "Sir, if you operate, can you fix him?"

The doctor nodded. "I'm pretty sure we can."

His dad opened his mouth to say something else, but didn't.

"Please, Dad...please," Billy begged. "I'll never ask for another thing again...ever!"

"Billy, we can't afford it."

"You never have to buy me another Christmas present or birthday gift. I'll even get a job and pay you back," Billy pleaded between sobs.

Still, the big man shook his head.

Billy's mom grabbed his dad's arm and whispered, "Norman, I don't think we can afford not to..."

The old man took a deep breath and was clearly thinking it over, which took a lifetime. He stood and looked at the vet. "Twelve hundred is extortion," he barked, "but go ahead and do it."

The vet nodded.

"But you'd better save the mutt," the big man warned; it was as close to a threat as Billy had ever heard from his father's mouth.

Overwhelmed with emotions he'd never felt or could even begin to define, Billy felt like he was going to collapse. He looked into his father's eyes; locked onto them for a moment. No matter what his father did or said in the future, regardless of what might come, Billy's love for his dad was sealed for all time.

Billy emerged from the vivid memory and looked at Vicki. "I later found out that my father put in two months of overtime to cover the vet bill." He smiled. "And I promised myself I'd never forget what he did for me...and Jimmy."

"Wow," she said, "he sounds like a great man."

"He's had his moments," Billy said and left it at that.

They sat in silence for a while. As Billy sprawled out on the blanket, he scanned the park. It was the very place that he, Charlie and Mark had claimed as their own when they were children—just a few years back. Now, he was acting all grown up, sipping iced tea and eating a sandwich, watching the kids run and scream and laugh and play. He looked at Vicki and felt both elated and peaceful. The sun was going down, casting a soft glow across her face and hair. *She looks like an angel*, he thought. *And I'm the luckiest guy on earth.*

Neither was in any hurry to leave. They lay back and watched as family after family packed up and went home for the night. Soon, they were alone in the fading light.

They kissed, passionately, Billy pressing his body against hers until he could not only feel her body heat but the thump of her excited heartbeat. He kissed her lips, her cheeks, her neck and her ears—soliciting a giggle. He lingered there a moment. She pulled him in tighter. After running his hand down her body, he let it rest between her legs. Vicki automatically flinched, pulling away from him. "What is it, Vicki?" he asked, immediately withdrawing his hand.

She sat up on the blanket, struggling to catch her breath.

"Are you okay, babe?" he asked. "I...I didn't mean to..."

She turned and grabbed his hand. "It's not you, Billy. Trust me. It's just an old trauma that I have to get past."

Billy swallowed hard. "If you don't want to talk about it, I understand but..."

Vicki shook her head. "I...I was young," she blurted, "maybe seven, when my Uncle Buddy touched me between my legs."

Oh no, Billy thought. "Did you tell your parents?"

Vicki nodded. "I did," she admitted, still fighting to keep the ancient monster behind the door, "but they pretty much brushed the whole thing under the carpet."

Billy gently placed his hand on her arm. "I'm so sorry," he whispered.

She shook her head. As she tried to breathe, her hands began to tremble and her eyes slammed shut. The first few tears rolled down her cheeks.

"If it's too difficult, Vicki," Billy said, "you don't need to..."

She opened her eyes. "But I do," she whispered. After taking a few deep breaths, she closed her eyes again and commanded every ounce of her strength and courage to go back to a time and place she'd obviously spent her entire life avoiding.

Dad wasn't around, as usual, probably working out on the road, she surmised. *Mom was also out, which was unusual...I think at some wake or funeral*, she tried to recall.

Uncle Buddy had made her and Barry mac and cheese, their favorite dinner, and had them put on their pajamas. He'd let them stay up a little later—past their bedtimes—to finish the movie, *The Lion King*. He put Barry to bed first and returned to the couch. "Do you want to watch something else, maybe another movie?" he asked her.

Vicki shrugged. She wanted to, of course, but knew her mother wouldn't approve.

"No one has to know but you and me," Uncle Buddy said, smiling. He patted the seat beside him on the couch. "Come snuggle with me," he whispered.

Vicki thought it was strange—*something feels wrong*, she thought—but it was her uncle. She took the seat beside him. The animated movie, which Vicki could no longer recall, was only a few minutes in when Uncle Buddy placed his hand on her knee. She remembered her body locking up, freezing in place. *Something is wrong*, she confirmed in her racing mind, while fear filled her small body.

"You look just like your mom," Uncle Buddy whispered, "... very pretty."

Vicki opened her mouth to reply when he slid his hand down her leg and rested it on her crotch, on her privates. As if she were spring loaded, she jumped up. "I need to go to bed," she whimpered, the first few tears already breaking free.

"Whoa, whoa," he said. "What's the matter, sweetheart? I didn't mean to..." He stood.

Vicki bolted down the hallway as fast as she could run, slamming her bedroom door behind her and locking it.

"Vicki, don't be silly. My hand slipped." He tried to turn the doorknob.

She froze again, terrified. She tried to scream but it got stuck in her throat. She felt like she was choking, as panic attacked her from within. She could hear his large hand on the door again.

"Open the door now!" Uncle Buddy said more firmly.

He's getting angry, Vicki thought but remained frozen in place.

"You're being foolish and your mom and dad aren't going to like it."

Her body was paralyzed; even if she'd wanted to unlock the door, she was physically incapable. She couldn't breathe right and felt dizzy.

Uncle Buddy pounded on the door one last time before stomping back down the hallway.

Vicki suddenly felt relieved, until she remembered Barry was alone in the room next to hers. *His door's unlocked*, she realized and tried to stand; the terror in her battled against her need to protect her little brother. She couldn't stand. Instead, she rolled herself into the fetal position and wept mournfully. *I can't help Barry*, she knew, unsure whether Uncle Buddy would do the same to him. In an instant, she was filled with more guilt than her young mind could handle.

It could have been minutes or hours—Vicki couldn't tell which in her hellish state—when there was another knock on her bedroom door. "Go away," she shrieked, surprised that she'd finally gotten the words out.

"Vicki, it's Mommy. Open the door, baby girl."

Bursting into tears, Vicki struggled to her feet to unlock the door.

Her mom rushed in. "What's the matter, babe? What happened?" She looked down at the floor, drawing Vicki's attention to a puddle of urine she didn't even realize she'd been sitting in. Her mom fell to her knees, pulling Vicki in for a hug. "You're okay now." She looked into her eyes. "Tell me, baby. Tell Mommy what happened?"

"Is Barry all right?" Vicki asked in a squeak.

"He's fine. He's fast asleep."

A few heavy pounds slid from Vicki's tiny shoulders. She then told every detail.

Vicki's mom scooped her up into her arms and carried her to the bathroom where she bathed and clothed her. "You can sleep in my bed tonight," she said. "We'll snuggle."

Vicki's body convulsed.

"You don't want to?" the woman asked.

Vicki shook her head. "I do, Mom. It's just that...that's what Uncle Buddy told me he wanted to do." She broke down in sobs again.

Her mom's face turned crimson red. She comforted Vicki before depositing her into the big bed. "I just have to call Daddy," she said, "and tell him..."

"No, Mom. Don't tell Daddy," Vicki pleaded.

"Oh sweetheart, you didn't do anything wrong. And Daddy needs to know."

Vicki tiptoed to the bedroom door and eavesdropped while her mom screamed into the phone. "I know the piece of shit's your brother, but either you do something about it or I'm calling the cops!"

Her mom returned to bed and they held each other close through the night. Vicki might have even been able to sleep had she not felt riddled with guilt for not being able to protect her little brother, Barry—a secret she decided to keep to herself.

Vicki awoke from the old nightmare and looked at Billy. "We never saw Uncle Buddy again," she said. "And no one ever talked about *the incident* again either," she added, painfully.

"What happened to your asshole uncle?" Billy asked, immediately sorry that he did.

Vicki took a deep breath. "From what I was told, my dad confronted him and don't you know...the piece of garbage denied it. He never came around again after that. I overheard that Dad beat him up pretty badly, though no one talked about it." She looked over at Billy and shook her head, her eyes filling with old tears. "And we never attended Uncle Buddy's funeral when he died from cancer."

Billy hugged Vicki tightly; there was nothing sexual about it—just a hug that showed his undying support.

Vicki wiped her eyes and gazed at Billy. "I've never told anyone this story," she whispered. "Not a soul."

Billy squeezed her tighter, realizing just how important this moment was for them, understanding that a deep trust was being forged between them. Conflicting feelings churned inside him; he felt so sorry for the pain she'd endured in her past, but he was equally delighted that she felt close enough to him to share it. *And I feel the exact same way about her*, he thought.

"Just be patient with me, okay?" Vicki whispered. She took a deep breath. "I love you very much and I promise I'll come around, but please be patient with me."

Billy gently kissed her cheek. "Of course," he whispered. "There's no hurry for anything. We'll take it as slow as we need to take it." He stared at his brave girlfriend and vowed, *I'm going to do whatever it takes to be there for you and I'll wait however long it takes.* "I love you so much, Vicki," he added, "and I'm not going anywhere... unless you're coming with me."

While more tears poured from her eyes, she hugged him. "I love you too," she whispered, "more than you'll ever know."

I know, Billy thought, feeling them grow as close as two people had ever been.

Even at the animal shelter—working hard enough to sweat— Billy was drifting along in a state of joy and wonder. Jimmy, on the other hand, chose to sulk in the yard. Just as Billy completed the morning feeding and was starting to mop the floors, Arlene returned from the road where she'd found a homeless family—a stray mutt, named Macy, and her pups—living between two dumpsters.

"She must have foraged for garbage and probably hunted small animals to feed her young," she told Billy. "From the look of her, she's lived a pretty rough life."

Billy could hear the empathy and understanding dripping from Arlene's words and suddenly recognized he felt the same. *Poor thing,* he thought, while Vicki's face immediately vanished from his thoughts.

"We'll keep the family together," Arlene added. "Can you imagine being split up from your family and put into separate cages?"

"God, no," he said, feeling angry over the thought of it.

Arlene reached out to touch one of the puppies.

Macy lunged at her hand like it was a honey ham at Easter dinner.

Arlene retreated just in time to save herself an emergency room visit and a half dozen stitches.

Teeth bared, tail straight back, Macy looked mean and nasty—displaying how fiercely protective she was of her young.

"I'd be aggressive too," Arlene said calmly, after nearly getting her fingers bitten off.

Her hackles raised, Macy growled, snarled and bared her teeth—issuing all the warning signs.

"We just have to win over Macy's trust," Arlene told Billy.

"How long do you think it'll take?" he asked, feeling discomfort in his soul over the unfortunate animal's predicament.

She looked at him sadly. "You'll be a real college boy long before she comes all the way around."

Billy nodded. *Well, that sucks,* he thought, continuing to feel the physical price of true empathy.

That afternoon, the vet inoculated each of the pups with Macy's suspicious gaze supervising from a leashed position. "See, we're just helping your babies," Arlene told Macy, talking to the barking dog each time one of her pups was picked up and handled.

Macy's growls and snarls were eventually reduced to quiet whimpers and whines. When the pups were all treated, Arlene put the entire family into one cage—without being attacked—and watched as Macy gave each one of them a thorough bath.

Arlene turned to Billy. "You know, she might come around earlier than I thought."

"I hope so," he said.

Just before the end of the shift, Billy stuck his head into Arlene's office. She was seated behind a cluttered desk, shaking her frustrated head. She looked up. "Please don't tell me any of the animals have escaped," she joked. "I'm at capacity and I don't think I can take another crisis right now."

Billy laughed. "No, they're all fine, Arlene." He nodded. "Fed, clean and happy. Most of them are out in the yard playing." He shrugged slightly. "I...I was wondering whether I could get your advice on something?"

Arlene immediately dropped the handful of papers onto her desk and sat up straight, offering her full attention. "Step into my confessional," she teased, gesturing for Billy to take a seat across from her, "and tell me what's going on."

Billy was talking before his back end hit the seat. "I have a friend, he's actually my best friend, who screwed up really badly at the start of the summer."

"How badly?"

"The worst," Billy whispered, swallowing hard, "and I've tried everything to get him to confess and make things right, but..."

"But he won't," Arlene said, finishing the sentence.

"That's right," he said, shaking his head. "The problem is... when the truth finally comes out, it's going to hurt someone I care about." His eyes filled and he could suddenly feel every ounce of the heavy weight he'd been carrying around. "It's going to crush her," he whispered.

Shaking her head, Arlene locked onto his eyes. "You say this is your best friend?"

"We grew up together like brothers," Billy explained.

"Let me give you a piece of advice that your best friend may not want to hear but needs to."

Billy nodded.

"I've been on this earth for more years than I care to admit. Trust me, the truth always comes out." She smirked. "And justice is karma's twin sister. They're both bitches when you keep 'em waiting."

Billy exhaled deeply, making his lips quiver.

"The longer it takes for this truth to come out, the more painful the consequences will be," she added. "Good or bad, it's just how things work."

"That's what I was afraid of," Billy said, picturing Vicki's sweet face contorted in pain over the real reason for her cousin's death.

"You need to tell your friend he's being selfish and that he's hurting people by withholding the truth."

"I have," Billy said, "believe me, I have." He nodded. "But I'll keep trying. Thanks, Arlene." He turned to leave.

"Billy?" Arlene called out.

He stopped, facing her again. "Yeah?"

"Would your best friend happen to be *you*? Are you the one who needs to confess to somebody?"

"No, it's my buddy who screwed up," he said, sorrowfully, "though at this point, I feel just as guilty for it."

Billy and Jimmy walked out of the animal shelter together to find a dark, unmarked cruiser parked alongside the Honda. *Oh no*, Billy thought. He was a few feet from his car when a massive man with a shiny scalp exited the cruiser and approached him. "Name's Detective Swanson," he introduced himself, discarding the toothpick that dangled from his lips. "And you're Billy Baker, am I right?"

Billy nodded, thinking, *I'm so screwed. I should have just left the car home and gotten a ride to work.* He could tell right away that Detective Swanson had been waiting for him; his heart began pounding in his chest.

Jimmy studied the man, without any reaction one way or another.

"I adopted a dog from this place a few years back," the older cop said with a smile.

"We did too," Billy said confused, patting Jimmy on the head.

"Have you seen Charlie Philips?" Swanson asked, putting an abrupt end to the small talk and kicking off an obvious interview.

"No," Billy lied, "I haven't seen him around for a while now." He swallowed hard, thinking, *I wish this cop was here to bag me for the loud exhaust pipe.*

Jimmy collapsed to his front paws and looked up, watching the tense exchange—but staying out of it.

Detective Swanson studied Billy's face for a few awkward moments, making Billy swallow even harder. Billy could feel himself blush. *I hope my face doesn't give me away*, he thought.

"Do you know anything about him having a problem with Dalton Noble?" the seasoned detective asked. "Maybe some bad feelings between them over a girl named Bianca?"

Although the big man had a friendly demeanor, Billy could tell he was asking questions for answers he already knew. "Not that I know of," Billy lied again, trying to avoid any extended eye contact. "At least he never told me about it."

"When's the last time you talked to Charlie?" the cop asked, writing into his spiral notebook with a ball point pen.

This guy's old school, Billy thought. "A couple of weeks ago," he replied.

"Where is he?" the cop fired back, picking up the questioning in both pace and volume.

Billy could feel Jimmy crawl closer to him; it actually felt like the dog gave him a nudge. "Home, I think. Like I said, I haven't seen him much this summer. I've been working a lot," Billy said, feeling the sweat drip down his back.

"Working a lot, huh?" Swanson repeated, peering into Billy's eyes again.

Billy quickly nodded.

With a smirk, Detective Swanson closed his notebook. "Let me ask you one more question."

"Sure."

"Do you know who Dalton Noble is?"

Billy swallowed hard again. "He's the kid who died in that bad car wreck on 88, right?" Billy said, surprised he could squeeze the words from his constricted throat.

"That's right. I met with his parents last week and they're in worse shape than he was the night he was lying on the hood of his car, bleeding to death." He searched Billy's eyes one last time. "Here's my card," Swanson said, handing it to Billy. "If you think of something you may have forgotten today, give me a call." He nodded. "I just came from Charlie's house. He wasn't home, but I asked his mom to have him come into the station so we can talk."

"Okay," Billy said, trying to limit the use of his shaky voice.

The detective bent down and scratched Jimmy's neck. "Good boy," he said, but he wasn't smiling.

Billy couldn't tell whether he was talking to him or the dog. And his skin crawled when the man took three steps before turning around and staring straight through him.

"Just make sure Charlie comes to see me, okay?"

Nodding one last time, Billy struggled for air but retained eye contact with the intimidating man.

As Detective Swanson slid into the Ford Crown Victoria's driver's seat, he muttered, "New inspection sticker. Smart kid." As he started the car, country music blared from its speakers.

After the unmarked cruiser left the parking lot, Billy sat with Jimmy in the Honda for fifteen minutes until his trembling ceased. *Damn you, Charlie,* he thought, and punched the steering wheel. "Damn you for all this bullshit!" he said aloud.

Jimmy lay on the front seat, his right paw covering his eyes. He even peeked out and whimpered a few times, as though he knew exactly what was going on.

"I know," Billy told the dog. "I know. This is really bad."

Billy turned the ignition and the Honda thundered to life. He looked around nervously. "And I can't drive this noisy pig again until it gets fixed," he told Jimmy.

Struggling to sit upright, the dog stuck his head out of the window, ready to catch a nice breeze on the way home.

Billy called Charlie's cell phone several times until he picked up. "There's a cop, a detective, who was waiting for me outside the animal shelter after work," Billy blurted. "He was asking about you...about the last time I talked to you."

"What did you tell him?" Charlie asked, panicked.

"I didn't tell him anything. I told him we haven't talked in a couple weeks."

"Oh man, this isn't good." Charlie was breathing heavily, nearly hyperventilating into the phone. "This isn't good at all," he repeated. "My mother told me that a detective just came by here, looking to talk to me," he said, thinking aloud. "Shit, it must be the same guy."

"He knows, Charlie."

"He knows what?"

"He knows you were involved in Dalton's accident or at least that you had a problem with Dalton over Bianca."

"You didn't tell him..."

"I didn't tell him anything," Billy interrupted in a volume just shy of a scream, "but I didn't have to. Just by the questions he was asking, he knows you had some bad blood with Dalton. He even mentioned Bianca's name."

"Oh God..." Charlie mumbled, and then there was silence. "Charlie?"

"Yeah?" he said, in the voice of a terrified five-year-old boy.

"You don't have a choice anymore. You have to turn yourself in." Billy cleared the emotion from his throat. "They'll eventually figure out what really happened that night and then it'll be worse for *everyone!*" Without realizing it, he nearly screamed the last word.

"I...I need time to...to think," Charlie stuttered.

"Just don't take too much time, Charlie," Billy said. "It'll make things worse."

Charlie dropped off the line.

Much worse, Billy thought, shaking his throbbing head. *You need to tell Vicki*, he told himself. *Somehow, you need to find a way to tell her.*

Charlie took a deep breath and reached under his bed for the shoebox. Removing the lid, he grabbed the .38 revolver and immediately placed it under his chin. *Just do it, you coward*, he told himself. *You're no good to anyone anymore. You were supposed to be an FBI agent, for God's sake. Now you're going to be a convict instead.* There were no tears this time; they'd dried up long ago. *It was no accident that night*, he told himself, finally facing the truth. *You killed that poor kid in a jealous rage and his family has suffered like dogs because of it.* With a steady hand, he jammed the snub-nosed pistol deeper into his flesh. *Just do it, chicken shit!* he screamed inside his head, feeling the cold steel against his skin. But he didn't squeeze the trigger; it wasn't for the lack of courage or even the will to live. Deep inside the recesses of his soul, he knew it would be the easy way out, cheating Dalton's family from any real justice. He pulled the gun down and looked at it. *They deserve better*, he thought. *They deserve closure.*

Chapter 11

The summer was more than half over, free falling toward autumn. Even being tormented over Charlie's terrible secret, Billy's feelings for Vicki were all-consuming. He awoke and immediately checked his cell phone. There was a text awaiting him from Vicki: the perfect start to a new day. *I love you so much.* It was only five words, but they were the greatest words Billy had ever read.

He typed back, *I love you more.*

Billy lay in bed for a few minutes with Jimmy, contemplating everything that had changed in just a few short weeks. "It's almost too good to be true," he told Jimmy, "but my relationship with Vicki is going better than I could have ever dreamed." When he and Vicki weren't together, they were talking on their cell phones or sending text messages to remind each other how they felt. Even still, every moment that passed, he was absolutely torn over his love for his girlfriend and his loyalty to his best friend. "I love Vicki so much, Lord knows I do," he told the attentive dog, "but I have no choice but to keep Charlie's secret." He shook his head. "Arlene's right though: the longer it takes for the truth to come out, the worse it's going to be for everyone involved...me and Vicki included."

Jimmy stood, yawned and hobbled off the bed. He looked up at Billy and whined.

"I'm coming," Billy said. "Hold your horses, I'm coming."

Vicki got a ride to Billy's house. She wasn't even through the door when she asked, "What are you planning, Billy?" She gave him a quick kiss, not realizing they were alone in the house. "I know you're planning something."

Billy shrugged. "I don't know what you're talking about."

Giggling, Vicki shook her head before locking onto Billy's eyes. "You're so stupid," she said. Even that statement made him feel like the luckiest man on the planet.

Billy could feel Vicki's love every moment he was with her. And being in love with her was not something he'd ever imagined was missing from his life. *There's no way I could have*, he thought. *I didn't have a clue just a few weeks ago. But now that I love her, there's no going back and life will never be the same.* That much he knew.

"I like your house," Vicki said, looking around the living room. "Can I get the grand tour?"

He shook his head. "I would, but my room's a mess right now," he said.

As if he'd caught it, Jimmy's head snapped up at the phrase *right now*.

"I can help you clean it," Vicki offered. "Remember the job we did on Mark's car?"

"Oh, I remember," Billy said, laughing. "But this is different. Unless you brought a dump truck, it wouldn't matter."

Her eyebrow stood at attention.

"There's no one else here, you know," he said, trying to redirect her thoughts.

They sat on the couch for a while, hugging and kissing— until Jimmy refused to be ignored and finally tapped in. Vicki petted Jimmy. Billy joined in and petted Jimmy. Once they stopped, the spoiled mutt pawed at them until they indulged him again. "You're such an attention vampire," Billy told the mutt.

Vicki laughed and kept right on massaging the drooling canine.

Billy watched her and, overcome with physical desire, he jumped in again—more aggressively this time.

"Did you make reservations?" Vicki asked, pinned under his full body weight.

"I did," Billy said, before kissing her one last time and rolling off of her to collect himself. "You're right. We need to get going."

While Billy and Vicki prepared to leave for their date, Jimmy whined like an angry tea kettle.

"Are you sure we can't take my boyfriend with us?" Vicki asked, stroking Jimmy's heavy coat again and peppering him with more kisses.

Shaking his head, Billy kneeled down to look Jimmy in the eye. "Sorry, buddy," he said, "but not this time." He leaned into Jimmy's floppy ear and whispered, "I'll tell you all about it when I get home."

Vicki chuckled, while Jimmy whimpered once more. It was his final plea to join them.

"I'm sorry," Billy said before grabbing his mother's car keys and escorting Vicki to the door.

Vicki loved art, so Billy had planned a secret date at the Muse Paint Bar downtown. After two long weeks, he needed a reprieve from the anvil he carried on his shoulders. He was thrilled when the night finally arrived.

It all started at Harry's Burgers and Beer, right next door to the paint bar, where he and Vicki ate hamburger sliders served at a high-top table in the back. It was a tiny joint, the walls lined with a menagerie of colorful beer taps. The burgers were hot and juicy, fried on a flat grill and delivered in record time. Each burger sat on a toasted potato roll, slathered in tangy house sauce and served with crispy sweet potato fries. The selection of craft beers was impressive, even if Billy and Vicki couldn't enjoy any of them. Instead, they ordered two hand-scooped vanilla shakes. Toward the end of dinner, Billy kept stealing peeks at his cell phone to check the time, concerned they might be late for their paint reservation. They'd had difficulty finding parking, which had really eaten into the clock.

Vicki gasped when they walked through the front door of the Muse Paint Bar. She turned and kissed Billy in front of everyone. "Thank you," she whispered. "Your thoughtfulness never ceases to amaze me."

Billy smiled widely, happy that he'd put in the time and effort.

Table-top easels with blank white canvases, six per table, were packed together like happy sardines. There were mostly women in attendance for a "Girls Night Out"—sipping wine and laughing loudly, as if they'd just been released from prison. "Oh, how sweet," one of them commented, referring to Billy and Vicki's arrival. "Young love."

Billy grinned slightly and then searched out his and Vicki's name cards. Sitting side by side on hard, mismatched chairs, they donned matching paint-stained aprons and exchanged a smile.

Garrett, the art instructor, was an earthy-crunchy type, his age betraying he was no more than one or two years out of art school—which was located just three blocks east. His hair was intentionally wild and unruly, mirroring his grungy clothes.

He started the night by pointing out each tool provided for the budding artists. A paper plate was used as a palate that had five globs of paint, along with a water can containing five brushes that ranged in various widths.

"Let's start with the filbert," Garrett said.

"Which one is that?" Billy whispered to Vicki.

She laughed and pulled it out of the water can. "Aren't you paying attention?" she asked.

"I am," he said, "but this guy could have been an auctioneer. He's talking so fast."

She laughed.

It was true. Garrett commanded the room and had a friendly demeanor, but he provided instruction like he was trying to sell heads of cattle at the best price; this only added to the laughter shared between Billy and Vicki.

"Be sure to clean your brushes with a paper towel before mixing new colors," Garrett said.

"Where are the paper towels?" Vicki asked, panicked.

"We don't have any at our table," Billy said and laughed aloud, catching a sideways glare from Garrett, who was in full motor-mouth mode.

"Details, details," Garrett said. "Let's see more blending and use your filbert."

"I'm so lost," Vicki sighed; frustrated, she blew a wisp of hair out of her soft eyes.

Billy looked around. Everyone was wearing the same comical facial expressions. "Everyone's lost," he whispered. "We just need to wing it."

It was warm in the place, too warm, and the matching aprons caused more sweat. Billy felt embarrassed by his growing sweat ring until he noticed Vicki's glistening forehead.

The painting began with a blue background; water on the bottom, sky on top. "Even brush strokes, side to side, and use lots of paint," Garrett said. "Don't let the canvas go dry."

Billy and Vicki mixed colors, which was a practice in trial and error, and took so much more time than Garrett allowed. They painted a white horizontal line three quarters up the canvas, adding in a range of gray mountains.

"And be sure to shade those," Garrett said, providing instruction like he presumed everyone was a seasoned artist.

Billy looked at Vicki. They laughed. "What a joke," he whispered.

Next, they added small green lines and blotches that were supposed to depict a thick tree line. Billy sat back and surveyed his work. *It looks like green lines and blotches*, he thought.

The lake consisted of strokes of blue, green and white, slathered in a sophomoric attempt to create the illusion of layers and depth. Every time Billy tried to make an improvement, he made things worse. He cursed himself under his breath, drawing giggles from his smiling date.

Vicki kept stealing peeks at his painting. In turn, Billy stole a quick glance at hers. *Yup, she's lost too,* he thought. They laughed again.

There were several more remarks about how cute it was to see the young couple out on a date. "You're the only guy in this whole place," one woman teased Billy. "If you'd come here alone, you would have had your pick of the litter."

Vicki's head snapped up, upset with the callous comment.

Billy shook his head. "But I did get the pick of the litter," he said sincerely.

Blushing, Vicki grinned and thanked him with her eyes— dabbing Billy's nose in mountain-gray paint. As they laughed together, she grabbed a paper towel and wiped away the paint from his face—though she could have never wiped away his smile.

Next, they painted a gray dock, with long posts on each side—which took much more attention and focus. The pine tree in the foreground was the final—and scariest—detail to tackle.

A quick bathroom break was the only way to enjoy the air conditioning in the place. Billy followed it up with a trip to the bar to purchase two bottles of cold water.

At the end of the night, each party took their turn standing up on Garrett's platform—a small stage with a red-bricked background—to take cell phone pictures of their finished masterpieces.

"Wow," the woman who took Billy and Vicki's photo said, "you guys did a great job!"

Too bad she's lying, Billy thought. He couldn't tell which painting was worse, his or Vicki's. *They're both horrible.*

Billy and Vicki stepped out into the humid night and stood in the shadows of the sidewalk, swapping paintings, along with a passionate kiss. "For me?" he asked, as he accepted her painting. The night air felt so good on his hot, sweaty neck.

She nodded. "I don't want it," she teased, and they both laughed.

He handed his painting to her. "Please tell me you'll keep it forever," he joked.

She nodded, her face serious. "I plan to."

For the second time that night, Billy struggled to take in air. He lifted her painting into the air and whistled. "Beautiful," he said.

She punched his arm and laughed, but he couldn't imagine owning a more valuable work of art.

They kissed again, more fervently—until they were mauling each other in the shadows of the night.

When she finally came up for oxygen, Vicki grabbed both of Billy's wandering hands and whispered, "Thank you for being so patient with me, Billy. I know it hasn't been easy." She kissed him again. "I want you just as bad as you want me, believe me, I do."

Billy nodded. "I know...and I'm ready whenever you are," he said, grinning.

Vicki leaned in and kissed him again. "Soon," she whispered. "I promise."

Billy suddenly felt lightheaded, as most of the blood in his head raced south toward his crotch. He smiled—on the outside. Beneath the surface, however, he fought the great battle of adolescence—coveted desires versus humility and selflessness. It was an all-out war, the body pitted against the heart and mind, struggling against desires that originated at the DNA level. As Billy gave Vicki's hand a gentle squeeze, his raging hormones pulled against the morals and ethics he'd been raised to believe. It was like he had an angel sitting quietly on one shoulder and a devil jumping up and down, screaming, on the other. "Soon," he said aloud, filled with hope. "How 'bout some ice cream then?"

"As long as I get to treat," she said.

He extended his hand.

She grabbed it.

"Good," he said, "'cause it may take a few sundaes to get my body temperature back to normal." While Vicki giggled, something in Billy's loins stirred again. *I'm not kidding*, he thought.

Billy had just lain down with Jimmy when he called Vicki's cell phone. "Please tell me you're thinking about me," he said.

"I'm thinking about you," she whispered.

"Good. Me too," Billy said, ignoring Jimmy's relentless pleas for attention. "And I'll be dreaming about you just as soon as I fall asleep."

Jimmy rolled onto his back and waited.

"I hope so," Vicki said.

Billy scratched Jimmy's belly. "Well, goodnight then."

"Goodnight," she whispered in her sweet voice.

As Billy worked Jimmy over, he could still hear Vicki's breathing. "Text me just as soon as you get up."

"I will," she promised.

"Okay then," he said, "goodnight." While Jimmy flipped over and prepared his nest, Billy reluctantly ended the call.

"What an amazing night," Billy told Jimmy, as he stared at the ceiling, recalling every magical detail. "We had burgers—that you would have really liked—for dinner. Then we..." He stopped.

The dog's snoring was light for a moment or two, but was picking up volume with each breath—like an old locomotive gathering steam.

Billy turned to his side and smiled. "Sorry to bore you, buddy," he whispered, "but you would have loved to hear about this one." Draping his arm over the dog's heaving chest, Billy closed his eyes and drifted off, thinking about Vicki to the rhythm of each breath.

It was Saturday morning. Billy grabbed his mom's car and headed straight to Charlie's house. By the third knock, Charlie answered the door; he remained in the threshold, not inviting Billy inside.

"Have you had enough time to think?" Billy asked, already feeling agitated.

"I went to see Detective Swanson yesterday," Charlie whispered.

Shocked, Billy's heart stopped for a millisecond. "You did?" he asked. "And what happened?"

Charlie lowered his voice until it was barely audible. "And I told him that I didn't have a problem with Dalton, and that I didn't know anything about the accident until I heard about it the next day."

"Oh Charlie," Billy said, his heart beating again—now from the pit of his stomach.

"What did you want me to tell him, Billy?" Charlie hissed, defiantly.

"Did he buy it?" Billy asked, shaking his head.

Charlie thought about it. "He asked me a few more questions," he said, shrugging, "but I think he might have. Either that or he doesn't have enough evidence to pursue it any further."

"Oh Charlie," Billy repeated, filled with disgust.

Charlie's eyes glazed over. "I went there with every intention of telling the truth, Billy, and doing the right thing for Dalton's parents," he whispered, torment plastered across his face, "but when I got there, I just couldn't do it. I was too scared."

"Who's at the door?" Charlie's mother barked from inside the house.

"No one, Ma," Charlie yelled, turning back to Billy. "I have to go," he said. "I'll talk to you later."

As the door closed in his face, Billy's head was spinning. "Sure you will, Charlie," he muttered, trying to exhale some of the toxins that poisoned him. "Asshole."

Ten minutes later, Billy met Sophie at the mall to pick out an anniversary gift for their parents. On his way, he forced himself to call Charlie's cell phone. It went right to voice mail. "Charlie,

I forgot to tell you that my mom's been asking why you haven't been around for dinner," he said, trying to sound friendly. "You might want to stop by and eat with us some night...if you want to that is." As he hung up, he thought, *Maybe if I can get him in my house, I can talk some sense into him.*

As Billy approached the mall's front doors, he spotted his sister sitting on the ground with her legs crossed, Native American style. "Hey," he called out. Sophie looked up but he could tell right away that his face didn't register for her. "Sophie?" he called out again, extending his hand. For a moment, she studied his face and then her distant eyes returned to reality.

"Billy..." she said with a smile. She grabbed his hand and, with Billy's help, jumped to her feet.

"Are you okay?" he asked, knowing something was wrong with her.

"Yeah," she said, "just daydreaming I guess."

"Did you wait long?"

She shrugged. "I don't know," she said and stepped into the mall, with Billy on her heels—confused.

Walking a few steps behind his sister, he suddenly detected the sweet stink of marijuana—again. *But it can't be,* he thought, and grabbed her arm, spinning her around to face him. "Sophie, have you been smoking weed?" he asked, smelling it on her but still not believing it.

She smirked. "Yeah, so what?" she asked, starting to turn around.

He yanked on her arm again. "Are you crazy?" he asked. "Do you have any idea how pissed Mom and Dad would be if..."

"Why, are you going to squeal on me, Billy?" she asked.

Billy's rising blood pressure was making him feel like the top of his head was about to pop off. He was so sick of that question. "No, I'm not going to squeal on you," he said, "but I...I just can't believe you're smoking pot, Sophe. I would have never thought..."

"...because you haven't felt the pressures of college yet, Billy," she snapped defensively. "Just wait until you're taking five classes and then working full time to pay for it. It's so stressful...you have no idea."

Billy still couldn't wrap his head around it. *No way, not Sophie*, he thought, but that perspective of her was clearly a delusion carried over from childhood.

"Grow up, Billy," she said, shaking her head. "It's only pot. It's not like I'm booting heroin to help me relax."

As she started to walk away, Billy took a few moments to realign his jaws.

For the next hour—while Billy tried wrapping his disillusioned head around his straight-laced sister using drugs as a crutch—they walked the mall, visiting one store after the next. From the strong smells of the leather shop to even more overpowering scents in the candle shop, Billy kept redirecting Sophie. "They're not going to want any of this crap," he said.

"How do you know what they want?" she asked.

"Well, I know Dad's not going to want a pumpkin scented candle. And I'm pretty sure Mom wouldn't appreciate matching leather vests." He shook his head. "Why don't we just get them a gift certificate or something?"

She considered it. "Maybe an overnight at a bed and break-fast?" she thought aloud. "It might be nice for them to get away for a night or two."

Billy snickered. "Dad at a bed and breakfast? Are you kidding me?"

"Whatever, Billy!" Sophie said, much too loudly. With a huff, she obnoxiously stormed away. "I'm hungry," she announced.

"What the hell..." he said, following after her. Before he knew it, they were standing in the food court.

Sophie made a beeline to The Wok and ordered sweet and sour pork.

Billy shook his head in disbelief. *She hates pork*, he thought, as he walked off toward the Italian vendor to grab a plate of bland ravioli.

They met at a small table in the middle. "You hate pork," Billy told his sister, as he took his seat. "And you hate Chinese food."

"Do I?" she asked, seriously. She took one bite and her face twisted in disgust. A moment later, she began picking at Billy's ravioli.

Shaking his head, he slid his plate over to her. "It's all yours," he said.

Sophie devoured the plate like she hadn't eaten in weeks, while Billy watched on—feeling both disgusted and amused. "What about something from Victoria's Secret?" she suggested, grinning. "They'd both enjoy that."

That's it, Billy thought. "Why don't we just get them separate gifts this year?" he said.

"Whatever, Billy," she barked again, making everyone in the food court stop and stare at them.

Billy stood and started for the mall exit. Although he found it easy to ignore all the bad looks sent his way, it was a little more difficult to process what he'd just learned about his sister—the angel.

Since he needed to get to work on time but had not yet been able to fix the loud exhaust on his car, Billy had no choice but to hitch a ride to the animal shelter. "Please, Mom," he pled, "why can't you drop me off on your way to work?"

"Are you ready to go right now?" she asked.

"Can't you just wait a half hour?"

She shook her head. "Your dad's not home until tonight and I need to get to the pizza shop *right now*," his mom told him. "Go next door and ask Mrs. Jacobs for a ride," she suggested with a smirk. "I'm sure she'd love to help out."

"Mrs. Jacobs?" Billy repeated. "Are you kidding me, Mom?"

She smiled. "You know what they say about beggars, right?"

"But her kids are animals."

"Which is probably why she'd love to get out of the zoo for a few minutes," his mom said, and smiled. "Besides, I thought you loved animals?" She grabbed her purse and headed for the front door.

"Yeah, the four-legged kind," Billy mumbled, before picking up the kitchen phone to call Mrs. Jacobs.

After securing the ride, he texted Vicki again. *I really wish I could explain how much I love you*, he wrote. *I'll call you just as soon as I get out of work.* He threw on his jeans and *Four Paws* t-shirt. He turned to Jimmy. "Ready to go to work, old man?" he asked.

The dog collapsed onto his belly, his snout lying flush to the floor.

"Come on now," he said.

Jimmy didn't budge.

"You're all done with that place, aren't you?"

Jimmy just lay there, staring off into space like Billy was invisible.

"I understand," Billy said. "That's fine." He scratched the scruff of Jimmy's neck. "How 'bout showing me that million dollar smile?"

Jimmy looked at Billy like he had a better chance of meeting God right there and then.

"Okay," Billy said, chuckling, "you don't feel like smiling. I get it." He started for the door. "I'll be back soon."

Jimmy stood, sighed once and, if Billy didn't know better, turned his back on him in disappointment.

Billy lingered at the front door for a moment, watching as Jimmy limped over to his plaid dog bed.

Mrs. Pringle stood up and hissed. Arching her back, she lifted her right paw with her invisible claws at the ready.

Jimmy tried to back up but was having a tough time, like his reverse gear was broken.

Billy shook his head. "Oh man," he muttered.

With his tail tucked between his legs and his head hung low, the passive mutt walked away from the vicious cat.

"Big baby," Billy whispered, closing the front door behind him.

Mrs. Jacobs' SUV was idling at the curb, with her three brats already screaming at each other in the back seat. "Oh man," he repeated.

Billy walked into the animal shelter, alone. "Jimmy quit," he informed Arlene.

She grinned. "The audacity of him," she joked, "no two-week notice or anything, huh?"

Billy laughed. "When Jimmy would rather hang out with Mrs. Pringle, you know he's made up his mind."

"I'd like to meet this Mrs. Pringle someday," Arlene said. "She sounds like a very strong female."

Billy smirked. "You can have her if you want," he joked.

Arlene laughed. "Still just a dog person, huh?"

Billy shook his head. "Not at all," he said. "Thanks to this place, I've learned that I love all animals." He shrugged. "But Mrs. Pringle is different. She's so manipulative, she's evil."

Arlene laughed hard. "A strong female indeed," she joked.

Billy laughed.

"Why don't you start on the interior kennels? I walked through there ten minutes ago and my eyes are still stinging from the stench."

"I'm on it," Billy said.

"And then you can help the vet with the inoculations when he comes in," she said. "You know how he gets if the animals aren't properly restrained."

Billy nodded. "I'll get the room cleaned up before he gets here." He thought about it and chuckled. "It probably sounds strange, but I actually like helping with the inoculations."

"It doesn't sound strange at all," she said. "There are few ways we can help these animals more."

Billy nodded. As he walked away, he realized—for the first time—that he was playing a vital role in the shelter's daily operations. *When I first started, I cleaned kennels, did tons of laundry and helped maintain the building and grounds.* He smiled proudly. *Now I help socialize both the dogs and cats, focusing on their health and adjustment.* He'd also become as comfortable with large dogs as he was with the smallest animals. *Which is a good thing,* he thought, *considering the majority of the shelter dogs are Labrador-sized.*

Two hours later, Billy rocked one of the whiny puppies—which had just received its shots—to soothe the trembling animal.

Arlene approached him, grinning. "Hey, I've been meaning to ask you," she said, "are you still floundering about what to take in school?"

Billy nodded. "If it were just school, I wouldn't be so freaked out. But I'm floundering about the future, you know...my life." While the puppy whimpered, Billy gently stroked its tan coat.

Arlene watched him rock the puppy in his lap. "I'm fairly certain it'll come to you before long, Billy," she said, smiling wider. "It might even slap you in the face when you least expect it."

Billy peered into his mentor's eyes. *She must know something I don't*, he thought. As if she already knew the answer, Arlene spoke with great conviction—like Billy's future was obvious and would become known to him soon. Although he had no idea what that answer was, he already felt better. "Thanks Arlene," he said and continued to pacify the tiny pup.

"My pleasure," she said, smiling so big she was starting to resemble a circus clown.

Staying later than his shift required—and not submitting the extra time to Arlene—Billy felt compelled to do everything he could to help. *I never realized how many animals get abused or abandoned*, he thought. Utilizing his years of computer experience, he updated the newsletter and put a new face on the Four Paws website. Once done, he posted photos and brief descriptions of the dogs and cats at the shelter that were available for adoption. He was becoming good at writing catchy blurbs in order to attract new pet owners. *But it's still not enough*, he thought. For a supposed menial job that started out with him cleaning cages, he now felt driven to help find homes for some of God's creatures that were at risk of being destroyed. *I need to do more*, he told himself, *whatever I can*.

Working deep into the early morning hours, Billy launched a social media campaign of awareness, as well as promoted several upcoming fund-raising opportunities. Somewhere along the way, his summer job had become a mission. *And my time* is definitely better spent trying to save animals than playing video games, he decided.

At one point, he looked up at the clock. *Shoot, it's later than I thought. I need to get home,* he thought. *Jimmy must be worried sick.* Billy picked up his cell phone and dialed his father. *He might get pissed at me,* he thought, *but he'll definitely come and get me.*

Billy was happy to forfeit sleep in order to spend time with Vicki. "Can I borrow your car?" he asked his mother the next morning.

"Where are you off to this time?" she asked.

"To see Vicki," he said, trying to keep his eyes open.

"Didn't you get in late last night?"

He nodded. "I had to work late." He smiled. "Sometimes the animals need help at night, too, Mom."

His mom opened her mouth to speak but nothing came out. She was speechless.

"I got a few hours of sleep," he said. "I'm fine."

"A few hours?" she repeated. "Wow, you must really like this girl."

Billy's yawn was challenged by his smile. *Oh, if you only knew,* he thought. "I have a question, Mom," he said.

"Well, let's hope I have the answer."

"When you and dad were dating, did he ever give you anything that sealed the deal for you guys?"

"What do you mean, sealed the deal?" she asked.

"You know, letting both of you know that you weren't going to kick it with other people."

"Kick it?" she asked again.

"Date...*go out* with...you know what I mean."

She smiled. "If you're asking, when did we start going steady, then it was when your dad gave me a hope chest."

"A hope chest? What's that?"

Her eyes lit up, as she went back. "It was a wooden cedar chest, intended to be filled with things that a couple would use in the future, together."

"I'm not looking to ask her to marry me," he said.

"I know that," the heavy-set woman said. "A hope chest was sort of a promise that..."

"That's ridiculous," Billy said, laughing. "If you're not going to help me, then..."

She shook her head. "Why don't you buy her a video game then?" she suggested sarcastically.

He laughed.

She grabbed the car keys from her purse and threw them to him. "Stay awake," she said, smiling.

"I will," Billy promised, as he headed for the front door. "Do they even make hope chests anymore?" he asked on his way out.

"I'm not sure," she yelled back. "You can have mine if you want." She then laughed loudly enough to wake the folks who lived on the next street over.

Billy jumped into the driver's seat, grabbed his cell phone and dialed. "Sorry about not calling you last night, babe, but I finished up late," he told Vicki. "I'll be there just as soon as I can."

"I can't wait," she said, "but please don't speed. I want you in one piece."

"I want you too," he said, hoping they were talking about the same thing.

She giggled. "Just hurry," she said, "but be safe."

He jumped off the cell phone and fired up his mom's car. It was hot out, the type of heat that made you wish you could peel off a few more layers. Billy stomped on the gas and headed straight to Vicki's.

I want her so bad, he thought, shifting a few times in his seat. While his subconscious took control of the steering wheel, his conscious mind pictured Vicki naked—finally pulling him onto her. *Oh my God*, he thought, *I want her so...* Suddenly, his eyes caught a ball of matted fur dart across a narrow alley. Instinctively, his right foot searched for the brake pedal and the car slowed to a crawl. *It's a dog*, he thought, immediately turning the car around to investigate.

Billy pulled up to the mouth of the alleyway and parked. He got out of the car and stepped lightly into the shadows. As he expected, a brown, mangy stray was half-concealed behind an overflowing dumpster. Billy whistled softly. The skeleton-thin dog wedged itself deeper into the corner. "It's okay, buddy," he whispered. "I'm not here to hurt you. I'm here to help you." Billy hurried back to his mother's car and grabbed the strip of beef jerky he'd spotted on the passenger seat—*probably meant for Jimmy*, he thought. Returning to the alley, he took a seat against the wall near the dumpster and threw a piece of the dried beef a few feet out in front of him. It only took a moment before the stray stirred behind the dumpster. "Looks like your nose works well enough," he told the hiding dog. It took a lot longer—three or four minutes—before the mutt peeked its head out, its eyes darting nervously between Billy and the beef jerky. "I won't hurt you," Billy whispered again, "I promise." He could see the anguish in the poor dog's eyes, as the animal weighed the pains of starvation against the risk of being abused at the hands of a stranger. Hunger finally won out and the mutt lunged for the beef. He hadn't chewed twice when Billy tossed him another small piece, not allowing the dog the time to retreat back behind the dumpster. "You're okay," Billy said calmly. "You're okay. I'm here to help you." One small piece of beef at a time, the emaciated dog crept closer to Billy, a fragile trust being forged between them with each small step. Nearly an hour had passed before Billy placed his hands on the trembling dog and gently petted him. Another half hour went by before he was able to entice the poor animal into his mom's car.

A cursory exam revealed two recent wounds, dark stains of blood disguised within the dirty, matted fur. "You've been in a fight recently," Billy told him, "and we need to get you fixed up before it gets infected."

Billy wrapped the mutt in a blanket, lay him on the passenger seat and was heading toward the shelter when he pictured Vicki's face again. "Oh shit," he told the dog and reached for his cell phone to discover that he'd missed five calls. "She must be very unhappy with me," he told the skittish dog. And that's when it hit him. One minute, he was fantasizing about having sex with Vicki and then for the next two hours he didn't give her gorgeous body another thought. Instead, his only concern was the safety and well-being of another lost, four-legged soul. "Vicki will get over it," Billy told the dog, nodding. "I'll call her later when we get to the shelter." He stroked the mutt's matted fur. "After we get you cleaned up and fed and treated by the vet."

As if he understood, the brown stray crawled a little bit closer to Billy.

"That a boy," Billy said, filled with a sense of purpose he'd never imagined feeling. "You're going to be as good as new before you know it." He laughed. *And now I'm starting to sound just like Arlene*, he thought, quickly adding, *and that's not such a bad thing.*

Billy called Vicki on his way to her house. *Wait 'til she hears what I just did*, he thought, his mind immediately returning to her beautiful body. *With any luck, we'll do some real celebrating tonight.*

"Hello?" she answered, clearly perturbed.

"I'm so sorry, babe," he blurted. "I was on my way to your house and..."

"Oh, Billy," she blurted, "thank God you're okay! I've been worried sick."

"I'm sorry, Vicki," he said. "I didn't mean to make you worry. On my way to your house, I saw a wounded stray that hadn't eaten in a while, so I had to stop and rescue him."

"That's wonderful, Billy, it really is," she said sincerely, "but why couldn't you take a minute to return my calls or texts?" The question was clearly more inspired by worry than anger.

"I'm sorry," he repeated. "My phone was on vibrate and the dog was in such poor shape that I became completely absorbed with saving him."

"I'm glad you saved the dog, babe," she whispered, her breathing changing from tense to relieved. "I am. It's just that I was scared and didn't know if something had happened to you."

"Something did," Billy said, excitedly.

"And what's that?"

"I saved an animal that needed to be saved," he whispered, proudly—conveying just how important the act was to him.

There was a pause. "I'm sorry, Billy," she said, her voice now gentle and loving. "I'm proud of you. It's just that when I hadn't heard from you, the first thing I thought about was my cousin's accident and..." She stopped.

"Oh, I'm so sorry," he blurted, his voice overwhelmed with more emotion than appropriate for the situation. Vicki's words were so sincere and unexpected that his eyes swelled with tears. The moment slapped him hard upside the head. *It's time to tell her*, he thought. *Just tell her and get it over with once and for all.* "We need to talk, Vicki," he managed. "I'll be there soon."

All twisted up inside, Billy rang the doorbell. The weeks of anxiety—being torn over divided loyalties and failed moral obligations—made him feel sick. As he tried running over some painless confession in his mind, Vicki's brother, Barry, answered the door—throwing him completely off guard. "What's up?" the muscle head said, stepping back to let Billy in.

"What's up?" Billy said, struggling to get a foothold on reality. "Hey, you'll be a senior this year, playing for varsity, huh?" he said, grasping to make a connection with the teenager.

Barry gawked at him, as though he was trying to summon enough interest to provide an answer. He finally nodded. "I started for varsity last year," he grumbled in response, clearly annoyed with having to waste his breath.

"Oh," Billy said, "what position?"

"Defensive end," he said, and started up the stairs. "Vicki, Billy's here," he yelled before slamming his bedroom door behind him

"All righty then," Billy said, while waiting alone in the living room. As he scanned past the photo on the mantel, he allowed his eyes—and mind—to remain on the dreadful declaration before him.

Vicki bounced down the stairs and threw her arms around his shoulders. She smelled clean and beautiful. "Hi, handsome," she said, kissing him.

Billy suddenly felt paralyzed with fear; every rehearsed word in his mind had vanished. "I need to tell you something, Vicki," he blurted, summoning every ounce of courage he could muster.

"What is it?" she asked, pushing away to look into his eyes.

Billy glanced back toward the picture on the mantel. "I need to talk to you about Dalton," he said in a hoarse whisper.

She squeezed his arm; it was clearly a negative reaction to the mention of her cousin's name. "Forgive me for bringing him up on the phone," she said. "I was just really scared, that's all. We don't have to..."

"It's not that," Billy said, shaking his head. "There's something I should have..."

She kissed him hard, stealing the rest of the confession from his lips. "Please, Billy," she pleaded. "I don't want to talk about Dalton. It's too painful and I'm tired of the pain." She shook her head, fighting off the mist that threatened to blur her vision.

"But Vicki, I..."

"No buts," she said, kissing him again. "Whatever it is, it's not going to change anything...or bring him back."

Billy gazed into her eyes and could see the deep hurt she'd suffered over her cousin's tragic death. *I don't want to cause her any more pain*, he thought, exhaling for the first time since he'd arrived at her house. *At least I tried to tell her*, he told himself, but he knew it was just another distortion of the truth. Part of him felt relieved that Vicki had let him off the hook; the rest of him, however, understood that the weight of the dark secret would still need to be carried. He felt so confused. *Just tell her*, he scolded himself. *Just...*

"Are you up for a movie tonight?" Vicki asked, yanking him further off the hook.

He shrugged slightly, his mind at war with itself.

"Come on, you saved a starving dog today, remember?" she teased. "You deserve some sort of award or prize..."

Instinctively, his eyes flew up and locked onto hers.

She giggled. "Sorry, but my parents are upstairs," she whispered, "and Barry doesn't look like he's going anywhere either."

Exhaling deeply once more, he surrendered with a simple nod. "A movie sounds like the perfect payoff," he said, feeling emotionally exhausted.

She leaned into his ear and whispered so softly that it tickled his ear lobe. "If you're a good boy, I might throw in some heavy petting," she teased, grabbing his hand and heading for the couch.

"I really like heavy petting," he said, making her giggle more and distancing them even further from the hideous truth of her cousin's death.

8.

They were halfway through *Wedding Crashers* with Vince Vaughn and Owen Wilson, when Billy feared he might pee his pants. While Vicki laughed and snorted, he looked at her in amazement. *I've never laughed so hard with anyone in my life,* he thought. *She really is one of a kind. How did I get so lucky?*

As promised, the laughter led to the heavy petting under a light throw blanket. Replaying the same old scene, Vicki's moans and groans preceded her pushing Billy away and jumping to her feet. Billy looked at her. She was panting and glistening in sweat. *She looks even sexier,* he thought.

"I'm sorry," he said.

She shook her head. "If you ever apologize again about us fooling around," she said, "it'll be the last time we do."

"Then I'm not sorry at all," he said with a grin and stood to leave.

At the door, Vicki asked him, "What date are you leaving for school?"

It was already August and Billy knew the days were ticking down, but he'd made a concerted effort not to think about it. Skype and text messages were good, but they could not replicate Vicki's distinct smell, or the way she grabbed for his hands when kissing him. "On the thirty-first. Why?"

"Good," she said. "There's a craft fair on the weekend before the thirty-first and I was hoping we could go together." She winked. "I already bought us the tickets."

"A craft fair?" he regurgitated, trying to smile. "Oh...okay."

She started laughing. "I was going to leave it a surprise, but I can't see you in this much pain."

"What?" he asked, confused.

She kissed him. "I got us a pair of Red Sox tickets before we both head off to school. And they're really good seats."

"Are you serious?" he asked, excited.

She nodded. "Four rows behind the home dugout."

He kissed her. "It's not the craft fair I was hoping for, but that'll work too." They both laughed. He hugged her tightly. "Have I told you how much I love you?" he asked.

She nodded. "You have, but it never hurts to hear it again."

He kissed her hard. "I wish I had the words," he whispered.

Chapter 12

That night—after making up for lost time with Vicki, but still leaving physically frustrated—Billy walked into the kitchen to find his mom sitting at the table with Jimmy by her side. Jimmy turned and spotted Billy; he was so excited to see his friend that his whipping tail was nearly spinning him like a top. Billy petted the dog's muzzle. "Hey buddy," he said.

The black mutt convulsed under his touch.

"Do you want to go for a walk?" he asked the dog, still fired up from his time with Vicki.

"Okay," his mom teased.

Laughing, Billy kissed her cheek, before grabbing Jimmy's leash.

Billy wasn't a block from his house when he looked back at Jimmy, who was struggling to keep up, facing the wind head-on. "Are you okay..." he started to ask the mutt when his cell phone rang. *It's Vicki*, he thought excitedly, fumbling to answer it. "Hey babe," he said, without looking at the phone.

"Don't *babe* me," Mark said in a serious tone. "You and I need to have a talk."

"I know, Mark. I know. We haven't seen each other. But between your summer classes and all the hours I'm putting in at the shelter..."

"That's not it," Mark barked.

"I know Vicki's taken up a lot of my time," Billy admitted, "but..."

"That's not it either," Mark barked louder, taking Billy aback.

"What's wrong?" Billy asked.

"How long have you known?" Mark asked in a strained whisper.

Without the need for further detail, Billy knew exactly what he was talking about. "When did Charlie tell you?" he asked.

"This afternoon in Nick's parking lot. He was blubbering away for a few minutes before I even realized what the hell he was talking about."

"Welcome to my nightmare," Billy said.

"Why didn't you tell me, Billy?" Mark asked, genuinely upset.

"Why, Mark, did you really want to know? I mean, are you happy you know now?"

There was a pause. "Not really," he admitted.

"Exactly," Billy said. "Besides, Charlie swore me to secrecy, which I've had to deal with for a lot longer than you." He took a deep breath. "It's been hell, bro, believe me."

"I can only imagine," Mark said, his tone much more friendly.

Billy thought for a moment. "Do you think we should tell the police?" he asked.

"Hell, no," Mark said without hesitation.

"Then like I said, welcome to my nightmare."

"This is so messed up," Mark said.

"You don't know the half of it," Billy said sadly.

"And how's that?"

"Dalton was Vicki's first cousin."

"You're shitting me?" Mark blurted.

"Nope, I'm not. I wish I were, but I'm not."

"Oh man, that's not good at all," Mark said, stating the obvious. "Talk about being stuck between a rock and a hard place."

"Oh, it's worse than that, I'd say," he said, bending down and scratching Jimmy's back.

"I'm sorry, Billy," Mark said, returning to his whisper.

"Me too," Billy said, feeling guilty that there was a part of him wishing Mark would just tell on Charlie and drag the truth out into the light, once and for all.

Jimmy collapsed onto his side, exposing his swollen belly for a rub.

In the morning—after hitching another mind-numbing ride from Mrs. Jacobs and her three screeching cherubs—Billy punched in for his shift.

He was in the middle of a flea bath with two of the newly-acquired strays, when the Levesque Family—Dad, Mom and young Timmy—arrived at Four Paws to adopt a family pet. Instantly, Billy recognized it as a strong reflection of his own youth. Old, deep emotions rose right to the surface.

While Timmy searched out his choices, his eyes quickly reached a yellow-haired mutt and lit up.

I remember making my pick like it was yesterday, Billy thought, picturing a much younger Jimmy.

Ironically, this dog was also a mix of Labrador retriever and something else, and the big oaf was maybe a year old. In that one magical moment, the boy and dog discovered each other. Everything and everyone around them was nothing more than white noise. Timmy hurried to the dog and collapsed to his knees, opening his arms to give the animal a hug.

"Don't," Mrs. Levesque said, "we don't know him. He could be..."

"He's very friendly," Arlene interrupted. "Trust me, that one's a lover, not a fighter."

Billy's eyes misted over, as he watched Timmy and the dog instantly fall in love.

Arlene sighed heavily, as if to say "another mission accomplished."

"I want this one," Timmy squealed. "Can we get this one?"

Mr. and Mrs. Levesque looked at each other. "Are you sure that's the one?" Mr. Levesque asked. "He's a big boy and I'm guessing he's only going to get bigger."

Timmy never looked up, but remained locked onto the dog's eyes. "He's the one," he said, as much to himself as to anyone else. "He's definitely the one."

He sure is, Billy thought.

Both Mr. and Mrs. Levesque nodded. "Fine," his dad said. "He's the one then."

Timmy looked up at Arlene. "Does he have a name?" he asked.

"Whatever name you give him," she said. "I've been calling him Romeo, but that's only because I have a crush on the big flirt."

Everyone laughed. Timmy studied the dog for a few moments. "I think I'll name him Buck," he said.

Billy joined the boy and the dog on the floor. "If you take good care of Buck," he told Timmy, "you won't believe how well he'll take care of you." Billy had said it with such conviction that everyone stared at him.

Timmy nodded and Billy could tell the boy was going to. Billy looked up at Arlene and, from her smile, he thought, *She must be thinking the same thing.*

Billy stood and smiled at the boy's parents. "Great choice, Mr. and Mrs. Levesque," he said. "You guys really picked a good one." Suddenly, Billy felt overwhelmed with a sense of love and purpose, confirming what he already knew. *This is very important work,* he told himself.

Mr. Levesque nodded proudly. "We wanted to teach Timmy some responsibility. He's at that age where he needs to think about others rather than just himself all the time."

Mrs. Levesque grinned, nodding in agreement. "And hopefully, Buck will look after him...help protect him, you know?"

Billy nodded. "Oh, you'll get all of that and so much more," he promised. "Trust me, Buck's going to help you raise your boy just like Jimmy helped raise..." He stopped, a pang of guilt ripping through him, leaving him speechless.

Arlene nodded and took over where Billy had left off. "Buck sure is," she said.

The parents smiled politely, clearly not convinced it was even possible.

Billy nodded, his mind still locked on Jimmy. "Just wait and see," he muttered, beating back the tears.

As the Levesques completed the paperwork and made their donation to the shelter, Arlene offered her parting words. "We recommend you feed Buck what he's been eating here, so that you can ease the transition." She handed them a five pound bag, which Billy knew they could hardly spare. "After Buck settles in, you'll need to talk with your veterinarian about switching him to the food of your choice."

They nodded gratefully and, as they prepared to leave, Billy got to the floor once more. This time, he spoke directly to the dog. "Watch over Timmy...the whole family," he said, "and love them as much as they're going to love you." He kissed the dog's forehead, causing a few surprised faces. "Now go do your job, Buck."

Arlene provided the family with a "go home packet," including behavior and animal care information which she handed to each adoptive family. Due to understaffing and lack of funding, there just wasn't enough time to provide verbal instructions and tips.

Once the family left, Arlene stared at Billy for a few seconds, a giant smile covering her kind face.

"What?" Billy asked.

She nodded. "Have I ever told you that hiring you here was one of the best decisions I've ever made?"

Billy half shrugged. "I don't think so."

She chuckled. "Well, I just did," she said.

"Thank you," Billy said, blushing slightly.

She nodded. "You're welcome," she said. "Now get over yourself and get back to work. Those new dogs still need help socializing."

Although he laughed, as Billy prepared to return to his chores, his mind and heart remained with Jimmy. *It's been too long since I've been there for you, buddy, and I'm sorry*, he told the dog in his thoughts. *But I'll make it up to you, I promise.*

When Jimmy had left the job at the animal shelter, there was even less time for him and Billy to spend together. Although the old mutt seemed to make the most of every moment they shared—and was always there for Billy, even when he was being pushed aside—Billy knew it wasn't enough. The irony was that Jimmy was just too old and tired to hang out with all the yapping puppies and whining strays. *But in the end*, Billy thought, *it's Jimmy who's been neglected.*

After the successful adoption, Arlene sighed. "Finally, an empty cage," she said.

Three minutes later, the avocado door's buzzer echoed through the building and Billy opened the door. A frazzled woman walked in, being pulled by a small Tazmanian Devil on a leash. It was a Jack Russell terrier mix that looked like he was fired up on an overdose of caffeine. With desperation in her face, the weary woman looked Arlene square in the eye and confessed, "I just can't do it anymore. I'm sorry, but I can't."

Arlene took a deep breath and held it. "What's his name?" she asked, exhaling.

Still trying to hold the leash—like a kite caught in a hurricane wind—the woman managed, "Spaz."

Arlene chuckled. "Of course it is," she said, turning to Billy. "Can you go make sure we have a clean room for the Spaz?"

Trying to contain his laughter, Billy nodded. "I'm on it," he said. "I'll go clean out Buck's cage."

Billy had just finished preparing the cage in the back when Arlene approached, doing all she could to hold on to the squirming terrier mix. He faced his mentor and took a deep breath. "Can I ask you a question, Arlene?"

"Anything," she said, managing to get the whirling dog into his temporary home, "you know that."

Billy nodded gratefully. "What do you do when you really want to achieve something, but you're not sure if you're capable of pulling it off?"

"Not capable of pulling it off?" she asked, locking the cage door. "Are we talking about college?"

He nodded. "Something like that," he admitted.

She smiled. "Knowing you'll wake up one morning, Billy, ten years from today, ask yourself, 'Where do I want to be? Who do I want to be?' Start working toward that goal and on that morning, when you awaken, smile. You can do anything, Billy. With your mind and heart, you can become whatever your dreams can imagine."

"Do you really believe that?" he asked.

"Of course I do," she said, chuckling. "How do you think I ended up working here?"

"Fair enough," he said, smiling.

Billy walked from the animal shelter to Nick's Pizza, which was much closer than walking home. Before he reached Nick's, he called in a take-out order for a small cheese pizza—to be delivered to his house.

When the delivery boy headed toward his car, Billy approached him. "Hey, do you mind if I hitch a ride with you?"

"Can't," the pimply-faced kid said, "I have a delivery right now."

Billy smiled. "Yeah, I know. That pizza's going to my house."

The kid laughed. "Then jump in," he said.

As they headed up the road, Billy thought, *This isn't a bad deal for a three dollar tip.* He smiled. *And a hell of a lot better than jumping aboard Mrs. Jacobs' crazy train again.* His cell phone rang. He looked down at the neon blue window. *It's Vicki.* He answered it. "Hi babe."

The pizza delivery driver looked over at him and smiled.

"Hey sexy," Vicki said, "when am I going to see you again? I know you must be tired from working so many long hours, but I already miss you like crazy."

Billy grinned. It was great to hear her voice, as well as her message. "Soon," he whispered. "I miss you too." In a world that could get dark very quickly, Vicki was a constant ray of sunshine.

Listening in, the young driver continued to wear his daffy smile.

"Is everything okay?" Vicki asked. "You seem distant, like there's something bothering you."

"I'm fine," he whispered, suddenly picturing Charlie's face.

"I'm here to listen if you need to talk," she said. "You can tell me anything, you know."

I wish that were true, he thought, her considerate tone making him feel even worse. "I know," he said, looking over at the grinning delivery boy, "but I'm getting a ride home right now and I can't really talk."

The teenage driver's smile disappeared.

"Oh, sorry," she said, sounding relieved. "I didn't know."

Billy nodded. "It's fine," he said, pausing. "I'm fine," he added, still feeling the full weight of her cousin's unsolved death in his guilty conscience. "I'll call you when I get home, okay?"

"How long?" she asked, playfully.

"Five minutes, max."

"Four minutes would be better," she teased.

In spite of himself, Billy smiled. "I'll shoot for four minutes then," he said, before hanging up. He looked left to see the delivery boy grinning again. "Women," Billy muttered.

As if he'd been struggling to hold it in, the kid laughed harder than he should have.

Billy returned home, surprised that Jimmy wasn't waiting for him at the front door. "Jimmy?" he called out and waited. The dog never came. "Jimmy?" he called again, feeling his heart sink. *Please God, don't take him yet*, he thought. *I don't think I can handle any more.* Billy ran through the living room and rounded the corner, only to discover Jimmy lying outside of Sophie's bedroom door. *Thank God*, he thought and, as he approached the mutt, detected the faint scent of marijuana seeping out from under the door. Shaking his head, Billy took a seat beside the dog. "Sophie's okay, buddy," he said, finally realizing that his sister was human.

Jimmy low crawled to Billy and placed his head in his lap.

"There are much worse crimes than smoking weed," he added, immediately picturing the two police cruisers securing Dalton's accident scene off of 88.

Charlie had spent weeks hiding out in plain sight. After answering Detective Swanson's terrifying questions, he forced himself out in public to avoid any further suspicion. It wasn't easy. As the weeks crept by, the buzz about Dalton's death had been reduced to a murmur. Even the questions around his break-up with Bianca had stopped. *Billy's crazy,* he thought. *I may actually get away with this.* As he tried to smile, the air was stolen from his lungs. Struggling to breathe, his heart pounded so hard in his chest he thought—and even hoped a little—that it might explode and finally put him out of his misery. A wave of adrenaline rushed through him, wave after overwhelming wave. While his extremities tingled, his mind plummeted into the depths of his guilty memory once again. He pictured Dalton's cracked skull and opened, judgmental eyes. He saw the growing puddle of blood. *Stop it!* he screamed at himself, but the reel continued to play. Dalton's mouth looked twisted, as if mocking Charlie for the pain he knew he would suffer. *Stop,* he heard echoing within his skull. Pacing back and forth, he tried to slow the hideous pictures that flashed in his mind. He was hyperventilating when a new picture—Billy's disappointed face—appeared. "What about Dalton's parents?" Billy asked. "Don't they deserve to know how their son died?" *Stop... stop...stop,* Charlie chanted, but it wouldn't stop. For weeks, it wouldn't stop. Suddenly, he heard a cynical laugh, which could have been his or Dalton's—he wasn't sure. *You got away with it, all right,* he thought. This time, he recognized the voice as his own, his guilty conscious passing the harshest judgment of all.

In the newly repaired Honda, Billy and Vicki kissed until they fogged out the rest of the world. While the music played softly, Billy asked her, "What do you think about getting into the back seat? There's more room." Even he could hear the hope in his voice.

She plunged her tongue back into his mouth and, to his surprise, nodded.

Billy's heart pounded out of his chest, while the sudden rush of blood headed south.

It took seconds before they'd both crawled over the front seat and were locked in each other's arms again. Kisses—once soft and sweet—were now hard and hungry. Vicki undid the buttons on Billy's shirt and began to caress his chest. More blood pumped into his crotch, throbbing painfully against his jeans. He returned the favor and removed her shirt and bra. She moaned softly. He felt dizzy, overdosing on oxygen, as he cupped her firm breasts in both hands and leaned in to kiss them. *Oh, my God*, he thought. *It's going to happen.* Her nipples were hard and erect, matching the surprise in his pants. As Vicki reached down to undo the button on his jeans, he slowly slid his hand between her legs—awaiting her reaction. She never flinched. Instead, she raised her hips to accept his advance. He gasped, trying to conceal his reaction with a fake cough. Her crotch felt hot to the touch. *Oh, my God*, he repeated in his swirling mind. *It's happening. It's really happening!*

Hyperventilating, Vicki reached down and grabbed his hand. "Billy, wait..." she said, trying to catch her breath. "I'm sorry, but I...I just need a little more time."

He pulled his hand away, trying to catch his own breath and make sense of what was happening.

"I love you, Billy, and I want to make love to you more than anything in the world, but..."

"I understand," he said, cursing Uncle Buddy in his mind. "It's okay, I understand," he repeated, surprised he could even speak.

"No, it's not that," she said, shaking her sweaty head. "It's just that I want the first time we make love to be perfect." She sighed deeply. "Not in the back seat of some car."

Matching her heavy sigh, Billy collapsed into the corner of the seat.

She dove after him, kissing him again. "You're the one, Billy...*my one.* I just want it to be perfect when we do it," she repeated.

More frustrated than he'd ever felt in his life, he nodded again—afraid he was going to explode.

"But that doesn't mean I'm going to leave you like this," she said, giggling.

While he watched on in awe, she finished unzipping his jeans and pulled them down to his knees, freeing his manhood. While she kissed him hard again, she took him into her hand.

Not a minute and a half later, they were scrambling for something to help clean up—both of them laughing with joy.

"That was awesome!" Billy said, at a loss for any other words.

After some long, deep kisses, Billy dropped Vicki off. "Thank you for tonight," he whispered. "It was unbelievable."

"Do you think we can make plans to get a room sometime soon?" she asked. "This way, we can finally be together the way we both want."

"Really?" Billy asked.

"Really."

Billy's head rattled up and down like a bobble-head caught in an angry windstorm.

She laughed. "I want to feel you inside me so bad," she said, kissing him again.

Billy swallowed hard, while his jeans grew tight again. "I'll plan the perfect night for us," he whispered, "and it'll be soon."

"Good," she said, "the sooner, the better."

After another kiss, Billy took a few steps toward the Honda. Suddenly, he stopped, turned and hurried back to her—planting another wet one on her puckered lips.

"What was that for?" she asked.

"I love you so much," he said. "You're everything to me. You know that, right?"

She searched his eyes for the longest time before she smiled. "I do," she whispered. "I feel it every time we're together."

Even before Billy reached the Honda, he decided to head over to Charlie's to brow beat him some more.

He fired up the car and started to pull the shifter down into drive when he noticed a blue envelope sitting on the dashboard. He left the shifter in park, leaned over and snatched the envelope off the dusty dash. As he swung it down in front of him, he detected a hint of Vicki's sweet perfume. *It's from her*, he thought, looking out the passenger window to see if she was still standing there on her front stoop. She wasn't. *She must have left it for me before I dropped her off.* Realizing Vicki had put some real thought and effort into the note, he tore it open and began reading.

> *Dear Billy,*
>
> *It's hard for me to tell you exactly how I feel sometimes. But I need you to know that I thank God every day that we met and I haven't stopped smiling since that Fourth of July parade. I wish we'd met earlier, but I also believe that we met exactly when we were supposed to. You've become more than my boyfriend—who I can hug and kiss. You've become my best friend, who I feel comfortable confiding in. There's nothing I wouldn't share with you, Billy, and I honestly can't wait to see what the future holds for us. Thank you for being you...sensitive and considerate and honest and kind. I can't imagine...*

As his eyes filled with guilty tears, Billy threw Vicki's letter onto the passenger seat, threw the shifter into drive and sped away from the curb. One block away, he grabbed his cell phone and dialed Charlie's number.

"What now?" Charlie said in a huff.

"What NOW?" Billy repeated in a hoarse yell. "You need to do the right thing NOW, Charlie...before you destroy more lives!"

Without a word, Charlie hung up.

Billy fired his cell phone onto the passenger seat, listening to it skip across Vicki's opened letter and crash into the passenger side door. "You son of a bitch!" he screamed. "You're going to ruin everything, Charlie."

As he drove home, Billy's mind spun in circles about what he should do. Each firing synapse led to the same place. *I can't give Charlie up*, he confirmed. *I just can't.* He looked sideways at his girlfriend's perfumed letter. "I'm sorry, Vicki," he said, as a pair of guilty tears threatened to roll down his crimson cheeks.

Chapter 13

While Charlie's shroud of darkness continued to hover over Billy, he was grateful it was so busy at the shelter. Arlene returned from the court with an abused dog named Peaches—a pit bull mix. Disgusted, she told Billy, "As her features are primarily pit bull, her thug owner tried to train her to fight other dogs. But the other blood in her wouldn't allow it; it went against her gentle spirit." She put her hand into the carrier to touch Peaches' left flank. The dog immediately cowered into the corner of the large carrier. "So the half-witted gangster tied her up with a heavy tow chain and nearly starved the poor animal to death." Arlene's eyes filled. "Even when he physically beat her, she wouldn't fight. The only thing the man's abuse accomplished was to make her fearful and untrusting toward all of us." She put her hand back into the cage and left it there for Peaches to sniff.

"Poor thing," Billy said, at a loss for more meaningful words but feeling the weight just the same.

With determination burning in her eyes, Arlene nodded. "That's okay," she said. "I'm going to work with Peaches for as long as it takes and give her a fresh start." She peered into the cage for a moment. "And from now on, her name's Sadie," she announced.

Billy nodded. "Sadie it is," he said, sharing Arlene's anger.

Arlene shook her head again, her mind still fuming. "I can't wait to testify in court against the piece of crap who abused Sadie. I can't wait to put the real animal in a cage where he belongs."

Billy immediately thought about Charlie's inevitable future and his eyes filled.

Arlene caught it and nodded. "I know how you feel," she said. "It breaks my heart."

No, you don't know how I feel, Billy thought and considered confiding in his mentor about Charlie's dismal secret, as well as the possible ramifications with Vicki. *But for what?* he decided, already knowing what Arlene would say, already knowing that Vicki's response was going to be devastating when she finally found out. His eyes filled more. "It breaks my heart too," he mumbled.

$\mathcal{8}$

After lunch, Arlene and Billy were working together taking inventory when they heard the angry barks and painful yelps of two dogs fighting.

"Damn it," Arlene said, handing Billy one of the long poles with looped rope attached to the end. Billy knew the poles were only used on dogs that acted out and were violent toward their peers, but he'd never used one. "Just follow my lead," Arlene said, as they ran for the yard.

Major, a German shepherd that had recently been saved from the streets, was locked in mortal combat with Gus, an even tempered husky-mix. "Damn it," Arlene repeated. Major was clearly getting the best of his bleeding opponent.

Billy watched as Arlene responded to the dangerous situation swiftly and firmly but also with great care. While she draped the rope around Major's neck and instructed Billy to do the same from the other side, the dog continued to snap his jaws, losing his mind to sink his sharp teeth into flesh—canine or human.

"Easy, boy," Arlene told Major, "easy now."

Slowly, she and Billy walked the aggressive dog into the building. *Isolation and containment*, Billy figured. He was right. As Major snarled and bared his teeth, he was escorted into the time-out cage. Billy turned to leave when he noticed that his mentor was staying behind.

Arlene took a seat outside the inmate's new cage and talked calmly to Major while he growled and frothed at the mouth. "It's okay, my love," she just kept telling the incensed dog in a loving and maternally soothing voice.

The crazed dog spun in circles, jumping up on the cage door and snapping his sharp teeth.

Billy watched her for a few moments before questioning it. "What are you doing, Arlene?"

She looked up at him and smiled. "Major's scared," she said, "and rather than bow to the fear, he's lashing out." She nodded. "Think about it. We have no idea where he's come from... what he's been through." She shrugged. "He could be a stray that's had a hard life, or he could have been abused and no longer trusts humans." She grinned. "And who could blame him for that?"

Billy laughed. "It's true," he said. "The more I learn about dogs, the less I like humans."

She nodded in agreement and looked back at Major. "This bad boy just needs to know he's safe here; that he's loved and no one's going to hurt him." She shrugged again. "Besides, it was my fault." She winked at Major. "Isn't that right, my love?"

The irate dog continued to snap at the steel mesh, trying desperately to get to Arlene.

"And how's that?" Billy asked.

"I should never have let him out in the yard with the others without getting to know him better," she said. "Can you please go check on Gus and tell him I apologize."

Billy nodded, still trying to process the lunacy.

"And if Gus needs medical care, call the vet and get it set up."

"I'm on it," Billy said.

It was just past dusk when Charlie drove two towns over—to the Noble residence in Berkley—hoping against all hope that Dalton's parents were anywhere but home. It was a raised ranch with an American flag blowing in the wind—typical middle class. *Please don't be here*, he thought, creeping along, *please*. But an ordinary mid-sized Buick was sitting in the driveway. Charlie slowed his car to a stop, almost directly across the street from the house. The living room light was on, as well as the intermittent flicker thrown off by a television. He threw the shifter into park, turned his body sideways and watched—struggling for each breath. Two faceless silhouettes sat on opposite ends of the couch, staring straight ahead—motionless and devoid of life. A pair of tears raced down Charlie's cheeks. "Oh God," he whimpered, "what did I do to you...to your family?" Although he could not see their faces, somehow he could feel all their pain. "I'm sorry," he sobbed, "I'm so sorry for what I did." But he knew it was not enough. The house felt shrouded in darkness and despair, a nightmare created by his hand. "I wish it were me who'd crashed and died that night," he told the two shadows. "I wish it were me and not your son!" The statues remained still, as if ignoring his plea for forgiveness. He cried and convulsed so hard that his chest began to hurt. As he pulled away from the curb, the larger of the two silhouettes walked to the window, pulled back the curtain and looked right at him. "I'm...I'm so sorry," Charlie whimpered, driving off to suffer alone.

In the morning, Billy's cell phone rang. Expecting it to be Vicki, he excitedly picked up. "Hey babe, I can't tell you how happy you've made me. I've read your letter a half dozen times already and..."

"It's me," Charlie said, followed by a ghostly pause.

"Charlie?" Billy asked, stunned.

"Yeah." He took a deep breath. "I've decided to turn myself in and talk to that cop, Detective Swanson."

"You have?" Billy said, shocked. "Really?"

"I'm heading over to the station right now," Charlie muttered.

"You don't have to do this alone, Charlie. Mark and I will meet you there."

"Okay," he said, "thanks." And then there was silence.

With Billy and Mark on each side of him, Charlie—his eyes filled with panic and his bottom lip quivering—told Detective Swanson, "I owe you an apology," he said, shaking his head at the absurdity of his words. "Actually, I owe more than an apology...to a lot of people." He took a deep breath. "And the only way I can start to make things right is to tell you the truth about what really happened that night." The last two words were delivered in a whimper; Charlie's body was already convulsing from the heavy sobs. "...the night Dalton died," he managed.

"I'm glad you came forward, Charlie. An elderly eye witness just offered testimony of a car chase on the night of the accident."

"It's true," Charlie blurted. "I was the one who..."

"Okay, son," Swanson interrupted, "before you say another word, I need to read you your rights."

"I'm under arrest?" Charlie asked.

"No, you're not. But it's important you know your Miranda Rights before you say another word...in the event that we do find cause to press charges."

"Okay," Charlie murmured.

"What's most important is that you know you have the right to an attorney." He lowered his voice. "...which I highly recommend, son."

"Okay," Charlie repeated, his face bleached to white.

A young uniformed officer removed a set of handcuffs from his utility belt and approached Charlie.

"There's no need to cuff him," Swanson told the cop, pointing to the rear of the police station. "Just take him to Interview Room Two. I'll be along in a few minutes."

Charlie was escorted toward the back room in the police station, while the stern police officer explained, "You have the right to remain silent..."

"I'm here for you, brother," Billy called out. "And that's never going to change."

"Ever," Mark yelled.

With his head hung low, Charlie nodded.

"You have the right to an attorney," the cop continued. "If you cannot afford one..."

Seconds later, Charlie disappeared behind the door and into the firm embrace of the justice system.

Billy and Mark stood alone with Detective Swanson, Billy feeling like Judas for talking Charlie into confessing.

"It may not feel like it right now," the old law man told Billy, "but you're a good friend."

While Mark patted his back, Billy's eyes filled with tears. "Sure I am." He shook his head. "What's going to happen to Charlie?"

"Well, we'll get his side of the story and, if we believe a crime was committed, we'll charge him. After that, it's in the hands of the courts."

"Oh man," Billy moaned.

"Trust me, Billy. The best thing Charlie could have done was to come forward on his own. The courts will see that and take it into consideration."

"Let's hope," Mark blurted.

Detective Swanson looked at them both and nodded. "I'll make sure they do, guys. You have my word on it."

"Thank you," Mark said.

Billy, however, was already picturing Vicki's face when she found out. "Now what do I do?" he muttered to no one.

Billy sat alone in the police station parking lot. *I have to call Vicki and tell her*, he thought. *It'll only be worse if she hears it from someone else.* It took two seconds to locate Vicki's cell number and twenty minutes to press the green call button. It rang twice before she picked up. Billy cringed.

"Hi babe," she said.

It was the first and only time he'd ever been sorry to hear her voice. "Are you home?" he asked.

"What's wrong?" she asked, picking up on his tentative tone.

"We need to talk."

"What is it, Billy?" she asked, sounding nervous. "Tell me."

He cleared the lump from his throat. "I don't want to discuss it on the phone."

She paused. "Okay, now you're scaring me," she said.

"Can I come over right now?" he asked.

"Of course," she said. "But can you at least tell me..."

"I'll be right over," he interrupted, hanging up.

Vicki was waiting for Billy, sitting on her front stoop. As he parked the car, she stood and waited for him. The short walk from the curb to her front door felt like a stroll to the electric chair.

As he reached her, there were no hugs or kisses, just a bombardment of nervous questions. "What is it, Billy?" she asked. "There's something wrong, isn't there? I can tell by your voice. What is it?"

He looked into her eyes and, to his surprise, he began to cry. He collapsed onto the front step.

She joined him, wrapping her arms around him. "Please tell me," she whispered, her eyes filling with his contagious tears. "Whatever it is, I'm right here beside you."

Billy looked up slowly and gazed into her eyes again; this time, he lingered there for a moment, like he was never going to see her again and knew it.

"Billy...please," she begged.

He shook his head and opened his mouth to speak. At first, nothing came out. He took a deep breath. "I just came from the police station," he said.

"Oh my God, what happened?" she asked, nearly sitting in his lap now.

He searched her face again and could feel his heart start to tear. "My friend Charlie..."

"Yeah? Has he been hurt?" she asked frantically. "Is he in trouble?"

Billy nodded. "He's in big trouble, Vicki. He...he just confessed..."

"Confessed to what?" she asked, her eyes wide with fear.

The tears were coming fast now, making it hard for Billy to see Vicki's face clearly. "He just confessed to running your cousin Dalton off the road the night he died."

Vicki convulsed slightly, her forehead creasing in disbelief.

Billy shook his head, like he still couldn't believe it himself, and blurted out the rest of it. "Charlie thought Dalton was seeing his girlfriend, Bianca, behind his back and...and he lost his mind over it. He followed Dalton home that night from the party and..." He stopped, knowing there was no reason for more details.

While Vicki took a moment to process what she'd just been told, Billy watched as her body naturally recoiled, moving away from him. "Vicki, please," he said, reaching for her hand.

She pulled away. "Charlie killed my cousin?" she said, still trying to make sense of it. "So Dalton was murdered?" She gagged at the truth of it. "My aunt and uncle are going to..." She stopped and gagged again, putting her hand over her mouth.

For a few horrific moments, Billy and Vicki sat together on her front stoop, their heads hung in pain. Billy's mind raced out of control, while Vicki dry heaved a few times.

Suddenly, she looked up at him and the deep hurt in her eyes nearly ripped his heart clean from his heaving chest. "Please tell me the truth, Billy." She hesitated a moment, as if in prayer.

"Did...did you know that Charlie ran Dalton off the road that night and killed him?" she asked, her tone a mix of desperate hope and betrayal.

While his eyes swelled with tears, he dropped his gaze. "Yes. Charlie told me about the accident..."

"Accident?" she squealed.

His head snapped up.

"How was that an accident?" she screamed. "You just told me that Charlie Philips killed my cousin in a jealous rage!" She studied Billy's eyes and, in one brutal moment, her love for him completely vaporized from her face.

A pang of fear ripped through Billy's core. *We're breaking up*, he realized, watching like a helpless victim as they did the irreversible dance of destruction. *We're never going to make love or kiss again or...*

"When did you know?" she asked, still trying to be strong but having trouble maintaining eye contact.

He shook his head in shame. "Charlie told me about it a few days after it happened."

"Oh my God!" she gasped, jumping to her feet. "You've known the entire time we were together?" Her voice was dripping with the pain that accompanies the worse betrayals. "I was at least hoping..." She stopped in mid sentence again and shook her head. "I guess it doesn't matter now what I was hoping."

Billy gasped and struggled to take in air. "I'm...I'm so sorry, Vicki," he cried. As he stood, the world started to spin and he wobbled on his unsure feet.

"I loved you so much," she said, backing away from him and starting to sob.

Loved, Billy thought, concentrating on the past tense. "Please, babe," he cried.

"Don't you dare call me *babe!*" she hissed, her voice laced with venomous rage. "I almost gave myself to you," she thought aloud, shaking her head. "Thank God I didn't."

Her words felt like knives slicing into Billy's flesh until they pierced his heart. "Please just give me a chance to explain. I told

Charlie right from the start that he needed to come clean, but he..."

But Vicki had already turned and started to walk into her house.

"Vicki, I tried telling you!" he pleaded, hysterically.

She stopped for a moment.

"The day I saved that stray dog, I came to your house and tried to tell you how Dalton died," he explained, "but you didn't want to hear it." He tried to catch his breath. "You...you wouldn't let me finish."

She turned back. "So then it's my fault you kept it from me?" she hissed.

He shook his head. "I'm not saying that. I'm only saying that I tried and..."

"You didn't try hard enough, Billy," she whispered, her voice thick with condemnation. The front door banged loudly behind her, like an angry wooden gavel deciding their fate.

"No!" Billy screamed out, with the desperation of an abandoned child. Tears cascaded down his cheeks. He wanted to pound on the door and chase after her, but he stopped himself. *I can't*, he thought. *I love Vicki too much to cause her any more pain.* Given how he'd hurt her so deeply, he knew, *Now it's my turn to pay. By finally telling Vicki the truth*, he realized, *I've completely destroyed any possibility at having a future with my true love.* His heart was now shredded; this was not a clean break but a jagged tear that would take so much longer to heal, if it ever really did. "No," he repeated in a defeated whisper, staggering off Vicki's stoop for the final time. "Please no..." He sat in his car by the curb—much longer than he should have—weeping like a wounded animal.

For hours, Billy drove around town—off to the beach and back again—and cried his eyes out. Filled with panic and desperation—and against his better judgment—he called Vicki's cell phone. She never answered. His greatest fears were continuing to unfold. *It's over for good*, he thought, but then did all he could to talk himself out of that negative thinking. *But we really loved each other. Maybe she'll forgive me?* Somehow, he knew better; every cell in his body was telling him differently. *She trusted me with her heart and her dreams...and even her body*, he thought, *and I betrayed that trust by choosing to keep Charlie's secret*. He called her again, leaving another message. "Please call me, Vicki," he said, trying not to sound desperate. "I know what I did was terrible, but please call me so we can talk about it and see if there's any way to get past it."

She didn't call.

His mind raced. He thought about calling Mark. *But I don't want him to see me like this*. He thought about going home to talk to his mother. *But she's working at Nick's and I'm not going there*. He felt so alone. *Sophie has her own problems and Dad would only lecture me. I could go see Arlene, but...* Not knowing where else to go, he ended up at the town dump. It was a vast and desolate patch of scarred land, the perfect place to suffer. *I feel like a piece of trash anyway*, he thought. As he sat atop a mountain of refuse, he realized this type of pain was alien to him. This wasn't road rash from a bicycle fall or a broken bone from jumping off the shed. This was a man-sized pain, throbbing with anguish and torment; it was a wound that would be invisible to the world but excruciating enough to steal the air from his lungs and thousands of beats from his heart—along with any sleep, appetite, sense of hope or well-being for the next second, minute, day or foreseeable future. He called Vicki again. "Forgive me for calling again," he said in the most pathetic voice, "but I can't lose you, Vicki. I love you with all my heart and..." He started crying. "Please just call me," he whimpered and hung up.

She didn't call.

With the car's gas needle on empty, Billy drove around—not caring whether he got stranded or even flipped the clunker into the same ditch Dalton had died in. *I can't live without her*, he thought. *She's everything to me*. He cried hard—until his insides felt like they were trying to get outside. *Vicki's taken the best part of my heart*, he thought. He picked up his cell phone again and considered another call. *Don't*, he told himself, trying to choke back the nightmare. *You're going to hurt her more*. Then, as if deciding to play some cruel joke on himself, he began to take an accounting of his magical summer with the girl of his dreams: *The parade and the picnic*, he recalled, *and all the dates...even getting caught in the rain. Her meeting Jimmy, the late night movies—laughing until we couldn't breathe...her confiding in me about her sick uncle*. Forcing his mind to stop, he grabbed his chest and tried to breathe; the heartache was so real it was paralyzing. He considered his options, realizing there were none. *Charlie did this*, he thought, and then caught his own reflection in the driver's side window. *No*, he thought, being honest with himself, *I did this. I could have told her the truth from the beginning, but I didn't*. He went over it again in his mind and couldn't decide whether he'd kept the secret from her to protect his best friend or because he knew Vicki would break up with him. *Either way, there's no changing it now*. Knowing there was no going back, he pulled over to the side of the road and jumped out of the car—just before his stomach kicked up everything he hadn't already digested.

It was way past dark when Billy coasted home on fumes. After letting Jimmy out to do his business, they went straight to bed. As Billy lay grieving, he told Jimmy, "She's gone, buddy. Vicki's left me."

Jimmy whimpered for a few moments. Then, as though the dog realized this wasn't about him, that it was about Billy's pain and that he needed to be there for his friend, he quieted down.

"She knows I knew about...about Charlie running Dalton off the road," Billy stammered between sobs, "and...and she's never going to forgive me for it." He began to wail, immediately pressing his face into his pillow to stifle his pain. "She's never going to want to see me again."

Jimmy nuzzled next to Billy and lapped his cheek—until he came out from the pillow.

"The woman I love with all my heart hates me, Jimmy," Billy said, crying more softly now. "She *hates* me!"

Jimmy added another coat of slobber.

"I screwed up bad, buddy, and because of that Vicki and I are done," Billy wept. "We're never going to be together again."

Deep into the night, Jimmy consoled his master with kisses, until mercy appeared in the form of sheer exhaustion and Billy finally cried himself to sleep.

For one torturous day after the next, Billy walked around like a zombie—destroyed mentally, emotionally and even spiritually. An internal war was waged, with him calling Vicki when he'd hit bottom each time. He checked his phone every three minutes. Just when he'd accepted the fact that he'd never hear from her again, his cell phone rang. He looked at the phone's small screen. *It's Vicki,* he thought, nearly dropping it when trying to answer the call. "Vicki?" he said, sounding pathetic once again. "Thank God you called. I was hoping..."

"Stop calling me," she whispered, clearly upset, "...please just stop." And the phone went silent. *She's already hung up,* he realized. *It's...it's really over.* Throwing the phone onto the floor, he began to wail. There would be no more loving texts or talking until the wee hours of the morning. There would be no more laughing until he couldn't breathe. *And we're not going to get a room together,* he thought, *ever.* As if they had just broken up for the first time, Billy slid to the floor, rolled himself into the fetal position and grieved until his entire body throbbed in pain.

Charlie was remanded to the House of Correction, awaiting trial for manslaughter and a very unsure future. His parents had no real means or interest to hire a good criminal lawyer. Instead, his future was in the hands—and benevolence—of a court-appointed defense attorney.

One stupid decision, Billy kept repeating in his head on his way home from the jail's visiting room.

After being greeted at the front door by Jimmy, Billy stepped into the kitchen to find his mom sitting at the kitchen table.

"One wrong choice," his mom said, "and your whole life..."

"I get it, Mom. Trust me, I get it."

"I know you do, sweetheart," she said. "I wasn't trying to lecture you. I..." She began to cry. "I love Charlie, too, you know."

"I know," Billy said, giving her a hug. "It's terrible...all of it, just terrible."

When his mom composed herself, she asked, "You still haven't heard from Vicki?"

Billy shook his head. "And I don't expect to...ever again."

"I'm so sorry," she said, her voice thick with empathy.

Billy took a deep breath, choking back the depth of his pain. "Me too."

"Unfortunately, we now live in a disposable society. Everything gets thrown out...cars, televisions, even relationships," she said, shaking her head. "Nothing gets fixed anymore."

Billy smiled politely, grateful for her support and willingness to take his side. *But this was my doing*, he thought. *I'm the one who chose to keep Charlie's secret all summer.* Understanding his role and responsibility in how everything unfolded made the break up with Vicki that much harder to accept.

The following afternoon, Billy was just walking out of Nick's Pizza with his tuna sub in hand when he spotted Vicki's dad and brother, Barry, in the parking lot. *They didn't see me yet*, he decided, and could have easily slipped past them. But something in him—something new—wouldn't allow it. *Time to man up and face them*, he thought. Before the scared little boy inside of him could talk him out of it, he marched straight toward them.

Vicki's dad spotted him first and slapped Barry on the shoulder.

As Billy approached them, he took a deep breath and blurted, "I am so sorry for not..."

The older man shook his head. "I'm disappointed in you, Billy," he said. "I thought you were one of the good guys, I really did."

Panic filled Billy, nearly drowning him. "But I am, sir. If you would please just let me explain..."

But the man would not allow it. "I'm very disappointed," he repeated.

Feeling crushed, Billy looked toward Barry, a part of him hoping that the bigger kid would just beat him up right then and there.

But Barry barely gave Billy a first look, never mind a second one. It was as if Billy wasn't worth a beating and Barry had known it the whole time.

"I'm sorry," Billy repeated.

Without another word, Billy's final two connections to Vicki turned and walked away.

Some dark days passed; long days filled with little hope and buckets of tears. Billy stood in the bathroom mirror, shaving his goatee. He finally decided to abandon the chin whiskers, coming to the conclusion that his acne had cleared and the goatee's bald spots would never fill in. After running a towel over his face, he lingered a minute staring into his eyes and trying to make sense of all that had happened.

Stuck between boyhood and being a man, Billy felt like a refugee without a country—like he'd been thrown from a boat and had no real choice but to flail around until he learned how to swim. It seemed like each decision he now made would prove to be a defining one in his life, with little to no room for making mistakes. *Should I have fun and hold on to the final moments of childhood, or should I choose responsibility each time?* he wondered. *Can there be a balance?* The days of making mistakes and saying "I'm sorry" with a cute grin were done. Thrown into the real world, he'd already learned that the keynote speaker at his high school graduation—the man he'd ridiculed only weeks before—had been right. *People don't care whether you can make it out in the world or not. Most of the time, they're doing all they can just to stay afloat themselves... playing the best hand they can with the cards they've been dealt.* People made their own choices and either enjoyed the consequences or suffered them as a result. *When I mess up,* Billy thought, *I'm messing up my own life and no one else's.*

He gave his reflection one last glance and shook his head. "They can keep this whole adulthood thing," he mumbled.

Long after Billy's mom stopped asking him if he was okay or Mark checked in on him, the pain remained—in strength and sharpness. Even with Jimmy by his side, night after night Billy learned that sometimes silence screamed the loudest and hurt the most.

He picked up his cell phone and accessed his voice messages, skipping two saved messages before reaching Vicki's sweet voice: "Hi, handsome, I can't wait to see you this weekend. I haven't thought about anything else all week. Call me later when you get a chance. Love you."

Love you, Billy thought, replaying the message on speaker phone over and over, long past the time he should have—and only stopped when Jimmy's whines turned to howls.

Billy threw the phone down onto his bed and began weeping again. It was amazing how Vicki's voice, which had once brought so much joy, could now cause such an unspeakable amount of pain.

Jimmy licked Billy's face until they both slipped into sleep, legs entwined.

On Friday afternoon, a known street thug called Razor walked into Billy's only refuge. "I want to adopt a dog," he announced.

While Billy watched on, Arlene sized Razor up. "What breed were you thinking?" she asked professionally.

"I've always been kind of drawn to pit bulls." Razor shifted his toothpick within his grin. "Do you have any of those?"

Arlene was right, Billy thought, shaking his head. *After everything I've experienced this summer, nothing surprises me anymore.*

"Not right now," Arlene lied to the hoodlum, "but we're always getting some in. Would you like to start the process?"

Billy was shocked. *She must be playing with him,* he thought. *At least I hope she is. This guy shouldn't have a dog and especially not a pit bull.*

As the punk took a seat across from Arlene, she asked, "Do you have any other dogs?"

Razor shook his head.

"Is your current residence suited to a pit bull?"

He grinned, leaning way back in the chair. "I got a sweet crib. Don't you worry about that."

"Oh, I'm not worried," she said. "How will your social life or work obligations affect your ability to care for a dog?"

"They won't."

"Do you work?" Arlene asked, pelting him with rapid fire questions.

"You could say that," Razor said grinning.

"We'll need proof of employment," she said.

Billy's jaw dropped. *What?* he thought. *She's so full of it.*

"How do the people you live with feel about having a dog in the house?" Arlene asked.

"They're down with it," Razor replied.

"That's wonderful," Arlene said, the word *wonderful* dripping with sarcasm. She even flashed the thug a fake smile.

She's going all out, Billy thought, hypnotized by his mentor's newest lesson. For a few moments, everything else faded away—even Vicki's face.

"Is there tension in the home?" Arlene asked. "Dogs can pick up on stress in the home and it can do a job on their health. Some even develop behavioral problems."

"Nope."

"Is there an adult in the family who's agreed to be responsible for the dog's care?"

"Me," Razor said, clearly getting agitated with the ongoing interrogation.

"Do you have the time and patience to work with the dog through its adolescence, taking house-breaking and teething into account?"

He nodded.

"Can you train the dog?"

Razor grinned again. "Oh, I plan to."

Billy could see Arlene's face flush. *Here we go*, he thought.

"We charge an adoption fee to help defray the cost of taking in unwanted or lost animals. And you'll also need to pay for your dog to be neutered before bringing him home," Arlene said.

"How much is that?"

She sighed heavily. "It's a hundred dollars for the adoption fee. And if there are no complications with the surgery, which there usually are, that'll run you another hundred and fifty bucks." Before he could respond, she began counting on her fingers. "At home, other expenses will include food and water bowls, a month's supply of food, a bed, routine veterinary care, licensing according to local regulations, a collar, a four to six foot leash and identification tags with your phone number on it, a carrier or foldable metal crate, basic grooming equipment and supplies which include doggy shampoo and conditioner, a brush, a canine toothbrush and toothpaste and nail clippers." She came up for air. "You'll also need absorbent house-training pads, a sponge and scrub brush, non-toxic cleanser, an enzymatic odor neutralizer..."

"What's that?" he asked.

She shook her head. "Trust me, you'll need one." She winked at him again. "And they're not cheap."

Trust me, Billy repeated in his head, grinning for the first time in a long while. *Very impressive, Arlene.*

Arlene went back to the finger counting. "Let's see, where were we? Oh yes, you'll need plastic poop baggies, the biodegradable ones are best...or a pooper scooper, a variety of toys like balls, rope and chew toys. You might want to mix up the dog's treats at first to see what he or she likes...cookies, rawhides...you know what I mean."

Razor sat staring at her, his eyes frosted over.

"And for pit bulls, we also mandate training classes."

The final blow, Billy thought. *And I'm betting it's a fatal one.*

"Mandated?" the prospective adopter asked, his voice reduced to a murmur.

She nodded. "Oh yes, believe it or not many people adopt pit bulls to fight them. We train pit bull owners so they can't claim ignorance when they're charged criminally and brought to court." She looked over at Billy. "I think I testified in two trials just last month, right?"

Billy nodded slightly, while the thug sat up straight in his chair. *She's finally gotten his attention,* he thought.

"What you must also consider before making your decision is that dogs need to be fed two to three times a day, more often in the case of puppies, and they need a constant supply of fresh water. You should spend at least an hour each day with your dog, whether it's training, exercising, grooming, or playing. Dogs with lots of energy, like pit bulls, need more time to exercise and someone to keep them entertained...or they'll tear your house apart." She smiled, knowing she was breaking him. "Dogs need to be taken out to potty several times a day. And in the beginning, they require additional bonding to let them know they're loved and safe. And you..."

The street thug waved his hand once in surrender and stood. "Listen," he said, "the more I think about it...this dog thing ain't for me."

"It's not?" Arlene asked, putting on her best surprised face. "What a shame."

Billy gagged, drawing both their attentions. "Sorry," he said. "I had a tickle in my throat." Just as he started to smile, Vicki's face popped into his head and the weight of the world came crashing down on him once again.

Razor wasn't three feet out the door when Billy said, "You were brutal with him, Arlene. Why did you even go through all that?"

She smiled. "If he left here without a dog, he would have just gone somewhere else and they might have let him have one."

"Clever," Billy said. "So that whole spiel was really about letting him know there were criminal charges for dog fighting?"

Arlene nodded and then laughed. "That might have been my best performance yet," she said, adding a wink.

Billy nodded solemnly.

Arlene stopped laughing. "Is everything okay, Billy? You seem blue."

"Blue?"

"Sad," she explained.

He thought about talking to her, but quickly shook his head. "I'm just not feeling well, that's all."

"Not feeling well, huh?" She studied his eyes. "Does it have something to do with that girl you've been seeing...Vicki?"

Billy nodded. "We broke up," he whispered, trying not to break down in front of his teacher.

"I'm sorry to hear that," she said, without prodding further. "Why don't you go home and get some rest? You haven't taken a sick day all summer. We'll be fine without you for one day."

He shook his head. "I appreciate it, but..."

"Go home," Arlene repeated; it was more of a command than a suggestion. "You need to grieve properly before you can heal."

Billy nodded. "Thank you," he said, starting for the door.

"You'll get past this, Billy," Arlene called out. "It'll take some time, but trust me...you'll survive it."

I don't know, Arlene, Billy thought, *it doesn't feel that way.* As ordered, he headed home to mourn.

Billy was moping around the house when he spotted Vicki's painting of the dock. His heart did a nose dive in his chest. He stared at the painting, remembering every moment of that magical night in vivid detail. Now, while his eyes misted over, he found that the painting was just another source of unspeakable pain.

Although Billy couldn't bring himself to throw it away, and doubted he ever would, he finally put it in the attic—out of sight.

As he descended the attic stairs, he began to think about his first date with Vicki at Agave Restaurant—*when we got caught in the rain*, he thought. He shook his head. *Don't you do it!* he scolded himself. It was such a perfect night and, by trying to remember it in detail, he knew he could never do it justice. *You'll either cheapen or ruin it*, he thought, preferring it to remain perfect. *Just let it go*, he told himself, as he did every time the thought popped into his head—swatting it away like some pesky house fly.

Although Billy refused to remember the date, he couldn't get Vicki's face out of his head. With Jimmy by his side, he logged onto Facebook and clicked on Vicki's home page to gawk at her pictures. "Oh God," he gasped. "She's so gorgeous," he told Jimmy, his voice raised an octave.

The old mutt immediately pawed at Billy's hand, as if trying to draw his attention away from the computer screen.

Billy felt like he was going to throw up again. He clicked off her page, promising himself to never visit it again. "No more cyber stalking," he told Jimmy. "I can't do it anymore. I just can't." But he knew better. *Right or wrong, Jimmy and I will be looking at Vicki's beautiful face again tomorrow.*

Jimmy continued to paw at him.

As Billy stood and headed for the backyard with the four-legged old-timer, he sensed that the break-up with Vicki had already changed him; matured him. He pondered all that had happened and told Jimmy, "Even if it did cost me big time, I did what I thought was right. And I'd do the same thing again." Just knowing this helped to define—for himself—the man he was becoming.

Chapter 14

Billy was taking Jimmy on a rare morning walk when he spotted Vicki on the sidewalk across the street. *Oh my God,* Billy thought, *it's her!* While she pretended not to see them—and Jimmy made it more difficult by barking his head off—Billy realized, *As much as she loved me just a few weeks ago, she hates me at least that much now.* Throwing embarrassment to the wind, Billy stood frozen and stared at her. *I miss you so much, Vicki,* he screamed at her in his head, hoping she would somehow receive his heartfelt message. But Vicki stayed strong, never offering so much as a slight glance in their direction. While Jimmy barked louder, pulling hard on his leash to visit his old friend, sharp painful tears filled Billy's eyes. Vicki suddenly glanced over and shot a longing look—at Jimmy. *Go talk to her!* Billy prodded himself, remembering that same desperate pep talk he'd given himself the afternoon of his graduation party. Vicki turned and began walking in the opposite direction. While Jimmy howled away, panic coursed through Billy's veins. *Talk to her now!* he pleaded with himself, *before it's too late.* But his feet stayed firmly planted. *I...I can't. It just wouldn't be fair,* he was thinking when he heard himself scream out, "Vicki!" For one brief moment, she looked over her shoulder and met Billy's gaze. The longing in her eyes was no longer there. She turned back around, picking up her pace. *Oh God*, Billy thought, feeling like she'd just broken up with him again, *it is too late*. His heart ached and his swollen eyes began to leak down his face. His true love's rejection of him was absolute and permanent. "Let's go home, Jimmy," he said, trying unsuccessfully to dry his eyes. "She's not coming back."

They weren't twenty feet down the sidewalk when Billy thought, *If she ever called and wanted me back, I'd jump at the chance.* And then he reprimanded himself for allowing that glimmer of false hope. *But it's never going to happen, you idiot.*

While Billy put in extra hours at the shelter, his mom looked out the kitchen window and noticed that the shed door was open. *Hmmm...* Throwing on her slippers, she went out and closed it.

Maybe an hour later, she realized she hadn't seen Jimmy. She went to the back door and called out, "Jimmy, Jimmy, come here, boy." But the dog didn't come. *That's odd*, she thought, trying to remember whether she'd let him out earlier. After scouring the house, she went to the back door and called out again, "Come on, Jimmy. Time to come in, boy." There was no response. *Maybe he's out gallivanting?* she thought, jumping into her car to search the neighborhood. Each loud summons produced the same results; there was no sign of the mutt.

She parked in the driveway, got out of the car and screamed, "Jimmy!" Still, there was no response. Her fear grew. After a few more screams, she decided, *He's lost!* She picked up her cell phone and called Billy. "Jimmy's missing," she said, her voice betraying her gut-wrenching fear. "I've looked everywhere and can't find him. I don't know what else to do."

Billy didn't even punch out. He sprinted toward the parking lot, yelling at Arlene over his shoulder as he went. "I have to go. Jimmy's missing."

"You need help?" she yelled.

"I'll call you if I do."

"Okay," she yelled louder, "but make sure you call me either way, okay?"

Billy nodded but was already in the Honda, speeding away.

Billy drove home at breakneck speed. After an unsuccessful spot check of the neighborhood, he skidded into the driveway, threw the shifter into park and sprinted for the house. *Where are you, Jimmy?* he wondered, his mind already wracked with fear. The frantic search was on.

A quick tour of the house confirmed that the aged dog had to be outdoors. Billy ran for the backyard. "Jimmy!" he screamed, "Come on boy." He waited. There was no response. It was twilight, the fading light painting long shadows across the abandoned yard. Billy's eyes struggled to pick up any slight movement. "Come on, Jimmy," he called out again. As each summons grew louder, the more panicky he felt—and his voice betrayed his fear. Nearly hyperventilating, tears began to blur his already limited vision. "Please, Jimmy," he whispered, sorrowfully, "come home, buddy."

It was getting dark fast. "Jimmy!" Billy screamed at the top of his lungs, scanning the yard for any movement. *Still nothing.* As he continued to call for his missing friend and the outcome started to look bleak, desperation filled his soul. Billy began to pray, realizing it had been a while since he'd talked to God. *We haven't spoken in a long while,* he said in his head, feeling bad about it, *and I realize there's nothing worse than talking to someone only when you need something from them...* He looked toward the dark purple sky. "Please forgive me, Lord," he said aloud, "but I don't want Jimmy to pay for my stupidity. Please just let me find him... soon."

As Billy searched, he scolded himself for neglecting the loving dog. "How would I feel?" he said aloud. And then it dawned on him. *The shed,* he thought, sprinting for it. As a boy, whenever Billy was sad, he and Jimmy went straight to the shed to be alone. They'd sit in the corner behind the lawn mower and a treadmill that had only been used twice; it was a safe campsite to think and cry and even scream, undetected.

After throwing open the shed door, Billy climbed over two boxes of Christmas decorations and a half bag of lawn fertilizer before he spotted Jimmy lying in the corner, wide-eyed and panting. Billy lunged the last few feet to reach his old friend. "Oh Jimmy," he said, hugging him tight, "I'm so sorry...for everything."

The old mutt stood slowly and looked at Billy, without a hint of judgment or resentment in his soft mocha eyes.

Pushing things aside, Billy helped Jimmy out of the shed and hurried to fetch him a bowl of fresh water. As they sat together on the shed's stoop, embracing each other, Jimmy lapped up the bowl while Billy wiped the tears from his face. "Sorry, buddy," Billy said. "I know I haven't been around all that much these last few weeks, but there's been a lot going on."

Jimmy licked Billy's face before placing his head in his master's lap.

"But that's no excuse," Billy said, kissing the dog's head. "You've always put me first and I need to start doing the same." He stroked Jimmy's silver muzzle. "I'm so sorry," he repeated.

Jimmy reached up and laid another kiss on Billy's cheek.

Billy locked onto the dog's gaze. "You've always loved me more than you love yourself," he told him, nodding gratefully and giving the mutt a strong squeeze. "You're mine and I'm yours and nothing can ever change that." He hugged the dog even tighter.

Billy's mom appeared from the shadows and interrupted the emotional reunion. She knelt on the ground and stroked Jimmy's coat. "You had us scared out of our wits," she told the dog. "The next time you want to sulk, do it in the house, okay?"

Jimmy raised his right paw, placing it on her thick thigh.

Billy shook his head. "There'll be no more sulking for Jimmy," he said, in a promise as much to himself as to his canine partner.

While the three continued to bond, Billy's cell phone rang. He looked at the number. "Shoot, it's Arlene. I forgot to call her." He answered the phone. "I found him," he blurted. "He's a little dehy-drated but fine." He listened. "I know, I know," he said, smiling, "I have the perfect trip planned for just the two of us."

Billy hung up the phone and looked skyward. *Even when you're being ignored, God, you still listen and care*, he thought. *And this time, you came through big time!* "Thank you, Father," Billy whispered.

His mom looked at him, but never questioned it. "Amen," she whispered.

Jimmy licked his paw and ran it across his dusty face.

Out of the blue, Billy's dad invited him on a two-day road trip. "We'll be hauling grain," he said, "and I'll pay you for your help. What do you say?"

"I'd love to, Dad, but I can't take any time off from the shelter."

"What are you saying...you don't get any days off?"

Billy nodded. "I do, but..." he said and then paused, his mind galloping.

The old man broke the silence. "You'll be off to college soon, so this'll give us some time..."

"Okay, but Jimmy needs to go," Billy blurted into the cell phone; it was more of a statement than a request.

"Of course," his dad said. "You know I love having that mangy mutt around."

Billy knew it was his dad's way of helping him out finan-cially, but two days and an overnight with his father could be an eternity. *Well, at least Jimmy's coming along*, Billy thought. "Let's do it, Dad," he said. "It'll be fun."

They drove in silence through nearly two full states, until Billy's dad began reminiscing about how fast the time had flown by and all the great memories they'd made along the way.

Their first stop, The Kozy Nook Restaurant, reminded Billy of the place he'd gone to with his father when he was a kid and was duped out of scoring a soda.

A row of chrome stools—topped with red, faux leather—sat beneath a long white counter sparkling with silver flakes sealed within it. Booths took up one side of the place, while tables seating six or more were situated on the other end. The walls were lined with dark paneling, dating the place. Eggshell-white paint covered the top half. But you could hardly tell. The walls were completely covered in nostalgic advertisements or framed photos of locals playing softball, fishing, bowling—engaged in one activity or another—with beers in hand. This was a working-class joint, blue-plate specials served with a smile to blue-collared workers.

Behind the counter, there was a soda fountain and Billy laughed when he saw it. And there was also a juice machine, orange juice circulating in one of the clear plastic containers and lemonade being recirculated in the other bin. A stainless steel milk fridge dispensed milk in three flavors: plain white, chocolate and coffee, a New England favorite. A mix of muffins and donuts was stacked within a glass, dome-shaped cake plate. A condiment rack, containing salt and pepper shakers, ketchup, vinegar and an assortment of jellies for the breakfast crowd sat atop each table, lining the length of the counter. A chalkboard was covered in multi-colored daily specials, penned in fancy script. Menus were protected beneath plastic sheets; some of the prices had been whited out and updated several times.

"I'll have a mug of hot coffee, black," the old man told the waitress before turning to Billy. "You want a tonic?" he teased.

Billy laughed, impressed that his dad actually remembered. "Nah," he said, looking up at the young waitress. "I think I'll get a cola," he said before going back in his mind.

It was their first road trip together. After turning eight, Billy had been invited to accompany his father on a short delivery run to

Boston. As kids, Billy and Sophie were never allowed to drink soda—only water, milk or Kool-Aid—so when the waitress came to the table and asked, "Would you like a tonic?" Billy was confused. He looked up at his dad for help.

"Order whatever you want," his dad told him, grinning.

Billy's mind raced at the possibilities, but he had no idea what *tonic* was. Disappointed, he ordered, "Chocolate milk."

"I'll have a tonic," his dad told the girl, "and make it a cola."

While the waitress walked away to fill the drink order, Billy looked up from the menu like he'd been backhanded. "Cola?" he asked.

The old man nodded. "In Boston, tonic is the word they use for soda."

Without thinking, Billy slapped the table while his dad laughed hard. It was the bitterest glass of chocolate milk Billy had ever tasted.

Billy looked up from his daydream to find the young waitress still standing there. She was probably a year or two out of high school, but old enough to be sporting some new body ink—several tattoos of Chinese symbols that she trusted was the message she'd wanted. She also had a message tattooed in some strange font, running the length of her forearm, which made it difficult for Billy to read—though he tried his best.

Billy ordered, "A patty melt, cooked medium, with onion rings."

The old man said, "I'll get the American Chop Suey," which was essentially macaroni and hamburger in a red sauce.

"Why don't you just ask her what the tattoo says?" his dad suggested after the third time Billy's neck twisted sideways.

"What fun is that?" Billy joked.

The big man laughed.

When the order arrived at the table, his dad went heavy on the grated parmesan cheese. "What's the latest on Charlie?" he asked, already tearing into his meal.

Billy shook his head. "He's in protective custody, still awaiting trial. It's going to be a rough road ahead for him."

The old man shook his head. "That's a damned shame.
Charlie's too pretty to serve time."

"I know," Billy said, feeling a chill over the truth of it.

The old man shook his head. "...surrounded by animals spit-
ting in his food and who knows what else."

"I get it, Dad," Billy said, starting to feel sick over the mental pictures flashing in his mind and wanting desperately to talk
about something else.

As if picking up on it, his dad devoured a giant forkful of
macaroni before changing the subject. "You ready for school?"
he asked, his mouth full.

Billy shrugged. "At the beginning of the summer, I was wondering whether I should even go to college..."

"What?" his dad said, his fork dangling in shock.

"It took forever," Billy said, grinning, "but I've finally figured out what I want out of college."

"You have?" he said, excited to hear more.

Billy thought about it for a moment and nodded. "You
know, when I first took the job at the animal shelter I thought
it was going to be just another meaningless summer gig. But
it hasn't been. It's been the furthest thing from meaningless."
He nodded. "I always knew I loved animals, but something's
happened since I started working there...something's changed,
you know?"

His dad remained silent, abandoning his meal to offer his
full attention.

"I really care about these animals and what happens to
them, Dad, and the shelter's become more than just a temporary
summer job." He nodded, confidently. "I now know that helping
animals will play a major role in my future."

The old man leaned back, nodding proudly. "Well, good for
you, son."

"And I've decided that I'm going to help save animals
on a much bigger scale. But to do that, I'm going to need a

formal education...a college degree in veterinary medicine." He shrugged. "Right now, I may not have what I need to make any real difference in the world," he said, smiling, "...but I will."

"I have no doubt," his dad said, clearly impressed. As he dove back into his pile of pasta, he nodded a few more times. "Good for you," he repeated. "The trick is getting paid for what really matters to you." He nodded. "Now that's a career worth fighting for."

Billy nodded. "Which is exactly what I'm going to do, Dad."

The old man looked up from his plate again and studied Billy's eyes. He grinned; it started slow before rolling over his face, becoming wide and proud. It was like he'd been waiting eighteen years to hear such a statement from Billy.

As if he were seven years old again, Billy was filled with pride.

"Do you think your car will hold up for a while?" his dad asked.

"I've already decided to sell the beater to a friend," Billy said, smirking. "Once I get my stuff moved in on campus, my buddy's going to throw me four hundred bucks for the junk."

"Four hundred bucks?"

Billy nodded. "That's right, enough to buy three college books." Billy shrugged again. "Freshmen aren't allowed to park on campus anyway." He smirked. "Besides, I can't afford to fix it anymore."

The big man nodded again. "If you say so."

Soft music played in the background, an easy listening station that set a relaxed atmosphere. As they ate, they settled into a comfortable silence. For the first time ever, Billy didn't feel the need to fill the dead air between them.

Toward the end of the meal, his dad ordered, "A chopped steak to go."

Billy nearly gagged on his last bite of blueberry pie. "For Jimmy?" he asked.

The big man grinned. "I'm guessing it's been a while since he's had one."

Once again, Billy caught a glimpse of his father's kindness. Although it was random and somewhat infrequent, it existed and it was great to witness it again.

Returning home, Billy and Jimmy took to the couch to relax. As Billy flipped through the channels, he happened upon a Red Sox game and left it on. "Oh good," he told Jimmy, "it's only the second inning and they're up by two." He kicked up his feet, prepared to settle in for the game when it suddenly hit him. While his heart skipped a beat, he jumped to the edge of his seat and pulled out his cell phone to check the date. "Today's the twenty-fourth," he said, thinking aloud. "This is the game Vicki bought us tickets to." He looked down at Jimmy, his eyes glazing over. "I was supposed to be at this game with her...four rows behind the home dugout." Shaking his head, he could feel the dull ache in his heart become inflamed. Tears sat waiting in the corner of his eyes. He grabbed the remote, hoping that this newest wave of sorrow would wash over him quickly.

I miss you, Vicki, he thought, flipping through the channels again. *I miss you so much.* While Jimmy snuggled in closer to him, Billy tried to hold back the tears. He finally let go of the remote control, landing on some random channel. *You've got to be shitting me,* he thought. It was the closing scene from *Dumb & Dumber.* Although he pointed the remote at the TV again, he never clicked off the movie. Instead, he forced himself to watch the last few minutes of the slapstick comedy. *This is crazy,* he thought. The mindless humor which had once brought him such unfettered joy now seemed completely asinine. He looked down at Jimmy again. "I don't think I'll ever laugh like that again," he said, "...not like I did with Vicki." And the tears finally broke through, dashing down his cheeks. Something told him that he had clicked with Vicki like no one he would ever click with again. "Not ever," he whispered.

As the TV went off, the old mutt low crawled even closer to Billy, where they sat together in silence.

On Billy's last day of work, he walked in and found Arlene cleaning out the kennels. "Hey, that's my job," he said, grinning.

She turned to face him. "No, sir, you've done your job." She smiled, studying his face for a moment. "So you survived *the pound*, huh?"

He smiled, thinking, *A few of them.* "And the shelter too," he answered.

Arlene laughed. "You got it, kid."

"So what do you want me to do today?" he asked.

"I want you to spend some time saying goodbye to the animals."

He started to laugh when he realized she was no longer smiling. "You're serious, aren't you?"

"Of course I'm serious," Arlene said, "and it'll be as good for you as it will be for them." She winked. "The trick to a happy life is to expect change and then try to make each transition as smooth as possible."

While Arlene pretended not to watch, Billy spent the next hour going from cage to cage, visiting his furry friends and bidding them a fond farewell.

"Feel better?" she asked him when he'd completed the peculiar task.

"Actually, I do," Billy said, surprised that he did. "But where's Major?"

"I decided to take him to my house and finish up the healing process there."

Billy smiled. "As another family member?" he asked.

She nodded.

Considering how she feels about her animals at home, Billy thought, *she must really trust him.* "I wanted you to know before I left that I made all the updates to your social media pages. The monthly newsletter and website are also up to date."

"Of course they are," she said smiling. "You really have no idea how many animals your online campaign has already saved, do you?"

He shrugged, blushing.

"That's amazing, considering the enormous difference you've already made," Arlene said, before changing the subject to stop Billy's face from turning blood red. "So did you learn anything at our summer school?" she asked, referring to the shelter.

He grinned. "I learned everything at summer school."

She laughed. "Well, that's probably not true but..."

"I learned that we all have the power to make a real impact on the world, whether it's some person's world or an animal's."

"Very good, Billy Baker."

"...and that you have to stand for something, or you'll watch your whole life drift by."

"*Very* good," she repeated in a whisper. "So where do you go to from here?"

"College," he answered confidently, "to become a veterinarian."

She opened her mouth to speak, but nothing came out. Her eyes filled. "Are you serious?" she asked.

He nodded. "I've never been more serious about anything in my life, Arlene," he said, "and I have you to thank for it."

She shook her head, as she tried to speak again. She couldn't.

"It may take me a year or two to get into the program, but I plan on getting the grades for it." Surprising them both, Billy wrapped his arms around Arlene and gave her a tight squeeze. "Thank you for inspiring me this summer, Arlene," he whispered. "I never imagined being this excited about the future," he said. "And now I can't imagine a future that doesn't include me helping animals."

"A veterinarian?" she thought aloud. "That's like an eight-year commitment, Billy."

"I know," he said. "Thank you for showing me the way."

She hugged him back, nearly emptying whatever air remained in his lungs. "You're welcome," she said as they parted, her voice muffled from emotion. "And in case you were wondering," she added, changing the subject again, "Sadie also found a great home."

Billy studied her face. "You're keeping her too, aren't you?"

Arlene shrugged. "She's probably napping on my pillow as we speak."

They both laughed.

"Then Sadie found the *best* home," Billy said.

Blushing, Arlene opened her mouth to reply but her words were clearly stuck again. While her eyes glassed over, she shook her head and turned her back to Billy. "I'm going to really miss you around here, Billy Baker," she muttered, before walking away.

"Me too," Billy forced from his lips, emotion raising his voice a full octave. *I'm going to miss everything about this place,* he thought and started for the front door. As he grabbed the doorknob, he looked back. "Hey Arlene," he said, "any chance I can work here again next summer?"

She stopped and turned. One of her eyebrows rose until it reached its peak. "You'd better work here again next summer," she said, shooting him the season's final wink.

Billy returned home from work. Not only did Jimmy not greet him at the front door, but he noticed that the dog's bowls were still full. *Neither one of them have been touched,* he thought and headed straight to his bedroom to find Jimmy already in bed. *Back to the sleeping patterns of a puppy,* Billy thought, placing both bowls at the foot of the bed. He patted Jimmy's neck. "How about dinner in bed tonight?" he said.

The dog struggled to get up and finally did, lying at the foot of the bed where his buffet had been placed.

"But let's keep it between us," Billy whispered.

Jimmy ate a few small bites before cleaning up with a wet paw across his face and ears.

Ignoring his video games, Billy ran his hand along the length of the dog's arthritic back, massaging him for a long time.

When it was time to turn in, Jimmy lay down on his belly, ready to sleep.

"No belly rubs tonight?" Billy asked, reaching under Jimmy's undercarriage to give him a few scratches.

The dog remained uninspired and just lay there, exhausted.

"Okay, buddy, we'll just go to sleep then," Billy whispered, placing his chest against his best friend's back and wrapping his arm around the dog. "You'll feel better in the morning after a good night's sleep."

The loving mutt licked Billy's hand.

"But you're never too sick or tired to bring the love, are you, Jimmy?" Billy said. For the next hour, he watched and worried about the silver-haired mutt. While Jimmy tossed and turned, his eyelids twitching to the mercy of his dreams, Billy held him close.

In the morning's first light, Jimmy barely climbed out of the bed. He stretched once and nearly went down on his arthritic legs.

"Go slow," Billy told him, yawning, "there's no fire."

Jimmy hobbled straight to the kitchen door and circled a few times; it was his signature move when he really had to go relieve himself. But the few minutes it took for Billy to open the back door were too much for the old-timer to take. Half-squatting, the dog urinated on the linoleum floor.

"Jimmy!" Billy began to scold him.

Whimpering, Jimmy's tail went straight down and his head slumped in shame. Even now, at his advanced age, the dog was an adult pleaser; when he was met with anything less than approval, he had a tough time handling it.

Billy immediately stopped, feeling badly.

His mom entered the kitchen and quickly grabbed the paper towels. "It's okay, buddy," she told the mutt sympathetically. "It happens. We're all getting older." She looked at Billy. "When you see that he has to go, you need to open the door right away. He can't hold it in anymore."

Nodding, Billy grabbed the paper towels from her. While he cleaned up after his friend, Jimmy headed straight to the corner of the kitchen to pout. "It's okay, buddy," Billy repeated, "it was only an accident. There's no need to punish yourself."

Jimmy looked out of the corner of his eye and sighed heavily, before turning back toward the wall—where he stayed for a solid two minutes in a self-imposed time-out.

Chapter 15

Billy was out with Jimmy for their morning walk when they spotted Vicki again. Jimmy barked a brief greeting. Vicki glanced over at them, but never responded. Billy realized that while she refused to look at him, he couldn't look away. Jimmy barked again, leaving it at that. As Vicki ignored them both, Billy also realized that the wound still hurt as badly as that life-changing afternoon on her front stoop. He wondered when it would start to clot and the healing process would begin. *But our relationship was the real thing*, he thought, *not some failed experiment that I might forget anytime soon...if ever.* He turned to Jimmy. "Come on, boy," he said, with an aching heart, "let's go home."

Jimmy turned his nose up at Vicki and followed Billy's lead, with his tail held high.

It was an overcast afternoon. Billy was at the kitchen table tallying all the money he'd made over the summer against his first year's college expenses. *I'm going to live like a pauper on campus,* he thought.

"Make sure you put money aside for your meals too," his mom told him.

Billy looked down at Jimmy and said, "I'm still going to be paying for my education when I'm your age..." The truth of it hit him like a sledge hammer.

The summer was nearly over and Billy and Jimmy had never made it to the beach. "I apologize," he told the old dog. "We never went camping or even visited the beach, like I promised." He thought about it, realizing, *We only have a handful of moments left*. "Thankfully, it's not too late," he said, smiling.

Within the hour, Billy had the tent packed, the cooler stocked and was heading out to spend an overnight with his best friend. He looked up at the ominous sky and told Jimmy, "With any luck, we'll have the whole place to ourselves."

As they drove to the beach, Billy thought about how all the days since his graduation had just flashed by. It seemed like it was Memorial Day when the Fourth of July rolled around. From there, it felt like he'd slept a few more times before waking up to Labor Day. The days had gone by so fast that he'd even confused Labor Day with Memorial Day. "So much has changed," Billy told Jimmy.

The mutt stuck his head out of the passenger window and let his tongue fly in the wind, splattering slobber all over the back window.

"Thank God for you, buddy," he told Jimmy, massaging the dog's hind quarter.

Jimmy kept his flapping tongue in the wind.

"Do your thing," Billy told him. "No worries."

From the look on Jimmy's face, he had none.

For the first time in a while, Billy's wish had come true. The beach was nearly deserted. After erecting their tent and establishing a cozy campsite, Jimmy trotted to the water. As Billy looked on, the silver-faced mutt walked in slowly—like an old man easing himself into a warm bath—the reckless abandon he'd once been known for completely gone.

Jimmy swam for a bit before sitting in the shallows with the water line at his chest.

Billy waded in and took a seat beside him where they sat for a long while, looking out onto the horizon. While the tide gently lapped at their chests, Billy wrapped his arm around Jimmy's shoulder. "This is the life," he whispered.

A seagull landed on the sand a few feet from them. Jimmy just sat there, watching the squawking bird with mild interest. "You *must be* tired, Jimmy. Back in the day, you would have chased that vulture until you collapsed."

Jimmy stood and took chase, but it was a haphazard effort.

"Half-stepper," Billy teased the dog and stood to go for a walk and dry off.

As they strolled along the coastline, Jimmy shook the salt water from his coat. He also took breaks, long breaks, acting like he was exploring.

"I know you're stalling," Billy told him, "and it's okay." *At least your spirit's still willing*, Billy thought, getting choked up.

When Jimmy slowed even more, Billy headed for the campsite. The sea grasses had lost their summer hue and were now brittle, snapping in half as Billy and Jimmy walked through the abandoned dunes.

They reached camp and sat together again where Billy discovered that the pads on Jimmy's paws were dry and cracked. One was even bleeding, which Jimmy licked for some time. Billy pulled the big moose into his lap. "Too many miles on those old tires, huh?" he whispered, before noticing the patch of missing fur on the mutt's hind quarter—a souvenir from a vicious fight he'd won in his glory days. A mean stray had swaggered into the backyard looking for trouble. Unwilling to let it go, Jimmy gave the growling stranger all the trouble he could handle. That one battle scar had been rubbed and patted thousands of times throughout the years, the family being forever grateful for Jimmy's sacrificial love and fearless devotion. As they sat side by side, Billy rubbed it again.

Resting his head in Billy's lap, Jimmy's eyes squinted while he enjoyed the heavy scratching.

Billy worked his hand up the old dog's body, stroking Jimmy's head and kneading the scruff of his neck. "I love you, buddy," he said. "You know that, right?"

Jimmy licked Billy's hand.

"And I need to go away pretty soon...to college."

Jimmy licked him again.

"The last thing in the world I want is to leave you, but I..." Billy stopped from going any further. A wave of tears was waiting to break on the shore just behind his eyes.

As though Jimmy understood, he nestled deeper into Billy's lap and began giving Billy's hand a thorough bath.

With his free hand, Billy rubbed Jimmy's chest up and down—fast and hard—exactly the way the old mutt liked it. As he did, he looked up and noticed a bank of even darker clouds had gathered above. "Looks like rain," he told Jimmy. "Hopefully, there's no thunder."

They napped in the tent, Jimmy appearing much less worried about his nails on the air mattress than Billy. They curled up together, the rain pitter-pattering on the light canvas above. "It's just a shower," Billy told him. *As good a guess as any meteorologist would make,* Billy thought, *though it doesn't matter either way.* As they began to nod off in each other's arms, Jimmy snored peacefully. Billy stared at his best friend's face, studying every nook and cranny—memorizing every crease and line. But it was silly. He knew Jimmy's face better than his own. *And I'm going to miss it something awful,* he thought, swallowing back the lump in his throat. While the rain picked up and began thumping on the tent's roof, Billy closed his eyes.

When they awoke from their afternoon siesta, Jimmy stood on the wobbly air mattress and yipped in pain. Once the sound of playful banter, Billy knew it was from pain now. "You okay?" he asked, massaging the dog's haunches and working out the knots as he'd watched Arlene do many times. "Feel better now?" he asked, stopping.

Jimmy reached up with his right paw and scratched Billy's hand, gesturing that he continue.

After a few more minutes, Billy stopped again. "Better?" he asked.

Jimmy licked Billy's face once before slowly stepping off the jelly-like mattress.

Billy hurried to throw an arthritis pill into a glob of peanut butter and fed it to the mutt.

When they came out of hibernation, the air was cool and fresh. The trees glistened from the rain. Billy looked up. The clouds had dispersed, leaving behind the last of the day's light.

The sunset was a palate of coral pinks and greens, with swirls of purple brushed in. The light softened—like the ambiance of an expensive romantic dinner, before fading into the distance and becoming twilight. There was a giant pause, as if the world collectively exhaled after filing another day into the history books. Billy and Jimmy sat together on a sturdy fold-out chair, silently sharing the magic. Billy took a deep breath and sighed.

Jimmy did the same.

Billy laughed. "Copycat," he whispered.

The beach had always been the place where Jimmy was free to romp and roam—to explore. And each year he did just that. But not this year. Jimmy nuzzled into Billy's lap again, where he awaited the attention Billy had always showered on him.

"You're a good boy," Billy whispered, as he scratched the gentle canine under his chin. He shook his head. "Although you haven't been a *boy* for a long time."

In what seemed like minutes, a million flickering stars covered the dark sky. Billy and Jimmy got up to take another stroll. They walked a few feet when they happened upon a giant puddle. Moonlight was trapped in the puddle, along with Billy and Jimmy's reflections—the two of them standing knee to shoulder. While Billy smiled, Jimmy bent at the water's edge and began to drink, sending ripples through the portrait. "Don't drink that, Jimmy," Billy scolded him. "You have fresh water back in the tent."

Jimmy paid him no mind and kept lapping loudly, slobbering all over himself and depositing an equal amount of back wash.

Billy shook his head. "Whatever, it's your stomach."

They made it down to the water's edge again and stood together in the silence for a long, long while. It was as though neither of them wanted the night to end, as though both of them needed more time together. Billy closed his eyes and listened to the tide. The ebb and flow was constant but random, like surround sound lapping the shore on the left, right and center.

The night grew cold, really cold for the time of year. Billy was surprised he and Jimmy couldn't see their breath. The drop in temperature was significant, reminding Billy once again that summer was quickly coming to an end. It was a cold slap to the face—literally. *I'm moving away in just a week*, he thought. *One week!* He looked down at Jimmy, glad that his furry friend had no concept or fear of time.

Billy built a campfire, which wasn't easy considering that everything was still damp from the rain shower. But sitting by a campfire had always been his and Jimmy's thing, the perfect atmosphere to spend quality time together, so he worked hard to get the fire going.

They sat together in silence for a long time, hypnotized by the swaying flames and the rhythm of the rolling tide. When it was time to turn in for the night, Jimmy licked his paw, running it across his face for the day's final bath. They both stood and stretched, leaving behind a handful of glowing embers and heading for the tent.

Kneeling beside the air mattress, Billy said his prayers. As he crawled in beside Jimmy, he left on the battery-operated lantern for his timid, four-legged friend, knowing that two D cell batteries would be killed in the process.

While Jimmy snored, Billy watched as their silhouettes moved randomly on the ceiling of the tent. He locked onto them, hypnotized by the shadows dancing above. His eyes grew heavy and he yawned. Within seconds, the shadows grew smaller until they disappeared.

Billy watched Jimmy—as a puppy—crying because the bedspread was covering his eyes. *Jimmy's claustrophobic*, he realized. "It's play time," he told the dog, tricking Jimmy into thinking they were going to horse around. The garden hose and bottle of dog shampoo, however, made the smart dog whimper. Billy laughed. When he looked back, Jimmy was stretched out flat on his belly, all four legs pin straight like he'd been strapped to the torturer's rack. Billy did a double-take and Jimmy was wearing the cone of shame so he didn't bite at his stitches after being neutered. *Poor guy*, Billy thought, and then yelled at the dog after he'd torn a pillow to shreds. In the next scene, an older Jimmy chomped on ice cubes, spraying them everywhere like a broken snow cone machine. And then they were fishing, both of them young again. Jimmy whined as he watched the small perch swim in circles in the bucket. He placed his paw on the lip of the pail, pulling it to him and dumping the flopping fish into the grass—in some sad attempt at freeing the prisoners. Billy laughed again and a moment later, he was watching on in horror as Sophie dressed the poor dog in some ridiculous outfit for one of her lively tea parties. Sophie played with Jimmy's ears, his paws, his tail; the mutt just lay there, as if he understood it was the price he had to pay for free meals. *Jimmy's the ultimate pilot fish.* Billy shook his head, while a water sprinkler soaked the summer grass and Jimmy exhibited another example of his terrible drinking habits. Billy could see himself falling out of the tree in the backyard and grabbing his arm; the pain was mind numbing. While he healed, Jimmy never left his side. Billy then looked down to find that his cast was gone. He looked up again and Jimmy was smiling at him, his teeth covered in tartar build-up. "Have you been kissing a skunk?" he teased the dog. "You have a bad case of gingivitis, buddy...or is it halitosis?" Billy passed the groomer's window and noticed that he'd grown tall. Jimmy was beyond ecstatic to see him; his nails had been clipped, his fur trimmed but his eyes were as wide as two chocolate pies. "What did she do to you, boy?" Billy teased the frightened dog.

Billy awoke, panting like a dog himself. He looked over at his tent mate, who was still snoring peacefully on the air mattress.

"Oh Jimmy," he muttered and wrapped his arm around the drooling heap.

Billy shook the cobwebs from his head and tried to make sense of it all. *It was just a dream*, he realized. Fragmented and confused in time and context, he'd dreamed about Jimmy. There were glimpses of the past and present merged together, as though Jimmy's life had been thrown into a blender and Billy was enjoying each experience with him a second time. He pushed himself closer to Jimmy until he could feel the rise and fall of the dog's breathing. "I love you so much, buddy," he whispered, before falling back to sleep.

They returned home, but Billy was not yet ready for his brief summer to be over. While Jimmy looked on, too old and stiff to follow, Billy grabbed his bicycle from the shed and jumped on it. It had been a few years since he'd ridden the old bike, which seemed odd considering the two-wheeler was like another body appendage most of his life. For years, the ten-speed was as important to him as his own feet, taking him everywhere. While Jimmy watched from the edge of the yard, Billy pedaled a few feet, allowing the wind in his hair to take him back in time.

Billy went off to tour his childhood: the baseball field where he, Mark and Charlie had played all those summers, the ice cream parlor they visited after every game, their hidden tree house down near the railroad tracks.

When Billy coasted home an hour later, he found Jimmy waiting patiently in the same shadows on the lawn's edge. With the dog on his heels, Billy put his bike away in the shed. The smell of charcoal lighter fluid and the half-empty plastic bottle sitting on a shelf triggered his memory of so many summers past. His dad liked to grill the old way; he always said the meat tasted better cooked over the gray, lava-hot briquettes.

Billy stepped out of the shed and scanned the backyard, picturing all he had experienced as a kid: the copper pot and the massive clam boils that cooked on two burners.

Billy pictured those who had passed away—faces that could never be replaced or erased from his memory. Their family was a unit, a clan—something bigger than any one of their measly existences. "Not so long ago, I thought all of it—even spending time with our family—was lame," he told Jimmy. "Now what I wouldn't give for one last clam boil with Grandma and Grandpa under that tree."

Jimmy glanced over at the tree.

"There was also a time when I thought I'd have nothing to do with my family when I got old enough to escape," Billy added. "How crazy is that?"

Jimmy still listened attentively.

Billy recalled his childhood friends: Charlie and Mark. Their time together had passed, gone with the wind, leaving behind countless mental pictures worth keeping. Billy looked skyward. "Please watch over Charlie, Father," he whispered, "and keep him strong."

Billy took a seat on the shed's stoop, while Jimmy dropped his head in Billy's lap. In that one moment, he felt overwhelmed with gratitude for all the people and experiences that had made up the whole of his life.

Billy was excited about what lay ahead, but he couldn't forget what lay behind him either. As he sat beside Jimmy, he took an inventory of the things he'd never imagined he'd miss but now realized he would: *cutting grass for a few bucks; drinking an iced-cold lemonade while looking over my work and feeling some strange sense of accomplishment; the money used to head off to the movies. Lying on the deck, listening to music on my headset, the sun on my face and a nice breeze keeping things cool. Climbing trees and building forts; playing hard. Our imaginations took us everywhere, without anyone questioning the silliness or judging the ridiculousness of it all. Riding bikes, swimming and even the Slip and Slide that caused as many bruises as it did laughs. Drinking from a garden hose and chasing fireflies. Mom's big Sunday breakfasts and the occasional church visit, inspired by the guilt of long absences. And late-night movies. 'Don't stay up too late,' Mom would say. 'We won't,' Billy, Charlie and Mark sang together. But they all knew otherwise.* Billy laughed aloud. "And you were right there with me to share it all," he told Jimmy, giving the mutt a hug. "We've had an amazing run, you and me," he whispered.

The dog licked his hand.

Billy's mom was finishing dinner, chicken mozzarella over penne pasta, when Billy and Jimmy entered the kitchen. "You've been sitting out there for a while," she said. "Is everything okay?"

He nodded. "Me and Jimmy just took some time to reminisce," he said.

She smiled. "Time well spent."

"Jimmy can't climb stairs anymore," Billy blurted sadly, rubbing the mutt's back.

She turned from the stove and nodded. "I know," she said, "but he doesn't complain all that much so I don't think he's in too much pain."

Billy recalled the dog's complaints during the camping trip but held his tongue. "Why do we have so little time with them?" he asked, still stroking Jimmy's thick coat. She opened her mouth to answer when Billy asked another question. "Why do you think dogs only live for a dozen or so years, Mom?"

She bent down to pet Jimmy's silver crown. "I honestly believe Jimmy will stay around for as long as we need him," she said.

That's what I was afraid of, he thought.

"Jimmy's known unconditional love his whole life," she said with a nod. "We're the ones who take much longer to learn it."

Billy's eyes filled.

"What is it?" his mom asked, taking a seat beside him.

"I'll be leaving for school soon. I'm just worried about him and..."

She placed her hand on Billy's arm. "Jimmy will be fine. I've already bought a night light for my room. He can sleep with me and Dad from now on."

"Does Dad know that?" Billy asked surprised.

"He'll find out when he gets back from the road," she said. "And if he doesn't like it, he can start sleeping on the couch."

Billy smiled. "Thanks, Mom," he said, feeling both grateful and relieved.

She rubbed Jimmy's head again. "He's my boy too," she whispered.

Billy stood and grabbed two plates. "How much pasta do you want?" he asked his mom.

She looked up, shocked. "You're going to serve me?" she asked.

He shrugged. "Sure, what's the big deal?"

"Two scoops," she said and then looked down at Jimmy. "It's amazing what a summer can change."

Jimmy whimpered once, begging for a free meal with his chocolate eyes.

She laughed. "And get our boy a plate too," she said, scratching Jimmy's muzzle. "No sauce."

With Jimmy snuggled tightly against him, sleeping, Billy lay in bed with his fingers locked behind his head. *College will be the real test, though,* he decided. *And it can't be easy, if it's caused Sophie to smoke weed.* With no more Mom and Dad around to take care of the menial details known as survival, he realized it would be a matter of give and take. Though he would have to learn to do his own laundry, there would be no need to make a bed. *It doesn't make sense anyway,* he thought, *to straighten out something you're only going to mess up again a few hours later.* Cooking promised to be a real treat. Billy could already picture the frying pan, lined in crusted lard, atop some old stove. He'd only need to heat it up and drop whatever he dared eat into the bubbling oil. Beer would become a staple in the diet to help learn the important lessons of overindulgence: bed spins, projectile vomiting and waking the following morning with a vice-like headache.

Billy continued to stare at his bedroom ceiling in deep thought. After all the summer's pain and suffering, he still felt grateful and content. He had no real idea what the future held, but there was no question about where he'd come from and everything that made Billy Baker who he was. And he also knew that he'd finally found his passion, his purpose—working with animals—which was all the direction he needed. *For someone my age*, he thought, *at this stage in the game, how could I ask for more?*

As he dozed off, his arm swung over the side of the bed. Instantly, his skin prickled and the tiny hairs on his arm stood on end. He pulled his hand up onto the bed, turned over and wrapped his arm around Jimmy. As ridiculous as it was, he would be taking the deep scars of childhood with him into adulthood. *Monsters don't exist*, he told himself, but a small voice deep inside of him still questioned it.

In the morning, Billy awoke with the sun, making Jimmy stare at him in confusion. After a quick bathroom break for each of them and a medication-laced breakfast, they returned to Billy's bedroom. Instead of grabbing the video game controller, Billy looked at Jimmy and grinned. "You feel like giving me a hand straightening up this dump?" he asked.

The tired mutt collapsed to the prone position, where he started his morning bath.

Billy laughed. "I don't blame you."

It took nearly two hours to see the carpet and an hour more before the room was thoroughly cleaned. Covered in sweat, Billy took a moment to appreciate his work. "I just hope it doesn't give Mom a heart attack," he told Jimmy, laughing.

Jimmy lifted his paw and placed it over his eyes.

Billy laughed harder. "You're still such a clown," he said, grabbing the overstuffed trash bag and swinging it over his shoulder. As they started to leave the room, Billy spotted a small white paper wedged into the corner of the room. He placed the trash bag down for a moment and reached for the paper. Right away, he recognized that it came from a Chinese fortune cookie. "Expect a season of change," he read aloud and snickered. "Confucius hit that one on the head, didn't he?" he said to Jimmy, throwing the fortune into the bulging trash bag.

Before Billy's dad set off for another long, cross-country haul, they said their goodbyes. "You have everything you need to make that dream come true, right?" he asked.

"I do," Billy said, knowing his father wasn't referring to money.

The old man hugged him tight. "I know you do, Billy," he said, his voice muffled from emotion. "I love you."

Billy's head snapped up. He knew it was true, always had, but when put into words it made his eyes instantly swell. "I love you, too, Dad."

The big man nodded. "Well, go chase it down then," he said, giving him one last hug.

The last few days of summer went by in a blur, filled with visits to the jail where Charlie awaited his fate, long talks with Sophie and a stop at Nick's Pizza, where Billy and Mark finally shared the lunch they'd talked about since high school graduation.

On Monday morning, Billy packed the last of his things into the Honda. Wearing a new *Four Paws* t-shirt, a going away gift from Arlene, he said goodbye to his tearful mother before taking Jimmy out to the backyard. As they sat together, Billy noticed that a few of the trees had already started to change color from green to yellow and red.

Jimmy sat close and whimpered a few times, sensing there was something wrong.

"Come on now," he told the old mutt, "let me see those pearly whites."

Jimmy curled his lip into a snarl and bared his teeth.

"You're so handsome," Billy said, chuckling. He patted the scruff of Jimmy's neck, massaging it a few times. Billy took a deep breath, his smile vanishing from his face. "Thanks for getting me through this summer, buddy. I don't think I could have made it without you." His eyes swelled with tears. "What am I saying? I can't imagine what the last twelve years would have been like without you...and I don't even want to try." He stroked Jimmy's coat.

The silver-faced dog nestled up closer and whimpered again, his milk-chocolate eyes pleading for Billy to stay.

"I know, buddy, I wish I could stay. But I can't," Billy said, shaking his head. "I'll miss you too," he added, his voice garbled from the knot in his esophagus. The first tear broke free and ran down his cheek. "It's not fair. I feel like I'm just getting started and you're..." He stopped and looked into his best friend's kind eyes. "But I don't have a choice, Jimmy. I have to go." He kissed the big mutt on the head. "I'll be back for Christmas break to watch you drink another pine tree dry, okay?" He got onto his knees, hugged Jimmy and whispered into the dog's floppy ear. "I love you with all my heart, Jimmy...you know that. And I'll be seeing you soon, okay?"

The old dog whimpered once, before the slightest twinkle flashed in his eyes—like a human who suddenly realized his life's work was finally done and his purpose fulfilled.

As Billy drove down the road, crying, his eyes were glued to the rearview mirror.

Jimmy howled once and took off after the overstuffed Honda, hobbling as far as his arthritic legs would take him. Within seconds, he was limping off to the side of the road, where he sat and whined in a mournful tone—an eerie wail loud enough for Billy to hear.

As Billy's mom approached the grieving mutt, Billy watched his best friend through blurred vision. "I'll miss you, too, buddy," he whispered and continued to cry.

Acknowledgments

First and forever, Jesus Christ, my Lord and Savior. With Him, all things are possible.

To Paula, my beautiful wife, for loving me and being the amazing woman she is.

To my children—Evan, Jacob, Isabella and Carissa—for inspiring me.

To Mom, Dad, Billy, Randy, Philip, Darlene, Jeremy, Baker, Jenn, Jason, Jack, the DeSousas—my beloved family and foundation on which I stand.

To Lou Aronica and Jessica Schmidt, for helping me to share this story with the world.

About the Author

Steven Manchester is the author of the #1 bestsellers *Twelve Months*, *The Rockin' Chair*, *Pressed Pennies*, and *Gooseberry Island* as well as the novel *Goodnight, Brian*. His work has appeared on NBC's *Today Show*, CBS's *The Early Show*, CNN's *American Morning*, and BET's *Nightly News*. Recently, three of Manchester's short stories were selected "101 Best" for the *Chicken Soup for the Soul* series.